ABOUT WRITING

Seven Essays, Four Letters,
and Five Interviews

Also by Samuel R. Delany

ABOUT WRiTiNG

Seven Essays, Four Letters,
and Five Interviews

Samuel R. Delany

Wesleyan University Press
Middletown, Connecticut

**This is for Marie Ponsot,
in return for the Djuna Barnes.**

Published by Wesleyan University Press, Middletown, CT 06459
www.wesleyan.edu/wespress

Printed in the United States of America   5
ISBN-13: 978-0-8195-6716-1 • ISBN-10: 0-8195-6716-7

"Teaching/Writing" first appeared as "Teaching S-f Writing" in *Clarion* (New York: Signet Books; New American Library, 1971).

"Thickening the Plot" first appeared in *Those Who Can*, ed. Robin Scott Wilson (New York: Mentor Books; New American Library, 1973).

"Characters" and "On Pure Storytelling" first appeared in *The Jewel-Hinged Jaw* (New York: Berkeley Windhover Books, 1977), 155–60, 161–70.

"Of Doubts and Dreams" first appeared in *Distant Stars* (New York: Bantam Books, 1981), 7–16.

"After Almost No Time at All the String on Which He had Been Pulling and Pulling Came Apart into Two Separate Pieces So Quickly He Hardly Realized It Had Snapped, *or:* Reflections on 'The Beach Fire'" first appeared in *Empire SF* 5.20 (summer 1980).

"Some Notes for the Intermediate and Advanced Creative Writing Student" first appeared in *Shorter Views* (Hanover, N.H.: Wesleyan University Press, 2000), 433–57.

"A *Para•doxa* Interview: Experimental Writing/Texts & Questions" first appeared as "*Para•doxa* Interview: Texts & Questions, with Samuel R. Delany" in "The Future of Narrative," ed. Lance Olsen, a special issue of *Para•doxa* 4.11 (1998): 384–430.

"An *American Literary History* Interview: The Situation of American Writing Today" first appeared in somewhat different form, as part of a symposium entitled "The Situation of American Writing Today" in *American Literary History* 11.2 (1999): 331–53.

"A *Poetry Project Newsletter* Interview: A Silent Interview" first appeared in *The Poetry Project Newsletter,* New York, March 18, 1999.

"A *Black Clock* Interview" first appeared in *Black Clock*, no. 1 (March 2004): 64–75.

"A *Para•doxa* Interview: Inside and Outside the Canon" first appeared as "*Para•doxa* Interview with Samuel R. Delany," in *Para•doxa: Studies in World Literary Genres* [Vashan Island, Washington] 1.3 (1995), ed. Lauric Guillard.

CIP data is available from the Library of Congress.

Contents

Part III FiVE INTERViEWS

Preface and Acknowledgments

If you are a writer, more and more you'll find yourself writing about writing—especially today, as creative writing classes at the university level grow more and more common.

Writers make their critical forays in many genres: letters to friends, private journals, interviews, articles for the public, general or academic, and at all levels of formality. Rather than try for an artificial unity, I thought, therefore, to give an exemplary variety. Today such variety seems truer to its topic.

After the preface and a general introduction, this handful of pieces on creative writing continues with seven essays, each taking up an aspect of the mechanics of fiction. (I am more comfortable with "mechanics" than "craft"; but use the term you prefer.) The first two, "Teaching/Writing" and "Thickening the Plot," grew out of Clarion Workshops many years ago, when the workshops were actually held in Clarion, Pennsylvania, under the aegis of their founder, Robin Scott Wilson. (For more than twenty years now they have been given every summer both in East Lansing, Michigan, and in Seattle, Washington. Since 2004, Clarion South, a third chapter, has been held at Griffith University in Brisbane, Australia.) "Characters" first appeared as an invited essay in a 1969 issue of the *SFWA* [Science Fiction Writers of America] *Forum*, when it was under the editorship of the late Terry Carr. "On Pure Storytelling" grew out of a comment made to me by Hugo and Nebula Award–winning novelist Vonda N. McIntyre, when I was privileged to have her as a writing student at an early Clarion. (The comment itself is recorded in "Teaching/Writing.") That essay was delivered as an after-dinner talk at the Nebula Awards banquet at the Claremont Hotel in Berkeley, California, in 1970. "Of Doubts and Dreams" is currently the afterword to my short fiction collection *Aye and Gomorrah* (Vintage Books: New York, 2003), though I wrote it initially in 1980 to conclude another anthology, *Distant Stars*. Thus you must put up with my self-references for a page or so. Finally, however, it turns to topics that might interest this book's readers.

"After Almost No Time at All the String on Which He had Been Pulling and Pulling Came Apart into Two Separate Pieces So Quickly He Hardly Realized It Had Snapped, *or:* Reflections on 'The Beach Fire'" was first requested by a fanzine, *Empire*, which endured a few years toward the end of the 1970s. Aimed at aspiring writers, each issue printed an amateur short story the editors had previously sent to a handful of professionals for comment. Most writers returned a paragraph of encouragement, in which they also pointed out one-to-three flaws. The editors printed these critiques along with the tale. I decided to send back, however, a fuller response. Incidentally, I have changed the name of the characters, the writer's initials, several of the tales' incidents, and the story title itself to protect the brave and laudable youngster, who, after all, was not yet seventeen when she or he first wrote it.

Something I don't mention in my piece on "The Beach Fire" (nor did any of the other three writers who sent in their much briefer notes): however unintentionally, the "alien-as-beach-ball" is lifted from John (*Halloween, They Live, Escape from New York* . . .) Carpenter's marvelously lunatic student film *Dark Star*, which was shown at hundreds of SF conventions throughout the seventies and eighties and which reduced auditoria full of science fiction fans to convulsive laughter. Since *Empire*'s editors, as well as its readers and writers, all came out of science fiction fandom, likely the author of "The Beach Fire" had seen, or at least heard of, Carpenter's spoof. Perhaps the plagiarism was inadvertent. But Carpenter's original was so telling and so widely known that the similarity would have immediately put the piece out of the running with any professional editor who recognized its source. I chose not to bring it up because to discuss what you can and can't take from other artists would have doubled, if not tripled, my essay's length. But even the nature of plagiarism has become a new order of problem in the last thirty years. From the eighties through the present, writers from age fifteen to age thirty-five have regularly handed me stories that were pastiches of William Gibson's *Neuromancer*, Tolkien's *Lord of the Rings*, or, more recently, Rowling's *Harry Potter*. Many do not even bother to come up with new names for the characters. Some have actually been quite skillful. But all these young writers were quite surprised when I told them that there was no hope of publishing such work outside a specifically fan context. More than one told me: "But whenever you read about movies or television, or even best sellers, everyone always says what producers and publishers want is something exactly like something that's been successful. That's what I thought I'd done . . ."

Without going further into the problem, let me say: this is a book for serious creative writers. That means it's a book for writers who have at least resolved that problem for themselves and come down on the side of originality; that is, writers who are not interested in formulaic imitation, at whatever level, however well done, fan to commercial. I stress, too: interest in formulaic imitation is not the same as interest in writing within one recognizable genre or another. What's here applies just as much to the mystery, the science fiction tale, or the romance as it does to the literary story, however normative, however experimental. Writers with genre interests are welcome among these pages. (Much of my own writing has been genre writing.) But the fine points of the difference between genre and the formulaic within a given genre are why such distinctions require thought.

The final essay, "Some Notes for the Intermediate and Advanced Creative Writing Student," deals with that all-important problem, structure. What is it? Why do you need it? How do you control it? That is to say, it speaks to the aspect of narrative that makes fiction an art—and an art whose elements here alone are clearly distinguishable from those of the poem.

Four letters to four different writers follow the essays. All are actual (or based closely on actual) letters sent at their particular dates (1997–2001; again, titles and identifying details have been changed). Two are to poets. Two are to fiction writers. One of the poets and one of the fiction writers are affiliated with universities. Two are out there on their own. Two are black. Two are white. Two are male. Two are female. Two are gay. One is straight —and I have no idea what the sexual orientation of the other is; statistics would suggest straight. But statistics *only* suggest.

Two of these letters answer writers who wrote me specifically for advice. In them (and in the closing interview on canon formation), I talk about reasons why the situation of the writer is what it is and how one might respond to it in order to negotiate it intelligently. One letter makes its point through criticism of a novel widely read today. All four to all four men and women deal, however, with an overarching truth about creative writing that is currently not a popular one, especially with most people picking up such a collection as this. I go into it, however, because it gives a flavor of what writers think about as they write back and forth. In their various modes, all four letters deal with the writer's current condition.

The collection proper closes with five interviews. For me interviews are largely a written form. In all five cases, I received the questions in writing and wrote out my answers. The first appeared in a special issue of *Para•doxa* on "The Future of Narrative," edited by Lance Olsen.* It deals with some specific problems and possibilities of experimental writing. (Be warned: I enjoy the genre.) The second interview answers a set of eight questions on "The Situation of American Writing Today," posed in 1999 by Gordon Hutner, the editor of *American Literary History.* It appeared as part of a symposium consisting of the responses to those same questions by a dozen-odd writers. Here my answers focus on the way writing relates to criticism. "A *Poetry Project Newsletter* Interview" is my attempt to talk about what art can actually *do* in our world—and what it can't. "A *Black Clock* Interview" focuses on questions of history, genre, and breakthroughs. The last interview, "Inside and Outside the Canon," is also "A *Para•doxa* Interview" and concerns the literary canon and literary canon formation. Specifically it tackles the ticklish question of how writers' reputations develop. By the way, it's the piece I refer "R—" to in the third letter here. As such, you may want to read it before that letter. I put it toward the end so it would be easy to find.

Finally an appendix, "Nits, Nips, Tucks, and Tips," cov-

---

* Since 1998, the journal has dropped the internal symbol, to become simply *Paradoxa: Studies in World Literary Genres.*

ers some topics the ignorance of which might easily hamstring a young writer, if no one has yet taken time to go over them with him or her: dramatic structure, how to punctuate dialogue, point of view, when to use first person and when not to, writing what you know, trusting your own images, and what makes characters believable or sympathetic, along with some minimal remarks on grammar and style.

I conclude this preface with something about "the basics" of creative writing—plot, character, setting, theme. Probably it's an overstatement to say that none of them exists—but certainly none of them exists *as* a basic. They are, *all* of them, effects. (Yes, even character.) As such, they may be basic elements for the *reader*. But, like a building that soars a hundred stories into the sky and lifts the eyes of passersby to the clouds, each needs some solid (and often largely invisible) foundation work. For the architect or the writer, the building of the foundation is what's basic. Certainly one can get so caught up in foundation building that one loses sight of those final effects. "Commercial" writers accuse "literary" writers of some form of this, repeatedly. But, if I may push the metaphor, the idea is to build an edifice that remains standing in the mind and does not collapse two hours after closing the book, magazine, or journal (more often, pieces of it coming loose and crumbling before the reader finishes the first chapter), so that its flimsy shell with gaping holes can only attract viewers during the season of its advertising campaign.

A reasonable concern—in many a worry; and in few a hope —is whether a creative writing teacher wishes to teach her or his students to write the way he or she writes. Emphatically that is not my enterprise. But the agenda here is no less personal. The thrust of these pieces is to teach writers to produce works I would enjoy reading. In the following introduction and even more in the pieces to come you will get a better sense of what I enjoy and what I don't, and thus be able to make a call as to whether—for you—this book will likely be helpful.

*   *   *

Finally, my acknowledgments: a number of readers have read over this manuscript, in whole or in part, and made more or less extensive comments. For their time and intelligence I would like to thank, particularly, Vincent Czyz, Carl Freedman, Maura High, Kenneth James, Josh Lukin (who, along with Vincent Czyz and Maura High, must be singled out for particular thanks for the thoroughness of his critique), Joan Mellen, Pamela Morrison, Rick Polney, and Elayne Tobin. As well I must thank my students of five years, graduate and undergraduate, in the Temple University Creative Writing Program, along with thirty-five-odd years of students at the Clarion Workshop, both East Coast and West Coast chapters, who have used now one section, now another, as auxiliary reading during one or another workshop, and who have offered their comments, sometimes heated, always helpful. Needless to say, eccentricities, overstatements, and outright gaffes are mine.

—New York City
2005

An Introduction

Emblems of Talent

I

In July of 1967 I waited in a ground-floor room, yellow, with dark wainscoting and wide windows giving onto Pennsylvania greenery. First, four holding notebooks, followed by three in sneakers, two more with briefcases, another six in sandals and Bermudas, then another three laughing loudly at a joke whose punch line must have come just outside the double doors, followed by two more in the denim wraparound skirts that had first appeared that decade, then still another two with foolscap legal pads, who looked as nervous as I felt, most with long hair except an older man and a middle-aged woman, both gray (and one woman, also in Bermudas and sandals with black hair helmet-short), some twenty-five students wandered in to sit on the couches circling the blue carpet. Behind a coffee table, I coughed, sat forward, said hello and introduced myself—and began to teach my first creative writing workshop. Repeatedly, in the thirty-five years since, I've been surprised how far and fast that July has fallen away.

For more than a decade (1988–99), at the University of Massachusetts at Amherst, now in a pale orange space—the well of a hall called Hasbrook—now on the stage of the Hurter auditorium above the university museum, I taught an introductory lecture course in the reading of science fiction, with, each term, ninety to a hundred-fifty students. Sometime during my first three lectures, I would step from behind the podium, look out over the space that, in the early 1960s, some architect had thought "the future" ought to look like, and ask for a show of hands from students interested in writing the kinds of stories we were reading. Perhaps five to ten people scattered throughout those hundred-plus would *fail* to raise a hand.

The rest were eager to write.

As well, for over half those years (usually in that same hall, but once in a cement cellar room with nozzles for Bunsen burners on the worn demonstration desk), to the semicircles on semicircles of students with their notebooks ranged around me, I delivered another lecture course on the reading of general short fiction. At the start of the term I would ask the same question to a similar number. Here, perhaps fifteen or twenty out of my hundred, my hundred-fifty students would admit to *not* wanting to be writers.

Among a notable sector of the country's college students oriented toward the humanities, the desire to write is probably larger than the desire to excel at sports.

Over the thirty-five years since I began to teach creative writing (with almost as many years writing about and teaching literature), I have asked hundreds of students why each wanted to write. By far the most common answer was, "I don't want to do what my parents do. I don't think they're happy in their work." Readily I identify with those feelings. Neither of my parents finished college—not uncommon during the Depression of the 1930s. For different reasons, both might have been happier if they had. Both were energetic and creative. Too much of that creativity was drained off in anxieties. Most worries are a matter of telling oneself more or less upsetting stories of greater or lesser complexity about one's own life. Turning that ability outward to entertain others, rather than inward to distress oneself, has to have *some* therapeutic value.

Even in a good university creative writing program, however, the number of graduates who go on to publish fiction regularly in any venue that might qualify as professional is below ten percent—often below five. Were we talking about medical school, law school, engineering, or any other sort of professional training, that would be an appalling statistic. Art schools fare better in turning out professional artists of one sort or another than creative writing programs do in turning out professional writers. But even with such distressing results, writing programs are currently one of the great growth areas of the modern university.

Though vast numbers of people want to write fiction, the educational machinery set in place to teach people how doesn't work very well.

While this book puts forth no strategies for correcting the situation, it discusses some reasons *why* this is the case—and why it might be the case necessarily. As well, it deals with three other topics and the relations between them. One—which it shares with most books on writing—is, yes, the art of writing fiction. The other two are far less often discussed in classes and rarely figure in such "how-to" books. First, how is the world structured—specifically the socio-aesthetic world—in which the writer works? Having said that, I should add that this is *not* a book about selling, marketing, or promoting your manuscripts. Rather, it is a book about the writer's world and how that world differs from the world of other people—as well as how that world is organized today differently from the way it was organized twenty-five, thirty-five, and seventy-five years ago, when most of the tales about writing that we still read today, the mythology of Pound (1885–1972), Joyce (1882–1941), Gertrude Stein (1874–1946), F. Scott Fitzgerald (1896–1939), T. S. Eliot (1885–1960), Ernest Hemingway (1899–1961), and the other high modernists, first sedimented. Second (and finally), this book discusses the way literary reputations grow—and how, today, they don't grow. (Clearly, they must grow in a very different way from the way they grew a hundred or two hundred years back, because the field in which they grow is so much larger and structured so differently.) In the letters and interviews here, I consider these last two questions—the writer's world and the writer's reputation—from the point of view of the writer who strives after high quality and who wants to be known for what she or he actually accomplishes. (I am not interested in reputations that develop when publishers decide they've found a "money-making" idea that they can flog into profit through advertising and publicity.) Frankly, I know of no other book on writing that treats all three (the art of fiction, how that art fits into the world today, and the nature of the writer's reputation), or shows the ways they interrelate. But I have tried to write one—because they do.

II

The essays here were written to stand alone. More or less, they introduce themselves. The letters and interviews following them —if only because it's somewhat unusual to include such documents in such a book—may need some intellectual context.

The first letter makes a point only in passing that is nevertheless fundamental. So I stress it now.

Though they have things in common, *good writing* and *talented writing* are not the same.

The principles of good writing can be listed. Many people learn them:

(1) Use simple words with clear meanings whenever possible. (Despite the way it sounds, this is a call for clarity, not a bid for simplicity.)

(2) Use the precise word. Don't say "gaze" when you mean "look." Don't say "ambled" or "sauntered" or "stalked" when you mean "walked." (And don't say "walked" when you mean one of the others.) As far as the creative writer goes, the concept of synonyms should be a fiction for high school and first- and second-year college students to encourage them to improve their vocabularies. The fact is (as writers from Georg Christoff Lichtenberg [1742–99] in the eighteenth century to Alfred Bester [1913–87] in the twentieth have written), "There are no synonyms."

(3) Whenever reasonable, avoid the passive voice.

(4) Omit unnecessary modifiers. As a rule of thumb, nouns can stand up to one modifier each; thus, if you use two—or more!—have a good reason.

(5) For strong sentences, put your subject directly against the verb. Preferably, when possible, move adverbial baggage to the beginning of the sentence—or to the end, less preferably. Don't let it fall between subject and verb. Except for very special cases (usually having to do with the intent to sound old-fashioned), do not write "He then sat," "She suddenly stood," or "He at once rose." Write "Then he sat," "Suddenly she stood," or "He rose at once."

(6) Omit unnecessary chunks of received language: "From our discussion so far it is clearly evident that . . ." If it's that evident, you needn't tell us. "Surely we can all understand that if

. . ." If we can, ditto. "In the course of our considerations up till now clearly we can all see that . . ." If it follows *that* clearly and we can all see it, we'll get the connection without your telling us we'll get it. If the connection *is* obscure, explain it. "It goes without saying that . . ." If it does, don't. "Almost without exception . . ." If the exceptions are important enough to mention, say what they are; if they're not, skip them and omit the phrase mentioning them. Make your statements clearly and simply. If you need to include qualifications of any complexity, don't put them in awkward clauses. Give them separate sentences.

(7) Avoid stock expressions such as "the rolling hills," "a flash of lightning," "the raging sea." "Hills," "lightning," and "sea" are perfectly good words by themselves. Good writers don't use such phrases. Talented writers find new ways to say them that have never been said before, ways that highlight aspects we have all seen but have rarely noted.

(8) Good writing rarely uses "be" or "being" as a separate verb. Don't use "be" or "being" when you mean either "becoming" (not "It had started to be stormy," but "A storm had started") or "acting" (Not "She was being very unpleasant," but "She was unpleasant"), except in dialogue or in very colloquial English. By the same token, avoid "There are" and "There were" whenever possible. Except in colloquial situations, don't write "There were five kids standing in line at the counter." Write "At the counter five kids stood in line."

(9) Don't weigh down the end of clauses or sentences with terminal prepositional phrases reiterating information the beginning already implies.

Here's an example of that last: "I turned from my keyboard to stack the papers *on the desk.*" Since the vast majority of keyboards sit on desks, you don't need that terminal prepositional phrase "on the desk." If you turned from the keyboard to stack some papers "on the floor" or even "on the kitchen table," that "on the floor" or "on the kitchen table" would add meaningful information to the visualization. But, in the context of the last three hundred years of office work, "on the desk" is superfluous.

You can consider this next a tenth rule, or just a general principle for good style: use a variety of sentence forms. Try to avoid strings of three or more sentences with the same subject—especially "I." While you want to avoid clutter, you also want to avoid thinness. Variety and specificity are the ways to achieve this. The rules for good writing are largely a set of things *not* to do. Basically good writing is a matter of avoiding unnecessary clutter. (Again, this is not the same as avoiding complexity.)

You can program many of these rules into a computer. Applied to pretty much any first draft, these rules will point to where you're slipping. If you revise accordingly, clarity, readability, and liveliness will improve.

Here again we come up with an unhappy truth about those various creative writing and MFA programs. If you start with a confused, unclear, and badly written story, and apply the rules of good writing to it, you can probably turn it into a simple, logical, clearly written story. It will still not be a good one. The major fault of eighty-five to ninety-five percent of all fiction is that it is banal and dull.

Now old stories can always be told with new language. You can even add new characters to them; you can use them to dramatize new ideas. But eventually even the new language, characters, and ideas lose their ability to invigorate.

Either in content or in style, in subject matter or in rhetorical approach, fiction that is too much like other fiction is bad by definition. However paradoxical it sounds, *good writing* as a set of strictures (that is, when the writing is good and nothing more) produces most bad fiction. On one level or another, the realization of this is finally what turns most writers away from writing.

Talented writing is, however, something else. You need talent to write fiction.

Good writing is clear. Talented writing is energetic.

Good writing avoids errors. Talented writing makes things happen in the reader's mind—vividly, forcefully—that good writing, which stops with clarity and logic, doesn't.

Talent appears in many forms. Some forms are diametric to each other, even mutually exclusive. (In *The Dyer's Hand,* W. H. Auden [1907–73] says most successful writers overestimate their intelligence and underestimate their talent. Often they have to do this to preserve sanity; still they *do* it.) The talented writer often uses specifics and avoids generalities—generalities that his or her specifics suggest. Because they are suggested, rather than stated, they may register with the reader far more forcefully than if they were articulated. Using specifics to imply generalities— whether they are general emotions we all know or ideas we have all vaguely sensed—*is* dramatic writing. A trickier proposition that takes just as much talent requires the writer carefully to arrange generalities for a page or five pages, followed by a specific that makes the generalities open up and take on new resonance. Henry James (1843–1916) calls the use of such specifics "the revelatory gesture," but it is just as great a part of Marcel Proust's (1871–1922) art. Indeed, it might be called the opposite of "dramatic" writing, but it can be just as strong—if not, sometimes, stronger.

Here are other emblems that can designate talent:

The talented writer often uses rhetorically interesting, musical, or lyrical phrases that are briefer than the pedestrian way of saying "the same thing."

The talented writer can explode, as with a verbal microscope, some fleeting sensation or action, tease out insights, and describe subsensations that we all recognize, even if we have rarely considered them before; that is, he or she describes them at greater length and tells more about them than other writers.

In complex sentences with multiple clauses that relate in complex ways, the talented writer will organize those clauses in the chronological order in which the referents occur, despite the logical relation grammar imposes.

Here is a badly organized narrative sentence of the sort I've read in dozens of student manuscripts handed in by writers who want to write, say, traditional commercial fantasy:

> (A) Jenny took a cold drink from the steel dipper chained to the stone wall of the corner well, where, amidst the market's morning bustle, the women had finished setting up their counters and laying out their tools, implements, and produce minutes after the sun had risen; she had left the sandal stall to amble over here.

The good writer would immediately want to break the above up into smaller sentences and clarify some antecedents:

(B) Jenny took a cold drink from the steel dipper chained to the stone wall. With the market's morning bustle, the women had finished setting up their counters and laying out their tools, implements, and produce. Only minutes after the sun had risen, Jenny had left the sandal stall and ambled over to the corner well.

Certainly that's an improvement; and it hides some of the illogic in the narrative itself. But a writer who has a better sense of narrative would start by rearranging the whole passage chronologically:

(C) Minutes after the sun had risen above the wall, amidst the market's morning bustle, the women finished setting up their counters and laying out their tools, implements, and produce. Jenny left the sandal stall to amble over to the corner well, where, from the steel dipper chained to the stone wall, she took a cold drink.

At this point, the two sentences *still* need to be broken up. But at least the various clauses now come in something like chronological order. This allows us to see that each fragment can have far more heft and vividness:

(D) Minutes after the sun cleared the market wall, footprints roughened the dust. Tent posts swung up; canvas slid down. Along the counters women laid out trowels and tomato rakes, pumpkins and pecan pickers. Jenny ambled from under the sandal stall awning. At the corner well she picked up a steel dipper chained to the mossy stones for a cold drink. As it chilled her teeth and throat, water dripped on her toes.

Talented writing tends to contain *more information,* sentence for sentence, clause for clause, than merely good writing. Example D exhibits a variety of sentence lengths. Yes, the images arrive in chronological order. But more than that, the passage paints its picture through specifics. It also employs rhetorical parallels and differences. ("Tent posts swung up; canvas slid down.") It pays attention to the sounds and rhythms of its sentences ("trowels and tomato rakes, pumpkins and pecan pickers"). It uses detailed sensory observation (the drink chills "her teeth and throat"). Much of the information it proffers is implied. (In D that includes *both* the bustle *and* the fact that we are in a market!) These are among the things that indicate talent.

I do not hold up D as a *particularly* good (or particularly talented!) piece of writing, but it shows a rhetorical awareness, a balance, a velocity, a particularity, and a liveliness that puts it way ahead of the others. Above and beyond the fact that they are logically or illogically organized, versions A through C are, by comparison, bland, formulaic, and dull. What distinguishes the writers of A, B, and C is, in fact, how good each is. But D alone shows a scrap of talent—and *only* a scrap.

Good writing avoids stock phrases and received language. Talented writing actively laughs at such phrases, such language. When talented writing and good writing support one another, we have the verbal glories of the ages—the work of Shakespeare, Thomas Browne, Joyce, and Nabokov.

Talented writing and good writing sometimes fight. The revisions necessary to organize the writing and unclutter it can pare away the passages or phrases that give the writing its life. As often, what the writer believes is new and vivid is just cliché confusion. From within the precincts of good writing, it's easy to mistake talent's complexity for clutter. From within the precincts of talent, it's easy to mistake the clarity of good writing for simplicity—even simple-mindedness. Critics or editors can point the problems out. The way to solve them, however, is a matter of taste. And that lies in the precincts of talent.

III

The early German Romantics—Schiller (1759–1805), the Schlegel brothers, Wilhelm (1767–1845) and Friedrich (1772–1829), and Ludwig Tieck (1773–1853), that is, the smart Romantics—believed something they called *Begeisterung* was the most important element among the processes that constituted the creative personality.

I think they were right.

Begeisterung is usually translated as "inspiration." *Geist* is the German word for "spirit," and "*Be-geist-erung*" means literally "be-spirited-ness," which is certainly close to "inspiration." As the word is traditionally used in ordinary German, though, it is even closer to "enthusiasm"—"spirited" in the sense of a "spirited" horse or a "spirited" prizefighter. For the Romantics, *Begeisterung* was not just the initial idea or the talent one had to realize it. *Begeisterung* was both intellectual and bodily. A form of spirit, it was also a mode of will. To the Romantics, this enthusiasm/*Begeisterung* carried the artist *through* the work's creation. If there were things you didn't know that you needed in order to write your story, your novel, your play, with enough *Begeisterung* you could always go out and learn them. If your imagination wasn't throwing out the brilliant scenes and moments to make the material dramatic, with *Begeisterung* you could arrive at such effective material through dogged intelligence, though it might take longer and require more energy. If you lacked the verbal talent that produced vivid descriptive writing, well, there were hard analytic styles that were also impressive, which you could craft through intellectual effort—though you would have to attack the work sentence by sentence. But however you employed it, *Begeisterung* is what carried you through the job. *Begeisterung* could make up for failures on other creative fronts.

Begeisterung is what artists share over their otherwise endless differences: enthusiasm for a task clearly perceived.

Over the range of our society the artist's position is rarely a prosperous one—certainly not in the beginning stages and often never. The increased size of the new, democratic field that today produces both readers and writers, the increase in competition for fame and attention—not to mention the increased effort necessary to make a reasonable living from one's work—all transform a situation that was always risky into one that today often looks lunatic. *Begeisterung*/enthusiasm is about the only thing that can get the artist through such a situation.

The decision to be a writer is the decision to enter a field where most of the news—most of the time—is bad. The best way to negotiate this situation is to have (first) a realistic view of what that situation is and (second) considerable *Begeisterung*. As Freud knew, *Begeisterung* is fundamentally neurotic. The critic Harold Bloom has suggested that what makes artists create is rank terror before the failure to create, a failure that somehow equates with death. When the artist discovers creation can, indeed, allay that fear, it produces the situation and form of desire that manifests itself as *Begeisterung.* When, from time to time throughout the artist's life, *Begeisterung* fails, often terror lies beneath.

Having mentioned the basic importance of *Begeisterung,* I'll go on to outline another use.

Let me describe two students in a midwestern graduate creative writing workshop I taught once. One was a young man of twenty-six from a solidly middle-class background, who had entered the university writing program with extremely good marks and high scores on his GREs (Graduate Record Exams). From the general discussion of the student stories we analyzed in the workshop, clearly he was an intelligent and sensitive critic. Certainly he was among the smartest and the most articulate of the students in the group. He was not particularly interested in publishing, however, and in a discussion during which I asked students what they wanted to do with their writing and where they saw themselves going, he explained that he wanted to improve his writing and eventually publish a collection of stories in a university series that was committed to doing graduate student and junior faculty work. He had no particular series in mind but was sure one such existed, which would accept his work, preferably without reading it, purely because some other writer—perhaps a workshop teacher—had judged him personally "ready for publication." When I told him I knew of no such series, nor had I any personal criteria for "publishability" other than finding a given story a rewarding and pleasurable read, he was not at all bothered. If such a series did not exist now, he was sure that in four or five years it would—because that was the right and proper way the world should work. Through continuing in workshops, he would eventually get his chance. If he didn't, finally it didn't matter. He felt no desire to have his work appear from a large commercial press, however, or from a small press *only* interested in supporting work it judged of the highest quality. As soon as any sort of competitive situation arose, he felt there must go along with it some bias based on nonesthetic aspects—actually an interesting theory, I thought. Though he sincerely wanted to improve his work for its own sake, he felt, when and if his work was published, it should be published because there was a place that published work such as his and it would simply be, so to speak, his turn. Competition, he believed and believed deeply, was not what art was about. He articulated this position well. The other students in the class were all impressed with his commitment to it—as, in fact, was I.

Myself, I had seen no evidence of what I could recognize as talent in his writing, however, and his stories struck me as a series of banal romances in which the hero either discovered his girlfriend was cheating on him and left her sadly, or another girl began an affair with a hero recently cheated on and stuck to him despite his gloom. They were well written, in precisely the sense I describe above, but they were without color or life—and always in the present tense. That made them, he explained, sound more literary. And that's the effect he wanted.

If I had seen what I could recognize as talent, I might have been even more interested in his aesthetic position. But personally I could not distinguish his stories from many, many others I had read in many other workshops. Nor did the fact that they seemed so similar to so many others bother him at all, since—as he claimed—competition was not the point.

Once he used the term "classical" about what he wanted to achieve in his own stories. "But," I said, "your model doesn't seem to be the great classical stories of the past, but rather the averaged banality of the present."

"Well," he said, "perhaps that *is* today's classical."

I couldn't take the argument much beyond that point. As a teacher, for me to say too much more would have been unnecessarily insulting—and I felt I had already come close to crossing a line I didn't feel was good for purely pedagogical reasons. I decided to let him have the last word.

In the same class was a young woman of twenty-nine, from a working-class background. She was no slouch either as a practical critic, but she had nowhere near the self-confidence of the first student. Her GREs were eccentric: high in math, low in English. Her written grammar was occasionally faulty. Often she seemed at sea when critical discussions moved into the abstract. Several times, in several descriptions in her stories, however, she had struck me as talented—that is, she had made me see things and understand things that I had not seen or understood before. Interesting incidents were juxtaposed in interesting ways in her stories. Her characters often showed unusual and idiosyncratic combinations of traits. Words were put together in interesting ways in her sentences. But it was also clear that her stories were pretty much an attempt to write the same sort as most of the other students in the class, which tended to be modeled on those of the first young man—in her case with the sexes more or less reversed. When I asked her what she wanted to do with her writing, she said she'd like to go on and "be a writer" and "publish books," but she offered it with all the hesitation of someone confessing to a history of prostitution.

At one point, after we had just read the story for class, I mentioned that Joyce had written "The Dead" in 1907, when he was twenty-five, though it was not published till 1914. I told them I would like to see their stories aspire to a similar level of structural richness and a similar richness of description of the various interiors, exteriors, and characters.

Immediately the young man objected: "You can't tell us that! That just paralyzes us and makes us incapable of writing anything."

But three weeks later, the young woman handed in a story she had gone home and begun that same night. It was far more ambitious than anything she'd done previously: incidents in the story had thematic and structural resonances with one another, and the physical description of the places and characters was twenty-five to thirty-five percent richer than anything she'd previously handed in. When I mentioned this to her after the workshop, she said, "I guess I went back to my math—that's what my degree is in. I made a little geometric picture of how I wanted the parts of the story to relate to each other. Has anybody ever done that before?" I said I often did it myself, but that it seemed too idiosyncratic to talk about in a general workshop. (Her comment is one of the things, however, that convinced me to write about it in the essay "Of Doubts and Dreams.") As well, it was the first piece I'd seen from her that was not basically a disappointed romance about a graduate student with no mention of how she supported herself. (The woman was happily married to a very successful and supportive engineer.)

Instead, she had taken another hint from Joyce and mined her own childhood material for her tale, in her case the Pittsburgh foundry where her Hungarian father had worked and the men and women who'd worked with him (I'd never known women worked at foundries before), whom she used to know when she was a child. She'd based her main character on a young woman, a few years older than herself, who'd had a job there, something that seemed to my student exciting and romantic. When she'd been twelve she'd desperately envied this young working woman of seventeen. A few years later, however, when she herself had reached twenty, she now realized this wonderfully alive young woman was actually trapped in a dead-end job by family and social forces, which led nowhere. Speaking to me privately after class, she said, "When you pointed out how old Joyce was when he'd done it, I realized there was no reason I couldn't do it, too." Though the fact was, her story shared nothing with Joyce's save the jump in descriptive and structural richness.

I have said most of the news about writing is bad. But much of the news—such as the age writers were when they wrote this or that work—is neutral. However neurotic its basis, *Begeisterung* or its lack is what turns these neutral facts into good news (Hey, *I* can do that!) or bad news (*Nobody* can do that!). Perhaps you can see from these last examples why the usual translation of *Begeisterung*—"inspiration," without the added energy of enthusiasm—doesn't quite cover the topic.

The idea that everyone can have a turn at publication is unrealistic—nor, outside a carefully delineated student context, do I think it's desirable. When our current-day democratizing urge works to render the competition fairer, I'm for it. But that is not the same thing as art without competition. Today many young writers see self-publication as a way to sidestep what they also see as the first round of unfair competition. Marcel Proust, Gertrude Stein, Stephen Crane (1871–1900), and Raymond Roussel (1877–1933) all self-published notable works—just as Edgar Rice Burroughs (1875–1950) self-published some commercially successful ones (the Tarzan series, for example). But that is only to say that, for them, the competition began *after* publication, not before.

The other important fact—important enough that I would

call it the second pole of my personal aesthetic, as *Begeisterung* is the first—is that literary competition is not a zero-sum game with a single winner, or even a ranked list of winners—that all-too-naive image of the canon in which, say, Shakespeare has first place and the gold cup, followed by Chaucer (c. 1343–1400) with the silver, in second place, Milton (1608–74) with the bronze, in third, with Spenser (c. 1552–99) and Joyce competing for who gets fourth and who gets fifth . . . The concept of literary quality is an outgrowth of a conflictual process, not a consensual one. In the enlarged democratic field, the nature of the conflict simply becomes more complex. Even among the most serious pursuers of the aesthetic, there is more than one goal; there is more than one winner. Multiple qualities and multiple achievements are valued—and have been valued throughout the history of the conflicting practices of writing making up the larger field called the literary. That multiplicity of achievement can value Vladimir Nabokov (1899–1977), and Samuel Beckett (1906–77), G. K. Chesterton (1874–1936), and Virginia Woolf (1882–1941), Seamus Heaney (b. 1939), and Meridel Le Sueur (1900–1996), George Orwell (1903–50), and Joanna Russ (b. 1939), Nathanael West (1903–40), Robert Louis Stevenson (1850–94), and Nella Larsen (1891–1964), Edmund White (b. 1940), and Grace Paley (b. 1922), Junot Díaz (b. 1960), Vincent Czyz (b. 1963), John Berger (b. 1926), and Willa Cather (1876–1947), Susan Sontag (1933–2004), J. M. Coetzee (b. 1940), Dennis Cooper (b. 1953), Amy Hempel (b. 1951), Michael Chabon (b. 1964), Ana Kavan (1901–68), Sara Schulman (b. 1958), and Kit Reed (b. 1954), Josephine Saxton (b. 1935), Erin McGraw (b. 1957), Harlan Ellison (b. 1934), Luiza Valenzuela (b. 1938), Mary Gentle (b. 1956), Shirley Jackson (b. 1919), JT Leroy (b. 1980), Thomas Pynchon (b. 1937), Linda Shore (b. 1937), Amy Bloom (b. 1953), Ursula K. Le Guin (b. 1929), Vonda N. McIntyre (b. 1948), Carol Emshwiller (b. 1921), Leonora Carrington (b. 1917), Lynn Tillman (b. 1947), L. Timmel Duchamp (b. 1950), Richard Yates (1926–92), Andrea Barrett (b. 1954), David Foster Wallace (b. 1962), Heidi Julavitz (b. 1968), Ben Marcus (b. 1967), Michael Martone (b. 1955), Hilary Bailey (b. 1936), Christine Brooke-Rose (b. 1923), Octavia E. Butler (b. 1947), Adam Haslett (b. 1970), Anita Desai (b. 1937), Zora Neale Hurston (1891–

1960), and Raymond Carver (1938–88), Malcolm Lowry (1926–66), and Wyndham Lewis (1882–1957), Tillie Olsen (b. 1912), and Raymond Chandler (1888–1959), Robert Glück (b. 1945?), and André Gide (1869–1951), Chris Offut (b. 1958), and Denis Johnson (b. 1959), James Joyce, Henry David Thoreau (1817–62), Lewis Carroll (1832–98), and Chester Himes (1909–84), Ralph Waldo Emerson (1803–82), and Wilson Harris (b. 1921), and Jean Rhys (c. 1890–1970), and John Crowley (b. 1943), Rikki Ducornet (b. 1943), Richard Wright (1908–60), and Djuna Barnes (1892–1982), Walter Pater (1839–94), Olive Shreiner (1855–1920), Thomas M. Disch (b. 1939), and Paul Goodman (1911–72), Oscar Wilde (1854–1900), Honoré de Balzac (1799–1850), Francis Bacon (1561–1626), and Rebecca Brown (b. 1955), Charles Baudelaire (1821–67), and Georg Büchner (1813–37), Michel de Montaigne (1533–92), and Naguib Mahfouz (b. 1911), Mary Caponegro (b. 1975), Marianne Moore (1887–1972), and Henri de Mantherlant (1895–1972), Melvin Dixon (1950–92), Daryl Pinckney (b. 1948), Roger Zelazny (1937–95), Randall Kenan (b. 1963), and Don Belton (b. 1956), Guy Davenport (1927–2005), and D. H. Lawrence (1888–1930), Hart Crane (1899–1931), and Jean Toomer (1897–1968), Ethan Canin (b. 1960), William Gass (b. 1924), Bruce Benderson (b. 1955), Ursule Molinaro (1923–2000), Paul West (b. 1930), Alan Singer (b. 1948), James Alan McPherson (b. 1943), Sandra Cisneros (b. 1954), Breece D'J Pancake (1879–1952), Michael Moorcock (b. 1939), and R. M. Berry (b. 1947), Edward Gibbon (1737–94), Richard Powers (b. 1957), John Galsworthy (1867–1933), and James Gould Cozzens (1903–78), Steve Erickson (b. 1950), Brian Evenson (b. 1966), Knut Hamsun (1859–1952), and Victor Hugo (1802–85), and any of the three hundred or five hundred or fifteen hundred others any literate reader would *have* to add to such a list. The greater their literacy, the more names they will add—*and* the more they will disagree over. Indeed, such a list only becomes useful as we read its biases and blindnesses, its gaps, its errors, its incompletenesses. The diversity and difference among such lists make the literary field rich and meaningful—not some hierarchical order that might initially generate one such list or another. Difference and diversity as much as education and idiosyncrasy will always defeat and shatter such a hierarchy after more than six or seven names are forced into it.

And that's a good thing, too.

When you have read widely among these indubitably good writers, you must make an average image for yourself of their inarguably talented work—and realize *that* is what your own work must be better than. And you must realize as well, one way or another, that is what they are all (or were all)—living and dead—doing.

IV

Begeisterung was formulated and written about by a group of Germans some two hundred years ago. But the nature of the literary world has changed mightily since.

I've already used the phrase "the enlarged democratic field." But what exactly are we talking about? Today the functionally literate population is more than fifty times the size it was 190 years ago in 1814, which is to say just at the time when ideas from Germany such as *Begeisterung* were first making their way through England and France both. It was after the Napoleonic wars but before the mid-nineteenth-century republican revolutions in Europe and the Civil War in the United States.

The Revolution of 1848 in France and the other uprisings within a few years of it throughout the continent (and, a dozen years later, the American Civil War) were armed battles between wealth concentrated in the old-style widespread *agricultural* capitalist system and wealth concentrated in the new-style widespread *industrial* capitalist system. Both in Europe and the United States, these conflicts were brought on by rising populations and changing technologies. First in Europe, then in the United Sates, new-style industrialism won.

Today a far higher percentage of the world's population lives in cities than ever before. Public education has made advances that would have been inconceivable a century ago, much less two centuries. In England toward the end of the first two decades of the nineteenth century, the major poets of that time numbered six: Wordsworth (1770–1850), Coleridge (1772–1834), Blake (1757–

1827), Byron (1888–24), Keats (1795–1821), and Shelley (1792–1822), all of whom were writing in the year 1814.

By general consensus some fourteen poets of considerable, if minor, interest were also writing then: Robert Southey (1774–1843), poet laureate in his day but known now only as the poet Lewis Carroll parodied in some of his *Alice and Wonderland* poems; Thomas Moore (1779–1852) was as famous as his close friend Lord Byron was in his day; he allowed Byron's journals to be burned—and is himself now unread, although his *Irish Melodies* receives a passing mention in Joyce's "The Dead"; during his lifetime Sir Walter Scott (1771–1832) was far better known as a poet than a novelist; his novels all appeared anonymously and he did not acknowledge their authorship till 1827; also there is Leigh Hunt (1784–1859), mostly of interest because he figures so importantly in Keats's biography. He was far better known than Keats during his lifetime. As well as his famous statement of radical reformist religious thought, "Abou Ben Adhem," he wrote a charming poem to Thomas Carlyle's wife, Jane, that sticks in the mind, "Jenny Kissed Me":

> Jenny kiss'd me when we met,
> Jumping from the chair she sat in;
> > Time, you thief, who loves to get
> Sweets into your list, put that in!
> > Say I'm weary, say I'm sad,
> Say that health and wealth have miss'd me,
> > Say I'm growing old, but add,
> Jenny kiss'd me.

Poets practically unknown in their time whom scholars have since rediscovered and found interesting include George Darley (1795–1846), Winthrop Mackworth Pread (1802–39), and John Clare (1793–1864). I've now named seven minor romantics. Someone might add another seven, to make, perhaps, fourteen. But today all fourteen concern a small group of professors and graduate students, enough to fuel the odd doctoral thesis and interest readers particularly focused on the period. At the time, however, when those six major and fourteen minor poets were writing, there were considerably less than 2.5 million people in the British isles who could read and write well enough to *be* poets of such ranking.

Today the current literate field (in American English, say)—at least twenty-five times the size of the field of 1814—might be expected to hold twenty-five times six major poets producing poems of an interest comparable to those of Blake, Coleridge, Wordsworth, Byron, Keats, and Shelley (that is to say, 150 major poets), and twenty-five times fourteen minor poets (or 350) of considerable interest.

That's about what the statistics are.

The fundamental difference between the world of 1814 and the world of the present day is that six major and fourteen minor poets is a knowable field. Arthur Symons's *The Romantic Movement in English Poetry* (New York: Dutton, 1909; Symons: 1865–1945) gives essays on 87 poets born after 1722 and dead by 1868—his own cut-off point for the romantics—arbitrarily as all such dates must be, but still eminently sensible. In a final chapter, "Minors," he mentions another 52 poets who fall within the same period. Though it may take a decade or more of reading, a single reader *can* be familiar with the totality of that field. No single reader can be thoroughly familiar with the works of 150 major poets and 350 minor poets. Symons's 340-page book could not cover the *major* English language poets alive today—much less give a comprehensive survey of both the major *and* the minor poets whose births and deaths were contained within the last 140 years. Thus, the doling out by the literate readership of fame, merit, or even simple attention is an entirely different process from what it once was.

When Lord Byron's poem *The Corsair* was published in 1814 (that year when all the romantic poets we've mentioned were writing), queues began to form outside London bookstores four and five hours before they opened, and, by the time the doors unlocked, those queues stretched around the block. *The Corsair* sold ten thousand copies on the first day of publication, and three hundred thousand in the next year. (That is to say, by the year's end, a copy was owned by just over a quarter of the people in the British Isles who could have actually read it.) And when the poet, novelist, and playwright Victor Hugo (b. 1802) died in Paris in 1885, his funeral was a four-day state affair, notably longer and finally grander than, say, the funeral of President Kennedy (b. 1917) on his assassination in 1963. Two years before, in 1883, when opera composer Richard Wagner (b. 1813) died in Venice, his funeral was not much smaller.

Today the deaths of artists simply do not constitute such national events. A far greater percentage of the society has seen the works of Steven Spielberg or George Lucas than ever saw Wagner's operas—or saw Hugo's plays or read his poems and novels. But though Spielberg's and Lucas's works cost more to make and make more when they appear, when at last these film directors go, neither is likely to have the same sort of final send-off as Wagner or Hugo—which is another way of saying that today even the most popular arts fit into the society very differently from the way they once did, a century or two centuries back.

From time to time all the major Romantic poets—and probably most of the minor ones as well—gave readings of an afternoon or evening in their homes or at the homes of their friends. Throughout the nineteenth century, writing their recollections of the French poets Rimbaud (1854–91) and Baudelaire, people described such occasions. The practice continued up through World War I and over the period between the world wars. William Merrill Fisher (1889–1969) writes about one such poetry reading "at home" in New York City, which the young Austrian-born American poet Samuel Greenberg (1893–1917) attended. From the sixties, I recall a woman who lived on Greenwich Village's Patchin Place telling about such a gathering when she was a student at Smith College in the late thirties, at which Edna St. Vincent Millay (1892–1950) read from her recent work.

I was born in the opening year of America's involvement with World War II. Only twice in my life have I been to such an "at home" reading. Once was with an elderly German woman in Vermont, when I was eighteen (I am now sixty-three). The second time was about a half-dozen years ago, when a bunch of graduate students at the University of Michigan dressed up in eighteenth-century costumes and gave a "tea," at which a few people read their poems. That is to say, it was in imitation of a discontinued practice.

Consider, though: while all of them gave readings at peoples' houses, neither Byron, Shelley, nor Keats ever gave a *public* reading of his poems during his brief life. (Prose writers such as Dickens and Wilde went on lecture tours, which even brought them to America, where they often did readings. But they did not come as poets.) A development of the last sixty years and almost certainly encouraged by the large number of returning soldiers to universities after World War II, the *public* reading, started at the 92nd Street Y in New York City in the years between the two world wars and was given a large boost by the popularity of the poet Dylan Thomas's public readings. The idea spread to San Francisco art galleries and Greenwich Village coffee shops through the forties and fifties. Today readings are a staple of college campuses and bookstores with any literary leanings whatsoever, so that even the likes of Barnes & Noble sponsors them. "Open mike" readings and poetry slams are a regular part of contemporary urban culture. Only a few nights ago, with my life-partner, Dennis, I went to see *Def Poetry Jam,* a staged reading on Broadway, at the Longacre Theater, by nine urban poets (one of whom I'd taught with out at Naropa University in Boulder, Colorado, the previous summer); the event grew out of the Home Box Office television series *Def Poetry Jam.* Now writers such as Maxwell Anderson (1888–1959), Robinson Jeffers (1887–1962), Ira Gershwin (1896–1983) and Dorothy and DuBose Hayward, Gertrude Stein, Langston Hughes (1902–67), and Dylan Thomas (1914–53) all had verse plays (or operas) on Broadway. But despite Fiona Shaw's one-woman presentation of T. S. Eliot's *The Waste Land* in 1996, this is the first time, I suspect, that contemporary poetry, read by the living poets themselves, has hit the Broadway stage. *Def Poetry Jam* received a wildly enthusiastic standing ovation. Once again, art and the artist—specifically the literary arts and the literary artist —fit into the society in a very different way today from the way they did in previous epochs.

When the change is this great, a phrase such as "the position of the artist has changed" no longer covers the case. Rather, such positions (where, as W. H. Auden once put it, "the artist is considered the most important of the state's civil servants") are no longer there for artists to fill—while other positions, however less exalted, are. This is tantamount to acknowledging that art—specifically poetry and prose fiction—has become a different sort of social object from what it once was, as English-language literature itself became a different social object when, shortly after World War I, it first became a topic of university study and so became the object we know today and more and more ceased to be the study of the philology of the language from Old English through Chaucer through Elizabethan English to the present—what "English Literature" had mostly meant before World War I, when it was taught at London and Edinburgh Universities in the 1880s and 1890s.

The things we look for "literature" to do in our lives, how we expect it to do them, and the structures of the social net in which it functions have changed. This is not even to broach the displacements, transformations, and borrowings effected by movies, television, or, most recently, the internet.

While these changes are very real, sometimes we can make too much of them. Art is a tradition-bound, tradition-stabilized enterprise. Often those folks newly alerted to the changes want to see a total erasure of the slate, allowing us to do anything and everything in completely new ways. But it is the traditions—especially (and paradoxically) the traditions of experimentation, originality, and newness—that make it so difficult for so many to see the changes in the actual object itself and that cause those caught up in the rush for originality to end up repeating, often to the letter, the experiments of the past and—save those among them familiar with more of the workings of art's history—producing works that are just not very original. Often they find the common audience bored or uninterested by their efforts—and the more sophisticated, unimpressed. No more than any other enquiry into aesthetics can this book solve such problems. But it does not ignore them either.

In his manifesto "No More Masterpieces" that forms the centerpiece for his influential collection of essays on art, *The Theater and Its Double* (1938), the French actor, writer, and director Antonin Artaud (1896–1948) wrote:

> One of the reasons for the asphyxiating atmosphere in which we all live without possible escape or remedy—and in which we all share—is our respect for what has been

written, formulated, or painted, what has been given form, as if all expression were not at last exhausted, were not at the point where things must break apart if they are to start anew and begin afresh.

We must have done with this idea of masterpieces reserved for a self-styled elite and not understood by a general public . . .

Masterpieces are good for the past. They are not good for us. We have the right to say what has been said and even what has not been said in a way that belongs to us, a way that is immediate and direct, corresponding to present modes of feeling, and understandable to everyone.

It is idiotic to reproach the masses for having no sense of the sublime, when the sublime is confused with one or another of its formal manifestations, which are moreover always defunct manifestations.

How could one not agree? Or not applaud? Or not run off to spread the news? But as the little history that I have already given suggests, in the seventy years since Artaud wrote his manifesto, the "masterpiece" as it was conceived of in the nineteenth century that Artaud is polemicizing against is by and large no longer part of the active aesthetic landscape. (We read *Ulysses* for pleasure and are even awed by it. But nobody would try to write out another one, full-scale, any more than someone would try to write another *Hamlet* in verse.) As well, no one has been able to get around the fact that the "masses" really *require* education.

Since Artaud wrote his manifesto, it has become widely evident that when the "masses" are left to themselves, the artists who are trying to "say what has been said and even what has not been said in a way that belongs to us, a way that is immediate and direct," are precisely the artists who most bore and bewilder the masses, who flock instead to the old, tried, tired, and true —not in terms of the classic sublime, but in terms of the formulaic, the violent, and the kitschy. Despite the fears of the moralists, the masses don't seem to retain any lasting interest even in works of pornography.

V

My education as a writer has been a diverse one. In just over forty years of publishing, I've read a handful of books about writing that I felt have saved me some time. (I've read many others that gave me little or nothing.) Among the ones I found useful were:

ABC of Reading (1934), by Ezra Pound: Pound's cranky, cantankerous, wildly opinionated, and wholly individual notions of literature can come as a vivifying breath to those who have endured the teaching of literature as an authoritarian enterprise done *this* way and *not* that way. He is *almost* always right and almost always interesting. Those whose literary educations took a more laid-back form sometimes have difficulty, however, conceiving of whom he could be polemicizing against. Indeed, Pound is a good example of what rebels sound like seventy or eighty years after they have been almost entirely successful.

The Autobiography of Alice B. Toklas (1933) and *Lectures in America* (1934) are both by Gertrude Stein. I devoured the first in a Vintage paperback shortly after I turned seventeen. In that book, Gertrude Stein tells the nineteen-year-old composer and writer Paul Bowles, "If you don't work hard when you're twenty, Paul, no one will love you when you're thirty." It's the first piece of literary advice I ever remember conscientiously deciding to take. The book also brought home to me a lesson without which it is almost impossible to become a professional writer: from it I first learned that the writers who wrote books, the writers who created published works, brilliant works, exciting works, were people. They had bodies. They lived in actual houses. They ate meals. They liked certain of their acquaintances and disliked others. They had personalities. They were neither gods nor primal forces—voices alone, moving, bodiless, through space and time. Their day-to-day humanity ceded them the material for their art. This was as true for Shakespeare, Chaucer, and Milton as it is for Jay Wright (b. 1935), Richard Powers (b. 1957), Angela Carter (1940–92), Michael Cunningham (b. 1952), Alice Munro (b. 1931), and William Ernest Gaines (b. 1933). Had I not suffered this revelation at seventeen, I wouldn't have published my first novel three years later at twenty.

Having read and so much profited from one of Stein's books at seventeen, at nineteen I gambled on a second, *Lectures in America*—and again lucked out. Among these half dozen meditations on English literature, Stein writes, "The paragraph is the emotional unit of the English Language."

There are myriad technical reasons to begin a new paragraph: another character speaks, the narrative switches focus to what another character is doing, the writer changes to a new rhetorical mode (from external action to internal reverie, from internal reverie to external description), and, of course, the all-purpose change of topic. But all are, finally, one form or another of movement between Stein's emotional units. In reading over his or her own prose, the writer who can forget the emotions that impelled the writing and can respond to the modulations in the emotions the words on the page actually evoke will generally be able to solve the problem of when to begin a new paragraph, that is, when the tenor of those emotions shift—and it's time for a new line and an indentation.

Stein was famous for writing in a kind of baby talk, with many repetitions and what was often taken as a childish disregard for punctuation. In that same collection, in what some critics during her lifetime called "Stein-ese," she wrote:

> The thing that has made the glory of English literature is description simple concentrated description not of what happened nor what is thought or what is dreamed but what exists and so makes the life the island life the daily island life . . . And in the descriptions the daily, the hourly descriptions of this island life as it exists and it does exist it does really exist English literature has gone on from Chaucer until now . . . That makes a large one third of English literature. (14–15)

Description (or psychological analysis, or any other rhetorical mode associated with fiction) without story to support it risks becoming interminable. But story without description soon becomes insufferably thin. "Good prose," Flaubert wrote his mistress, the aspiring writer Louise Colet, "is stuffed with things"—another observation of what I suspect is only a different aspect of Stein's perception.

The more I read and reread Gertrude Stein, the more I am convinced that, for writers, she is the most important critic-writer between Walter Pater and Antonin Artaud—with both of whom, indeed, she overlaps.

I have always found George Orwell's (1903–50) essay "Politics and the English Language" (1948) a wonderfully clarifying document. In certain circles, during the 1970s and 1980s, Orwell's piece was used widely as a writing aid for college freshmen and sophomores, most of whom were neither sophisticated nor widely read enough to take in its points. It has never been a popular text with beginning writers (an audience it was never intended for). As well, if you read it carelessly, it can be taken as attacking some of the cherished pleasures of those of us who enjoy the rarified heights of literary theory and its attendant complex rhetoric. But Orwell's essay is for people who seriously want to write—and who have done enough general reading in fiction, journalism, and criticism so that it is possible that they might even succeed; the essay offers little help to writers who still must learn how to put together grammatical or logical sentences or a coherent argument. Orwell's piece is specifically for people who *can* write what passes for "competent" prose, but who need someone to point out why their "competent" efforts are so often empty or worthless. The essay has occasioned a barrage of recent attacks. But the best I can say for them is that most of the essays I have read are notably more muddled than Orwell's. What these academics are muddled about is why Orwell's bit of eminent good sense does not turn students who can't write into thinkers who can. They fail to see that their students have not read enough, while Orwell's piece is addressed to people who have read too much—specifically too much of the wrong thing, and in the wrong way.

When the writing of literary theory is bad (and often at the general academic level it is), what usually makes it bad is something Orwell's essay points to—what Orwell calls "operators" or "verbal false limbs," which save the writer the trouble of "picking out appropriate verbs and nouns, and at the same time pad the sentence with extra syllables which give it an appearance of symmetry" (130).

Often when graduate students find themselves having to

write about a difficult passage from, say, Flaubert or Heidegger, which is developing a point (or, more usually, a portion of a larger point) that the graduate only dimly understands, again and again I have seen one or another of them break the passage up all but arbitrarily and put "On the one hand he writes" in front of the first part and "But on the other hand, he says" before the second—or, indeed, any other possible verbal limbs that effect the same suggestion of symmetrical contrast—establishing the idea that a single passage outlining a development actually expresses contrasting or contradictory ideas. The rest of the student's paper—or section of the paper—will cite other examples of one or the other of these "two contradictory ideas," sometimes through the medium of a shared word or phrase or sometimes just through hazily similar notions.

Only yesterday morning, while marking a Ph.D. preliminary exam, I found one such false contrast—not in the student's answer but in one of the questions posed by a colleague: "D. H. Lawrence called the novel 'the bright book of life.' Contradicting this, however, he also said that the novel was the receptacle of the most subjective responses to the world. Choose three novels written between 1850 and 1950 in which subjectivity is foregrounded and discuss them in terms of the formal techniques the writer employs to present or invent the modern subject." The fact is, there is no contradiction between the novel's function as 'the bright book of life' and its presentation of subjective responses to the world—since subjective responses to the world are part of life. It's far too limited a reading that would assume "the bright book of life" referred only to the object world around us. The relation is one of "as well as," not one of "contradicting this." The point is to understand how B follows from A, not how it contrasts with it. But such careless articulation often suggests to someone whose critical lens is not highly focused that the discernment of such "contrasts" represents "close reading," or that finding contrasts that aren't there is the way to trace out some "problematic" or "aporia" (Greek for "contradiction") in the passage, when all it does is sow confusion on top of misunderstanding. One *can* write clearly about complex notions. Those complexities still require concentration, repeated reading, and careful articulation to get them clear.

Orwell discusses this process in the context of political journalese, in which the commentator will use "the appearance of symmetry" to set up conceptual antitheses where no antitheses exist. But today this is what makes three out of four graduate student papers (not to mention too many "higher thoughts" from the already securely tenured) reaching after the heights of theory flounder off into fogged failures of logic, leaving their works all-but-pointless exercises in verbiage.

Again, it's professors, journalists, graduate students, and critics who *do* write for others who need Orwell's piece—not undergraduate students who don't.

I am a lover of the verbal sensuality and conceptual richness of Jacques Derrida (1930–2004), Michel Foucault (1926–84), and Jacques Lacan (1901–81), just as I enjoy William Faulkner (1897–1962), John Cowper Powys (1872–1963), and Charles M. Doughty (1843–1926). I delight in reading them and rereading them, in teaching them and teaching them again; and I enjoy equally John Ruskin (1819–1900), Thomas Carlyle (1795–1881), Edgar Allan Poe (1809–49), and Walter Pater (1839–94).

Still I think, basically, Orwell is right.

Another fine and informative book for people who write regularly and understand the mechanics of writing is Jacques Barzun's *Simple and Direct: A Rhetoric for Writers* (1975; revised 1985). Rich in the history of words, the book is particularly good at explaining why some mistakes are, indeed, mistakes. Here's an analysis from Barzun's book that dramatizes particularly well one of Orwell's points, using the example "They said they had sought a meaningful dialogue on their demands, which, as they made clear before, are non-negotiable."

> *Meaningful* is usually quite meaning*less*. Does the writer mean *productive, fruitful, satisfactory, fair-minded?* It is hard to say; the word *dialogue* is too vague to suggest its proper epithet, and taken together with *non-negotiable,* it lands the writer in self-contradiction; for what is there to discuss if the issues are not subject to negotiation? The only tenable sense is: "They faced their opponents with an ultimatum." This result is a good example of the way

in which the criticism and simplifying of words discloses
a hidden meaning.

Barzun's chapter on frequently confused words is far more thor-
ough than, say, the one in the ever popular Strunk and White
(*The Elements of Style*, 1959), and it lets us know something about
the history of those confusions, which are often more complex than they appear. "Restive," for example, does not mean
restless—or at least up until the Second World War, it didn't.
It was the adjective from "rest" and meant fixed, immobile, or
stubborn. Now it means almost anything. Barzun points out
how the poor use of words by careless writers makes writers
more sensitive to the language less willing to use them for fear
of being misunderstood. Barzun's book is not a remedial text.
It's another grown-up text for grown-up writers.

Other works that I have found useful and stimulating include
the essays in W. H. Auden's *The Dyer's Hand* and *Forewords
and Afterwords*; William Gass's *Fiction and the Figures of Life*
and *The World within the Word* and *Habitations of the Word*;
Guy Davenport's *The Geography of the Imagination*, *Every Force
Evolves a Form*, and *The Hunter Gracchus*; and Jorge Luis Borges's *Other Inquisitions* and *This Craft of Verse*; as well as Hugo
von Hoffmannsthal's *The Lord Chandos Letter* (1902). This last
is a fictional letter from a young Renaissance writer, presumably
to Sir Francis Bacon, explaining why the twenty-eight-year-old
young man is giving up literature. If you are feeling discouraged, Hoffmannsthal's text is all but guaranteed to make you
want to get back to writing. Also a turn-on in two very different
modes are G. E. Lessing's *Laocoön* and Laios Egri's *The Art of
Dramatic Writing*.

As well, I'm a fan of E. M. Forster's 1927 meditation *Aspects of
the Novel*. We'll get to that one shortly.

In his astute and useful essay "On Writing," Raymond Carver
says he doesn't like tricks, cheap or otherwise. Yet the creation
of a certain order of particularly vivid description is a trick. (I
discuss it in two essays, "Thickening the Plot" and "Of Doubts
and Dreams.") It is one of the many tricks that, in his own writing, Carver generally eschews. While he was an extraordinary

creator of moving and poignant miniatures, and while his descriptions are always adequate for his own narrative purposes, few would cite him as a master of description per se.

Yet the "trick" I speak of was used by Flaubert and Chekhov and the great American short-story writer Theodore Sturgeon. Buoyed by a raft of other descriptive planks, Joyce uses it particularly effectively in *Ulysses* and "The Dead"; all Virginia Woolf's mature fiction relies on it more or less heavily, as does Richard Hughes's, Harry Matthews's, William Golding's, Vladimir Nabokov's, John Updike's, Lawrence Durrell's, William Van Wert's, Gene Garbor's, Antonia Byatt's, Robert Coover's (particularly in his early "realist" novel *The Origin of the Brunists*), William Gass's, John Gardner's, Angela Carter's, Harlan Ellison's, Luisa Valenzuela's, Guy Davenport's, John Crowley's, Charlotte Bacon's, and Rikki Ducornet's—indeed, just about every writer known for both beauty of language and vivid scene painting. The reason to call it a "trick," rather than a technique, strategy, or method, is because it doesn't always work in every instance with every reader every time. It rarely works in the same way with the same reader in repeated readings of the same text. Because it's fundamentally psychological, its success tends toward a statistical existence across a general audience. Yet, statistically, readers find it highly pleasurable, even though three or four readers will often argue over why it works and when, indeed, it doesn't. This book several times discusses how it's done. If you can wrap your mind around it, it's interesting to try.

Before we get on to the "how," though, let's talk a bit about the "why" and the "what."

VI

During a recent conversation I was having with a friend, he picked up his well-read Vintage paperback of *Ulysses*, opened it to page 36, and said, "Listen to this: 'On his wise shoulders through the checkerwork of leaves the sun flung spangles, dancing coins.' Now, I love that sentence. But why is it better to write that than, say, 'Sunlight fell on him through leaves'? Or even to omit it altogether and get on with the story, our day in Dublin?"

Actually my friend had already given the reason: *because* he loves it. A possible reason to love it is because it makes two things pop up in the mind more vividly than does the sentence "Sunlight fell on him through leaves." One is what specifically happened at *that* particular time when light fell through *those* particular leaves; it has been described. In some light, in some venues, when someone walks under a tree, the bits of light simply slide over him or her. In others, such as this one, when, yes, a breeze is passing, they dance. The second thing that pops up is your awareness of the possibilities for the person *in* that space of shadow and light—in Joyce's case the jocularly anti-Semitic Mr. Deasy, whose know-nothing claim that there are no Jews in Ireland sets up a controlling irony for the novel: Leopold Bloom, who represents Ulysses to Stephen's Telemachus, *is* a Dublin Jew. The combination of specific description and strong implication (in this case, the irony in the word "wise") is one that, to a statistically large sampling of readers, affords a more vivid reading experience than the simple "statement of information." As well, because the sentence mimes what it describes—that is, it dances—in a manner I discuss in the essay "After Almost No Time at All the String on Which He had Been Pulling and Pulling Came Apart into Two Separate Pieces So Quickly He Hardly Realized It Had Snapped, *or:* Reflections on 'The Beach Fire,'" it calls up a chain of further implications about the way perceptions and words dance and are flung about through the day, which the reader can take as far as he or she wishes.

Now, such combinations of presentation and implication are a trick—though it's one used by the J-Writer who wrote many of the really good parts in the early books of the Bible (the story of Adam and Eve in the Garden of Eden, for instance), by Homer throughout the *Iliad* and the *Odyssey*, and by Shakespeare in his plays and sonnets; also by Joyce, Woolf, and Nabokov. (Pater located it as an element in the true genius of Plato, above and beyond any of his specific philosophical arguments.) I persist in calling it a trick because of these, yes, intermittent successes. But it works for enough readers, enough of the time, to keep writers such as G. K. Chesterton and Djuna Barnes in print, when the political (or, in Chesterton's case, religious) content of their work has become highly out of favor, if not downright repellent.

We love a sentence only partially because of *what* it means, but even more for the manner and intensity through which it makes its meaning vivid.

People with whom the trick tends not to work include people who are just learning the language and/or who have no literary background in their own or any other language before they start. It tends to include people who know exactly what they're reading for, and who are not interested in getting any other pleasure from a book except the one they open the first page expecting.

The vividness comes from a kind of surprise, the surprise of meeting a series of words that, one by one, at first seem to have nothing to do with the topic—striding under a tree on a June day—but words that, at a certain point, astonish us with their economy, accuracy, and playful vitality. Again, some of it will work on one reader, whereas others will only find it affected. But it's managed to remain of part of literature for several thousand years.

Now, "Sunlight fell on him through leaves" has a precise economy and its own beauty. We can enjoy that, too. But the other—through that combination of specific statement and implication—puts a higher percentage of readers closer to the pulse and texture of the incident. Rhetorically, it makes a greater number of educated readers feel there's a shorter distance between words and occurrence. What we are talking about here is the (very real) pleasure of good writing versus the delight of writerly talent.

If an early nineteenth-century essayist had written, "The true and the beautiful are largely the same and inextricably entailed. That is one of the few self-evident facts of the modern world. Indeed, I believe, if you have understood that, you can pretty much negotiate the whole of modern life," I doubt anyone would remember it today.

But around 1820, at the conclusion of his poem in five ten-line-stanzas, "Ode to a Grecian Urn," Keats wrote:

> Beauty is truth, truth beauty,—that is all
> Ye know on earth and all ye need to know.

The economy, symmetry, and specificity here—the performance of its meaning through implication, accuracy, and bodily rhythm (the rhythmic and alliterative emphasis on "all," "need," and "know"; its encompassing of both wonder and "on earth" despair)—lift it to a level of immediacy that won't shake loose from the mind. "Beauty is truth, truth beauty," is, of course, in the same rhetorical mode as "Sunlight fell through leaves." But "—that is all / ye know on earth and all ye need to know" is a statement that *implies* a broad and complex argument. As you unravel those implications, you can find yourself facing a declaration of the tragic limits of what, indeed, *can* be known: you really *don't* know anything else, and the bare sufficiency of that basis for knowledge has been the universe's great gift to humanity, a gift from which all law and science and art have been constructed. For behind all we presume to be knowledge, whether correct or incorrect, some correspondence between elements in the world must have been noted at some time or other, a correspondence that was once assumed beautiful, fascinating, or at least interesting—before anyone could go on to judge it useful, efficient, or functional. A correspondence must be *noticed* before it can be evaluated, can be judged. What makes us notice anything is always some aspect of the aesthetic. The three categories—the useful, the efficient, the functional—already must at least *begin* as aesthetic constructions, which, only after they have been established through aesthetic correspondences, can go on to support usable judgments on what subsequently we can find in them. That is how all knowledge—however useful—has its basis in the apperception of the beautiful—even to the hideously ugly and the painful. When Keats's words have impelled my thoughts in this direction, his lines have made me weep the way the tragic knowledge we took with us on our expulsion from Eden occasionally does.

To have that response to the Garden of Eden story, I have to read the text very slowly, leaving out the first chapter of Genesis that contains the famous seven days of creation (introduced by the P-Writer—or Priestly Writer—some three hundred years later). I have to follow what the J-Writer in the eighth century BCE alone put down, word by word, phrase by phrase; and I have to follow the Hebrew version beside two or three English translations, as my own Hebrew is simply not good enough to read it in the original unassisted. I have to pay particular attention to the humor of the text ("I bet you thought snakes *always* crawled on the ground," the J-Writer, who first wrote her tale in the later years of the Court of David, jests with her audience; "I bet you thought *all* human beings had been born out of women for all time." Critic Harold Bloom and biblical scholar Richard E. Friedman both feel that the J-Writer was likely a sophisticated court lady in the late years of King David's court). I have to pay particular attention to the multiple meanings of the infinitival intensifiers in the Hebrew, sometimes indicated by italics in the King James version, as well as all the specific information we learn from overhearing the words of YHWH, first in his poetic explosion at the serpent, and finally in his anxious mutterings as he sets the angels with their flaming sword to guard the way back into Eden—which mutterings, of course, reveal to us, after the fact, the *most* important thing that Adam and Eve (she gets her name only after God gives her and Adam clothes of skins) learned when they ate of the tree of the knowledge of what's good and what's bad (*etz hada'at tov v'ra*): "We are doomed fools; we made a tragic choice; we ate from the *wrong* tree! We ate from the tree of the knowledge of *tov* (good) and *ra* (bad), and the *ra* (the bad thing) we now know in our bones is that we should have eaten from the *other* tree—the perfectly licensed tree of life! We now know our choice was *mortally* bad —for immediately we had to become too busy with our shame to compensate for our error: the knowledge of our mortality (one with the knowledge of how we missed out on immortality), which we have just gained—the knowledge that shuts us out of the garden."

Those textual details lead me through the implications that such are the inevitable repercussions of all human learning. To learn anything worth knowing requires that you learn as well how pathetic you were when you were ignorant of it. The knowledge of what you have lost irrevocably because you *were* in ignorance of it *is* the knowledge of the worth of what you have learned. A reason knowledge/learning in general is so unpopular with so many people is because very early we all learn there is a phenomenologically unpleasant side to it: to learn *anything* entails the fact that there is no way to escape learning that you were formerly ignorant, to learn that you were a fool, that you have already lost irretrievable opportunities, that you have made wrong choices, that you were silly and limited. These lessons are not pleasant. The acquisition of knowledge—especially when we are young—again and again includes this experience. Older children tease us for what we don't know. Teachers condescend to us as they instruct us. (Long ago, they beat us for forgetting.) In the school yard we overhear the third graders talking about how dumb the first graders are. When we reach the third grade, we ourselves contribute to such discussions. Thus most people soon actively desire to stay clear of the whole process, because by the time we are seven or eight we know exactly what the repercussions and reactions will be. One moves toward knowledge through a gauntlet of inescapable insults—the most painful among them often self-tendered. The Enlightenment notion (that, indeed, knowledge also brings "enlightenment"— that there is an "upside" to learning as well: that knowledge itself is both happiness and power) tries to suppress that downside. But few people are fooled. Reminders of the downside of the process in stories such as that of Adam and Eve can make us—some of us, some of the time, because we are children of the Enlightenment who have inevitably, successfully, necessarily, been taken in—weep.

We say we are weeping for lost innocence. More truthfully, we are weeping for the lost pleasure of unchallenged ignorance.

Before the Enlightenment stressed the relationship between knowledge and power, there was a much heavier stress on the relationship between knowledge and sex. Freud retrieved some of that relationship in *Leonardo da Vinci and a Memory of His Childhood*. (The first intellectual problem almost all children take up, Freud pointed out, is where do babies come from, the pursuit of which soon catapults us into the coils and turmoils of sexual reproduction.) It perseveres, of course, in the concept of "knowing" a woman or a man sexually. It is there in the J-Writer's version of the Adam and Eve story as well: To know that sex leads to procreation is immediately to want to control it (especially among beleaguered primitive peoples), to set up habits (covering the genitals or other body parts) to dampen the sexual urges. But any effort to keep them under control is to instill habits that produce shame and embarrassment when violated, even in pursuit of procreation itself, to say nothing of innocent, guilt-free copulation. As a deeply insightful "pre-Enlightenment" text, the Adam and Eve story figures this aspect of the tale forcefully just as it figures that death will come before we can do anything about it: that knowledge *is* the burning blade preventing reentry into the garden and a return to the tree of life. The tragic implications repeatedly produce real tears in me—as I suspect they have for many readers over the centuries.

The story of Eden is a short, ironic tale to teach children a religious tradition—that can make an adult (and, in my case, an adult who happens to be an atheist) weep. That's among the things that, through statement and implication, stories can do. Such implications as nestle in Keats's ode and the J-Writer's Eden story are so broad that, today, most of us would probably figure, "Don't even *try* it!"

But both work.

When one approaches Keats's conclusion about truth and beauty through the historical set-up of *Ode to a Grecian Urn*'s previous 48 lines, his observation can take the top of your head off. Keats is, after all, *the* master of accuracy and implication among the English romantic poets, working toward vivid immediacy. Indeed, like Joyce's story "The Dead" and Lawrence's tale "Odour of Chrysanthemums," Keats's poem is one of the gentlest, one of the most powerful *retellings* of the tale of the Edenic expulsion implicit in the gaining of any and all knowledge (in Keats's case, it is the particular knowledge called happiness implicit in domestic social beauty).

Again, not everyone is affected by these texts in this way; nor is each reader affected by them in the same way every time she or he reads them. But enough readers find that they work enough of the time to preserve specific description and withheld implication as valued techniques of the literary, both in prose and poetry. Writings that employ those techniques generously often seem more immediate, more protean, and more vibrant over the long run than works that eschew them for a safer rhetoric and more distanced affect.

I think of myself as a reader with broad, if not actually catholic, tastes. When I have tallied it up, I find that I spend as much on reading matter weekly as I do on food—now that my daughter is grown—for a family of two. That includes a fair amount of eating out. As much as I love to read, however, I enjoy reading far fewer than one out of twenty fiction writers. (That's currently living and publishing fiction writers.) Certainly I read more books than I actually like. Telling you a bit more about the kind of reader I am will, then, suggest something about the strengths—and the limitations—of the book to come.

VII

My approach to story is conservative—all but identical to the one E. M. Forster (1879–1970) put forward in his 1927 meditation, *Aspects of the Novel*. (I said we'd return to it.) Because Forster says it well and succinctly, I quote rather than paraphrase. Only then will I point out the few ways in which Forster and I differ.

> If you ask one type of man, "What does a novel do?" he will reply placidly: "Well—I don't know—it seems a funny sort of question to ask—a novel's a novel—well, I don't know—I suppose it kind of tells a story, so to speak." He is quite good-tempered and vague, and probably driving a motor bus at the same time and paying no more attention to literature than it merits. Another man, whom I visualize as on a golf-course, will be aggressive and brisk. He will reply: "What does a novel do? Why, it tells a story of course, and I've no use for it if it didn't. I like a story. Very bad taste on my part, but I like a story. You can take your art, you can take your literature, you can take your music, but give me a good story. And I like a story to be a story, mind, and my wife's the same way." And a third man he says in a sort of drooping regretful voice, "Yes—oh, dear, yes—the novel tells a story." I respect and admire the first speaker. I detest and fear the second. And the third is myself. Yes—oh, dear, yes—the novel tells a story . . . The more we look at the story (the story that is a story, mind), the more we disentangle it from the finer growth it supports, the less we shall find to admire. It runs like a backbone—or may I say a tapeworm, for its begin-

ning and end are arbitrary . . . It is a narrative of events arranged in their time sequence—dinner coming after breakfast, Tuesday after Monday, decay after death and so on. *Qua* story, it can only have one merit: that of making the audience wonder what happens next. And conversely it can only have one fault: that of making the audience not want to know what happens next. These are the only two criticisms that can be made on the story that is a story . . . When we isolate the story like this and hold it out on the forceps—wriggling and interminable, the naked worm of time—it presents an aspect both unlovely and dull. But we have much to learn from it. (25–28)

And we have much to learn from Forster's description of it, as well. Paradoxically, story itself does *not* have a beginning, middle, and end (though any *particular* story must have these in order to be satisfying): story itself, however, is "interminable" and (incidentally) chronological, "the naked worm of time." The famous "beginning" and "end" (of the "beginning," "middle," and "end" triad) are simply narrative strategies for mounting the endless train of narrative and strategies for dismounting. When writers try structurally to harmonize the beginning and ending strategies with what is going on in the mid-game, we approach the problems grouped under the rubric "narrative art."

Within his ellipses (the parts I have elided with the traditional three dots), Forster talked about the age, strength, and power of story, for which he had much respect. So do I. (Sheherazade of *The Thousand Nights and a Night* is the heroine of the passages I've omitted. Look them up.) But in terms of the problems before us, that is not to the point. Indeed, what *is* to the point is that, in most of the narratives we are presented with today, be they sitcoms, TV miniseries, movies, or even news accounts, the stories we get are mostly bad. With some extraordinary exceptions throughout the history of all these fields, most comic books, TV series, and action movies don't have good stories. Neither do most published novels, and for the same reason: the logic that must hold them together and produce the readerly curiosity about what will happen is replaced by "interesting situations" (or an "interesting character"), which *don't* relate logically or developmentally to what comes before or after. That is to say, they are wildly illogical. We cannot follow their development, even—or especially—if we try. If we look at them closely, they don't make much sense. The general population, day in and day out, is not used to getting good stories. This has two social results.

First (on the downside), it probably accounts for why there is so little political sophistication among the general populace. Political awareness requires that people become used to getting rich, full, complex, logical, and causative accounts of what is going on in the world and, when they don't, regularly demanding them. But with television and most films and books, they get little chance.

Second (on the upside), it produces a relatively small but growing audience interested in and hungry for experimental work. Paradoxically, most experimental work is simpler than the traditional "good story." As far back as 1935, in his introduction to his selected poems, Robinson Jeffers called the techniques of modernism "originality by amputation." Formally, it's still a pretty good characterization—which is probably why normative fiction (and figurative painting) persists. What it leaves out, however, is that the nature of the experiment is rarely a negative one. It's a positive one. E. E. Cummings (1894–1963) began his lines with lower-case letters throughout his career—as has Lucille Clifton (b. 1936) throughout hers. But the experiment is only secondarily about not beginning your lines with upper-case letters. It's about the effect *gained* by beginning your lines with lower-case letters. It is a matter of exercising the attention to focus on smaller elements that, in a "good story," would only be perceived in concert with many others. The long-term effect of experimental work is the heightening of the microcritical abilities among readers, so that, among other things, we get better at criticizing those "good stories" that turn out to be, in reality, not so good after all.

I do *not* believe the only purpose of the contemporary, the experimental, or the avant-garde is to increase our appreciation of the traditional. Both have rich and distinct effects, pleasures, and areas of meaning. But as the legacy of high modernism (through which most of us come to the contemporary and the avant-garde) makes clear, the normative and the experimental relate; they nourish each other.

What distinguishes story from a random chain of chronological events that all happen to the same character, or group of characters, is causal and developmental logic. This logic alone is what makes one *want* to find out what happens next. Most beginning writers are, however, unaware of how fragile the desire to know what comes next actually is—or how easily it's subverted.

Turning readers' attention from the future to the past with a flashback will almost always slay that desire, unless that flashback answers a clear question set up in the previous scene—and answers it clearly and quickly.

In my creative writing classes today rarely do I get a short story of more than six, eight, fifteen pages that doesn't have at least one flashback in it. Rarely does it work. Understand, I have no problem with *realistic* flashbacks—but in life, flashbacks are just that: flashes. They last between half a second and three seconds, ten at the outside. Thus, in texts, they are covered in a phrase or two, a sentence, three sentences, or five sentences at most.

Try to think about a single past event concertedly for *more* than ten seconds, without the present intruding strongly. Unless you are talking about a specific past event with another person, who is stabilizing your attention with questions and comments (or, indeed, unless you are writing about it, so that your own recorded language helps stabilize your thought), it's almost impossible. Indeed, what's wrong with most flashback scenes in most contemporary fiction is that they are simply unrealistic: by that I mean the scene where, on Friday night, Jenny sits in front of her vanity putting on her makeup, in the course of which she thinks back over the *entire* progression of her relationship with Steve—for the next six pages!—whom she is going to meet later that evening; or the scene where Alan is walking down the street Monday morning, during which he runs over the last three months' growing hostility with his foreman, Jeff—for eight pages!—whom, when he arrives at work, he will confront to demand a raise. Nine times out of ten, both these stories simply begin at the wrong place. The first really starts with Jenny's meeting Steve. The second begins the first time Jeff's hostility manifests itself to Alan.

The "subjectivity of time" that writers and philosophers have been going on about for the last hundred years or so has to do with whether or not time passes quickly or slowly—not whether it passes chronologically. Of course conscious and unconscious memories constantly bombard our passage through the present. The web of unconscious memories and associations is what makes the present meaningful, decipherable, readable. That web is why a frying pan on a stove, a book on a shelf, and a broom leaning in the corner register as familiar objects and not as strange and menacing pieces of unknown super-science technology from a thousand years in the future. Spend some time observing how these memories arrive, how long they stay, how they add, expand, subvert, or create present meaning before you plunge into another flashback. It may save you time and preserve believability as well as free you from a bunch of stodgy fictive conventions.

I want to be clear—because several readers have misunderstood me in earlier versions of this same argument. What I'm arguing against here is not flashbacks in themselves. Even less am I against a conscientious decision to tell a story in something other than chronological order. (To repeat: I enjoy experimental fiction. For me to come out against nonlinear storytelling would simply be a contradiction.) What I object to is the scene whose *only* reason is to serve as the frame for an anterior scene because the writer has been too lazy to think through carefully how that anterior scene might begin and end if it were presented on its own, and so borrows the beginning and ending of the frame scene, which—equally—has not been chosen because anything of narrative import actually happens in it. What I'm reminding you is that flashbacks themselves began as a narrative experiment: If you're *going* to experiment, one that has a reason will always win out over one without any thought behind it, one we simply indulge because, today, that's the way everyone *else* does it.

Here is a rule of thumb that can forestall a lot of temporal clutter in your storytelling. Consider the scene in which the flashback occurs. Ask yourself, "Has anything important happened *in the scene* before the flashback starts? Has any memorable incident taken place? Have we seen any important change? Has the character done anything more than sit around (or walk around) and think?" If the answer to *all* these questions is no (and thus the only purpose of the present scene is to allow the character to remember the past incident in the flashback proper), consider omitting the frame and telling the flashback scene (after deciding on its true beginning and a satisfying conclusion) in the order that it occurred (often it's the first scene—or one of the first—in the story) in terms of the rest of the narrative's incidents.

The fictive excuse for the flashback is that it is a product of memory. The reason for fiction, however, is that it provides the explanatory force of history. This may seem like an overly grand statement. But give it a little thought.

We *live* our lives in chronological order.

When we *remember* them, however, our mental movement is almost entirely associational.

Listen to people who are not trying to solve a particular problem reminisce with one another. One good meal leads to another. One sadness leads to another sadness, till suddenly it becomes too much and the conversation leaps to pleasure or silliness or gossip. It's only when human beings want to solve a problem or figure out the causality behind something that they carefully try to reconstruct chronological order.

If you've ever done it with someone else, you know how hard it can be.

Why did we lose the war? Because before we marched off to fight we didn't start out with good weapons and well-trained men. Why was last year's crop so good when the crop before that was so poor? Because the river flooded and left a deposit of silt over the land that promoted rich growth—while just before the year of the poor crop no flooding occurred at all. Chronological causality is how history begins, and that can only be supplied by chronological order. Only the concomitant cross-checking and stabilizing by notation and the pressure to be accurate and exact that two or more people remember in dialogue with one another creates history. What one person remembers by himself, while it may be a contributing element to history, is precisely *not*-history until it enters into such a dialogue. Chronology is our first historical mode.

Fiction is an intellectually imaginative act committed on the materials of memory that tries for the form of history.

That's why a political climate pushing the individual to see her- or himself as autonomous and self-sufficient is, by definition, a climate unsupportive of rich and satisfying fiction. (This is not the same as an individual writer in her or his work pushing against a climate of conformity and security to assert her or his individuality.) A climate that discourages research and open discussion is usually pretty distrustful of good fiction as well.

However much, as readers, we lose ourselves in a novel or a story, fiction itself is an experience on the order of memory— not on the order of actual occurrence. (History is an even higher level of abstraction.) It *looks* like the writer is telling you a story. What the writer is actually doing, however, is using words to evoke a series of micromemories from your own experience that inmix,* join, and connect in your mind in an order the writer controls, so that, in effect, you have a sustained memory of something that never happened to you.

That false memory is what a story *is*.

Among other things, the writer's art comprises various techniques to make that unreal memory as clear and vivid as possible. That clarity, that vividness, is entirely dependent on the order and selection of her or his words. Again, one might say that the fiction writer is trying to create a false memory with the force of history. The problem with the flashback is, again, that we don't have too many memories of memories that we recognize as such—or, when we have them, rarely are they the most vivid *among* our memories. Thus, the flashback is a tricky technique. Think about its problems if you're going to use it. When you find yourself telling your story out of chronological order,

---

* At John Hopkins University, in October 1966, the French psychiatrist Jacques Lacan discussed this all-important signification process in a paper entitled "Of Structure as an Inmixing of an Otherness Prerequisite to Any Subject Whatsoever" (reprinted in *The Structuralist Controversy*). This "inmixing," this "intertrusion," this "conjoining," is what allows scenes, sentences, and even words to signify.

ask yourself if it adds anything truly necessary or important to the telling, or is it just laziness or bad habit, a failure to think through the tale logically to (and from) a beginning.

Here, now, are the places I differ from Forster. First, I, too, am the reader who says, "Yes—oh dear, yes—the novel tells a story." I too very much fear the second reader. ("I like a story. Very bad taste on my part, but I like a story. You can take your art, you can take your literature, you can take your music, but give me a good story. And I like a story to be a story, mind, and my wife's the same way.") But while I fear him, unlike Forster, I don't detest him. For while I believe (one) that the second reader is profoundly mistaken and needs to be the focus of most of today's educational energy and (two) that he is the audience that most corrupts both critical and commercial approaches to the popular arts, I also feel that such audience members *are* educable, in a way that Forster probably didn't. Today, this reader's haunts are not golf courses but rather the active fandoms of TV, comic books, science fiction, and other venues particularly appreciative of paraliterature or popular culture. The fact is (which puts me close to Forster once more), I recognize that without *some* story—temporal, developmental, logical—most writing is simply not recognizable *as* fiction. But having said that (and this moves me away from Forster, even as it sets me in antagonistic opposition to Forster's golfer), I see no particular reason why all writing, even if it begins by appropriating the name "novel," "story," or, indeed, "poem" or the name of any other genre, needs to be immediately recognizable as belonging to the genre label it carries. I have gotten great pleasure from "short stories" that were nothing but sequences of numbers, random words, or abstract pictures, not to mention comic books—a medium I love. I've gotten pleasure from J. G. Ballard's "condensed novels," which are collections of impressionistic fragments running only seven or eight pages each (see *The Atrocity Exhibition*, 1967). I have gotten pleasure from poems where the words were chosen by any number of games or operationalized systems or semantic or aesthetic tasks or within any of a variety of constraints. But all this will be discussed in its place. Genres are ways of reading, ways of understanding, complex moods, modes, and chains of expectations—discourses, if you will—and as such there is as much aesthetic pleasure (and use!) to be found in opposing those expectations as in acquiescing to them.

Sixty years ago, that witty and sensible critic Leonard Knights ("How Many Children Had Lady Macbeth," 1948) noted: "Only as precipitates from memory are plot and character tangible; yet only in solution has either any emotive valency." This is what Forster's dull, ugly worm is all about. Plot, character, and the structure that constrains and embodies them are the solutes that effloresce into emotive force within the solution of those "finer growths." Those "finer growths" through which the plot and characters achieve their emotive fullness are, themselves, controlled by structure. Most of the interminable discussions of plot in writing texts are useless because finally plot has no existence by itself; it is only a single aspect of a more complex process (which I call structure); and if the writer tries to deal with only the plot by itself, he or she ends up twisting at that dried-up little worm, which, when it effloresces, may or may not swell to proper shape and effect, depending entirely on the solute—the finer growths—it arrives in.

This book teases apart how writing works: what the process of its making consists of; and how its making is made by and remakes the world.

These are huge topics.

As the reader can see, this is not a large book.

My comments about them are suggestive rather than definitive. Still, with what notions we can harvest here—the ones we can speak of intelligibly—I hope my readers can begin to figure out how to do what they want on their own.

VIII

What sorts of stories do I enjoy?

What do I read for?

I read for information. Clearly, forcefully, and economically given, information constitutes my greatest reading pleasure. I cotton to Ezra Pound's oft-quoted dictum, "Fundamental accuracy of statement is the ONE sole morality of writing." (Raymond Carver quotes it in his fine essay "On Writing.") Notice, however, Pound says "morality," *not* value. The first information I read for, at least in fiction, is usually visual and generally sensual. I want to know *where* I am, and in particular what that place looks like, smells like, sounds like, and feels like. If the writer can make me sensorily aware of his or her setting—trick me into seeing/hearing/smelling it vividly (again, vivid description is a trick, and a more complex trick than simply laying out what's there), so much the better. Throughout my fictions I want Stein's one-third "description simple concentrated description not of what happened nor what is thought or what is dreamed but what exists and so makes the life the island life the daily island life"—or, if not, then something that I will find equally interesting.

The next kind of information I read for is any tone of voice in the writing that is informative itself about the story, about how the story is getting told. Just who is the narrator? Should I trust that narrator? Should the narrator awake my suspicions? Should I like the narrator or not like the narrator? Should I look up to the narrator? Or should I assume the narrator is my equal? What is the narrator's attitude toward the characters who occupy the foreground of the fictive field? And toward those in the background? And to the other characters? And the situation and the setting itself? If the writer keeps giving me those shots of vocal and sensory information, forcefully and with skill, I can be happy with any one of the narrative stances above, because I am disposed to trust the *writer* creating that voice and painting the pictures—whether I "like" a character or not. Even if the narrator gives me mostly vocally modulated analysis (Proust, James, Musil . . .), I can be happy with the tale—though probably a reader other than I will have to *discover* that book and alert me to its excellences before I read it. (Proust, James, and Musil are not writers I'd have been likely to pick up on my own and stick to without some critical preparation. Joyce or Nabokov I might well have.) Those fictive works that make their initial appeal through tone of voice—often a tone solidly bourgeois, educated, ironic—can take on more complex concepts and explore them through a level of formal recomplication that is often richer than the relatively direct fiction writer can achieve. But the greatest failures in this mode occur when the voice runs on and on without ever managing to erect the narrative structures that create beauty, resonance, and finally meaning itself. These failures usually hinge on a misunderstanding we have already seen: the confusion of "the literary effect" with an effect of tone rather than an effect of form that can even contour the tone (a confusion I would say my very smart twenty-six-year-old male creative writing student had fallen into).

Writers working in this mode, however, should avoid creative writing workshops. Little or nothing in such works can be criticized on the workshop level. Often the resonating structures take 60, 130, 300 pages to construct. By the same token the most successful works in this mode (Proust, late James, Dorothy Richardson's *Pilgrimage,* Anthony Powell's *Dance to the Music of Time,* Joyce of *Finnegans Wake,* Gertrude Stein of *The Making of Americans* and *Lucy Church Amiably,* Marguerite Young's *Miss McIntosh, My Darling,* James McElroy's *Plus* and *Men and Women,* William Gaddis's *The Recognitions* . . .) do not find their audience quickly. (In his *Alexandria Quartet,* Lawrence Durrell tried to have it both ways and was, I feel, remarkably successful—though the reader has to commit himself to the *whole* thing. Moreover, most of Durrell's theoretical folderol about axes and so forth is simply distracting nonsense.) Those structures have to be built just as clearly—in their own larger, more generous terms—and the writing must eventually seem just as economical, if such works are to garner a readership.

When I read, I am also aware of tone (apart from tone of voice) and mood, and often a quality that can only be called beauty. Still, a writer who tries to go for them directly without giving me a hefty handful of writerly *stuff* on the way is usually not going to make it.

> He walked into the room and saw Karola sitting there.
> She was beautiful. He thought of flowers. He thought of
> butterflies. He thought of water running in the forest.

The writer who begins a story with these sentences is probably very aware of tone—but is not really giving me, as a reader, much else. (I would be getting even less, if it were in the present tense—"He walks into the room and sees Karola sitting there. She is beautiful. He thinks of flowers. He thinks of butterflies. He thinks of water running in the forest"—more "tone" and even less voice.) It is much easier for me to be interested in a story that begins:

He walked into the little room with the white plaster ceiling and the wooden two-by-fours making rough lintels above its three windows. Karola sat at a small table, her forearm in the sunlight. When he looked at her ear, he remembered the pink and white flowers in his aunt's kitchen garden back in New Zealand. By her tanned cheek, some of her white-blond hair lifted and shook in the breeze, and he remembered the flaxen butterflies flicking in and out of the sunlight and shadow of the big Catalpa outside in the green and gray Bordeaux landscape they'd been staying in three summer months now. Just standing there, just looking at her, he felt the same surge of pleasure he'd felt, a year before, when he'd come around the rocks in the twelve acres of forest his aunt had purchased for the farm in that last, sweltering New Zealand winter, and he'd seen the falling water for the first time, how high it was, how it filled his head with the sound of itself, how cool it looked in the winter heat. Karola did that to him.

Although I can't know or even be sure, I suspect the first writer wanted to describe something as interesting and richly detailed as the second writer, but was afraid to, or was just imaginatively incapable of it—or, perhaps, had gotten distracted by thinking only about tone. But as a reader, I find the second more interesting.

As I said, the vocal approach I can also find interesting:

He stepped into the room—Jesus, it was so white—but Karola was sitting there. If you'd asked him, later, what he'd been thinking right then, he would have answered, "I don't know what to tell you. I thought she was beautiful. I did, really. It's stupid, yeah. But I thought about flowers. You think about flowers, you think about butterflies. That's just what's going to happen with some guys. And waterfalls in the forests, that kind of thing—I thought about them, too." But then—*right* then—standing just inside the door, a dozen memories flickering in and out of his consciousness, he thought only: "She's *beautiful.*"

Here, in terms of direct information about the scene described, this third writer is giving no more than the first one. But what it lacks in specific detail and associative richness, it starts to compensate for by giving a sense of a person, with a voice, that lets us know a fair amount about the character, either as it infects the narrative voice ("Jesus, it was so white!") or directly ("I don't know what to tell you. I thought she was beautiful. I did, really").

Personally I find the tone and the mood of the second and third examples much more interesting than the tone and mood of the first. In all three cases, tone and mood would be things not to violate, as the story—or at least the scene—progresses. With number 3 ("He stepped into the room—Jesus, it was so white—"), I'd probably want something to start happening on Forster's "pure story" level faster than I would with number 2. (In number 1, I'd want something to happen almost by the next sentence, or the tale would lose me.) Too much of number 3's foot shuffling and embarrassment grows quickly tiresome though. Soon I'd want some proof that this personality, this sensibility, this observer was worth my time to stay with. He's got perhaps another three sentences in which to observe something interesting and tell it to me in an interesting way. Almost certainly I'd have more patience with the second narrator—because what he gives me is informatively richer. I'm more willing to let the second narrator take time to build up my picture of where these people are, who they are, what their relationship is, and suggest how, in the course of the tale, it's going to develop. So the second narrator has about *five* more sentences in which to let me know a lot more about the woman at the table (or let me know why the narrator doesn't know it). Wouldn't it be interesting if, say, in either example 2 or 3, Karola turned out to be a Palestinian and six or seven years older than our narrator? As soon as her hair began to turn white, she bleached it platinum. There, in France, with her current young New Zealander, who finds her so fascinating, she's working on a book about her country's archaeology . . .

Still, with examples two and three I have more trust in the

writer than I do with example 1—a trust that, in terms ranging from mood to plot, either writer 2 or 3 may still betray with the next sentence. However promising I find their openings, both tales *could* dissolve, equally and easily, into clutter. Unless the writer is really setting us up for a very conscious effect, number 1 telegraphs a general thinness that is the hallmark of contemporary dullness. And if the narrator *doesn't* win my trust soon, I'm likely to enjoy only a narrator whose tone *and* character I personally like. And if the narrator never gains my trust, however much I personally like the narrator or sympathize with his or her politics or recognize the situation, for me the work remains—if I keep reading, and most of the time I don't— an entertainment, rather than a work of art. Finally, I want all this information—whether sensual or tonal—given me economically. If, after even three, five, seven sentences, I have not gotten one or the other of these orders of information, and I find myself spotting extraneous words and phrases that tell me nothing of interest, phrases that withhold information rather than present it, expressive clumsinesses and general lack of writerly skill, then I am disgruntled. (Vast amounts of fine literature wait to be read. Many more skilled writers exist than I can read in a lifetime. Unskilled writers don't hold much interest for me. Bad writing makes me angry.) If the elements of the sentence could be better arranged so as to give the information more swiftly, logically, forcefully, I am equally unhappy. (I don't particularly enjoy having to rewrite the writers I read, sentence by sentence. I want the writer to have done that work for me.) In my experience, three such clumsy sentences in a row usually indicate that the text will be littered with them. Despite whatever talent is manifested, they signal that the imaginative force needed to develop an idea clearly and explore it richly is likely lacking. In turn this means that even should I enjoy the story, I am not likely to point it out as an exemplum of one idea or another (unless it's an example of what *not* to do); nor am I likely to sketch out the development of its idea as praiseworthy in any of my own critical writing. (As Emily Dickinson wrote, "Nothing survives except fine execution.") While any of the information I enjoy might be worked up to form what might easily be called a good story, if I don't enjoy the economy and force of the presentation (the word for this level of presentation is "style"), from experience I know the tale will simply not be worth the time and energy I must put into reading it. These are the books—the nineteen out of twenty—I put down and rarely come back to.

Fortunately there are other readers who read—no less critically than I—for a different order of writerly and readerly priorities and pleasures. In their critical writing, such readers are always guiding me to things I might have missed, as I hope, in turn, now and again I can guide *them* to something interesting. Of course what is *likely* the case is not *absolutely* the case. Three dull, bland, or clumsy sentences don't *always* mean an impoverished work. I would have missed out entirely on the considerable pleasures of Leonid Tsypkin or W. G. Sebald had I only read the opening page or pages of either, under my own critical regime—not to mention Theodore Dreiser, a great novelist (for many readers, including me) despite his style.

Nevertheless, the above represents my own priorities. It outlines my own aesthetic gamble, if you will, in the greater process of working to sediment the new or revised discourses that stabilize the systems of the world and make them better. (The purpose of fiction in particular and art in general is not to make the world better, directly and per se. But, despite the protests of all the apolitical critics, they [art and fiction] still help, if only because, as critics from Pater to Foucault have acknowledged, they *do* make life more enjoyable—specifically the time we spend reading them. If they didn't, we wouldn't bother.) In pursuit of such ends, the above gives the parameters around which my own set of dos and don'ts for fiction are organized—and thus suggests where their limits lie. Unless another critic has alerted me to pleasures that will only come after 50, 75, 150 pages, these are the texts I'm likely to abandon after a few thousand words or so—if not a few hundred.

Although I believe thirty-five years of teaching creative writing have helped me become more articulate about my readerly responses than I might have been without them, and while there are many other good readers of types different from mine, I do not think I am all that uncommon. I believe the kind of reader I am has a contribution to make in the contestatory wrangle producing that social construct, literary quality. But because human beings are a multiplicity, there can be no fixed and final canon, despite whatever appearance of stability any given view of the canon suggests. This is why no single book can tell folks how to write fiction that will join the canon. Having seen the canon change as much as it has in the years between my adolescence and the (I hope) forward edge of my dotage, I'm content with the forces that retard that change as much as they do.

Balzac, Dreiser, and Sebald; Lawrence, Barthelme, and Bukowski are all extraordinary writers, for extraordinarily different reasons. All are writers who at one time or another I've gorged on; but all are writers about whom I end up feeling, finally, that a little goes a long way. To enjoy any and all of them requires a fertile and lively mind; fertile and lively minds find things of interest, and thus may also find greater or lesser amounts of what's in *this* book interesting. They may also find some things here painful, if not crashingly irrelevant, even as they marvel that someone could go on at such lengths as I do about fiction while spending so little time on fiction's oh-so-necessary social content.

Because in the realm of art all absolute statements *are* suspect, the most I can say is that I am still willing to gamble on the fact that, by and large, *most* of the writers whose works I would lay down and not return to are ones who don't contribute very much (except by their all-important negative examples), and the exceptions are precisely those glorious ones that prove, in the sense of test, the rules and principles on which my overarching aesthetic rests.

The less interested either we or our characters are in their jobs, incomes, families, social class, landlords, friends, neighbors, and landscapes (i.e., how they are connected to the material world around them), the less we have to write about. This may be why the highly individualistic but highly isolated heroes of genre fiction—from Conan the Conqueror to James Bond—often seem so thin in relation to those of literary fiction. This is why the strength of such stories that feature them tends to be on an allegorical—i.e., poetic—level, rather than on the level of psychological (not to mention sociological) veracity.

IX

I've already suggested that the desire to hear our stories in chronological order may begin with the desire to have our fictions take on the image of history. Eighteenth-century novels such as Fielding's *Tom Jones* (1749) were often called histories (the novel's full title is *Tom Jones, the History of a Foundling*). Readers of the twenty-four-years-earlier *Robinson Crusoe* (1726) initially flocked to the book because they thought they were getting the thinly fictionalized "history" of the actual adventures of a sailor named Alexander Selkirk, who had famously spent time on a desert island, as had Crusoe; Defoe even encouraged the rumor that he had interviewed Selkirk in order to write his book, though almost certainly that was untrue and just a publicity move.

Supporting him through fourteen meaty novels, Dickens's great discovery in the nineteenth century was that what happens to us as children directly influences the adults we turn out to be, both in terms of our strengths and in terms of the shortcomings we must overcome. Thus plot in the novel in particular—and in fiction in general—became, for Dickens, part of a structure of incidents that not only tell the story but also move us among the kinds of incidents that explain what happens in terms of certain kinds of causes as well as the given moments of history needed to understand them: in Dickens's case, particular childhood incidents and (later in his novels) the adult happenings particularly affected by them.

The fictive discovery of the eighteenth century was that the forces of history were themselves large determinants of our interests, wants, and desires. Nor is that lesson forgotten during the nineteenth. In Stendhal's *The Red and the Black* (1830), Julien Sorel's life is entirely determined through having to live in the social retrenchments following the expansions of the Napoleonic wars. In *Les Misérables* of 1862, Victor Hugo shows how the social advancement of working-class criminal Jean Valjean is as dependent on the turmoil accompanying the early years of the age of republican revolutions in Europe in general and France in particular as that advancement is dependent on Valjean's own character—while seven years later, in 1869, almost as if it were posed as a counterargument by Flaubert, *Sentimental Education* details how its middle-class hero, Frédéric Moreau, misses out on opportunity after opportunity to behave as a moral hero over the period that includes the revolution of 1848, through his own romantic daydreaming coupled with his personal inhibitions.

The nineteenth century's particular addition to the novel might be seen as a realization that the conflicts between social classes and the desires that cross class lines—along with the aforementioned Dickensian discovery of family and childhood as a complex force in the creation of character—propel the machinery of the world.

Beyond the one-third that is "description of the daily island life," the glory of the nineteenth-century novel was its ability to present dramatically, in logical if not chronological order, the complex of reasons that cause things to work out as they do: What elements in his own miserly character interact with his disappointments in the world to make Ralph Nickleby hang himself? Bitter and rigid police inspector Javert is obsessed with his belief in Jean Valjean's subhumanity and fundamental evil. How and why, then, after Valjean saves Javert's life, once they meet just outside the Paris sewers during the Revolution of 1832 does Javert subsequently go to pieces, finally allowing himself to fall from a bridge into the Seine and drown? How does the brilliant provincial inventor David Séchard end up a happy man, even though most of the profits from his discovery of the way to make paper from artichoke fiber have been stolen from him? How does David's childhood friend, the aspiring poet Lucien Chardon, end up a miserable suicide in a Paris jail cell, where he has been imprisoned for murder?

The dramatic richness and resonance with which these questions are answered contribute to making *Nicholas Nickleby* (1838–39), *Les Misérables* (1862), and *Lost Illusions* (1834) great novels.

Drama suggests that if we simply *hear* what Ralph, Javert, David, and Lucien say to other people and watch what they do, we shall understand their fates. The novel adds: For full understanding, we must also know how they think and feel, as well as how they are enmeshed in "the daily island life." In short, it adds the most productive parts of psychoanalysis and Marxism to the historical mix.

The twentieth century's particular refinement on these exploratory and explanatory novelistic structures, from Proust and James to Joyce and Woolf, was that, in the lives of real people, all these elements were now further granulated across the individual play of swirling subjectivity, either dramatically though artfully rendered stream of consciousness techniques (as in Woolf and Joyce), or through precise analysis (as in James and even more so in Proust), on an even more nuanced, more complex level. By adding the focus on the subjective, however, such writers do not forget the social.

If one or more (or indeed all) of the *characters* in a story are unaware of the sociohistorical levels that contour where they are and the choices they have open to them in the world, it doesn't particularly matter. But, as the *writer* is less and less aware of these sociohistorical levels in the course of structuring her or his tale (that is, when the structure of the story does not carry us through a set of incidents, places, and descriptions that, apart from or in conjunction with the "plot," help explain those positions and those choices), the tale seems thinner and thinner, regardless of its subjective density.

To generalize all this and say that fiction that is unaware of the historical dimensions, both of the genre and of the aspects of life it chooses to portray, tends to be thin and relatively uninteresting sounds hopelessly high-falutin', even arrogant. But there it is. Certainly this is the failing of the "sin and sex in the suburbs" genre, which over the sixties, seventies, and eighties produced such a memorable amount of unmemorable writing. Its plots so rarely moved the characters through any situations that allowed the characters (or the readers) to see what had stalled these characters in that landscape, or what was preventing them from leaving it, or why they could not transform it into something more humanly satisfactory. Similarly it is the major failing of the genre that has come largely to replace it through the culture of university creative writing and MFA programs: "sin and sex in graduate school," where, in story after story, the characters never consider the absurdly low exploitative salaries they are actually teaching for, how they supplement those salaries into the possibility of living, what they hope to achieve through the sacrifice, and what in all likelihood the overwhelming majority will *actually* achieve—and the discrepancies between vision and actuality.

The non-high-falutin' way to say it is to point out that from the beginning of fiction as we know it, the basic way to produce a richly interesting fictive situation is to take a person from one social stratum and carefully observe him or her having to learn to deal with folks from another, either up or down the social ladder: the bourgeois young man who must learn how to live and work among sailors (Kipling's *Captains Courageous,* 1887) or the poor working-class fellow who must learn to negotiate society (Jack London's *Martin Eden,* 1913); Becky Thatcher's social rise from impoverished poor relation to society's heights in *Vanity Fair* (1848) or Odette de Crécy's rise from *demi-mondaine,* through a stint as the cultured Swann's mistress, till finally she becomes the Duchesse de Guermantes, which provides the running story thread through the grand tapestry of *Remembrance of Things Past** (1913–27). Fiction feels most like fiction when it cleaves most closely to such situations—and, as its stories stray further and further from such interclass encounters, it feels thinner and thinner.

Another way to sum up much of what we have said above is another unhappy truth:

One way or the other, directly or indirectly, good fiction tends to be about money.

Whether directly or indirectly, most fiction is about the effects of having it or of not having it, the tensions caused between people used to having more of it or less of it, or even, sometimes, the money it takes to write the fiction itself, if not to live it. Supremely, it's about the delusions the having of it or the not having of it force us to assume in order to go on. Like Robert Graves's famous and equally true statement about poetry, however ("All true poetry is about love, death, or the changing of the seasons"), the generality ends up undercutting its interest. Like Graves's statement, one either recognizes its truth or one doesn't. Both need to be acknowledged. Neither needs to be dwelled on.

*More recently translated as *In Search of Lost Time.*

Probably I am drawn to such overgeneralizations—"All true poetry is about love, death, and changing of the seasons," "All good fiction is about money"—because I am *not* a poet, and not (primarily) a writer of realistic fiction. Thus I like statements that do a lot of critical housekeeping for me—possibly, certain poets or fiction writers might argue, too much to be useful.

"All good fiction is about money" probably appeals to me because, while I acknowledge the necessity of the economic register in the rich presentation of social life (like Forster's necessity for *some* story if we are to recognize the text as fiction at all), the economic is, nevertheless, not the *most* interesting thing to me as a reader personally (in the same way that story is not the *most* interesting thing either to Forster or to me). But stories that *never* address money or the process by which we acquire it—if not directly then indirectly—are usually stillborn.

As far as all fiction being about money, the good news is that over the last three hundred years so many indirect strategies have been developed to indicate the money that controls the fiction that often the reader—sometimes even the writer—is not aware of the way the monetary grounding that functions to elicit the fictive "truth effect" is actually present in her or his tales. Still I think it's better to know than to gamble on its happening. When the writer doesn't know, and can't provide such information directly or indirectly, allowing the reader to sense the economic underpinning of the tale through the representation of work or otherwise, the fiction usually registers on the reader as thin or lacking in staying power.

The better news is that, regardless of guidelines people writing about it lay down—guidelines that I or my students have from time to time found useful—they are *only* guidelines. There are no rules. The truth is, fiction can be about anything. I don't believe the best of it changes the world directly—though many people felt that works such as *Uncle Tom's Cabin* (1851) and *Les Misérables* (1869) were pretty effective in their day. (When President Lincoln was introduced to Harriet Beecher Stowe, he reputedly met her with the words, "So this is the little lady who made this big war!" And the popularity of Hugo's novel is often counted as influencing many people to support late 19th century welfare reforms.) One of New York's historical public catastrophes, resulting in twenty-three deaths and over a hundred wounded, the Astor Place Riots of 1849 were sparked by two rival productions of *Macbeth*, playing in New York on the same night, in theaters half a dozen blocks apart, one starring the American Edwin Forest and the other featuring the Englishman William Macready. Again, art no longer functions in the society the way it once did: it functions in *different* ways. And it can help people understand how those who live and think in ways different from themselves can manage to make sense of the world. The pleasures from writing fiction—and even more, the pleasures from reading it—easily become addictions. Some of the guidelines above may, I believe, have something to do with why our society continues to organize itself so that such addictions are not only common and continuous but often flower in such wonderful ways, ways that manifest themselves in provocative and satisfying stories and novels across the range of genres, literary and paraliterary.

—Buffalo, Philadelphia,
Boulder, and New York
July 2000–April 2005

Partial List of Works Cited

Artaud, Antonin. "No More Masterpieces." In *The Theater and Its Double*. New York: Grove Press, 1958.

Barzun, Jacques. *Simple and Direct: A Rhetoric for Writers*. Rev. ed. Chicago: University of Chicago Press, 1994.

Borges, Jorge Luis. *This Craft of Verse*. Cambridge: Harvard University Press, 1998.

Carver, Raymond. "On Writing." In *Fires*. New York; Vintage Books, 1983.

Egri, Lajos. *The Art of Dramatic Writing*. New York: Simon & Schuster, 1972.

Forster, E. M. *Aspects of the Novel*. New York: Harcourt Brace Jovanovitch, 1927.

Hofmannsthal, Hugo von. *The Lord Chandos Letter*. Translated by Russell Stockman. 1902. Marlboro, Vt.: Marlboro Press, 1986.

Lacan, Jacques. "Of Structure as an Inmixing of an Otherness Prerequisite to Any Subject Whatsoever." In *The Structuralist*

Controversy: The Languages of Criticism and the Science of Man. Edited by Richard Macksey and Eugenio Donato. Baltimore: Johns Hopkins University Press, 1972.

Orwell, George. "Politics and the English Language." In *In Front of Your Nose (1945–1950): The Collected Journalism, Essays, and Letters of George Orwell*, vol. 4, edited by Sonia Orwell and Ian Angus, 127–40. New York: Harcourt Brace Jovanovich, 1968.

Pound, Ezra. *ABC of Reading.* New York: New Directions, 1934.

Stein, Gertrude. *The Autobiography of Alice B. Toklas: Selected Writing of Gertrude Stein.* 1933. New York: Vintage Books, 1975.

———. *Lectures in America.* 1935. New York: Vintage Books, 1975.

Part I **SEVEN ESSAYS**

Teaching/Writing

The young painter who has set about learning to paint "realistically" is often surprised that the eye must do the learning; the hand more or less takes care of itself. "But I can *already* see what's there! Tell me what I'm supposed to do to set it down."

Keep your hand still and look more closely.

As "realistic" painting does not exhaust art, neither does the comparatively high resolution of narrative storytelling exhaust fiction. But the young writer who has decided to utilize his or her experience of the world at this comparatively high resolution, for like reasons, is always surprised when he or she is told to go back and reexamine his or her experience.

"But I want to know how to write an exciting piece of action!"

Examine your reactions when you are excited; as well, when you are bored.

"But how do I create a vivid character?"

Look closely at what individualizes people; explore those moments when you are vividly aware of a personality. Explore the others when you cannot fathom a given person's actions at all.

"No, no! You don't get the point. Tell me about style!"

Listen to the words that come out of your mouth; look at the words you put on paper. Decide with each whether or not you want it there.

But it will always be a paradox to the young artist of whatever medium that the only element of the imagination that can be consciously and conscientiously trained is the ability to observe what is.

Teachers of narrative fiction fail or succeed according to the ingenuity with which they can present the above in as many ways as possible—a success or failure that, alas, has nothing to do with their own writing ability.

A teacher at the Clarion Writers' Workshop,* you may live in the dormitory with the students, or room in a separate building. The students are energetic, dedicated, writing and revising throughout the six weeks. The solution to most literary problems is time and thought. But if someone can be there immediately to suggest where thought might be directed, so much the better. I chose to room in the student dorm. I had given occasional lectures and one-day seminars. Summers ago I had taught remedial reading to a volunteer class of adolescents at a community center. But Clarion for five days was my first formal teaching experience. A handful of the students were older than I. Several had sold stories and novels already.

The situation would intrigue any teacher of fiction.

A writer of fiction, I could not resist it.

The real worth of that summer, as with any intense, living experience, is in the texture of the experience itself.

I had set up exercises and discussion topics for the formal three-hour morning classes. Part of this time was set aside for the group discussion of stories handed in the previous days.

In my first class, we began by discussing some complex ideas about the way information is carried by and between words. We read some sentences, a word at a time, to see just what the information given was—tone of voice, mood, order of presentation, and importance—and at which points in the sentence this information became apparent. I tried to examine just what happened in the microleaps between words. I had notes. But there were great silences in the discussion when I and the students were at a loss for what to say next. Afterward, I was very relieved when two people came up to discuss ideas of their own that more or less took off from things I had said in class. But later, when I asked two others, whose comments had

*The Clarion Writers' Workshop is a writing workshop, held annually since 1967, that specializes in imaginative writing, fantasy, and science fiction. It runs for six weeks during the summer, June through July, with a different professional writer in attendance as instructor every week, with one branch held at Michigan State University and the other, Clarion West, held annually over the same period, in Seattle, Washington. Since 2004 Clarion South has been held in Brisbane, Australia.

seemed the most astute, what they thought of the session, I was cheerfully informed they hadn't the foggiest idea what I was talking about.

The next morning in class, a young woman whose writing had already struck me as among the most talented* asked guardedly, "But what do you feel about just pure storytelling?"

I wasn't quite sure what to say, so I came out with "I like it a whole lot!"

Then we spent five seconds wondering if we should say anything more, and decided on a truce.

An exercise fared better.

I asked the students to choose partners. Limiting themselves to written words (pencil, pen, and paper; or typewriters), each was to collect material from the other for a brief biography. "Write a question, exchange papers with your partner; write down your answer to her or his question (or your comment or request for further explanation of the question), then give the paper back. Read what you've obtained, and write down another question, and continue the process until you feel you have enough information for a short biography. If possible, conduct the experiment without seeing your partner—for example, pass your papers back and forth under a door."

The dorm hall, usually filled in the evening with frisbees and laughter, tonight was oddly quiet. I passed some four couples sitting on the hall floor, exchanging notebooks, and one young man with his typewriter before a closed door, sliding out a sheet of yellow paper.**

Several people gave me rather odd looks. One girl, coming out of her room to deliver a paper to a boy in another, asked with somewhat amused belligerence, "Where did you get this idea, anyway?"

Next morning in class, I asked for someone to read the questions and answers. No one raised a hand.

---

* Vonda N. McIntyre, whose story "Of Mist, and Grass, and Sand" four years later would win a well-deserved Hugo.
** The then-sixteen-year-old Jean Marc Gawron, who three years later was to write *An Apology for Rain* (1974), and three years after that, *Algorithm* (1978).

"Someone must have done the exercise," I said. "I saw too many of you working on it."

People shifted in their chairs, glanced at one another.

Momentarily I suspected I was the victim of a practical joke.

But when a discussion did, haltingly, begin, it seemed that, almost without exception, the twenty-five very bright, very sensitive young people had found, when their communication was limited to the written word, that almost in spite of themselves they had shunted into personal areas and intensely emotional parts of themselves that felt too uncomfortable for oral display . . . though no one was averse to my or another's *reading* these papers.

As the discussion progressed, some people volunteered to read sections out loud. Even from this, it became clear that when a one-to-one situation was fixed between information wanted and information granted, with the communicants checking out one another after each step, the result was a strange freedom, an obsessive honesty, a compelling and rising clarity. The general superiority of the prose style to most of their fictional attempts was duly noted.

This was certainly what I had hoped the point of the exercise would be. But I had never tried it in this way. *I* was surprised by the emotional force behind the point.

Another exercise we did in class.

"This morning," I said, "I want you all to look around the room—get up and walk around, if you'd like. Observe the people in the room with you, very closely. Keep looking until you notice something about one of your classmates that you've never noticed before. Now examine this thing about them, this aspect of her behavior or his appearance, until you see something about it different from the way anyone else you've ever seen exhibits this feature of appearance or behavior. Then write down what you've seen in a sentence or two."

I drank two styrofoam cups of coffee from the urn in the corner while the class milled and prowled by one another. One girl came up to me and said, "But I just don't *see* anything!"

"Make up something," I told her softly, "and see if anyone notices."

Twenty minutes later, most people were seated again. I suggested we bring the class to order and hear some of the examples. If there was any embarrassment here, it was of a lighter tone. Before we started, there was some humorous anticipation of the crashing triviality of what had been observed. But by the third example, the giggles had ceased. People were leaning forward in their chairs, or looking back over their own examples with renewed attention.

If the previous exercise had discovered a lucid, working prose, this one, in example after example, pushed language to the brink of the poetic. The readings, as we went about the room, became a torrent of metaphors—how many of the unique things noted were resemblances between something present and something else! And those that were not metaphorical still had an astonishing vividness, the gesture, expression, or turn of speech caught with the stark economy of the tuned ear, the fixed eye.

There were other discussions on the economic significance of story setting, the natural tendency of words to say things other than you intend and obscure your meaning, and the necessity for rendering your fictional incidents intensely through the senses. Whenever one of my convoluted arguments brought us to a point of confused silence, Robin Wilson, who led the half of the class devoted to story discussion, patiently and kindly extricated me from the snarls of my own inexperience.

The high point of the five days' classes for me was when, after a discussion of the way the vividness of fictional characters usually lies *between* rather than *in* the facts we know about them, one young woman produced a character sketch of an aging, alcoholic midwestern lady with bohemian pretensions. I had asked the class to put together these sketches of fictional characters through a collection of actions—purposeful, habitual, and gratuitous—which should be observed with the same astuteness with which they had observed one another. Unfortunately I cannot reproduce the sketch here. But when it was read, among the dozen or so other examples, the class was silent in that way which makes someone who has previously been uproariously applauded feel he has turned in a poor showing after all.

I left Clarion aware just how short five days were—I had actually been on campus five days and two weekends. Besides the three hours a day of classes, I had read some sixty-five or seventy student stories (and one novel) and had managed at least one story conference with each student—in some cases, with the more prolific, three, four, or five. It was stimulating, intense, even numbing. Most of the students seemed to feel that the individual work with particular stories was the most valuable part of the workshop. The most repeated exchange in these sessions was:

"Now in this paragraph/sentence/section here, can you tell me just what you were trying to say?"

Answer . . .

"Well, I think it would have been better if you'd *written* that . . ."

In perhaps three or four cases I was able to reassure some people who had worked very hard that the work, at least, was evident. For the rest, I just felt very flattered.

Rilke says in a letter that in the end all criticism comes down to a more or less happy misunderstanding.

I suspect he is right—which is why the literary worth of a workshop like Clarion cannot be defined by simply reviewing what, critically, went on.

—New York City
1970

Thickening the Plot

I distrust the term "plot" (not to mention "theme" and "setting") in discussions of *writing*: it (and they) refers to an effect a story produces in the *reading*. But writing is an internal process writers go through (or put themselves through) in front of a blank paper that leaves a detritus of words there. The truth is, practically nothing is known about it. Talking about plot, or theme, or setting to a beginning writer is like giving the last three years' movie reviews from the Sunday *New York Times* to a novice filmmaker. A camera manual, a few pamphlets on matched action, viable cutting points, and perhaps one on lighting (in the finished film, the viewer hardly ever sees the light sources, so the reviewer can hardly discuss them, but their placement is essential to everything from mood to plain visibility) would be more help. In short, a vocabulary that has grown from a discussion of effects is only of limited use in a discussion of causes.

A few general things, however, can be noted through introspection. Here is an admittedly simplified description of how writing strikes me. When I am writing I am trying to allow/construct an image of what I want to write about in my mind's sensory theater. Then I describe it as accurately as I can. The most interesting point I've noticed is that the *writing down* of words about my imagined vision (or at least the choosing/arranging of words to write down) causes the vision itself to change.

Here are two of the several ways it changes:

First—it becomes clearer. Sudden lights are thrown on areas of the mental diorama dark before. Other areas, seen dimly, are revised into much more specific and sharper versions. (What was vaguely imagined as a green dress, while I fix my description of the light bulb hanging from its worn cord, becomes a patterned, turquoise print with a frayed hem.) The notation causes the imagination to resolve focus.

Second—to the extent that the initial imagining contains an action, the notating process tends to propel that action forward (or sometimes backward) in time. (As I describe how Susan, both hands locked, side-punched Frank, I see Frank grab his belly in surprise and stagger back against the banister—which will be the next thing I look at closely to describe.) Notating accurately what happens *now* is a good way to prompt a vague vision of what happens *next.*

Let me try to indicate some of the details of this process.

I decide, with very little mental concretizing, that I want to write about a vague George who comes into a vague room and finds a vague Janice . . .

Picture George outside the door. Look at his face; no, look closer. He seems worried . . . ? Concerned . . . ? No. Look even closer and write down just what you see: *The lines across his forehead deepened.* Which immediately starts him moving. What does he do? . . . *He reached for the* . . . doorknob? No. Be more specific . . . *brass doorknob. It turned* . . . easily? No, the word "brass" has cleared the whole knob-and-lock mechanism. Look harder and describe how it's actually turning . . . *loosely in its collar.* While he was turning the knob, something more happened in his face. Look at it; describe it: *He pressed his lips together—* No, cross that line out: not accurate enough. Describe it more specifically: *The corners of his mouth tightened.* Closer. And the movement of the mouth evoked another movement: he's pressing his other hand against the door to open it. (Does "press" possibly come from the discarded version of the previous sentence? Or did wrong use of it there anticipate proper use here? No matter; what does matter is that you look again to make sure it's the accurate word for what he's doing.) *He pressed his palm against the door* . . . And look again; that balk in his next movement . . . *twice, to open it.* As the door opens, I hear the wood give: *You could hear the jamb split—* No, cross out "split," that isn't right . . . *crack—* No, cross that out too; it's even less accurate. Go back to "split" and see what you can do; listen harder . . . *split a little more.* Yes, that's closer. He's got the door open, now. What do you see? *The paint—* No, that's not paint on the wall. Look harder: *The wallpaper was some color between green and gray.* Why can't you see it more clearly? Look around the rest of the room. Oh, yes: *The tan shade was drawn.* What about Janice? She was one of the first things you saw when the door opened. Describe her as you saw her: *Janice sat on the bed* . . . no, more accurately . . . *the unmade bed.* No, you haven't got it yet . . . *Janice sat at the edge of the bed on a spot of bare mattress ticking.* No, no, let's back up a little and go through that again for a precise description of the picture you see: *Janice sat on the bare mattress ticking, the bedding piled loosely around her.* Pretty good, but the bedding is not really in "piles" . . . *the bedding loose around her.* Closer. Now say what you have been aware of all the time you were wrestling to get that description right: *Light from the shade-edge went up her shoulder and cheek like tape.* Listen: George is about to speak: *"What are you doing here . . . ?"* No, come on! That's not it. Banal as they are, they may be the words he says, but watch him more closely while he says them. *"What—" he paused, as though to shake his head; but the only movement in his face was a shifting*—Try again: . . . *a tightening* . . . Almost; but once more . . . *a deepening of the lines, a loosening of the lip—"are you doing here?"* Having gotten his expression more accurately, now you can hear a vocal inflection you missed before: *"are you doing here?"* There, that's much closer to what you really saw and heard. What has Janice just done? *She uncrossed her legs but did not look at him.* Ordinary grammar rules say that because the sentence's two verbs have one subject, you don't need any comma. But her uncrossing her leg and not looking up go at a much slower pace than proper grammar indicates. Let's make it: *She uncrossed her legs, but did not look at him* . . .

Now let's review the residue of all that, the admittedly undistinguished, if vaguely noirish bit of prose the reader will have:

> The lines across his forehead deepened. He reached for the brass doorknob. It turned loosely in its collar. The corners of his mouth tightened. He pressed his palm against the door, twice, to open it. You could hear the jamb split a little more
>
> The wallpaper was some color between green and gray.

The tan shade was drawn. Janice sat on the bare mattress ticking, the bedding loose around her. Light from the shade-edge went up her shoulder and cheek like tape.

"What—" he paused, as though to shake his head; but the only movement in his face was a deepening of the lines, a loosening of the lips—"are you *doing* here?"

She uncrossed her legs, but did not look at him.

And if you, the writer, want to know what happens next, you must take your seat again in the theater of imagination and observe closely till you see George's next motion, hear Janice's first response, George's words, and Janice's eventual reply.

A reader, asked to tell the "plot" of even this much of the story, might say, "Well, this man comes looking for this woman named Janice in her room; he finds the door open and goes in, only she doesn't talk at first."

That's a fair description of the reading experience. But what *we* started with, to *write*, was simply: George goes into a room and finds Janice. (George, notice, at this point in the story hasn't even been named.) The rest came through the actual envisioning/notating process, from the interaction of the words and the vision. Most of the implied judgments that the reader picks up—the man is looking *for* Janice; it is *Janice's room*—are simply overheard (or, more accurately, overseen) suppositions yielded by the process itself. Let's call this continuous, developing interchange between imagination and notation, the *story process*; and let us make that our topic, rather than "plot."

A last point about our example before we go on to story process itself: by the time we have gone as far as we have with our "story," all this close observation has given us a good deal more information than we've actually used. Though I didn't when I began (to momentarily drop my editorial stance), I now have a very clear picture of George's and Janice's clothing. I've also picked up a good deal about the building they are in. As well, I've formed some ideas about the relationship between them. And all of this would be rescrutinized as I came to it, via the story process, were I writing an actual story.

The general point: the story process keeps the vision clear and the action moving. But if we do not notate the vision accurately, if we accept some phrase we should have discarded, if we allow to stand some sentence that is not as sharp as we can make it, then the vision is not changed in the same way it would have been otherwise: the new sections of the vision will not light up quite so clearly, perhaps not at all. As well, the movement of the vision—its action—will not develop in the same way if we put down a different phrase. And though the inaccurate employment of the story process may still get you to the end of the tale, the progress of the story process, which eventually registers in the reader's mind as "the plot," is going to be off: an inaccuracy in either of the two story process elements, the envisioning or the notation, automatically detracts from the other. When they go off enough, the progress of the story process will appear unclear, or clumsy, or just illogical.

It has been said enough times so that most readers have it by rote: a synopsis cannot replace a story. Nor can any analysis of the symbolic structure replace the reading experience that exposes us to those symbols in their structural place. Even so, talking to would-be or beginning writers, I find many of them working under the general assumption that the writer, somehow, must begin with such a synopsis (whether written down or no) and/or such an analysis.

This, for what it's worth, has not been my experience. At the beginning of a story, I am likely to have one or more images in my mind, some clearer than others (like the strip of light up Janice's arm), which, when I examine them, suggest relations to one another. Using the story process—envisioning and notating, envisioning and notating—I try to move from one of these images to the next, lighting and focusing, step by step, on the dark areas between. As I move along, other areas well ahead in the tale will suddenly come vaguely into light. When I actually reach the writing of them, I use the story process to bring them into sharper focus still.

As likely as not, some of the initial images will suggest obvious synopses of the material between (one image of a man on his knees before a safe; another of the same man fleeing across a rooftop while gunshots ring out behind; a third of the same man, marched between two policemen into a van) that the story process, when finished, will turn out to have followed pretty closely. But it is the process, not the synopsis, that produces the story. The synopsis is merely a guide.

Writers are always grappling with two problems: they must make the story interesting (to themselves, if no one else), yet keep it believable (because, somehow, when it ceases to be believable on some level, it ceases to be interesting).

Keeping things interesting seems to be primarily the province of the conscious mind (which, from the literature available, we know far less about than the unconscious), while believability is something that is supplied, in the images it throws up into the mind's theater, primarily by the unconscious. One thing we know about the unconscious is that it contains an incredibly complete "reality model," against which we are comparing our daily experiences moment to moment, every moment. This model lets us know that the thing over there is a garbage can while the thing over there is a gardenia bush, without our having to repeat the learning process of sticking our nose in them each time we pass. It also tells us that, though the thing over there *looks* like a gardenia bush, from a certain regularity in the leaves, an evenness in its coloring, and the tiny mold lines along the stem, it is really a plastic model of a gardenia bush and, should we sniff it, will not smell at all. The story process puts us closer to the material stored in our reality model than anything else we do besides dream. This material is what yielded up the splitting door jamb, the strip of light, the mattress ticking. This model is highly syncretic: reality is always presenting us with new experiences that are combinations of old ones. Therefore, even if we want to describe some Horatian impossibility "with the body of a lion and the head of an eagle," our model will give us, as we stare at the back of the creature's neck, the tawny hairs over the muscled shoulders, in which nestle the first mottled, orange-edge pin-feathers. Come to it honestly, and it will never lie: search as you want, it will not yield you the height of *pi*, the smell of the number seven, the sound of green, nor, heft hard as you can in the palm of your mind, the weight of the note D-flat. (This is not to suggest that such mysterious marvels aren't the province of fiction, especially science fiction; only that they are mysterious and marvelous constructions of the equally mysterious and marvelous *conscious* mind. That is where you must go to find out about *them*.)

When writers get (from readers or from themselves) criticism in the form "The story would be more believable if such and such happened" or "The story would be more interesting if such and such . . . " *and* they agree to make use of the criticism, they must translate it: "Is there any point in the story process I can go back to, and, by examining my visualization more closely, catch something I missed before, which, when I notate it, will move the visualization/notation process forward again in this new way?" In other words, can the writers convince themselves that on some ideal level the story actually *did* happen (as opposed to "should have happened") in the new way, and that it was their inaccuracy as a story-process practitioner that got it going on the wrong track at some given point? If you don't do this, the corrections are going to clunk a bit and leave a patch-as-patch-can feel with the reader.

Writers work with the story process in different ways. Some writers like to work through a short story at a single, intense sitting, to interrupt as little as possible the energy that propels the process along, to keep the imagined visualization clearly and constantly in mind.

Other writers must pause, pace, and sometimes spend days between each few phrases, abandoning and returning to the visualization a dozen times a page. I think this is done as a sort of test, to make sure only the strongest and most vitally clear elements—the ones that cling tenaciously to the underside of memory—are retained.

Masterpieces have been written with both methods. Both methods have produced drivel.

In a very real way, one writes a story to find out what happens in it. Before it is written it sits in the mind like a piece of overheard gossip or a bit of intriguing tattle. The story process is like taking up such a piece of gossip, hunting down the people actually involved, questioning them, finding out what really occurred, and visiting pertinent locations. As with gossip, you can't be too surprised if important things turn up that were left out of the first-heard version entirely; or if points initially made much of turn out to have been distorted, or simply not to have happened at all.

Among those stories that strike us as perfectly plotted, with those astonishing endings both a complete surprise and a total satisfaction, it is amazing how many of their writers will confess that the marvelous resolution was as much a surprise for them as it was for the reader, coming, in imagination and through the story process, only a page or a paragraph or a word before its actual notation.

On the other hand, those stories that make us say, "Well, that's clever, I *suppose* . . . ," but with a certain dissatisfied frown (the dissatisfaction itself, impossible to analyze), are often those stories worked out carefully in advance to be, precisely, clever.

One reason it is so hard to discuss the story process, even with introspection, is that it is something of a self-destruct process as well. The notation changes the imagination; it also distorts the writer's memory of the story's creation. The new, intensified visualization (which, depending on the success of the story process, and sometimes in spite of it, may or may not have anything to do with the reader's concept of the story) comes to replace the memory of the story process itself.

Writers cannot make any wholly objective statement on what they were trying to do, or even how they did it, because—as the only residue of the story process the reader has is the writer's words on the page—the only residue of the story process in the writer's mind is the clarified vision, which like the "plot" synopsis, is not the story, but the story's result.

—New York City
1972

Characters

Here are two points about characterization. Both, however, grow from a particular concept of story. A story is ultimately not what happens in the writer's mind that makes her or him write down a series of words (that is the just discussed "story process"). Rather, it is what a given series of words causes to happen in the *reader's*. And I might mention a minor corollary: it is only by seriously examining the things we can't make happen in the reader's mind that we begin to gain fine control over what we *can*. For example, there is no way, with words, to make a reader *see* the color red, but we can make the reader *remember* the color . . . In short, the experience of a story is a mental phenomenon of the order of memory, not immediate sensory apprehension, and an analysis of why some memories are more vivid, pressing, or moving than others is much more likely to lead to a vivid, pressing, and moving story than all the accurately reported first-hand experience in the world. A story is of the order of memory, and that is why it takes place in the past, even when set in the future. A story is a maneuvering of myriad micromemories into a new order.

It was the red of bricks.

It was the red of an Irish setter.

It was the red of Hawaiian Punch.

It was the red of smeared cherry pulp.

The point is, of course, all these are different reds. We remember them all differently.

But characterization?

My first point has to do with psychological veracity.

Any two facts clustered around a single pronoun begin to generate a character in the reader's mind:

She was sixteen years old, and already five-foot eleven.

Though only a ghost, she is already more or less vivid depending on the reader's experience. As soon as we get ready to add a third fact, however, we encounter the problem of psychological veracity. All subsequent information about our character (let's call her Sam) has to be more or less congruent with what already exists in the gap between these two facts. I have no particular problem if I continue adding facts thus:

She was a shy girl, and tended to walk around with her shoulders hunched.

The character, remember, is in our minds, not on the paper. She is composed of what we have seen or what we have read, which in this case has to do with what we know about the height of most sixteen-year-olds, as well as the general behavior of adolescent girls who are different from their peers.

If I wanted to, instead of making Sam shy and stooped, I could have said:

Lively, self-assured, she was cuttingly witty, though always popular; active physically, though always gentle.

If I did, however, in order to compensate for the tension that forms immediately with our sense of psychological veracity, I would have had to add (with an implied "For you see . . ."):

She was the middle child of seven, with siblings taller than herself on either side. It was a close and boisterous family, so that when Sam first came to Halifax High her stubby classmates amused her, and she was big-hearted enough to try to amuse them back. That and her basketball prowess made her very popular.

But if I had made her shy and stooped, I would not have needed the above. In the same way that the physically unusual needs explanation, so does the psychologically unusual. Practically any combination of physical and psychological traits can exist beneath a single persona: but the writer's instinctive feel for psychological veracity has to determine which combinations need further elucidation to cement their juxtaposition, and which simply work by themselves to generate a character, without further embellishment. All too often the plot simply calls for someone near six feet (because she has to be able to see over Mr. Green's fence when Henry runs out the French windows), sixteen years old (so that she isn't allowed in the movie house, where Green is the day manager Tuesday mornings), and self-assured (so she can calm down the people who rush out into the lobby on Saturday night when Henry shoots the blank air gun . . .), and so on.

But if the writer has violated the reader's sense of psychological veracity, he will have a fine and exciting tale moving around a Sam-shaped hole . . . even if the character in the writer's mind is quite real.

Ideally, all the plot information should contribute to the realization of the characters. All the character information should move the plot: if we *need* that sprawling, emotionally supportive family to make Sam real, it would be a good idea to have them take part in the story as well (Henry is Sam's oldest brother, who is living on the other side of town and doesn't get along with his parents at all; let us look a little more closely at Sam's happy family, and at Sam's apparent self-assuredness . . .). But this is how short stories turn into novels: this is what writers mean when they say characters can run away with the story.

My second point about characterization appears rather paradoxical in light of the first. Once a reader catches, by his or her own sense of psychological veracity, the character from what generates between the facts scattered about a name, vividness and immediacy are maintained, essentially, through what the character does: her actions (and particularly that subgroup of actions prompted by things outside her: reactions).

A character in a novel of mine—that most dangerous of creations: a novelist writing a novel—observed that there were three types of actions: purposeful, habitual, and gratuitous. If the writer can show a character involved in a number of all three types of actions, the character will probably seem more real.

This occurred to me when I was trying to analyze why some writers who can present perfectly well-drawn males cannot present a convincing female to save themselves—heroines *or* villainesses. I noticed with these writers that while their heroes (and villains) happily indulge in all types of actions, if there is a villainess, she is generally all purpose; if there is a heroine, she often does nothing but habitual actions, or nothing but gratuitous ones.

Assuming one has one's characters clearly visualized, the writer has to expose them to enough different things so that the characters can react in her or his own ways.

Often, in the rush to keep the action going, writers who specialize in what are seen as adventure stories forget to confront their characters (especially the women) with enough objects/ emotions/situations or give their characters space enough to react in a way both individual and within the limits of psychological veracity.

Ten years ago, before I had had any novels published, as a rule of thumb I constructed a small list of things that I thought all major characters in a novel should be exposed to and allowed to have individual reactions to, to make them appear particularly vivid.

Food: How does the character behave when eating with a group? If possible, how does she or he react when supplying food for others?

Sleep: What particularizes his/her going to sleep, his/her waking up?

Money: How does he or she get his/her shelter, food, and how does she or he feel about how she or he gets it?

Society: How does he or she react to somebody who makes substantially more money than he or she does, and how is this different from the way he or she acts to an economic peer (and believe me, it is different, however admirable)?

How does she or he react when she or he meets somebody who makes substantially less money than he or she does (and ditto)?

In a short story, of course, one may not have time to explore all these particular aspects of this character. But I can't think of one great novelist, from Madame de Lafayette (*La Princesse de Clèves* [1678]) through Joyce (*Ulysses* [1922]), who does not particularize her or his characters through at least some of these situations, somewhere or other through their books.

Now one can take the "list method" of character development and run it into the ground. When I was seventeen, a writer of successful juvenile novels gave me an eight-page mimeographed form he claimed he used to help him construct characters. In proper Harvard outline form were questions like:

I. How does he react outdoors?
    A. To weather?
        1. To rain?
        2. To sleet?
        3. To sun?
    B. To geography?
        1. In the mountains?
        2. By the sea?
II. How does he react indoors . . . ?

As an experiment, I took a character in a story I was working on (a skindiver, I remember, who had come with an American team to work on underwater oil wells off the coast of Venezuela) and wrote out nineteen pages of "characterization," following the guide.

Needless to say, I lost all interest in completing the story.

Leaving my particular points to generalize a bit:

The confusion in following most sorts of literary advice usually comes from the author's confusion as to what is happening in the author's mind and what he can effect in the reader's.

I don't think the writer has to understand the characters to write about them. The writer does need to *see* them. The *reader*, however, does need to understand them; if the reader figures them out for herself, the writer has "created" all that more vivid a character than if the writer explained them away. The writer must see and put down those things that will allow (not *make*: you can't *make* the reader do anything—not even open the book) the reader to understand. If you can (figuratively) close your eyes and see Sam as sixteen, six feet tall, and heroically self-assured, fine. But you will have to pay more attention to the vision of the story than certainly most adventure plots allow for.

The juxtapositions of traits that make up a "hero" are, alas, comparatively rare. That is why a "heroic" hero needs a good deal of characterization if our sense of psychological veracity is not to be strained past the breaking point very fast—precisely because she is a psychological (as well as a statistical) anomaly.

I don't think a writer's understanding is going to hurt the writer's (or should I say, the reader's) characters, in and of itself. However, what we understand with exhaustive analytical thoroughness we are not too likely to be interested in enough to fictionalize about with intensity—since the actual fictionalizing process itself is a form of synthetic analysis.

The thing to remember about characterization—direct characterization, in which you write about a person's psychology and the specific things which have shaped it to its particular form—is that, in most stories, a little goes a long way. As Oscar Wilde noted more than a hundred years ago, the more characterization you have, the more your character comes to sound like everybody else. Therefore what most writers want (Proust, Henry James, and Robert Musil notwithstanding) is a little very telling characterization, rather than lots of very precise characterization.

It is intriguing that the writer of the past hundred years to discuss most systematically what goes on in the writer's mind when creating was the French poet Paul Valéry, and that he produced an amazingly hard-headed aesthetic in which the words "precision" and "scientific" appear over and over. He himself began as an engineer. Mathematics and engineering supply most of his nonliterary specimens of the creative process.

A poet, his particular concern was poetry. But much of the impetus behind fiction is close to the poetic impulse. In an essay on La Fontaine's *Adonis*, he says in passing: "Follow the path of your aroused thought, and you will soon meet this infernal inscription: *There is nothing so beautiful as that which does not exist.*"

Whether she is writing about what she thinks could, should, or might someday exist or might have once existed, or whether he is dallying with some future fantasia so far away all subjunctive connection with the here and now is severed or is writing about the most nitty-gritty of recognizable landscapes, the writer has still become entranced with and dedicated her- or himself to the realization of what is not. And all the "socially beneficial functions of art" are minimal before this aesthetic one: it allows the present meaning; it allows the future to exist.

—San Francisco
1969

On Pure Storytelling

—for Vonda N. McIntyre

[Talk delivered at the 1970 Nebula
Awards Banquet in Berkeley]

I think the trouble with writers writing about writing (or speaking about it) is the trouble anyone has discussing his or her own profession.

I first came across this idea in E. M. Forster's *Aspects of the Novel* (1927): you'll do better writing about something you've only done a little of, because you still preserve those first impressions that make it vivid, even to someone who has been doing it for years. If you write about something you have been doing day in and day out, though you would recognize those impressions if someone else were to recall them to you, you yourself tend to pass over them as commonplaces.

Therefore, contemplating what I was going to say this evening, I tried to go back and capture some of my initial impressions about the whole experience of writing stories, or even my first encounters with the whole idea of stories and storytelling.

The catalyst for my ideas this evening was a book I passed recently on the shelves of the Tro Harper bookstore. It was a large-sized, quality paperback, with a red cover, published by Dell: *The Careless Atom* by Sheldon Novick.

Sheldon Novick . . .

The last time I heard Sheldon Novick's name was fourteen years ago. He was several years ahead of me at the Bronx High School of Science. There was a strange half dozen years when the Bronx High School of Science held a whole gaggle of fascinating people at once, including, among others, Stokeley Carmichael, Bobby Darin, Todd Gitlin, Peter Beagle, Norman Spinrad, someone else who is currently writing the motorcycle column for *The Good Times* under the nom de plume of The Black Shadow, and Marilyn Hacker.

As I said, that was the last I'd heard of Shelley, till two weeks ago.

The first I'd heard of him was several years before that. We were at summer camp. Some dozen of us had taken an evening hike from a place named, for unknown reasons, Brooklyn College, to another known as The Ledge.

There was a campfire.

Several marshmallows had, by now, fallen into it. We were a quarter of the way up the back of a forested hill, pretentiously called Mount Wittenburg. And it was dark and chilly. You know the situation: smoke in the eyes, your left cheek buttered with heat, your right shoulder shivering.

Somebody said, "Shelley, tell us a story."

"What do you want to hear a story for?" Shelley said with disdain, and licked marshmallow from his fingers.

"Tell us a story, tell us a story!" There wasn't any stopping us. "Tell us a story. Tell us the one about—"

"Oh, I told you that one last week."

"Tell it again! Tell it again!"

And I, who had never heard Shelley tell anything at all, but was thoroughly caught up by the enthusiasm, cried: "Well, then, tell us a new one!"

Smiling a little in the direction of the rubber on his left sneaker toe, Shelley rose to take a seat on a fallen log. He put his hands on his knees, leaned forward and said, "All right." He looked up at us. "Tonight I shall tell you the story of . . ."

The story that he told was called *Who Goes There?* He told it for an hour and a half that night, stopping in the middle. We gathered outside Brooklyn College the next night and sat on the flagstones while he told us another hour's worth. And two nights later we gathered in one of the tents while he gave us the concluding half hour under the kerosene lantern hanging from the center pole.

"Did you make that up?" somebody asked him, when he was finished.

"Oh, no. It's by somebody called John W. Campbell," he explained to us. "It's a book. I read it a couple of weeks ago."

At which point our counselor told him, really, it was well past lights out and he simply had to go.

Our counselor blew out the light, and I lay in my cot bed thinking about storytelling. Shelley was perhaps thirteen, back then. I was nine or ten, but even then it seemed perfectly marvelous that somebody could keep so many people enthralled for four hours over three nights.

Shelley was the first of those wonderful creatures, "a Storyteller," whom I had ever encountered.

A summer camp is a very small place. Shelley's reputation spread. Some weeks later, he was asked to tell his story again to a much larger group—bunk five, bunk six, and bunk seven all collected in the amphitheater behind the long, creosoted kitchen house. On a bench this time, once more Shelley told the story *Who Goes There?* This time it took only a single hour sitting.

We who'd heard it before, of course, had the expected connoisseur reaction: Oh, it was much better in the longer version. The intimacy of firelight and roasted marshmallows vastly improved the initial sequence. And lanterns were essential for the conclusion to have its full effect. But the forty-odd people who, that evening, heard it for the first time were just as enthralled as we had been. More important, I got a chance to look at how Shelley's tale was put together.

The first thing I noticed the second time through was that the names of all the characters were different from the first time. And when I got a chance to look at the novel myself a year or so later, I realized with amusement that the names in neither of Shelley's versions corresponded with those of Campbell's.

The second thing I noticed was that a good deal of the story was chanted—indeed, in the most exciting passages very little was actually happening; and you had sections like:

They walked across the ice, they slogged across the ice, there was ice below them and ice all around them . . .

Or, when the monster was beginning to revive, I recall:

The fingers rose, the hand rose, the arm rose slowly, a little at a time, rose like a great green plant . . .

Needless to say, you will find none of these lines in the book.

What Shelley was giving us was a very theatrical, impromptu, and essentially poetic impression of his memory of the tale.

When I did encounter Shelley again in Bronx Science, I had just joined the staff of the school literary magazine, *Dynamo.* I was delighted to discover him. That was one of the first times I made the discovery that three years difference in age is a lot more at nine or ten than it is at fourteen or fifteen.

At any rate, I bumped into Shelley—literally—behind the projection booth in the auditorium balcony. We recovered, recognized each other, enthused for a while, and I asked him if he would be doing any fiction or poetry for *Dynamo.* He looked quite surprised. No, he hadn't thought about it. Actually his interests were in theater.

I was quite surprised. But creative writing, he explained, had never particularly attracted him.

Later, Shelley turned in quite a credible performance as Jonathan in the senior play, *Arsenic and Old Lace.* And a few weeks ago, after having not seen him since, I learned, via the blurb on the back of *The Careless Atom*, that "Sheldon Novick is Program Administrator of the Center for the Biology of Natural Systems at Washington University in St. Louis. He is also Associate Editor of the journal *Scientist and Citizen* and is a frequent contributor of articles dealing with atomic energy." I can recommend the book to anyone interested in the recent developments of the practical side of reactors and reactor plants. (Even more recently, Novick is the author of a fascinating and controversial biography, *Henry James: The Young Master* [Random House: New York, 1997], as well as a life of Oliver Wendell Holmes. He is also editor of Holmes's collected works. –SRD, 2005)

But let's get back to "storytelling."

The second "storyteller" I encountered was Seamus McManus. He was the grandfather of one of my elementary school classmates. Mr. McManus had been born in Ireland. His father had been a professional storyteller who went from cottage to cottage and, for lodging and meals and a bit of kind, kept the family entertained in the evenings with what were called "faerie stories," in which an endless number of heroes named Jack, always the youngest of three brothers, set out to seek their fortune and, after encountering multiple old women, magicians, giants and elves, magic mills, and enchanted apples, married the beautiful princess and lived happily ever after.

Mr. McManus had made the reconstruction of these classic Irish folk tales his hobby. He told them at children's parties—indeed, it was at his grandson's, Fitzhugh Mullan's, birthday party that I first heard him. Sunlight streamed through white organdy curtains while the gray-haired gentleman sat forward in the armchair, and the rest of us, sitting on the rug and hugging our knees, were bound in the music of his brogue. Over the next few years, I heard him several times more, once at a children's library, and once in a program in the school's auditorium. And, after the initial magic, again I got a chance to look at what was going on.

The action in these stories—and you always left a McManus storytelling under the impression that you had just been *through* the tremendous and hair-raising adventures—the action, when you looked at it up close, was usually dismissed in a sentence or two: the typical battle between Jack and one of his numerous adversaries was usually handled something like this:

> "You want to fight?" said Jack. "Well I'm a poor sort of fighter but I'll do my best, and the best can do no more."
> So they fought, and they fought, and they fought, and they fought, and—(here Mr. McManus would snap his fingers)—Jack slew him with a blow.

There was your action.

On the other hand, the things that stuck, the things that remained, indeed the things that took up most of the time, were the ritual descriptions and incantatory paragraphs, the endless journeys that all went from tale to tale, from story to story:

> So they lifted up their bundles, and set out in high spirits. And they traveled twice as far as I could tell you, and three times farther than you could tell me, and seven times farther than anyone could tell the two of us.

And when, in a year or so, I first read the *Iliad*, I think this contributed much to my understanding of those ritual descriptions that are repeated word for word throughout the poem—like the sacrifices that come with exactly the same words nearly a dozen times, at each point the Achaeans are called on to perform one:

> When they had made their petitions and scattered the grain, they first drew the heads of the animals back; they cut open their throats; they flayed them. Then from the thighs they cut slices and wrapped them in fat folds with raw meat above them. These the old priest burnt on the wood, and he sprinkled wine on the fire, and the young men gathered around him, five-pronged forks in their hands. When the thighs were burnt up, and they had all tasted the organs, they carved the remains into small pieces and pierced them with boughs and they roasted them well, then pulled them out of the flame. Work done, the meal ready, they fell to eating hungrily, all with an equal share. And, when their thirst and their hunger were satisfied . . .

When their thirst and their hunger were satisfied, the Trojan War got under way again.

Mr. McManus published several books of his stories. The one I recall most readily was *Bold Heroes of Hungry Hill.* If you read them, I suspect you will find them a little flat—though they are word for word as Mr. McManus told them.

While I considered the flatness, I was taken back to Mr. McManus at FitzHugh's party. Afterward, we'd asked him questions about himself, about the stories, about Ireland. "After all," I remember him saying, "the tales are hundreds of years old, passed on by word of mouth. We had some good storytellers, and some not so good. But the thing to remember—" and he sat back in his armchair again—"the tale is in the telling."

The third storyteller I remember from that terribly odd, angular, and hyperlogical time called childhood was my geography teacher, John Seeger. He was the older brother of the folk singer Pete Seeger. They have practically identical speaking voices. Any one of you who caught Pete Seeger on the Johnny Cash show a few weeks back will have some idea of the terribly arresting quality of that voice. John—my elementary school was one of those fifties strangenesses where children called the teachers by their first names—John taught a good deal of his geography through storytelling.

They all followed the same form. Two children, a boy and a girl, variously named Pat and Pam, or Bill and Barbara, or John and Judy, along with their crotchety governess—the only one of her many names I remember was Miss Powderpuff—would get separated from their parents in a foreign country, and John would regale us with the economics, the geography, the landscape, the morals and mores of the country in a fusillade of fascinating anecdotes.

John's stories were incredibly popular with the students. Twice a week, the geography room would stay open after school, and forty or fifty of us would squeeze into the circle while John, mimicking first this character, then another, with much slapping of the knees and clever gesticulations, would take his alliterative hero and heroine through Athens, Beirut, Calcutta, Damascus, Edinburgh, Frankfurt, and Geneva. I think John's stories were the most enjoyable of the three. Besides being educational, they involved a great deal of audience participation. Whenever a new character entered, John would first describe him—a Greek musician, a French banker, a Turkish ambassador's son—then he would turn to us and say, "And what should we call him?"

We would cry out names, and whichever one seemed most appropriate would stick with the character through the story.

During this time, I was indulging in my own first experiments with writing. I had even gone so far as to put down a hundred-odd pages of a novel, in cramped scrawling pencil, about an elderly gentleman of fifteen who spent a lot of time looking at the sea and taking long walks alone in the city. Sometime or other during its composition, it occurred to me that, besides spelling and grammar, something else was missing from the sorrows of my youngest of Werthers (it was called *Lost Stars*). But what . . . ?

Once, after one of his more fascinating storytelling sessions, I went up to John and asked him if he had ever written any of his stories down.

All the other students had gone, and tall, gangling John and I walked down the hall toward the elevator. John looked surprisingly pensive. "I've tried," he explained. "But somehow, I just can't tell stories to a typewriter. And there isn't the interplay back and forth between me and you kids."

I was precocious. "Have you ever tried to record them?" I suggested. "Then you could transcribe—" (I had just learned the word two weeks ago and was using it now at every opportunity—) "you could transcribe them, and then they'd be just like you told them."

"It's funny you should suggest that," John said. "Last year, I tried that. And once I forgot about the microphone, the telling went pretty well. Then I got my wife to type it out. And you know what?"

"What?" I asked.

"They were perfectly dreadful!" Then the elevator came.

I believe that was my first practical lesson in fiction writing. Indeed, I'd go so far as to say that everything I know consciously about writing—and I'm painfully aware how little that actually is—has to do with the difference between written and spoken language.

I feel that I was lucky to have been exposed to so much purely verbal storytelling as a child, because it pointed out some essential differences between sitting, with a bunch of people, at the feet of a marvelous and magical raconteur, and sitting in one's room, by oneself, with a book.

The aural art of storytelling, like theater, is essentially communal. People come together to hear stories. And the storyteller has the whole theatrical battery, including elements of dance and song, to compel his listeners' attention.

Reading is very much a do-it-yourself entertainment. It's private. There is no way for an author to *compel* the reader to do anything. Any call to the phone, or even a passing thought, can interrupt. On the other hand, the reader can determine his or her own pace at reading, can go back and reread; indeed, as a rule, the reader is far more conscious of details than the hearer.

In speech, incantation, invocation, and repetition are practically a must. But what the ear finds supremely enthralling the eye finds dull.

On the other hand, such a tiny part of the visual capacity of the eye and brain is used in scanning black print on white paper that practically the whole pictorial imagination is left free—so that in written texts, *evocation* becomes almost the entire process, the conjuring up of pictures, tones of voice, resonances, implications, and reminiscences.

Reading, as opposed to listening, requires a far higher level of attention, and the McLuhan formula, "Low resolution equals high involvement," governs the whole play. Traditional phrases that weigh heavily on the ear, to the eye are mere clichés. The reader wants the information once and at the highest intensity, rather than beat into the tympanum with chanted repetition.

As much as tone of voice is part of writing, the infinite nuances that various vocal tones can give to a single phrase are totally lost on the page. The scant dozen punctuation marks in the English typesetter's box are just inadequate to handle the job. (A couple of weeks ago, Greg, Joan, Don, Quinn,* and I were contemplating a new punctuation mark: a "sarcasm mark" which, when it appeared at the end of a sentence, would indicate that the sentence should be read in such a way as to imply the exact opposite of its denoted content. Perhaps a small tilde over a period?)

Aural language depends on repetition, of intravocalic sounds, of sound patterns, of ideas.

In written language the beginnings and the ends of sentences are the place for that sentence's most important words. In speech the most important word in the sentence has to be surrounded on both sides by an aural bolster of padding, to prop it up, to buoy it up, to keep it afloat in our minds. Let me repeat that, because I'm speaking: in speech the most important word in a sentence has to be rumti-tumped and bumti-bumped in padding, to scuba-duba, to oh-calcutta, to rumplestiltskin it in the hootchy-kootch. (Hear what I mean?)

In written language, one doesn't *begin* to hear it until a certain *visual hardness* (or density) is achieved. And when the ear does come into play, I think it is on a much subtler level. It is listening to an essentially unsung music.

When we listen, we want the ideas interlarded with noise—

* Greg and Joan Benford, Don Simpson, and Chelsey Quinn Yarbro.

all those meaningless words and phrases like "essentially," "practically," "on the other hand," "almost," "seems," "more or less," "suddenly"—the words that give us time to think.

On the page, the same words are abhorrent, ugly, and, even in reported dialogue, more times than not get in the way.

When I was a child, I was a perfectly dreadful storyteller. I wanted very much to be a good one. Storytellers are amazing and wondrous people. Anyone who has not encountered a fine tale-teller has missed out on a very basic, important, and rewarding cultural experience.

Several times I tried to tell stories.

People fidgeted.

I kept forgetting the plot.

I have this creaky, asthmatic laughter (as with the canned studio responses to situation comedies, the storyteller must lead and guide the audience's laughter at the tale, so that a large and generous laugh is essential to the art), and I usually talk too loud.

I suppose that's why I became a writer.

You know, I think about being a child, listening to stories. Then I think about all of us, gathered here for this banquet tonight. You know, a lot of funny things happened on my way here this evening.

But I'm damned if I'm going to *tell* you about them.

—San Francisco
1970

Of Doubts and Dreams

[First written in 1980 as a preface to a collection of my stories, *Distant Stars* (1981), today this piece appears as an afterword to my collection of short stories, *Aye, and Gomorrah*, published in 2003 by Vintage Books.]

The request to write about your own work—to comment on a collection of your own fictions, say—is, to most writers, an occasion for distractionary tactics. What you do when you "write a story," like what you do when you bleed or heal, is too simple and too complicated for the mid-level exposition most such pieces presuppose. ("We want something informative, of course—but don't get *too* technical . . .") What makes it simple *and* complicated is not, oddly, what you do when you write. It's what people have said about writing over many years. To be simple is to say, in whatever way you choose, that they are, all of them, right. To be complicated is to explain that they are wrong, and why.

Simply? You sit down to write a story. The excitement, the sweep, the wonder of narrative comes over you, and, writing as fast as you can, you try to keep up with it till the tale is told.

The complicated part?

Just try it. You see, what comes as well, along with the narrative wonder, is a lot of doubts, delays, and hesitations. *Is* it really that wondrous? Is it even a decent *sentence?* Does it have anything to do with the way you *feel* about the world? Does it say anything that would at all interest you were you *reading* it? *Where* will you find the energy to put down another word? What do you put down *now?* Narrative becomes a way of negotiating a path through, over, under, and around the whole bewildering, paralyzing, unstoppable succession of halts. The real wonder of narrative is that it can negotiate this obstacle path at all.

A baker's dozen years back I first found myself, through a collision of preposterous circumstances, in front of a silent group of strangers, some eager, some distrustful, but all with one thing in common: all had registered for a writing workshop I had been hired to teach. And I became formally, articulately, distressingly aware how little I knew about "how to write a story."

The workshops recurred, however; and finally I found my nose pressed up against the fact that I knew only—perhaps— three things about my craft. Since I filched two from other writers anyway, I pass them on for what they're worth.

The first comes from Theodore Sturgeon. He put it in a letter he wrote in the fifties to Judith Merril, who quoted it in an article she wrote about Sturgeon in 1962. To write an immediate and vivid scene, Sturgeon said, visualize everything about it as thoroughly as you can, from the dime-sized price sticker still on the brass switch plate, to the thumbprint on the clear pane in the unpainted wooden frame, to the trowel marks sweeping the ceiling's white, white plaster, and all between. Then, do *not* describe it. Rather, mention only those aspects that impinge on your character's consciousness, as she or he, in whatever emotional state she or he is in (elated buyer seeing it for the first time, bored carpenter anxious for lunch . . .), wanders over the squeaking planks beside the paint-speckled ladder. The scene the reader envisions, Sturgeon went on to explain, will *not* be the same as yours—but it will be as vivid, detailed, coherent, and important for the reader as yours was for you.

Number two comes from Thomas Disch, who suggested it at a Milford science fiction writers' conference in 1967 during a discussion about what to do when a story or novel runs down in the middle and the writer loses interest. The usual half-hearted, half-serious suggestions had been made, from "take a cold shower" to "kill off a main character." Then Disch commented that the only thing you can do in such a situation is to ask of your story what's really going on in it. What are the characters' real motivations, feelings, fears, or desires? Right at the point you stopped, you must go down to another level in the tale. You must dig into the character's psychology deeply enough (and thus build up your vision of the story's complexity enough) to reinterest yourself. If you can't, then the story must be abandoned.

Number three has to do with the preparatory story stages, though it can also be used with smaller sections of a tale during the actual writing. It's the one writing notion I've put together more or less on my own. At some point, when the story is still only an idea, an image, or a topic, ask yourself, what is the most usual, the most traditional, the most cliché way to handle that particular material. Ask yourself what are the traps that, time and again, other writers have fallen into when handling the same matters, that have made their work trite, ugly, or dull. Can you think of any way to avoid precisely those traps? How do you want your work to differ from the usual? How is your work going to deal with this material in a way no one has ever dealt with it before? Locating a precise writerly problem to avoid (or to solve), or situating a particular writerly approach that will set your work apart, can often provide the excitement to write it.

I've run into other rules of thumb about writing. When stuck for something to say in a writing workshop, I've even passed them on. Occasionally someone else has claimed to find them helpful. But these three are the only ones I have ever personally used. They exhaust my very tentative, firsthand, "how-to" knowledge.

What you learn in a creative writing workshop, of course (especially if you're the teacher), is how *not* to write. And when writing is looked at as a series of don'ts, then even the three suggestions above turn over to reveal a more familiar side:

Sturgeon's point, when all is said and done, really boils down to "Don't overwrite."

Disch's point, by the same reduction, becomes "Don't let your writing become thin or superficial."

And my own is simply "Don't indulge clichés."

Suddenly none sounds very original. Notice also, as soon as the advice is rendered negatively, it begins to suggest the same list of doubts with which we began. Indeed, whenever you find yourself writing a cluttered, thin, or cliché sentence, you *should* doubt, and doubt seriously. And once we are in this negative mode, we can put together a whole list of other things to doubt as well, hopefully to one's profit. Myself, I doubt modifiers, especially in bunches, particularly when they are prepositional phrases ending sentences. I doubt verbs that get too far from their subjects. I doubt story endings so violent no character left is in any state to learn anything from what has occurred. I doubt story endings so poetic you begin to suspect, really, there was nothing to learn in the first place. I doubt descriptions put down "exactly as they happened." And I doubt descriptions so badly put down they couldn't have happened at all.

What does this doubting mean? It means a writer *may* just let any one of them stand. After all, that extra adjective may not be clutter but an interesting catachresis that allows us to see something unusual about the object. That sentence or paragraph may not be thin, but rather a synoptic account that highlights a quality we might otherwise miss. That cliché may make an ironic comment on a certain kind of banality that is, itself, what you want to write about. But it means you'd better be convinced.

It means you don't give any one of them the *benefit* of the doubt.

I suspect one reason creative writing classes and workshops are not more successful than they usually are has to do with *when* the doubting takes place.

A unique process begins when the writer lowers the pen to put words on paper—or taps out letters onto the page with typewriter keys. Certainly writers think about and plan stories beforehand; and certainly, after writing a few stories, you may plan them or think about them in a more complex way. But even this increased complexity is likely to grow out of the process of which I'm speaking. The fact is, almost everyone *thinks* about stories. Many even get to the point of planning them. But the place where the writer's experience differs from everyone else's is during the writing process itself. What makes this process unique has to do directly with the doubting.

You picture the beginning of a story. (Anyone can do that.) You try to describe it. (And anyone can try.) Your mind offers up a word, or three, or a dozen. (It's not much different from what happens when you write a friend in a letter what you did yesterday morning.) You write the words down, the first, the second, the third, fourth, fifth, sixth, seventh—suddenly you doubt.

You sense clutter, or thinness, or cliché.

You are now on the verge of a process that happens only in the actual writing of a text.

If the word you doubted is among those already written down, you can cross it out. If it's among the words you're about to write, you can say to yourself, "No, not that one," and either go on without it, or wait for some alternative to come. The act of refusing to put down words, or crossing out words already down, while you concentrate on the vision you are writing about, *makes* new words come. What's more, when you refuse language your mind offers up, something happens to the next batch offered. The words are not the same ones that would have come if you hadn't doubted.

The differences will probably have little or nothing to do with your plot, or the overall story shape—though they might. There will probably be much to reject among the new batch too. But making these changes the moment they are perceived keeps the tale curving inward toward its own energy. When you make the corrections at the time, the next words that come up will be richer—richer both in things to accept *and* to reject. And the process doesn't end. Frequently something you've arrived at through this process on page six will make you realize that you now doubt something back on page two. Perhaps it's cluttered—maybe a whole sentence can go. Perhaps it's thin— maybe a whole incident must be added.

If there is a privileged moment somewhere in the arc of experience running from the first language an infant hears, through the toddler's learning that language, to the child's learning to read it, learning to write it, to the adolescent's attempts to write journals, tales, dramas, poems—if there is a moment, rightly called creative, when the possibility of the extraordinary is shored up against the inundation of ordinary rhetoric that forms, shapes, and is the majority of what we call civilized life, it is here. This is the moment covered—in the sense of covered over—by the tautology against which so many thousands of would-be writers have stumbled: "To be a writer, you must write." You must write not only to produce the text that is the historical verification of your having written. You must write to project yourself, again and again, through the annealing moment that provides the negentropic organization which makes a few texts privileged tools of perception. Without this moment, this series of moments, this concatenation of doubts about language shattered by language, the text is only a document of time passed with some paper, of time spent pondering a passage through a dream.

A teacher can take a page from a story written the night or the month before, focus in on a few sentences, and point out three superfluous adjectives, a dangling modifier, and a broken-back sentence (Damon Knight's term for a sentence carrying too much baggage, often lodged between subject and verb). Truly enlightened, the student may cross out the adjectives, reshuffle the clauses—and the sentence or sentences may now evoke their object with a bit more grace and precision. But the student will not get the immediate charge from having made the corrections at the time of writing, an energy that will manifest itself among the three sentences written next.

Narrative sweep, then, is not only being able to make your criticisms on the run, as it were, but being able to work with the resultant energy.

Doubting over a longer period also, however, produces its changes. One story in this collection [see head note], for example, is both among the oldest stories here and is also the fantasy short story most recently completed. I first wrote it some time around 1962—that is, I wrote out a version in longhand in my notebook (doubting and rejecting all the way), then went back, reread it, doubted some more, and made some more changes. I typed up a rough draft, which involved much doubting and rewriting as well. Then I reread it, wrote in *more* changes; then I typed up a final draft, in which I made even more changes.

The story never placed—which is to say, for reasons mainly involving forgetfulness, it was only submitted once. In 1967 I discovered it in a file cabinet drawer the same week a fanzine editor asked me for a fiction contribution. I reread it, doubted, and wrote in a lot more changes. Then I retyped it, making still more. Another rereading made me write in a few more. Then I gave the story to the fanzine.

When I read the fanzine's mimeographed version, I recall making a few more changes on my own copy—but that copy was shortly lost. Still, by now I'd decided I *liked* the story. Last month, after a twelve-year hiatus, I ferreted out a Xerox copy of the fanzine version, reread it, and, to assuage a few more doubts, made still more handwritten corrections. Then I typed up a draft, which included those corrections plus numerous ones in response to a whole new raft of doubts. Then I typed still another "final" draft, incorporating just a *few* more changes. There were a few more rereadings over the next few days, each one of which produced three to five new changes—and that, along with a few doubts about my typing from the copy editor, is the version here. Copy editor excluded, that's at least twelve layers of doubts spread over seventeen years. I know I enjoyed first drafting the story back in '62. And I certainly enjoyed the re-writes. Yet frankly, the story still strikes me as . . . slight—which is to say the doubting process I've been describing is finally interesting not because it *guarantees* accomplishment, but merely because it happens. At this point we may even begin to doubt the doubting process itself, whereupon narrative becomes only the habits of mind, for better or worse, the writer goes through while writing; and reason is only the principal among those distractionary tactics mentioned at our opening. Slight as the story is, however, my view of the characters, the landscape, the buildings, and the general decor is clearer for me than it was seventeen years ago. And if Sturgeon's point is correct, the reader's may be clearer than it would have been, at least from the first version.

So much for long-term doubting.

The French novelist Flaubert is known for the immense effort he put into his style. The late Roland Barthes once quipped that Flaubert brought the whole notion of labor to fiction, which made the conservative French middle classes begin to trust it more. Once, Flaubert worked for several days on a single sentence, at the end of which time he had only removed one comma. Still dissatisfied (still doubting?), he continued to work on the sentence, and at the end of several more days, he had put the comma back. But now, Flaubert concluded in one of his letters, he knew *why* the comma was there.*

I suspect even this belongs among the simple things one can say about writing. The work, not to mention the final knowledge, is not on the rational level that produces the academically acceptable explanation, but rather in that oddly blurred area where linguistic competence (the knowledge of the language everyone who can speak it shares) is flush with the writer's individual suspicions about how words can be made to mean more accurately and intensely. That's hard to talk or write about. That's why it *is* work.

In conversations about writing, I've occasionally said writing strikes me as a many-layered process, only the top three or four of which have anything directly to do with words. This, however, is another easy metaphor. And when you analyze through introspection, it is always hard to know *how* metaphorical you are being. I do know that just under the verbal layers there is a layer that seems to me much more like numbers than like words. It is a layer controlling pure pattern, where, among other things, places are set up for words that are going to be the same (or very much alike) and other places are set up for words that are going to be different (or highly contrasting). Frequently these places are set out well before the actual words that will fill them are chosen. Once, writing a novel, I realized I wanted a description of a highway light moving down the pockmarked face of a truckdriver at night, forming shadow after shadow, to mirror a description of the sun moving down the face of a tenement building at evening, windowpane after windowpane flaring gold. I wanted one description to be near the beginning of the novel and the other to come around the midpoint. The midpoint of this particular novel turned out to be about 450 pages away from the opening. When I decided this, I had no idea what the actual words of either description would be. But once both sentences were written, whenever one description would be revised, 450 pages away, the other one would have to be revised too—as I recall, both went through over a dozen rewrites. Then

* More recently I have heard this tale told about Oscar Wilde.

a proofreader's error destroyed the symmetry in the published version, which is why it weighs heavily enough on me to mention it here.

Another example of this same mathematical layer at work: toward the beginning of a previously published story, included in this collection, a character slips on a rock and gets a foot wet in a stream.

"Why," demanded my original editor,* who was plagued with length restrictions and who wanted to see the story cut, "do you need *that?*"

Because later on in the story another character does *not* slip on that rock and does *not* get a foot wet. The two incidents served as a kind of mutual characterization, an *en passant* comment on the two characters' contrasting abilities to maneuver through the landscape. But (as I was too flustered to explain to the editor at the time—which is probably why I mention it now) that is why I couldn't cut the one—at least not without cutting the other. And again, the incidents' positions in the story and their contrasting nature were determined, at this mathematical level, long before I knew what the incidents or the words that would realize them were. I think, then, that a good deal of the "sweep" part of narrative sweep is the creation of some formal pattern—a structure, if you will—and the subsequent urge to fill it with language that will manifest it.

Besides the fact that both of these cases were challenged by the world (one by a printer's slip and one by an editor), which makes them, among the thousands and thousands of such cases that underlie any writer's text, remain in mind, another aspect of their exemplary quality is that the patterns stayed fairly clear from conception to execution. Yet even on this mathematical level, the writing down—and the rejecting—of language produces revelations and revisions in the most formal organization of the story. At any time, on any level, at any moment where you can doubt, at any place where you can say, "No, I want something better, other, different . . . ," this sharpening and reenergizing process can take place.

* Edward Ferman, then editor and publisher of *The Magazine of Fantasy and Science Fiction.*

Freud, in his *Interpretation of Dreams* (1900), describes a phenomenon you can check for yourself if you have a cooperative friend, patience, and a cassette tape recorder. Catch your friend within minutes after she or he wakes and ask the person to describe a dream into the recorder. Now immediately have the person describe the dream again. Then have the person describe the dream a third time. It is important that this be done within five or ten minutes of waking—after twenty minutes, or an hour, the phenomenon is far less noticeable. The number of changes in the three descriptions, however, will often be astonishingly high. Sometimes the sexes of minor dream characters will alter. Or the number of characters will vary. Often what people were wearing or what they looked like will shift markedly between retellings. Often the settings will become more specific, while character motivations will become more complicated. Most people, if asked to spot changes in their own accounts, will accurately notice two or three. But the number actual transcription reveals is frequently unsettling. What Freud saw was that, as the descriptions changed, the memory of the dream in the dreamer's mind seemed to change as well.

Dreams, as Freud knew, are closely allied to language. They frequently turn on puns, alternate meanings, rhymes, or other plays on words having to do with something said or read, to or by the speaker, during the previous day. A young woman who has planned to go camping tomorrow dreams she is walking by a post office where she sees an American flag wrapped around the flagpole, which, as she passes, suddenly unrolls to drop a slumbering woman to the street. In this dream a sleeping bag— which our prospective camper, the day before, was wondering how she was going to obtain for the trip—has become a sleeping flag.* As the French psychiatrist Jacques Lacan has pointed out,

---

* One afternoon some years after I had written the above, I was on a bus from Amherst, Massachusetts, to New York City. I was very tired, and, to pass the time, I was reading a magazine article about rock and roll, when the phrase "weeping and wailing" passed under my eye— moments before I dozed off . . . and I began to dream I was standing on the deck of a rocking ship in full sail. I was sweeping the deck with a broad push broom. I swept my pile of refuse to the deck's edge, where

the analyst does not analyze the dream itself so much as the language with which the dream is recounted. Freud proposed that, on waking, often the dream is not really complete in the dreamer's unconscious—especially a dream that is remembered. The dreamer's own language, then, reenters the unconscious mind and, through more wordplays, puns, and alternate meanings, joins with the still malleable dream material, and the content of the dream is actually emended, even while we are awake. This explains the great changes between these various early accounts and why the changes are so hard to catch except in transcription —since the actual memory of the dream is changed along with them.

Imagining a scene in a story and then writing it is certainly not identical to dreaming a dream and then telling it. But they share enough characteristics that it seems feasible they might be subject to the same mental process. In both cases one imagines. In both cases one responds to that imagining with language. In both cases the language one accepts (or, indeed, rejects) may go back to affect the imagination directly, which in turn affects the subsequent language by which we continue our narration. With writing, however, because of the whole doubting process (even when it doubts itself), we have a way to discipline our imaginings through disciplining our language—an endless process of doubts, of rejections, of things avoided, things not done.

These stories, then, include a number of fantasies and a number of science fiction tales in which I have, well . . . tried to avoid an amount of clutter, thinness, and cliché. The places I've failed, despite my aim, some may find instructive—a modestly direct statement.

The simple ability to write, active talent, and writerly genius

———

I saw an immense whale had been roped up against the boat. As the boat rolled deeply, I stepped from the deck onto the whale's gray back and continued sweeping—whereupon I woke in the trundling bus. The words "weeping and wailing" had generated a dream about sweeping and whaling, rocking, sailing, rolling . . . Dreams, Freud tells us, are often put together like a rebus puzzle. From this arose Freud's famous advice as to the best practice for anyone who would work to analyze them: "Do word puzzles."

lie on a line—and genius is far off and hard to see. In his wonderfully readable *Laocoön*, in which he alerts poets and sculptors to the greater strength of esthetic effects posed through suggestion over those embodied in statement, G. E. Lessing made an aspect of it vivid and visible when he characterized genius as "the ability to put talent wholly into the service of an idea." (In 1766, twenty-two-year-old Johann von Herder read Lessing's book—famously—cover to cover, in the afternoon and again in the evening of the same autumn day it arrived at his Königsberg bookshop.) Today, wherever we or others—they never coincide —see ourselves on that knotty line, a statement such as the previous paragraph's is as direct as a writer can risk if the distractions are not to become more than the fictions can bear.

—New York City
September 1980

After Almost No Time at All the String on Which He Had Been Pulling and Pulling Came Apart into Two Separate Pieces So Quickly He Hardly Realized It Had Snapped, *or:* Reflections on "The Beach Fire"

I am going to be fairly tough in this story. You may find yourself asking, "Does Q— E— really deserve this horse-whipping?" Frankly I doubt it. Though I don't think I've ever met him, chances are he's a pretty nice guy. Chances are he comes off pretty bright, even in a room full of bright people. Chances are his feelings about the Palestinian question, gay liberation, or the Iranian hostages (I write this on day 106) are close enough to mine for significant simpatico between us; or, if they're not, he probably has some information to back up his position it wouldn't hurt me to listen to, even if we don't agree. Chances are, over a Coke at a late-night party we could have a good discussion about the place of topology in modern mathematics, life messages to be learned from playing Dungeons & Dragons, or even the problems of writing SF short stories. Chances are he's got things of real insight to say on all these topics—or, if not on them, then on ten others twice as interesting.

Why, then, am I going to put him—and you, and me—through this?

Mainly because the writing business is a tough one.

If you're going to stay in it, you must build up calluses against criticism—criticism from readers, from other writers, from reviewers, from editors, and from critics. Yes, praise is fine and fun. But one has to field, again and again—*and* again—someone telling you your work's not very good. That's your absolutely best work, which you've rewritten and retyped and blue-penciled and rewritten and retyped *again*. After three years, or five years, or a dozen years trying, there may be publication. If it's a novel, there may even be reviews—someone may even write you a letter saying she or he liked it. But the day-to-day diet, from others and, more important, from the little critic we all carry on our own shoulder, is a grim one. And it has to be so.

If there's anything useful *in* the criticism, that's gravy.

But the calluses must grow for survival and sanity's sake.

They aren't developed by appreciative pats on the head.

A broken baseball bat brings them out faster.

I'll start with some remarks on technique.

We're all more or less aware of it for poetry. Frequently, though, we forget it for prose. In good fiction sentences must dramatize what they are about as well as simply say it. Also, a sentence describing the most objective action must suggest (*not* tell!), by pacing, by word choice (diction), by its consonantal clatter and its assonantial coo, what is going on with the characters' feelings. The sentences in a story tell us a progression of events and occurrences. At the same time, these same sentences are busy gesturing, miming, and generally carrying on about a supportive countertext that gives the story we're reading all its resonance, highlighting, and intensity. Talent for writing fiction, however consummate, however clumsy, is the ability to control text *and* countertext with the same words. If you can't, you'd better try journalism or, better still, some nonwriting profession, because, in matters writerly, the countertext is always there. Sometimes it works to help the text, to reflect it clearly and luminously, to suggest depths and highlights. But sometimes it merely mumbles against the text, providing a glare of logically unconnected associations, which, like mixed metaphors, shadow it in contradictory obscurities if they don't drown it in incoherence.

When we read a story where the sentences do not dramatize themselves or the characters' feelings, where the sentences do not provide an illuminating and supportive countertext, the story soon becomes dull. We suspect that something's missing. After we read such tales, we forget them quickly.

Encounter a sentence whose countertext is absolutely at odds with its overt meaning (such as the burlesque I've concocted for my title), and you may even laugh out loud.

There are many such sentences in "The Beach Fire."

Bill woke up, snapped into consciousness by nothing of which he was immediately aware.

This sentence has neither snap nor immediacy. It needs both if it is going to work, there, in the story, where it is, doing its particular job.

Bill jumped at the closeness of her voice.

You couldn't get "Bill" and "her voice" farther *apart* in the sentence; yet the sentence is about how *close* they are! A rule of thumb may help you here: when possible, avoid attributive nouns ("closeness," "smallness," "redness"); they're logically weak and phonically clumsy for most jobs we might want them to do.

The sentence describing the alien's feelings, "A rising panic shot through its neurons," and the sentence describing Bill's feelings, "Bill jumped to his feet as a frustrating mixture of shock, irritation and concern pulsed through his brain," both have the same thing wrong: by the time we've been told about the neurological workings, we've lost all sense of panic or pulse.

Though the sentences "Bill's first inclination was to run. Instead, he helped his fiancée to her feet, his eyes nervously jerking left and right. He wasn't sure what to expect" *tell* us Bill is nervous, they loll over one latinate word after another ("inclination," "fiancée," "nervously," "expect"; latinate words can often dramatize hidden embarrassment—they don't dramatize overt nervousness). Read these sentences in an emotionally neutral tone to a French- or German-speaking person. Then ask (in French or German) whether they are more likely about a man and a woman in a house gone mad, or about someone applying suntan lotion in the last few beach days of August. Intuitively, from the pacing and sound, we know which choice the non-English speaker will make. If you want to complete the experiment, ask the same question of *these* sentences read in the same neutral tone: "The tube cap . . . where . . . ? There . . . ! The lotion dripped, dripped, dripped down her flank. Gritty sand ground under the blanket. She rubbed. Beautiful." For ordinary narrative purposes, the pace and sound of both sentence sets are mutually inappropriate.

There are many ways to talk about the problem we've been discussing. One is "clichéd writing." Another is "received language." Another is "wooden prose." All these terms can be applied to this story, more or less accurately, from beginning to end, sentence by sentence, phrase by phrase. I've been trying to talk about it, however, in a way that at least suggests a solution. At some time between first and final draft, you must ask yourself of each sentence, "What is it saying?" and "What is it doing?" Next, ask if there is any way to make it say it more intensely, or do it with more bravura. Even better, is there any way to make the sentence *be* an example of what it's about? Failing that, is there a way to get the sentence to say, do, or be something that supports the basic statement in an interesting way? Ask yourself if any part of the sentence gets in the way of (prepositional phrases, frequently toward the sentence's end, are often the worst offenders—also, parenthetical phrases or dangling ideas) the sentence's doing its job as economically as possible. Can that part be reduced or eliminated?

This kind of thinking won't make a style-deaf writer into a Nabokov overnight. But it will put you on the thruway running from leaden language to your own stylistic domain at whatever entrance you're ready to get on. It will take you along that way as fast as you, personally, can go.

Though it's a specialized case of what we've been talking about till now, I'll say a few words about the story's dialogue.

Once the supernatural question enters, the conversations, which till then have been almost adequate, veer completely into the wooden.

Other than some snootier undergraduates at a beer-soaked session of "I can out-arch you," I've never heard *any*one say, "I think she's to be believed." And it's certainly not the right diction for a frightened parent in an all-but-haunted house. "Her trembling voice!" is a ludicrous (and overliterary) exclamation. Both of these make the confused antecedent of "she" (the medium? Rosie?) and the redundant "powers" in the fourth sentence register as bathetic clumsiness rather than as a possible realistic touch:

> "I still remember the astonished look on that medium's face when she saw Rosie. Her trembling voice! She warned me, then and there, Rosie could have special powers. She's reputed to have some incredible powers, Bill. I've checked her out since then and damned if *I* could find any trickery. I think she's to be believed."

Finally the dialogue just careens into the preposterous:

Outside the crazed cabin with a sobbing, sleepy child in her arms (and no other adults around), "Valerie wondered aloud, 'If the uproar continues in Rosie's absence, then how could she be . . . ?'"

Sure, with the slightest turn of plotline, any writer faced with explanations to be gotten across in dialogue may find themselves* in the midst of something like:

---

* The official term for the lack of agreement between the singular "writer" and the plural "themselves" is "the sexually aspecific demotic exemplary"—if anyone ever asks.

"You see, George, the left-handed knob on the gazimbo had to control the krager-laser because every time I turned the right-handed one, nothing came out but blue zibner-fants. It's the only explanation!"

First off, it's never the *only* explanation: suggesting that it is merely nudges the reader to consider others. And whether it's a *necessary* explanation for the story or not, it's awful writing.

It's awful in Heinlein.

It's awful in Le Guin.

It's awful in me.

It's awful in Q— E—.

The only thing a writer can do about such passages is to keep one part of the mind off to the side, ready to point them out, sneer at them, and jump up and down jeering should one of them slip in under the typewriter ribbon—while, of course, the rest of the mind is reveling in the joy of creation.

But when this special part (the critic on the shoulder) starts to jeer, you listen, you cross out, and you write over. And over. And over *again,* if necessary.

That special part has to be kept fairly small—otherwise you'll never write anything at all.

It also must be kept sharp—otherwise you'll never write anything worth reading.

A passing note: Valerie has done research in, and written articles on, the supernatural. But though the tables are overturning and the knick-knacks are flying off the mantel, she never thinks of the possibility of a poltergeist. This certainly doesn't help the believability of an already logy discussion.

Some words about the story in general:

An SF story creates an alternate world and/or an alternate consciousness functioning in that world. If the world is different enough from ours, then the most familiar of consciousnesses will eventually perceive and behave differently. If the consciousness starts off differently enough, the most familiar of worlds will look different. The latter is what this story does—at least in the beginning: the alien roog perceives the most familiar of beach scenes in an unfamiliar way. That's basic material for good science fiction. And though the writing itself is devoid of any life or writerly imagination, this initial right choice of material propelled me as a reader through more than the first dozen pages of the manuscript. (It's akin to developing a character voice.)

Often, however, when I am reading a story with an eye out for analysis, whether the story is published or in manuscript, I'll put a mark in the margin at the place where, were I not reading with a critical eye, I'd put the story down.

I finish reading it anyway.

Then I go back to my mark and try to figure out what, if anything, went wrong at that point. My marginal exit mark for this story comes on page 14 of the typescript, right after the sentence, "I've done several articles about the supernatural."

Clichés and stilted dialogue aside, up till then the story seems to be about what it's about: a family coping with a series of catastrophic occurrences at their beach house. After that, it seems to be about something else: the same family determining the supernatural element involved. (As a rule of thumb, the supernatural fits awkwardly into science fiction and should be avoided.) The fundamental tension in the story is between the alien's view of our world and our view of it. Eventually what the alien does knocks our (or our human characters') view for a loop. Dragging in an offstage medium to validate some supernatural possibility is, first, a red herring; second, it just lets all the energy run out of the story, at least for me.

What I'd probably do if the story were mine is not have Bill so busy smooching at the beginning. Rather, I'd have him *see* Rosie going after the ball—which is acting so strangely on the beach—and I'd let this put the first nagging possibility in his mind that Rosie is . . . well, weird. As the story progressed, I'd have Bill more and more caught up in the notion of supernatural possibilities until he finally bolts. I'd have Valerie, on the other hand (possibly because she *has* done supernatural research and knows most of it's hogwash), cling to sanity through it all while trying to save her child. This would mean any references to an offstage encounter between Rosie and some medium would come off with a very different flavor, or would just not occur at all.

Finally, to satisfy my own sense of closure, I'd have to insert *some* encounter, no matter how baffling, incomprehensible, and opaque, between Rosie, Valerie, and the roog. Just before they get into the car to drive off, Valerie might see on the cabin window what she first takes to be one of those flat, round, plastic defraction lenses. It wasn't there before . . . and somehow she's drawn to it. But when she looks through, instead of the wreckage inside the cabin, distorted through the striations, she sees stars, novas, luminous nebulae, the hydrogenous sweep of the galactic arm . . .

> She tightened her arms around Rosie's back.
> "Oh, mommy . . . " said Rosie. "Oh, mommy, *look!*"
> Beside the lens, something flickered in the sagging drape. Then one, then five, then fifty bright fingers tugged at the curtain, clawed over the rug, grasped the torn webbing on the bottom of the overturned sofa.
> "*Mom*-my . . . !"
> But Valerie was already scrambling through the japonica, over the loose sand toward the car. Smoke rolled from the open cabin door . . .

At any rate, *some*thing like that. (Though the supernatural fits awkwardly in SF, a little cosmic mysticism can go quite a ways.) And maybe the roog feels that something has been communicated, too . . . ?

For me, somehow this would make the final split with Bill more satisfactory, though I don't really dislike it the way it is.

For my final point, I'll comment about a factor that will be invisible to anyone who doesn't have the manuscript to hand; so let me describe it.

In the upper right-hand corner of the first page, the writer has typed:

> First North American Rights
> Approximately 5750 words

Aside from the intriguing coincidence that about twelve years back I wrote an essay with nearly the same title as Q— E—'s word count,* there is something here that will let any editor or first reader at *Analog, Fantasy and Science Fiction,* or *Galaxy* know we've got ourselves a rank beginner—or a suicidally careless typist.

From *Playboy* to *The New Yorker,* U.S. magazines that buy any sort of fiction at all purchase first North American *serial* rights. ("Serial" is an old term for periodical.) *F&SF* usually includes a proviso that amounts to saying if they should want to repurchase your story for their annual best-of-the-year anthology, you won't give them an unduly hard time. But because this *is* the tradition, there's no need to mention any rights at all on your MS. I don't know any professional writer who does. To be on the safe side, certainly you should glance at the permission form that accompanies your payment or acceptance and make sure first North American serial rights are specified. But if you *are* going to put the rights for sale on the MS, at least put down the proper ones! There are many different first North American rights. Besides first North American serial rights, there are first North American anthology rights (exclusive and nonexclusive); there are first North American television rights; there are first North American film rights; there are first North American graphic version rights (comic books to you and me); and there are probably half a dozen more that have simply slipped my mind. If, however, you're fool enough to offer *all* first North American rights for sale and somebody decides to buy them (at 3 cents to 5 cents a word), then these rights *no longer belong to you.*

This means that you are entitled to *no money* that comes from the subsequent sale of any of these rights.

Who is?

Whoever bought the story.

What that "First North American Rights" tells me—and any magazine editor who notices it—is that at one time or another Q— E— probably heard something about first North American serial rights, but didn't understand it, or misremembered

* "About 5,750 Words," by Samuel R. Delany, in *The Jewel-Hinged Jaw,* Berkley Books, 1977.

the phrase. Most SF editors would just smile and, if they wanted the story, send him the right contract anyway. But this field has had its schemers. All an editor would have to do is return a memo to Q— E— saying, "Upon receipt of X dollars, the author agrees to sell all first North American rights to the story titled 'The Beach Fire' . . . " and that would be the end of all possible future profit from the story to Q— E—. If somebody wanted to reprint it in another magazine, or use it in an anthology, or develop a prime time sitcom from it, or base a $12 million movie on it, not a penny would Q— E— get. Now $10,000, $50,000, or a $150,000 movie or TV sales are not that common for short stories. But they have happened and will happen again—sometimes to the oddest tales.

I said it before: Q— E— is probably a nice guy. I wouldn't want to see him do himself out of all possibility of profiting from such a sale should one come along. With all I've said about it, the story isn't *that* bad. But this is precisely what Q— E— has laid the groundwork for on the upper right-hand corner of his first page.

Okay. I've punched and kicked and hit. The places where Q— E—'s calluses are, or will shortly be, have been given a good working over.

I will say this by way of the smallest consolation: "The Beach Fire" is good enough so that if I came across another story over the same by-line, I'd probably read it. Fact is, my marginal exit mark on most stories, published or not, comes in the first three pages. Page 14 then . . . ?

—New York City
1980

Some Notes for the Intermediate and Advanced Creative Writing Student

Write as simply as you can for the smartest person
you can imagine.
—Blanche McCrary Boyd, OutWrite, Boston, 1998

You write simply, we might add, so that your assumed intelligent reader can more quickly catch you out when you write down idiocies—and, if that reader is generous enough, so that he or she can bracket those idiocies and go quickly to what's interesting among the suggestions in your work. From time to time (or again and again) the writer must write directly against that simplicity to enhance and control just the suggestiveness in which, for such a reader, much of the work's worth will reside. The tension between clarity and connotation is one reason many writers have two voices. With his shaved head, ivory suit, and orange sunglasses—the first I'd seen—Dudley Fitts explained this to us in a poetry lecture at the Breadloaf Writers' Conference. He sat in a wood-frame wheelchair, in front of the stage to the right. (It was the summer of 1960; the stage of the Middlebury College meeting house was not wheelchair-accessible back then.) In a wide-ranging lecture that analyzed a poem by the contemporary poet Claire McAllister and that explored the significance of the family members of Aeneas (Anchises, his father; Creusa, his wife; Ascanius, his son . . .), Fitts used Henry Reed's moving poem on Adamic pretensions in the light of World War II, "The Naming of Parts," as a particularly clear example of the double-voiced poem, more than half a dozen years before anyone this side of the Atlantic had even considered the Lacanian idea of a split subject.

I have written the following notes as simply as I can. What use they may have, if any, will be entirely in what they can suggest—as much as if I had written them with the recomplications of some of my examples.

What is literary talent? To what extent should it be treated as a skill?

A skill may or may not be something to be mastered. Certainly the physical ones require strength, muscles, and, in general, those faculties that must be built up by repetition.

My feeling is that literary talent is definitely *not* something that involves mastery in any way, shape, or form. Thus the treatment appropriate to the mastery of a skill is wholly inappropriate to the training of literary talent. Both encouragement and the proffering of *judgmental* criticism in the early stages are equally out of place—though the student may desperately want one, the other, or both.

As far as I can see, talent has two sides. The first side is the absorption of a series of complex models—models for the sentence, models for narrative scenes, and models for various larger literary structures. This is entirely a matter of reading and criticism. (And, yes, that means criticism by the writer of his or her own text as well as criticism by others.) Nothing else affects it.

To know such models and what novels, stories, or sentences employ them certainly doesn't hurt. Generally speaking, however, the sign that the writer has internalized a model deeply enough to use it in writing is when he or she has encountered it enough times so that she or he no longer remembers it in terms of a specific example or a particular text, but experiences it, rather, as a force in the body, a pull on the back of the tongue, an urge in the fingers to shape language in one particular way and avoid another. To effect this one must encounter that model or structure again and again in other texts and experience it . . . well, *through* the body. Clumsy, inadequate, and not quite accurate, that's the only way I can say it.

These models must be experienced through what the early German romantics called *Begeisterung*—the sine qua non for the artist, more important than intelligence, passion, or even imagination, and the foundation for them all. Literally "inspiritedness" and often translated as "inspiration," it carries just as strongly the sense of "spirited," so that it is more accurately designated by the English word "enthusiasm." *Begeisterung*—inspiration/enthusiasm—can alone seat these models in the mind at the place where they can, with like energy, forget their sources, grasp new language, and reemerge with it.

The training of literary talent requires repetition of the experience of reading, then; but it does *not* require repetition of the experience of writing (other than that required to achieve general literacy) in the same way that piano playing or drawing does. Far too many writers have written fine first novels without ever having written anything that would have fixed their place in literary history before—Jane Austen, Emily and Anne Brontë, J. D. Salinger; the list goes on. A number of writers who did write one, two, or a handful of comparatively mediocre works before they started producing much better ones—Flaubert, Woolf, Lawrence, Balzac, Cather, Faulkner—frequently tell of a sea change in their conception of what the novel actually *was* or *could be* that is responsible for the improvement. They realized there were more complex models to submit to. But once they had them, submit to them they did. In none of these cases was it just a matter of the simple improvement or strengthening of a craft or skill.

Which brings us to the second side of talent. The second side is the ability to submit *to* those models. Many people find such submission frightening. At the order, even from inside them, "Do this—and let the model control the way you do it," they become terrified—that they'll fail, fall on their face, or look stupid.

If the body could do it entirely on its own, we'd all be very lucky. Though sometimes, for a passage or—more rarely—even for a story or an entire book, your body seems to take over and all but does the writing for you (it's called inspiration; it's called self-expression—but what it *is* is submission), fundamentally writing is done with the mind. To say it seems unnecessary—but the mind plays an active, complicated, and intricate part in the process, a part *far* more complex than simply thinking up what to write about. *Most* of what the mind does is think about and give instructions for controlling the conditions under which we *do* our writing. This is where, frightened or made anxious by aspects of the writing process, your mind will repeatedly sabotage your writing project. If it does go with the project, probably it's because your mind becomes, as it were, addicted to the pleasure of writing—but that addiction, devoutly to be wished, only happens if consciously and carefully you put writing first before all other responsibilities; which is to say, while the pleasure is there (it's unique, very real; all writers experience it), the truth is, it isn't *that* great. You need lots of it to effect the "addiction" that will keep you at it. Though the practice of writing *has* the structure of an addiction, it's a mild one—one remarkably easy to wean yourself away from, even accidentally or through inattention. Thus, count on internalization of models rather than addiction to the process; addiction without the proper internalized models explains why bad writers often write so much so compulsively.

Acknowledging that there *are* models to submit to is much the same as realizing there are standards to be judged by. That you yourself must exercise the first and possibly harshest rounds of judgment on your work is not a situation most of us would characterize as fun. Rather, it's a situation most people find endlessly anxiety-producing and unpleasant. But the writer must revel in it and grow. This takes a particular personality type most people just don't have. If you don't get some major satisfaction from such autolacerations, however, you might as well try something else which does not demand such constant self-critique. This is (only) one reason why, ten years after every creative writing class, most (often, all) of the participants have given up writing for a less taxing profession.

When people have not internalized the models at the bodily level, often they develop a stubborn streak, usually based on insecurity and fear: while they have a recognition awareness of the models, they're afraid they'll lose something of themselves if they give in to them. This is especially true when someone else with a sense of what might be done to help a piece of fiction makes a suggestion to them for improving it: the writer knows his critic is right—but would rather do anything in the world than follow the suggestion. Well, for them, stubbornness and fear must be taken as one with *lack* of talent. A teacher can do only so much to allay such insecurities—although we do what we can. When the writer does have a deep sense of the model that's controlling her or his work, however, and someone makes a criticism that points up where the model has, for a moment, not been followed, often the writer can hardly wait to make the suggested change. (I've seen writers sit down on the classroom floor to correct a manuscript before leaving the workshop.) Having made these points, however, I must also stress, most criticism is not so dead-on. The writer should respond enthusiastically to that which is useful. Still, most (and often all) of the criticism the writer gets has to be ignored. Though models are rarely referred to directly by either writers or their critics, it is the deep sense of the model that tells the writer what criticism is useful and what is not. For many years, I have told creative writing classes that the writer must be able to *hear* the criticism if it is to be useful. But, clearly, *when* the writer "hears" it, something so much more active than *just* hearing is going on, it would be unfair not to point it out. Similarly, when the writer does not hear it, and there is no deeply internalized model to guide him or her, the confusion, resistance, and hostility are often great enough to note.

To write a novel or a story means that one takes one of these internalized models and adjusts it, often with a good deal of thought, to the material at hand. That, yes, means changing the model somewhat. This is what produces new work. Sometimes it even produces new kinds of work. But it is not an accident that so many of the writers we associate with the production of whole new kinds of writing—Gertrude Stein, Virginia Woolf, T. S. Eliot, Ezra Pound, James Joyce—were articulately aware of the tradition they were developing from/breaking with. (We shall come back to this notion.) The sad truth is, there's *very* little that's creative in creativity. The vast majority is submission—submission to the laws of grammar, to the possibilities of rhetoric, to the grammar of narrative, to narrative's various and possible structurings. In a society that privileges individuality, self-reliance, and mastery, submission is a frightening thing.

When looked at in terms of the submission to internally absorbed models, only a few things can go wrong with writing.

Maybe you've never absorbed the particular model you need. Sadly, that too is tantamount to having no talent—or not having enough talent or the right sort of talent. If that's the case, you have to give it up. Sometimes one has absorbed a model, but it needs time to come forward and take over the material. Time, then, *can* help. But many people read widely and voraciously without *ever* absorbing the models from the fiction they read at a depth that will allow them to *write* any fiction of interest on their own. They might store those models in recognition memory, so that they recognize the patterns that fiction makes and enjoy them immensely as readers. But that doesn't mean they have necessarily internalized them to the extent needed to become creators. We recognize our friends' faces. Few of us, however, can produce a likeness on paper—though we recognize it when someone else does. In this one sense, then, the creative writer is closest to the concert performer playing a composer's score and making it sound out at its most beautiful.

For the writer, the model comes forward in the mind as a kind of vaguely (or, sometimes, very strongly) perceived "temporal shape" that takes the "material"—whatever it is the writer is writing about—and organizes it, organizes it rigorously. These models function on several "levels" at once. They are there to organize the words (the sounds and multiple meanings associated with the words) into sentences. They are there to organize the different kinds of sentences into scenes. They are there to organize the different kinds of scenes into subsections (chapters or parts). They are there to organize the chapters or parts into a novel. I say, "They are there . . . " But if they are *not* there, then the novel stalls at a certain point; and unless the writer can summon forth the proper model, the work will get clunky and awkward from that point on—if it progresses at all. Sometimes the model is clearly expressible: "The book will begin with three chapters devoted to the main characters, in the central one of which they encounter or observe some minor characters; then a fourth chapter will be devoted to those minor characters alone; the next three chapters are devoted to the main characters (with, again at the middle of those three chapters, the main characters encountering the minor characters); then, yet again, another chapter gets devoted to the minor characters alone. Then there will be still three more chapters devoted to the main characters (with, again, the middle chapter of those three linking major and minor characters), followed by a minor-character chapter once again; the book will close with three chapters, in the first of which the actions of the main characters will resolve; again the centerpiece of these three chapters will resolve the minor characters' story in terms of an encounter with the major characters, and, in the final chapter, the emotional fallout of the whole story is resolved among the main characters. End of novel. That's fifteen chapters all together, with three devoted directly to the minor characters and four devoted to tying them in with the main characters, who in turn command eight chapters by themselves."

Let's look at a chart of this narrative structure where _____ represents a chapter about the major characters alone, / / / / / / / represents a chapter about the minor characters by themselves and - - - - - - represents a chapter about the major and minor characters interacting:

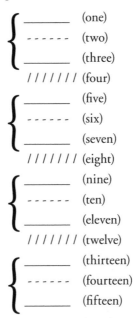

When we chart it out, we can see that the narrative progresses in four three-chapter units devoted to the major characters, punctuated with three chapters devoted to the minor characters alone. The chapters that deal with the minor and major characters together nevertheless produce an overall structure in which the minor characters are on stage every other chapter, starting with chapter 2 and ending with chapter 14. The chapters themselves, of course, are going to have to be structured, since most novel chapters usually contain more than one scene. The progression of scenes within chapters will also have to be taken into consideration and structured. Possibly every chapter contains three scenes. Or five. Or every other chapter contains three and the alternate chapters contain only two, in which case we have to figure out, in the - - - - - chapters, which scenes get devoted to the minor characters and/or to the major characters, and so on. At this point, someone may say, "Look, just tell your story." But the sense that you *are* telling a story and not just presenting a random progression of incidents is controlled by (among other things) such patterns.

Rarely, however, does narrative structure (another name for those models we began by discussing) manifest itself even this clearly; and this is already fairly complex.

The all-important social range over which the novel takes place has to be structured as carefully as any other element. (Is the book about a young man's or woman's rise [or fall] in society? Do the minor characters move in the same direction, up [or down] the social scale, as the main characters? Or do they move in the opposite direction?) At the same time, like a through-composed opera, leitmotivs consisting of repeated phrases, parallel incidents, running metaphors, and the like must be carefully placed throughout this dual story, so that they can recall and mirror one another.

Only a certain amount of this structuring can be externally imposed on the fictive material. The material must call up an appropriate structure, rather, that is already inscribed, as it were, wherever the writer keeps his or her inner feel for fiction. Yes, there can be a certain amount of conscious adjustment. But if the writing strays too far from the model, there may just be no other one there to catch the material up and control it—and the result will be either stasis (that awful thing, writer's block) or chaos.

Notice that not once, in all this, have we spoken of *what* a given novel is about. This is not because the structure *must* precede the novel's subject matter. But the structure certainly *can* precede much of the plot—and also control it.

Our democratic society believes strongly in educational opportunities made available over the range of our country. All people should have the opportunity and education needed to enjoy the variety of the arts. Another idea, however, has grown up along with this: as many people as possible should be given the chance to *make* art themselves. In terms of writing, we've seen the last twenty-five years' explosion of writers' workshops and MFA programs. But there's a possible built-in failure in this program: while many—or even most—people can internalize a range of literary models strongly enough to recognize and enjoy them when they see them in (some) new works that they read, *very few people* internalize them to the extent that they can apply them to new material and use them to create.

Lots of people want to.

But not many people can.

Most of you who read these notes—the vast majority—will discover, sometime fairly soon (that is, in the next three, four, or six years), that you are not really writers. The very few who do not discover this then, will—sometime around the age of fifty-five, sixty, seventy, or seventy-five—discover that, with the general deterioration of the mind that accompanies the second half of your lifetime, you are no *longer* a writer. (So no one escapes.) It is not a pleasant discovery no matter when, in life, it comes. The only consolation anyone can give is this: there is nothing wrong with not being a writer—that is, not being one who has, however briefly, been able to submit. It doesn't help that, among people who control the machinery of narrative dissemination, most editors, all publishers, and especially TV and film producers, no one wants to speak of the reality of artistic submission. All "professional" rhetoric about writing is organized, rather, around an illusory phantom called artistic mastery, which involves meeting deadlines, being totally "in control" of your "craft," and making anything happen in a story you want (or anything that anyone who can pay you tells you that he or she wants), however externally imposed or at odds with any particular model that happening or incident is.* These same people are then willing to lie through their teeth (and often pay exorbitant amounts of money for it), declaring that the product is great—when the actual result, visible to everyone in the audience, is that *nothing* either believable or interesting is happening at all in the butchered narrative.

By and large, because she or he must work constantly against this rhetoric of mastery, the writer must be someone who can be more or less satisfied with the pursuit of personal excellence at the expense of personal happiness when the two, as they will again and again, conflict. There are, of course, a few exceptions to this rule of thumb: most of those are *truly* tragic.

If you're going to write well, you will do a lot better if your prose models are F. Scott Fitzgerald, Vladimir Nabokov, late Dickens, Raymond Chandler, Virginia Woolf, Nathanael West, Joanna Russ, Theodore Sturgeon, William Gass, Ethan Canin, and Guy Davenport (with a few reminders from E. B. White thrown in)—certainly you'll do better than if your models are James T. Farrell, Theodore Dreiser, Pearl Buck, John Dos Passos, Sidney Sheldon, or John Grisham; or even Henry James or William Faulkner. (From the last two you might absorb other, higher-level literary models.)

If your models have come only from the ironic experimenters and minimalists in short fiction of the last thirty years, who run from Donald Barthelme and Raymond Carver up through Ann Beattie and Lorrie Moore, whose work exists only as delightful and graceful—and sometimes poignant—commentary directed in delicate pinpricks against the foibles of the Great Tradition, when you try to write a serious novel about topics of social import, you will come out with a disaster that doesn't even make it to the level of good TV sitcoms or comedy sketches (the best of which are also instructive).

* Those who wish to explore this further should see S. R. Delany, "The Politics of the Paraliterary," in *Shorter Views* (Middletown, Conn.: Wesleyan University Press, 1999).

Things to remember about some common criticisms:

1. If your character is thin, the character is thin *now*. What the character does in the next chapter or scene is not going to help that current thinness.

2. If your plot is incoherent, what happens in the next chapter or scene is not going to make it suddenly cohere. Incoherence is neither mystery nor suspense. (These are *controlled* responses that the writer evokes.) Incoherence is produced by the writer's *losing* control of the material.

3. A bad or incoherent short story will not make a good opening novel chapter. Rewrite that short story and try to make it better. Don't just keep maundering on, hoping that, somehow, later material will repair the damages readers have noted earlier. It doesn't work that way.

4. Stories (and plots) emerge from novels. But novels are not primarily stories. They are ragbags of various discourses (descriptive, dramatic, narrative, reflective, analytic) structured in some inventive and interesting way against a matrix of rhetorical expectations.

5. It is almost impossible to write a novel any better than the best novel you've read in the three to six months before you began your own. Thus, you *must* read excellent novels regularly.

6. Excellent novels set the standards for our own. But bad novels and bad prose are what teach us to write—by setting strong negative examples. You must read both, then—and read them analytically and discriminatingly.

7. Much of good writing is the avoidance of bad writing. (Most bad writing by people who write easily comes from submission to demonstrably poor models.) Get together a list of prose-writing errors that *you* refuse to make any more. Choose them, perhaps, from the most common errors people make in your writing workshop. Before you hand anything in or send it out, read your work over for your own personal list of errors. When you inadvertently fall into them (and you will), correct them. (This is the best example I have, by the way, of what I mean by "submission to an aesthetic model." It also explains why such submission is work.)

8. The novelist who wants to do anything more than paint a portrait of a contemporary character or detail a more or less limited situation—who wants to show the effect of a situation over a range of social conditions—but has only read the short fictions of the last fifty years with any care starts with four strikes against him or her.

9. The San Francisco renaissance in poetry of the middle fifties and sixties was predicated on the aesthetic principle "Good art makes great art look better. Thus, it benefits the great to encourage the good."

10. You need to read Balzac, Stendhal, Flaubert, and Zola; you need to read Austen, Thackeray, the Brontës, Dickens, George Eliot, and Hardy; you need to read Hawthorne, Melville, James, Woolf, Joyce, and Faulkner; you need to read Tolstoy, Dostoyevsky, Turgenev, Goncharov, Gogol, Bely, and Khlebnikov; you need to read Stephen Crane, Mark Twain, Edward Dahlberg, John Steinbeck, Jean Rhys, Glenway Wescott, John O'Hara, James Gould Cozzens, Angus Wilson, Patrick White, Alexander Trocchi, Iris Murdoch, Graham Greene, Evelyn Waugh, Anthony Powell, and Michael Cunningham; you need to read Nella Larsen, Knut Hamsun, William Demby, Saul Bellow, Lawrence Durrell, John Updike, John Barth, Philip Roth, Coleman Dowell, William Gaddis, William Gass, Marguerite Young, Thomas Pynchon, Paul West, Berthe Harris, Melvin Dixon, Daryl Pinckney, Daryl Ponicsan, and John Keene, Jr.; you need to read Thomas M. Disch, Michael Moorcock, Carole Maso, Edmund White, Jayne Anne Phillips, Robert Glück, and Julian Barnes—you need to read them and many more; you need to read them not so that you will know what they have written about, but so that you can begin to absorb some of the more ambitious models for what the novel can be.

The first move the more experienced creative writer can make toward absorbing these models is to realize that "plot" is an illusion. It's an illusion the writer ought to disabuse her- or himself of pretty quickly, too, at least if she or he ever wants to write anything of substance, ambition, or literary richness. (There *is no plot.*) That is to say, plot is an *effect* that other written elements produce in concert. Outside those elements, plot has no autonomous existence.

What there is, is narrative structure.

Here is a formal statement of the reason plot doesn't exist:

No narrative unit *necessarily* corresponds to any textual unit. Plots are always and only composed of synoptic units.*

I'll try to demonstrate with examples.

Again: What we call "plot" is an effect produced by (among other things) structure. But many, many *different* structures can produce the *same* "plot."

(Structure *does* have textual existence. You can point it out on the page: "See, this comes first. This follows it. This takes five sentences to say. This takes two. This sentence concerns the character's action. This subordinate clause gives the character's thoughts . . . " These are all comments on narrative structure. Structure exists because a given narrative text exists in its actual and specific textual form.)

All of the following, A through G, have the identical plot. All of them have radically different structures:

(A) Joe woke. He tossed the covers back. A moment later he was standing by the bed on the rug.

The plot so far might be synopsized here: "Joe gets out of bed." A different type of story—with a different intent, a different focus, and a different development—might take any of the three microincidents in the above mininarrative, however, and atomize one or another of them. One of the most important things

---

* A recent riddle demonstrates what analysis can also reveal—why plot neither has definitive existence nor indicates any necessary information about its text:

From the following account of the plot, identify this classic American Depression film:

"An unwilling immigrant to a New Land of Opportunity, a dissatisfied young foreign woman kills an older woman whose face she never sees. After she recruits three equally dissatisfied strangers, together they go on to kill again . . . "

Answer: *The Wizard of Oz*

that such atomizing does is accent the crispness and brevity of the presentation of the *other* textual units:

(B) Waking assailed Joe and retreated, a wave foaming up and sliding from the sands of day. At its height, there was a sense or a memory of dark green sheets beneath his belly, his knees, the pillow bunched under his shoulder, the quilt across his ear. Rising and retreating at an entirely different oscillation was sexual desire, now an unfocused and tugging emptiness, now a warm fullness in the groin, a sensitivity within his slightly parted lips under the susurrus of breath. Somehow the cycles met. He opened his eyes—aware of the room's silence. (But what had he been aware of before . . . ?) He could feel the dawn moisture drying along his lower lids. Pulling one hand from beneath the covers into the chill, he twisted the heel of his thumb against one eye socket.

Then he tossed the covers back. A moment later he was standing by the bed on the rug.

(C) Joe woke.

Pulling one hand from beneath the covers into the chill, he twisted the heel of his thumb against one eye socket. Then he snagged his fingers around the coverlet's edge. He raised it—and the chill slid down his arm, along his side some eighteen inches. Dragging in a breath, he raised the covers further. Somewhere below, something put two cold palms over his kneecaps. He heard breath halt a moment in his throat. The bedding beneath his shins was suddenly *so* warm. He gave the quilt's rim a toss and began to kick free even before it fell, off below the bottom of the T-shirt he slept in these November nights. One foot made it from the mattress edge, then the other—as the first slid from under the blanket to hang an instant, an isolate entity out in the cold room. He pushed into the pillow with his fist, so that his shoulders rose; his feet lowered.

A moment later he was standing by the bed on the rug.

(D) Joe woke. He tossed the covers back.

He pushed into the pillow with his fist, so that his shoulders rose; his feet lowered.

The shag rug's nap tickled his soles, till the weight of his legs crushed it away beneath. Every damned bone in his feet had to move this way or that a couple of millimeters, it seemed, to get into the right position—and in the left foot, that hurt! He pushed himself forward, the hem of his limp T-shirt swinging over his upper thighs. As his body lifted, a cold blade of morning slid beneath his buttocks and down toward the back of his knees. (Somewhere the springs clashed, muffled below the mattress.) It felt as if someone were shoving at his right kidney with the flat of a hand. He put his own hand there to rub the feel away. He blinked, standing in the silent room, flexing chill toes on the rug, aware (or was it more a memory of something he'd been half conscious of before waking?) that he had to go to the bathroom.

A, B, C, and D generate identical plots, but in each case the elements that do the generating are structured differently. (Their content is, of course, different too. But right now that is not our concern.) There are still other effects to be achieved, however, by the use of these *same* structural variants. For example:

(E) Waking assailed Joe and retreated, a wave foaming up and sliding from the sands of day. At its height, there was a sense or a memory of dark green sheets beneath his belly, his knees, the pillow bunched under his shoulder, the quilt across his ear. Rising and retreating at an entirely different oscillation was sexual desire, now an unfocused and tugging emptiness, now a warm fullness in the groin, a sensitivity within his slightly parted lips under the susurrus of breath. Somehow the cycles met. He opened his eyes—aware of the room's silence. (But what had he been aware of before . . . ?) He could feel the dawn moisture drying along his lower lids. Pulling one hand from beneath the covers into the chill, he twisted the heel of his thumb against one eye socket.

Then he tossed the covers back.

The shag rug's nap tickled his soles, till the weight of his legs crushed it away beneath. Every damned bone in his feet had to move this way or that a couple of millimeters, it seemed, to get into the right position—and in the left foot, that hurt! He pushed himself forward, the hem of his limp T-shirt swinging forward over his upper thighs. As his body lifted, a cold blade of morning slid beneath his buttocks and down toward the backs of his knees (somewhere the springs clashed, muffled below the mattress). It felt as if someone were shoving at his right kidney with the flat of a hand. He put his own hand there to rub the feel away. He blinked in the silent room, flexing chill toes on the rug, aware (or was it more a memory of something he'd been half conscious of before waking?) that he had to go to the bathroom.

And finally:

(F) Waking assailed Joe and retreated, a wave foaming up and sliding from the sands of day. At its height, there was a sense or a memory of dark green sheets beneath his belly, his knees, the pillow bunched under his shoulder, the quilt across his ear. Rising and retreating at an entirely different oscillation was sexual desire, now an unfocused and tugging emptiness, now a warm fullness in the groin, a sensitivity within his slightly parted lips under the susurrus of breath. Somehow the cycles met. He opened his eyes—aware of the room's silence. (But what had he been aware of before . . . ?) He could feel the dawn moisture drying along his lower lids. Pulling one hand from beneath the covers into the chill, he twisted the heel of his thumb against one eye socket.

Then he snagged his fingers around the coverlet's edge. He raised it—and the chill slid down his arm, along his side some eighteen inches. Dragging in a breath, he raised the covers further. Somewhere below, something put two cold palms over his kneecaps. He heard breath halt a moment in his throat. The bedding beneath his shins was suddenly *so* warm. He gave the quilt's rim a toss and began to kick free even before it fell, somewhere below the bottom of the T-shirt he slept in these November nights. One foot made it off the mattress edge, then the other—as the first slid from under the blanket to hang an instant, an isolate entity out in the cold room. He pushed into the pillow with his fist, so that his shoulders rose; his feet lowered.

The shag rug's nap trickled his soles, till the weight of his legs crushed it away beneath. Every damned bone in his feet had to move this way or that a couple of millimeters, it seemed, to get into the right position—and in the left foot, that hurt! He pushed himself forward, the hem of his limp T-shirt swinging forward over his upper thighs. As his body lifted, a cold blade of morning slid beneath his buttocks and down toward the backs of his knees. (Somewhere the springs clashed, muffled below the mattress.) It felt as if someone were shoving at his right kidney with the flat of a hand. He put his own hand there to rub the feel away. He blinked, standing in the silent room, flexing his chill toes on the rug, aware (or was it more a memory of something he'd been half conscious of before waking?) that he had to go to the bathroom.

Still an entirely different structure (with an entirely different affect) can be achieved by casting the whole "story" so far into the mode of indirect discourse:

(G) Earlier that morning, Joe had waked, tossed the covers back, and stood up by the bed on the rug. Now he
. . .

None of these versions is *necessarily* any better—or any worse—than the others. While each highlights different and particular details, strives after a different sense of immediacy, presents a different pacing of sensations and incidents, with different juxtapositions (all structural qualities), none is more narratively accurate than any of the others. The only thing that will decide which approach you use in a particular tale is what else is going on—structurally, not plotwise (for, again, all seven *plots* are identical)—in the remainder of the narrative.

When we write a story, we often (though not always) start with a more or less vague sense of "what happens" in it. Writing the tale out, however, is a matter of modulating that "what happens" into a specific structure. (And *not* into various other structures!) The structure, finally, *is* the story—even if a reader, asked to synopsize it, can come up with more or less the same "what happens" that you went into it with when you began writing. The overall aesthetic pleasure the reader takes from the story is going to depend largely on how pleasing the reader finds the story's overall structure.

A story or a novel has an overall structure as well as smaller structural patterns. The repetition—or variation—of small structural elements is what produces the overall structure. In general, structure will always produce *some* sort of plot—coherent or incoherent, interesting or dull. Plot is no guarantee, however, of *any* sort of structure, pleasing or otherwise. Be aware of the "plot," sure, in the back of your mind as you write. But be aware of it as you are aware of an *illusion you are creating.* Don't think of it as a reality out there that will somehow write the story for you. The particular problems you write *through,* as it were, while you are actually first drafting a text in your notebook or typing at your word processor, are the structural elements and their relations.

Also, there are a *lot* more kinds of elements to be shaped into a structure than simply detailed observation versus synoptic account.

Here is another example of narrative structure, in this case juxtaposing a series of sequential present actions with a series of equally sequential memories:

> (H) Under a cold aluminum sky, Joe hurried along the November pavement.
>
> Last night, bundled in blankets on the couch, Margery had coughed and coughed, till finally he had been able to pay no attention at all to the TV sitcom.
>
> At the corner, he looked down from the light as it changed to green, then started across for the far curb.

Where in the world *was* it? (There was the leather bag store. And the bodega just after it. And down there was the blue and white marquee of the Greek coffee shop.) It couldn't be more than three streets from the house. He'd passed it hundreds of times—only now that he was actually looking for it, it seemed to have moved, or secretly slid further off by a couple of city blocks.

Last night, when, finally, he'd phoned Mark—Mark, his cousin, Mark the doctor—he'd felt like a fool. But Mark, who was basically a good guy, had said: "If it's a dry cough and she's not bringing anything up, then it's just a little flu. Get her some Cloraseptic. It comes over the counter—and it's good stuff. It'll cut the soreness." Waving an arm from her plaid cocoon, Margery had insisted, still coughing, that he not go out for it that night but—it was past eleven and the drugstore was closed— wait till morning.

There it was—at the corner where it had always been! Hands deep in his anorak, Joe hurried by the window, filled with pale plastic shampoo bottles, a bronze pedestal of nail polishes and lipsticks, and a mannequin arm lying across crumpled Mylar, its elbow in an Ace bandage.

He pushed through the door; warmth puffed against his face—and a bell rang.

The structure of this narrative is:

Present, past, present, past, present . . . where each of the first four elements is slightly longer than the element before. They converge in the final present element in a particularly satisfying way: one of the pleasures of this particular structure is the mystery, very soon resolved, of what Joe is looking for and why.

There are a number of ways we could restructure this, for different effects—again, depending on the rest of the story development. (And if we do decide to restructure the elements, we will lose the micropleasure of that little mystery, finally resolved.)

We could, for example, put everything in chronological order:

(I) Bundled in blankets on the couch, Margery coughed

and coughed, till finally he could pay no attention at all to the TV sitcom.

When, finally, Joe phoned Mark—Mark, his cousin, Mark the doctor—he felt like a fool. But Mark, who was basically a good guy, said: "If it's a dry cough and she's not bringing anything up, then it's just a little flu. Get her some Cloraseptic. It comes over the counter—and it's good stuff. It'll cut the soreness." Waving an arm from her plaid cocoon, Margery insisted, still coughing, that he not go out for it that night but—it was past eleven and the drugstore was closed—wait till morning.

The next day Joe woke. He tossed back the covers. A moment later he was standing by the bed on the rug.

From the far side of the bed, Margery coughed.

Minutes on, under a cold aluminum sky, Joe hurried along the November pavement.

At the corner, he looked down from the light as it changed to green, then started across for the far curb. Where in the world *was* the drugstore? (There was the leather bag store. And the bodega just after it. And down there was the blue and white marquee of the Greek coffee shop.) It couldn't be more than three streets from the house; he'd passed it hundreds of times—only now that he was looking for it, it seemed to have moved, or secretly slid further off by a couple of city blocks.

There it was—at the corner where it had always been! Hands deep in his anorak, Joe hurried by the window, filled with pale plastic shampoo bottles, a bronze pedestal of nail polish and lipsticks, and a mannequin arm lying across crumpled Mylar, its elbow in an Ace bandage.

He pushed in the door; warmth puffed against his face—and a bell rang.

I've used the initial example, "Joe woke. He tossed the covers back . . . " as a subnarrative within this larger one, to remind us that the material of any subsection can be structured in any number of ways. Note that, structured as it is here, the same textual unit plays a much smaller part in the plot than it would if it introduced the story.

What would happen if we used one of our first six (A to F) structures? Basically, if the remainder of the story is going to focus on the relation of Margery and Joe [and/or Mark], we probably want what we have now or something close to it. That is to say, we want to get Joe back to Margery as quickly as possible, so they can start interacting. If, in the remainder of the story, however, Joe is deflected from returning home from his drugstore mission and the major events happen outside, away from the house, with new characters whom we have not yet met, one of the other more detailed renderings of Joe's waking, throwing the covers back, and standing—depending on the nature of that adventure to come—might work better to focus us on Joe's internal state and prepare us for his responses to these nondomestic happenings; also, the nondomestic story might well be considerably longer than the domestic one, so that it admits of more development all through it. But all of these are *structural* decisions. Plot will depend on which ones the writer makes.

Whether one goes with a story about Margery, Mark, and Joe, or a story about what happens to Joe outside the house while he's going to pick up some cough syrup for Margery, there is another way beginning writers often structure the sort of material in the narrative above. It is one of the *most common* and the *weakest* of narrative structures for the opening of stories or scenes. It should be avoided like the plague:

(J) Under a cold aluminum sky, Joe hurried along the November pavement.

Last night, bundled in blankets on the couch, Margery had coughed and coughed, till finally he had been able to pay no attention at all to the TV sitcom.

When, finally, Joe phoned Mark—Mark, his cousin, Mark the doctor—he'd felt like a fool. But Mark, who was basically a good guy, had said: "If it's a dry cough and she's not bringing anything up, then it's just a little flu. Get her some Cloraseptic. It comes over the counter— and it's good stuff. It'll cut the soreness." Waving an arm from her plaid cocoon, Margery had insisted, still coughing, that he not go out for it that night but—it was past eleven and the drugstore was closed—wait till morning.

The next day Joe woke. He tossed back the covers. A moment later he was standing by the bed on the rug.

From the far side of the bed, Margery coughed.

Minutes on, Joe had on his anorak and was outside.

At the corner, he looked down from the light as it changed to green, then started across for the far curb. Where in the world *was* the drugstore? (There was the leather bag store. And the bodega just after it. And down there was the blue and white marquee of the Greek coffee shop.) It couldn't be more than three streets from the house; he'd passed it hundreds of times—only now he was looking for it, it seemed to have moved, or secretly slid further off by a couple of city blocks.

There it was—at the corner where it had always been! Hands deep in his anorak, Joe hurried by the window, filled with pale plastic shampoo bottles, a bronze pedestal of nail polish and lipsticks, and a mannequin lying across crumpled Mylar, its elbow in an Ace bandage.

He pushed in the door; warmth puffed against his face—and a bell rang.

This structure is *so* common among young writers, I've given it a name: "the false flashback." What's wrong with it?

The opening element ("Under a cold aluminum sky, Joe hurried along the November pavement") is simply wasted, functioning only as a distraction from the far more logical purely chronological version. The transition points—first from present to past, then from past to present—are particularly weak. What's happened, in this third and weakest version, is that likely the writer began to imagine Joe on the street and only filled in the back story in his/her imagination moments later—then wrote it down in the same order he or she thought it up.

(Possibly the writer had some intimation of the possibilities of our first, five-part structure, but lost it while actually writing the opening sentence.)

Well, the order in which you figure out what's going on in your story is *not* privileged.

If you came up with a good twist for the ending of a mystery, and only later figured out how to set it up and make it function, you wouldn't start your story off by telling the end. The same goes for a scene that you suddenly realize needs something before it—even if that scene is only a sentence, or a paragraph, or indeed a page or two, long.

You shouldn't do it there, either.

Generally speaking, it's best to tell your story from *beginning* to *end*—*unless* there's a clear structural reason to tell it otherwise. Make your structural choices because they provide a more economical way to tell the story, and because they add certain pleasures (mystery, humor, suspense—*not* incoherence) to the tale.

In our first version (H), there was a clear and distinct structural pleasure to be gained by telling the story in two small flashbacks interspersed among the three sections of present narrative: the creation of a small mystery (what is Joe looking for?) resolves by the convergence of past element two with present element three. Also it's more economical—that is, it's *shorter* than versions two (I) or three (J). In version one (H) you don't need the transitional wake-up scene, which would be missed in version two (I). (If the bulk of the story is set outside the house, without Margery, and is fundamentally humorous, and itself involves a larger mystery to be eventually solved, version one might well be the *best* opening—because, highly economically, it prepares us for what is to come.) But in neither our second nor our third version can the mystery be maintained. So the *single* flashback of version three is purely superfluous. The initial element ("Under a cold aluminum sky, Joe hurried along the November pavement") is just not long enough or weighty enough to create any continuing sense of fictive life. Nothing is gained in the third, flashback version (J) that isn't there in the second, chronological version (I). The displacement in time is unnecessary and confusing.

Don't do it.

Other fictive elements that must be structured into a tale include:

Dialogue. Directly described first-level foreground action. Revery. Indirect reportage of action. Analytic thought. Emotional description of responses. Exposition. Social information.

(An action described directly and the same action reported indirectly often generate the same plot—but they produce *vastly* different reading effects!)

One reason structure is so important is because it creates expectation: if a reader reads a novel, and chapter 1 is told from Joe's point of view, then chapter 2 is told from Margery's point of view, then chapter 3 is told from Joe's point of view again, already there is an expectation that chapter 4 will be told from Margery's. The writerly fulfilling of readerly expectations—especially at the structural level—is pleasurable to the reader. (From one point of view, a novel is nothing *but* a concatenation of structural readerly expectations. The writer's task is to fulfill those expectations at the structural level in such a way that nevertheless lets the text generate an unexpected plot or story.) If the reader is right and chapter 4 turns out to be from Margery's point of view, the reader will experience a bit of structural pleasure. As well, this will strengthen the expectation that chapter 5 will be told from Joe's point of view.

Here is the place to remind the writer of a terribly important reality: writing takes longer than reading. A novel can take six months, a year, or five years to write. The same book can be read over two to twenty hours. In six months, not to mention five years, *you* may grow tired of the structural pattern you have committed yourself to. Nevertheless, if suddenly—in a novel that's been going along in alternating chapters between Joan and Jim—a chapter comes up from Billy's point of view, the reader—surging through the text in an evening or three—is going to experience a stretch of structural *disruption* and *displeasure.* Plot developments or other things may lay other pleasures over it; but that displeasure is still going to be there. It's going to mar the reading experience that finally *is* the novel you write.

There are more complicated structures than simple alternating chapters. For example, in a novel of thirteen chapters, chapters 1 through 6 might alternate between Joe and Jane. The seventh, central chapter might be told from Frank's point of view. Then the final six chapters might alternate between Joe and Jane once more—or even, perhaps, between Mike and Milly. You still have a formal, symmetrical and apprehensible structure that the reader can pick up on. Nevertheless, to *abandon* your structure in the midst of your story or novel—or to change it radically, without going back and restructuring what has occurred up to that point—is simply to write a badly structured book, no matter how interesting the plot (or plot synopsis: I believe the two are synonymous) is.

Almost as common as the false flashback among young writers is the story or novel that begins by exhibiting a perfectly lucid and clear structure that, after a third, a half, or three-quarters of the tale is done, is then thrown away. Again and again, when questioned about it, young writers have explained to me: "Well, I just got *tired* of doing it that way. I wanted to try something different."

However sympathetic one is with the tired writer, such derelictions still produce bad work. Your job as a writer is to write a good story, a good book. Don't abandon your structure midway. To think you can get away with it (or that the reader will be just as tired of it as you are and welcome the change) is to confuse writing with reading. It's to forget that a story or a book is to be read—and the much briefer time that the reading takes. (The poet Valéry once remarked, "All art is a disproportionate act." It's the name of the game. If, in practice, the fact upsets you too greatly, it only means you should take up another line of work.) One of the most important pieces of advice a young writer can receive is: choose material—and work toward a structure—that is rich, varied, and complex enough to sustain your interest, if not your enthusiasm (the old *Begeisterung*), for the extended time it will take to write the work in question.

If you don't, the writing itself will be painful to undergo, and you will be tempted to cut corners and move off in directions that will only weaken the work. Or, if they *are* actually more interesting than the original conception, you still have the problem of reconceiving the beginning material to bring it in line with where you've decided to go.

Now of course the reader can get tired of a structure too —one that isn't doing anything in terms of the material— alternating chapters, say, that still don't throw new and interesting light on what's going on. But if the reader is going to get tired of it, the answer is not to change it midstream. The answer is to go back, start over again, and choose a different structure that is richer and works better with the material.

Writing fiction *is* work. And hard work, at that.

If you're *not* prepared to work hard, think seriously about doing something else.

Many writers structure their narrative in the following manner or something close to it: a sentence of action, followed by a sentence of emotional response, following by a sentence of action, followed by a sentence of emotional response . . . and they continue on in this way for large blocks of text, now and again breaking things up with passages of dialogue. (An even more prevalent structure is a sentence of action, *three* sentences of emotional response, a sentence of action, *three* sentences of emotional response . . .) Generally speaking, this is not a very interesting narrative structure. (And page after page of the one-three, one-three narrative structure is *deadly!*) Even if, sentence by sentence, the writing is clean and polished, the overall effect tends to become gray and homogenized because of the fundamentally boring and repetitive structure. Writers can produce more varied and far stronger effects if they will work with larger rhetorical units, as well as structuring those larger units in more interesting and imaginative ways.

We spoke of structure as a way of creating expectation, a few pages back. This is the place to note that, to the extent the novel and the short story are forms (that is, structures), each exists as nothing but various sets of structural expectations. These expectations have been set in place by the history of the respective genres. One of the strongest structural expectations shared by both short story and novel is that, somewhere at the beginning of the text or comparatively near it, the writer will let us know what economic bracket the main character is currently in (and what bracket that character has come from). This expectation has been put in place by three hundred years of novels and stories that have answered this question within the first few pages. Because this expectation is so strong in fiction, the ways a writer can answer it have become very subtle. The kinds of paragraphs that are obligatory toward the start of any Jane Austen novel ("A single man of large fortune; four or five thousand a year. What a fine thing for our girls!") need not occur in every novel today. It can be done by the mention of a manila envelope from the VA (Veterans' Administration) or Social Security sticking out from under the coffee grounds in the garbage pail. It can be done by the mention of a bunch of checks stuck in a savings bank passbook on the back of the kitchen table. It can be suggested by the clothing someone wears, by the kind of house a character lives in, the mention of a profession or a line of work, or any of hundreds of other devices. But if that information is not stated or implied—and stated or implied clearly—the reader will feel the same sort of structural displeasure as he or she does when an internal set of structural expectations is violated.

The notion of structure runs from how words and phrases are organized within the sentence (even how sounds are organized throughout various phrases), to how sentences are organized within the narrative, to how larger units such as chapters are organized to make up the overall tale. It even covers the larger question of what fiction, what a story, what the novel actually *is*.

Edgar Rice Burroughs, in Tarzan novel after Tarzan novel, adhered to a simple and clear narrative structure: chapter 1 told about the villains of the story; chapter 2 told about what Tarzan was doing; chapter 3 told about the doings of the villains again; chapter 4 went back to Tarzan, who now discovered what the villains had done in chapter 1; chapter 5 went back to the villains, who by now were aware of Tarzan and were trying to trip him up; chapter 6 showed Tarzan again righting what the villains had set wrong two chapters before and going on to find what they'd done in chapter 3; chapter 7 showed the villains at it again; chapter 8 showed Tarzan straightening out the mess of chapter 6 and pursuing the villains, only to encounter the results of chapter 7 . . .

This alternating chapter structure went on throughout the novel, back and forth between Tarzan and the villains, until the last chapter, in which Tarzan gets to fight the villains directly —and triumphs. The structure supported Burroughs through dozens of Tarzan novels—and made him a millionaire several times over. It was simple and effective; suspense was built into it—and the readers never tired of it. But while the *structure* of the novels was the same, the *plots* of all the Tarzan novels—what the villains are after, who they are, the various ways Tarzan foils them and cleans up their mess—are as different as can be.

It's a lot easier to talk about plot than it is to talk about structure. Plot exists as a synopsis that often has no correspondence to text. (Where, among the pages of Kafka's *Metamorphosis*, can you point to the deadening, boring routine of Samsa's work? Or to Samsa's character? Or to his sister's? Or to his father's? Or to his family's decisions to take in boarders? But it would be hard to discuss the plot in any detail without reference to all of these.) Structure exists, however, *only* in terms of a particular text, so that to talk about it in any specificity or detail you must constantly be pointing to one part of a page or another, at these words or at those: structure is specifically the organization of various and varied *textual* units.

Structures are there, certainly, to be talked about. But if they are to be useful to the writer, they must be *felt*.

(We find out that Samsa's family is now taking in lodgers in the last clause of the third sentence of the ninth paragraph of *The Metamorphosis's* third chapter—suddenly and without any access to the decision itself, as Gregor must have discovered it: that is to say, the structure of the narrative parallels the *experience* of the point-of-view character—*without* directly recounting it—and as such represents the smallest of structural elegances in the many that make up that extraordinary narrative performance.)

As hard as structure is to talk about, when actually writing the writer must accustom him- or herself to thinking about structure—and to thinking about it constantly. I don't mean that the *word* "structure" must be in your mind while you write. But, while writing, you must constantly be thinking such thoughts as: As I write this section of my story, is there another section that must be more or less the same length (or much shorter; or much longer) in order to balance it? Given the feel of this section, is there another section that, for the story to be satisfying, should have the *same* feel? Is there a section that must have a markedly *different* feel? How does this section differ in feel from the previous section? How should the next section differ in feel from this one? Finally, and perhaps most importantly, how does a previous occurrence cause the reader to regard the one I'm currently writing about?

These are all structural questions—and are the questions the writer has to ask *while* writing. You have to hold on to the answers, too. In my experience, mulling on these questions during the writing process often precedes any knowledge I have of what, specifically, is actually going to *happen* in a given scene or section later in the tale. (Often deciding on the answers *leads* to a decision about what happens.) These kinds of questions must be wrestled with, usually while the pen is in hand or the fingers are knocking at the typewriter keys, if the story is to come out with a sense of shape, provide readerly pleasure, and project writerly wholeness.

In the canon of great nineteenth-century European novels, the most pyrotechnically structured is Flaubert's *L'Éducation sentimentale.* The novel begins and ends with comparatively benign anecdotes, both organized around the adolescent protagonist, Frédéric Moreau. The first details Frédéric's journeying on a steamer from Paris, a traditional ship of fools, returning to his provincial home, Nogent-sur-Seine. The last, recounted by the now-middle-aged Frédéric, is a reminiscence of an incident that takes place even before that initial journey home—and describes Frédéric and his somewhat older friend Charles Deslaurier's attempt to visit a provincial bordello, a visit that goes awry because Frédéric is too embarrassed and, at the last moment, runs away. Because Deslaurier has no money of his own for the adventure, he must flee as well. In between, Flaubert recounts half a lifetime of Frédéric's (and Deslaurier's) adventures that carry him through the republican revolution of 1848, during which Frédéric would seem to be an up-and-coming young man, cutting a swath among Parisian women, both in the center of French society and on its outskirts. Because of his hopeless love for Madame Marie Arnoux, however, Frédéric never gets what he wants. Each triumph is soured at its high point through the interplay of chance, half-understood malice, and misdirection from others. But to speak of the book on such a level is to speak of it in terms of plot—rather than structure. In terms of plot, *Sentimental Education* moves from social success to social success. It climaxes when Frédéric refuses to marry an unbelievably vicious—if extremely wealthy—woman, Madame Dambreuse, and gains his freedom as a man. In terms of structure, it moves from failure to failure, each new one more devastating than the last, each demanding a greater accommodation and deformation of Frédéric's soul for him to endure. Although by the end Frédéric is a free man with a good house and a place in Parisian society—and at least some of his fortune intact—one can only assume, from his last encounter with Madame Arnoux, that perhaps his earlier encounter with Madame Dambreuse at the auction house has left him wounded in ways that put him finally and wholly outside the possibility of receiving the benefits Madame Arnoux's love might have given him had he and she been able to come together. If Flaubert had simply *explained* how each social triumph was in reality a failure, the novel would have been banal. Again and again, however, its structure justifies Robert Baldick's claim at the opening of his introduction to the Penguin edition that the book is "undoubtedly the most influential French novel of the nineteenth century" and makes it the novelist's novel from its time. That structure is what makes the book about so much more than the social adventures of one moderately callow youth and turns it, rather, into the analysis of the dilemmas of an age.

Most people who write novels—that is to say, people who write and publish the workaday novels, the mysteries and romances, the best sellers, or, among the more adventurous readers, the science fiction and the occasional "serious fiction" that, from time to time, fall into the lap of fiction readers and make up most of our reading—absorb a few, simple novelistic structures. And they can more or less submit to them. Rarely have they absorbed the range of structures, however, from the possible play of sounds in sentences, to the necessary structures for a variety of scenic resonances, to the structures for the interplay of texts and countertexts in tension with one another that make the novel into the richest of symphonic art forms. Usually the structures they've absorbed are at the mid-range, and are just visible enough to keep us reading through reams of unbelievable dialogue, pointless internal "characterization," and the like, under the illusion we are trying to find out "what happens." We aren't. We are following a mid-range structure that promises that "what happens" at a certain level will be revealed. And, in one form or another, usually it is.

These particular structures can best be characterized as "formulaic." Indeed, the vast majority of fiction that we read *is* formulaic. And formulaic fiction is rarely *good* fiction.

Constructing a new model is always a matter of revising an old model. Certain elements are adjusted. Others are negated. What happens if, for example, one abolishes the tyranny of the subject (Robbe-Grillet), radically displaces the position of irony (John Ashbery, Kenneth Gememi, James Schuyler), rebels against the tyranny of reference (Hart Crane, Charles Bernstein), the tyranny of narrative progression (Ron Silliman, Lyn Hejinian, John Keene), or even the tyranny of the letter (Richard Kostelanetz) . . . ? In such enterprises poetry and prose, as well as literature and pictorial art, begin to lose their hard and bounded distinctions. But if, for fiction, say, you were to construct an *entirely* new model, the chances are *overwhelming* you'll come up, rather, with an awkward (and probably old-fashioned) model for dry cleaning, for archaeological research, or for political lobbying before you come up with one for fiction. The fact that you—and possibly a very few aesthetically sophisticated members of whatever limited audience you might command—can recognize the results as belonging to the realm *of* fiction (or art—or whatever) in the first place *means* you have retained some signs—if only a label, if only the placement of the object in a context (publishing it in a journal, scrawling it on a wall)—that bespeak it a text. And "text," as most of the readers of this essay will know, already has a distressingly wide interpretation—far beyond what can fit on walls, screens, pages, or stages.

Nonsense is conservative. If your wish is to be radical, think about that. Radicalism resists aesthetic entropy in the same way it resists the formulaic and the cliché. Through irony, there are radical ways the cliché can be welcomed into art. But irony requires more, not less, thought to respond to than ordinary humor, sentiment, or any of the last three millennia's narrative tropes.

To extend our discussion beyond this point, however, where

cliché and formulaic structures are distinguished from the relatively neutral structures of genre and the more ambitious sort of good art, we would have to enter a discussion about the violation of structural expectations—a violation that is finally just as important as cleaving to them. (Advice: If it strikes *you* as well structured, as clearly structured, or as interestingly structured, go with it. If it strikes *you* as cliché and formulaic, avoid it.) Indeed, it is the combination of fulfilling *and* violating structural expectations that makes fiction not just a craft, but an art. If there is a distinction to be made between good art and art that we think of as great, often it lies in the area of what structural expectations to violate. But the violation of expectations very quickly, over a period of ten or fifteen years, can turn into an expectation itself—one reason it is so hard to talk of, when negativities turn out to be positivities after all. These questions are, however, beyond the scope of such limited notes as these, even though they are just as important—and just as intimately bound up with the idea of narrative.

—New York City
February 1996

Part II FOUR LETTERS

New York City
December 10, 2001

Dear P—,

What a pleasure it was to read with you at La Taza this past Saturday, there on Market Street in Philadelphia. The night's feeling was rich, informal, and literary in a way I liked. The piece I heard you read was smart, witty, and foregrounded a political apprehension I found very winning.

It was also warming to discover we shared a publisher.

When I got home, I dove into the copy of your book of criticism that you had given me. The opening essay on Gertrude Stein is a knock-out and wonderfully clarifying.

Some thoughts on questions that it raises have been zipping around the old lizard brain awhile. I hope you don't mind if I share some of them with you.

Do you know the critical work of the late poet Gerald Burns? A Harvard grad, professional magician (for a while he made much of his living performing at children's birthday parties), and general ne'er-do-well, he died in '95 at age fifty-four. In an all-too-thin little book he published with Treacle Press (*Toward a Phenomenology of Written Art*, New Paltz, 1979), in a piece he called "The Slate Notebook," Burns wrote:

> Some writers know a great deal about how words should come at a reader, others study the ways words come to a writer. The second is likely to please passionate readers more, if only because the first is more likely to be vulnerable to literature as rule book, a catalogue of other men's effects. What saves him sometimes is reading very little. The second, whether reading or writing, is likely to pay less attention to the book of rules than to grass and how the ball looks coming at you, and the oddity of lines painted on a field. What he explores is the act of writing, as readers explore the act of reading. There is nothing contemptible about traditional writing, but its readers are more likely to

ignore the act of reading as part of the experience of what is. In the first quarto *Hamlet* Corambis* asks: What doe you read my Lord? And Hamlet says, Wordes, wordes. In the Folio he says, Words, words, words. It's not only funnier, it's truer, to his and our experience. The scribe may hate his pen as the painter his paint, but in another mood he will imitate Van Gogh and drink ink. (22)

In Burns's terms, I believe Stein is very much interested in how words come to her as a writer. As someone who claimed herself a genius on so many occasions, Stein set herself the project, I'm sure, of showing how words—how language itself—*come to* a genius. As your essay demonstrates, words come to the genius—came to Gertrude Stein—simply, one at time, and with many inculcating repetitions. They came in the way language comes to a young child, of two, two and a half, or three—when, as we know, the child's mind is learning at a genius rate it will never reach again. The knowledge, which your essay highlights, is that they come as well in all the specific rhetorical forms that language comes to a person who is (always already?) learning that language for the first time—whether as a child or as a foreigner.

Paradoxically, we can contrast this to the way language comes to your average U.S. college freshman. For her or him, language arrives as ill-thought-out chunks of already assembled phrases. For him or her, languages come in "received-language" gobs, which fall together with inappropriate syntax and, now and again, individual words placed in the demonstrably incorrect position.

The way language comes to *most* adolescents-to-adults *most* of the time is what bad writing *is*.

The real trouble with genius (to appropriate Bob Perelman's title) is that, consciously or unconsciously, genius wants to democratize the entire art-making and art-receiving process. At the level of desire, I'm sure, this is one with the desire to create a larger audience *for* the geniuses. Often, however, ge-

---

* "Corambis" of the first quarto edition of *Hamlet* becomes Polonius in later folio editions.

niuses don't think through the consequences—consequences that hinge on the unhappy truth nestled in that single-sentence paragraph just above this one. As Jacques Barzun noted as far back as 1958 (in *The House of Intellect*), what makes the democratizing urge problematic is this: The democratizing process invariably lowers the general level of education and sensibility; it dilutes and minimizes the shared information armamentarium in direct proportion to the population expansion of the educated. It stifles the general ability to manipulate the elements of that armamentarium. While it raises the general level of intellectual proficiency of *some*, nevertheless, by squashing competitions among our students, by appreciating a greater range of idiosyncrasy among them, and therefore rewarding a lower and lower level of demonstrable accomplishment with higher and higher (and therefore more and more meaningless) marks, it lets into the field (along with truly creative idiosyncrasy) more and more of what we can also recognize today as flabby thinking, inaccuracy, and error—errors that range from the grammatical to the logical.

Two summers ago, while at Yaddo, I found an interesting definition of "genius" in G. E. Lessing's wonderful essay on sculpture and poetry from the 1750s, *Laocoön*. (It was on a shelf of books outside my door. Pages were still uncut. I doubt anyone had cracked this particular volume in forty or fifty years.) "Genius," Lessing wrote, "is the ability to put talent wholly into the service of an idea." Looking around at the various writing workshops that have both nourished and plagued me since that luxurious August in the art colony mansion, it occurs to me that I can (with a squint) locate three levels of writerly accomplishment:

First, there are people with the *ability* to write. Second, there are people who are *talented* at writing. Third, there are people—quite as rare now as they ever were—with *genius* at writing, in Lessing's sense.

Today, in the wake of the general democratization process, when someone with the ability to write—which, after all, is by no means universal—turns up in, say, a midwestern class of high school seniors, or, indeed, is noticed in some inner-city group of underprivileged kids, often, by comparison with those around, that person seems truly talented. People suggest he or she may be a . . . writer. Writing as a profession seems to offer such young people freedoms and rewards workaday jobs can't.

When people with the ability to write persevere, often they end up published—with reviews, articles, essays of one sort or another. Sometimes they even publish fiction or poems. Today, because of the democratizing urge throughout the greater social machinery, some even publish a novel or two—or three. If their writing ability extends to a general clarity, sometimes these books are even well received by local and not-so-local reviewers.

Today, because of the competition, because of the money involved, rarely does one come across a technically bad acting job in a commercial film—even if most of the films themselves are not very good. (While the directorial conception of the character may be a botch for the film the producers ended up making—though often it was fine for the film they began with—usually the stable of working Hollywood actors can deliver rich, believable performances of the characters they are asked for. Otherwise, they don't work again.) But—again because of the money involved—the making of films is probably the least democratic (and the selling of film scripts, in the general imagination, among the most romantic) of enterprises. The amount of real talent available in the commercial film industry is staggering. What it lacks, of course, is precisely Lessing-style genius—the ability to put that talent totally into the service of a single overarching idea. In terms of film directing, this failure has to do largely with the fact that the whole enterprise is such a collaboration of talents and that finally the power is not with the director (who may or may not be a genius) but with the producer (who almost never is).

In fiction, today, the situation is the opposite of that in commercial films, even as it produces similar results. Most published novels—that is, most novels published as serious fiction—are unreadably poor. (Many—though, by no means, all—commercial works are notably better than these "serious" works, on just about any aesthetic scale.) Because the writers have no more than ability, however, "it" never really happens in their books, and—after a few tries—their careers are generally over because they have produced no sizable percentage of intensity of excitement and pleasure high enough to produce, in turn, the socially stabilizing situations we acknowledge as quality (always conflictual, never—in its larger form—a consensus phenomenon). There is neither talent nor genius to discipline what writerly ability is there (and, unlike writerly ability, talent is as varied and as multiplex as light flickers across a jeweler's tray). The few writers who have one form of talent or another often get a coterie of readers, and manage to build something of a reputation, with a string of workshops, led, taught, attended, and even—sometimes—loved by the aspiring writers who follow them. But talent is what makes fiction more interesting than a newspaper article on the same topic.

Talent's great paradox is that it is entirely social. This is another of those unpleasant truths that immediately begins to undercut the young writer so terrified of competition that she or he cannot even acknowledge it, and who hides, therefore, from that terror before the world's complexity by deciding to write entirely for him- or herself. (Writing for oneself is the retreat of those with the ability to write but not much else.)

When I say, "Talent is social," I mean that, while good writing manifests itself as similarity to other good writing, talent per se can only manifest itself as difference.

In that sense, it is closely allied with information: the talented writer tends to get more information into the writing with fewer words. Difference *cannot* manifest itself unless it is a difference *from* something. What talented writing is different from is the range of published writing around. This means that talent only registers on readers educated to a familiarity with that "normal" range. This is why the college freshmen and sophomores, on whom we keep trying out those books that we as teachers find talented and even exciting, keep responding to those books with yawns and ho-hums—unless they already happen to be wide-ranging readers themselves. The sociality that contains, governs, and manifests what talent there is and what it can be is only the sociality of the aesthetic; but it is social, nevertheless, no matter how it is manifested by a single practitioner. Talent is something that can only be read, and what can be read is always and only the social.

In the same way that the ability to write and talent in writing are not the same thing, a "reader" is not the same as a "wide-ranging reader"—another reason why, so often, our text selections register so poorly in the new, welcoming democratic classroom, with its barely functional field of literacy. It is only relatively wide-ranging readers who *can* respond to writerly talent, because they alone can experience what it is different *from*.

Indeed, the most widely ranging reader has the most intense and exciting experience of writerly talent in the presence of its specific difference. The conflicts and debates that produce categories of quality must be among educated readers—that is, readers with a broad experience of the literary field. People who read only mysteries, or, indeed, only eighteenth-century novels, are not likely to have much input into the contestatory dialogue about which contemporary works are worthwhile and which works aren't.

This is the basis, by the way, for my feeling that both the aspiring fiction writer and the aspiring fiction teacher must read widely in the range of published fiction and nonfiction. Any responsibility on the shoulders of the aspiring writer to publish begins here: should you have talent—or even should you have only ability—you have some social responsibility to help shape the greater field that not only makes other talent stand forth, but that is the creator itself of such talent; that, indeed, makes the talent meaningful, manifest, readable, and significant, and allows it to be other than meaningless sounds and scrawls on paper.

Historically, the writers that we read today tend to have been ambitious for fame and, if not for a vastly wide readership, a large readership that understood what they were doing. They felt what they were doing was important enough to put out there. The nonambitious writer who simply feels it would be nice to write, that writing might help in some vaguely conceived inner project of self-actualization, but that greatness is not a reasonable goal, is largely a product of the democratization process in the arts. Over the last decade and a half, however, such writers have come to dominate the creative writing workshops that proliferate across the academic landscape.

Poets of the San Francisco Renaissance of the late 1940s and

1950s* often expressed their sense of the sociality of art in a motto worth preserving: "Good art makes great art look better." This became a reason for established poets (or poets who were self-confident enough to consider themselves great) to help younger and struggling writers whenever they could—an early plank of the current democratization platform. An awareness of this fuels the publishing writers' sense of responsibility to teach these ever proliferating workshops. But the proliferation itself seems to have greatly changed the sort of young writer attracted to these workshops and has produced a field, as well, in which anything recognizable as ambition is regarded as something between a sickness and a crime. And while it's always good to keep a grip on the reality of any situation, this one does not strike me as healthy for the general art-making landscape.

Often, in these non- or even anti-ambitious workshops, the mistaken idea develops that bad writing is something done *out there*—among the freshmen and sophomores, say, or in magazines and newspapers—while what *we* do is, somehow by definition, good writing. No. This is not the case. People who simply can't write are not even in the running. The point is, people with the ability to write, even at a highly refined level, still make the same mistakes as the freshmen and sophomores, only within the rules of grammar, usage, and elementary rhetoric. That's because words still come to them in the same way they come to the freshmen and sophomores: in bunches. They only doctor the bunches a little better.

Because people who have the ability to write often have such an unclear notion of the distinction between what they do and what talent and genius do above them (largely because today's antiromantic** critics talk so little about these elements), they find it easy to repress this fundamental fact of art: (again) the competition is not with the illiterate. Rather, work by those with the ability to write constitutes the normative range of clut-

* The Berkeley and San Francisco Renaissance of the late forties and fifties included the poets Jack Spicer, Robert Duncan, and Robin Blaser, and also played host to many of the Black Mountain School as well as the Beat Generation and a whole subsequent generation of poets.
** In the preface to his play of 1830, *Hernani*, which many took as the

tered, thin, cliché writing—dull, bad writing, that is—which talent and genius must distinguish themselves from. Whether they like it or not, those with the ability to write are the enemy, save when art seduces them and they are carried away by it, to support it, to praise it, to cherish it. Or, to put it more generously: only as they are part of a constitutive global process, which produces the social bodying forth of talent and genius that is, alas, not them.

The talents that particularly excite *me* (as a relatively wide-ranging general reader) are those that make the writing wittier, more vivid, and more economical than the range of ordinary writing. (How does one put across to one's students that to aspire to write at an ordinary level of competency is to aspire to write badly—that in art, the ordinary defines what poor or bad art is?) Equally exciting, however, is writing that is simpler, more direct, and more focused than the norm. This is what, intermittently, propels writers such as Stein, Hemingway, Beckett, or Carver into the stratosphere of aesthetic accomplishment. It is also the proof that, indeed, aesthetic achievement is a matter of conflict, not of consensus. We honor writing that is more efficiently ornamented than the norm; we honor writing that is more efficiently stripped down than the norm. Difference manifested in still another direction makes experimental work—that of a Ron Silliman, a Lyn Hejinian, a Christian Bök, or a John Keene, and many others—almost unbearably exciting and, indeed, of compelling interest.

I like Lessing's description of genius.

There in the green fury of early romanticism, it's humble; it's nonarrogant. It comes from an epoch when the number of people in the running for the title "genius" was smaller than it is today. It's all but devoid of the romantic baggage that would accrue to the term over the next 250 years. If it makes the process seem simpler than it is, at least it gives a sense of its goal.

Though I don't express it in the same way, forty-five years after Barzun wrote his polemical exploration of the democratiz-

---

clarion call officially opening the Romantic period in France, Victor Hugo called Romanticism "nothing other than liberalism in literature." I think it's a good characterization; nor have we emerged from it yet.

ing urge in education, I have the same problem that Barzun had: I applaud the efforts and the goals of educational democratization (even in the making of art), while I am still troubled by the concomitant falling away of intellect, a falling away that often seems to menace the production of intelligence—not to mention art—itself.

I do not know how this can be resolved. The only answer is, I suspect, inventively creative pedagogy. Teaching must become a far more respected profession, where those who do it well are encouraged and those who do not do it well are encouraged to do something else. Simply taking folk of high intelligence and general cultural exposure and telling them to break their classes up into smaller discussion sections doesn't do it.

I remember my cousin recounting to me his first anatomy class in medical school. His anatomy professor stood in front of the students, holding a yardstick. Suddenly he raised it, then snapped it in half. (Everyone in the lecture hall sat up!) "The average human spinal column," he began, "is *exactly* eighteen inches long." Then, in his fist, he held up one of the yardstick's pieces.

Said my cousin, he never forgot it. Probably you won't either. I haven't. But that's the kind of dramatic pedagogy we need about nouns and verbs, history, philosophy, Latin, political science, and Greek. It requires as much creative thought as good writing.

(Also it requires students who already know that a yard contains thirty-six inches and that half of thirty-six is eighteen.)

Maybe, however, like the spread of the human population itself, we are simply mired within a self-destruct process—and art, as we know it, will finally vanish, or at least change its form and use within the social to a point where those of us born in the twentieth century will not recognize it by the time those born later in the twenty-first move ahead into the twenty-second.

On the upside, we're all beginning to recognize "talents" of a sort that, in a more formal art-making field, might have looked simply eccentric at one time and thus have gotten no attention or recognition at all. But we want more, and more intense, such talents—and let's see how words come to *them*, as well as what they can do with them once they arrive!

Well . . . this is outcome, excrescence, efflorescence, and up-growth from what our evening together in Philadelphia settled and set free in me. Once again, it was a delight to meet you and to have a chance to hear you read. Maybe we shall run into each other in New Orleans at MLA.

All my best wishes, and—once more—it was a wonderful night and a wonderful opening-up, which your autonomous readings (of your own work, in your own voice, and of your readings of other writers in your essays) have given me.

All good thoughts
for all good things,

(*signed:*) Samuel R. Delany

East Lansing, Michigan
October 28, 1997

Dear Q—,

We are two days beyond the first snow. When, this morning, I left my room (I think I told you, Dennis and I have been housed in the back hall of a girls' dorm), outside stood six rows of bicycles, their handlebars, wheels, and seats piled and puffy, making waist-high arches, white interlocked waves.

Pines and maple branches were still bowed down to the cottony ground and, in many places, joined it.

I walked the wooded thirty yards between the campus and Grand River Avenue under falling splotches and splatters. From the tall pines, nonstop, sun-silvered ice chips glittered down, in fifty-foot curtain after curtain. A city boy, I'd never seen that before—not to such an extent.

Grand River Avenue's brick sidewalks were clear, with only a graying gabbol at the curb. (I don't think there *is* a word "gabbol." But there ought to be: it means something lumpy, uneven, and cold, and it's equally applicable to old, shoveled-up snow as to the rougher surfaces on oatmeal, when, abandoned on the kitchen table and left three hours in the bowl, you scrape it out into the Disposall.) My "free bagel" card was all filled up; so, this morning, at Bruegger's I got my Santa-Fe-turkey-on-a-spinach-herb bagel for nothing.

A friend of mine has just completed a book on the crafting of alternative fiction. In writing me about it, he's several times said that most writing textbooks teach the subject as though no fiction has been written since 1830. But I wonder if his "1830" metaphor—which he's repeated in several letters, now—can do the job, vis-à-vis alternative fiction, he asks of it.

I have just finished rereading Toni Morrison's *The Bluest Eye* (1970) for a class I'm visiting the day after tomorrow. I think it's a bad book. It's bad in some particularly contemporary and characteristic ways. But it could not have been written in 1830—in terms of style, content, or structure.

If you're going to fight the aesthetic failings of our day, it occurs to me, the proper place to aim your brazen arrows is not at the fiction of 1830. (I also think Cather's *O Pioneers!* is a bad book—while her *My Ántonia* is a beautiful one, as are most of Cather's subsequent novels, especially *My Mortal Enemy*—which ranks with Joyce's *The Dead*, Joanna Russ's *The Second Inquisition*, Glenway Wescott's *The Pilgrim Hawk*, and Guy Davenport's *Dawn in Erewhon*, among this century's finest English-language novellas.) A good deal of what passes for "good" or even "excellent" contemporary fiction could benefit from a somewhat larger helping of the virtues of (the best) fiction of 1830. I can easily imagine the editorial suggestions the George Sand (an infinitely smart polemical writer) of *Indiana* (1832) would have made to Morrison in '63 to '69, when she was writing *The Bluest Eye*. Those suggestions could only have improved it.

(The problem with actual writing workshops is the far more important writers' workshop they keep the writer from forming, where the suggestions come from Huysmann and Proust and Ernest Gaines and Anne Brontë and Olaudah Equiano and Mrs. Gaskell and John O. Killens and Émile Zola and James Gould Cozzens and Dashiell Hammett and Frank Norris and Stephen Crane and Willa Cather and Sarah Orne Jewett and Charles Chesnutt and Kate Chopin and whoever else is needed, because they have already wrestled with the problem you are now confronting and have learned something that left, in dramatic form, a lesson in their texts . . . a lesson you can only read if you have also read another writer who has failed before the same problem.)

First, Morrison's novel is a bad book on the level Matthew Arnold specified when he explained that, for the novel to be meaningful, the novelist must convince us the actions the main characters perform and the incidents befalling them are characteristic of at least some group of actual people. If they are not characteristic (i.e., believable), then the book is about purely idiosyncratic and eccentric people and happenings and thus not of any relevance.

Well, as a black man who grew up, not in a small town but in New York City's Harlem during the forties and fifties (and certainly I have enough relatives and have visited enough friends in various small towns, from Greenwood Lake, New Jersey, to Hopewell Junction, New York, to the Bronx and New Rochelle, and Raleigh and little places outside it in North Carolina), I just don't *recognize* anyone in Morrison's book, save Claudia, Frieda, and their mother. I recognize a certain rhythm to the dialogue of (most of) the women in the book, as well as a density of detail in some of the writing. But neither their ideas nor their material persons seem to me particularly (or interestingly) real. Miss China, Miss Poland, and Miss Marie ("the Maginot Line"), the three whores, are not believable prostitutes. They are cleaned-up and prettified fairytales, so scrubbed, perhaps from a desire to present some "strong women." But since, once they come on stage, they don't *do* anything in the novel, all their prettification and suggested strength finally serve no novelistic end.

Morrison's novel is a bad book at the level Lukács identifies in his *Theory of the Novel* (1916), when he wrote, "The novel is the only art form where ethics *is* the aesthetic problem." As Morrison's covey of mixed-race villains, Maureen Peal, Geraldine, Junior, and Soaphead Church, terrorizes, oppresses, and befuddles the simple and innocent, dark-skinned Pecola, they are contoured, the lot of them, from a white racist trope straight out of *Birth of a Nation*: the archetypal melodrama where all the purely evil black villains are also pointedly of mixed blood, stirring up all the otherwise happy and contented *echt* blacks to violence against the kind and good-hearted whites, because they (the mixed bloods) want what the white man has that they, of course, lack—rights, privileges, and material goods that "true" blacks would never think of wanting for themselves.

Historically, mixed-blooded blacks have often led the fight for racial equality. (In one sense, *Birth of a Nation* is *more* accurate than Morrison.) Thus, at the behest of a white theory of racial purity, they were particularly demonized by white racists. Their dissatisfactions were attributed to their "impure blood," rather than to white oppression. It was their perverted desire to *be* white that, presumably, betrayed and oppressed the good darkies of the world.

In terms of the book to hand, far more dangerous than the

myth she attacks is, I think, the one she buys into: that good blacks are very black and/or illiterate or powerless children, while light-skinned blacks spend all their time betraying and terrorizing dark-skinned blacks because the light-skinned blacks want to be white—while darker skinned blacks couldn't possibly want what whites so clearly have. Certainly I never wanted to be white—for more than five minutes. Though, the truth is, I remember my occasional five-minute fantasies, and I don't feel Morrison has captured even those. It was like wanting to be a fireman or a policeman (and, yes, those are romantic power images), only this one you were not allowed to articulate in my house. My parents would probably have beaten me if I'd expressed such a wish. And both my parents *were* light enough to pass for white—and both would have died before either would have considered doing so. (That's not a metaphor. Both marched on picket lines in the thirties and forties, where my mother was regularly arrested and even jailed for taking part with other blacks in political protests.) But my whole "mixed-blooded" family was like that. So was every other light-skinned black family I knew.

In their highly differing approaches, radical and conservative, to improving the condition of black men and women in America, both W. E. B. Du Bois *and* Booker T. Washington were regularly demonized by whites for their white blood or white cultural component—presumably the source of their dissatisfaction with the black man's lot. A step beyond the history books' hagiography, you'll find it.

Because all the people (except Cholly) whom Morrison presents as doing selfishly evil deeds that torment Pecola (because *they* want to be white even more than she does; she would be satisfied with blue eyes) are characterized as of mixed blood, they register as *aesthetically* redundant. Their aesthetic redundancy *makes* their appearance in the novel a statement about the characteristics of a group—because, in the novel, they *form* a group. This is what the twenty-seven-year-old Wittgenstein meant when, in the same year as Lukács's book appeared, he jotted down in his notebook during a trip to Norway, "Aesthetics and ethics are one."

(Morrison allows herself to express "love" for the insane,

mixed-blood Soaphead—as she does for the father/rapist Cholly; but that does not mitigate the evil of what they actually *do*: the dog-murdering repressed-homosexual pedophilic evil mulatto Soaphead *is* as crazy [he writes a letter defending himself to God] as Pecola *ends up being*.)

It pains me as a black man (and a mixed-blood black man at that) to see a black writer such as Morrison (or a black filmmaker such as Haille Gramas, director of the film *Sankofa*) buying into these white racist and historically indefensible tropes.

The Bluest Eye is supposed to occur in 1941—that is to say, just before the Second World War. (If it were happening any time from '65 on, someone would doubtless tell Pecola: "You want blue eyes? Save your money, get some contact lenses—and boogie down!") But if this is a historical novel, why don't I get any sense of prewar life? Where is the ice man, with his wheelbarrow and his tongs, delivering his twice-weekly cube of ice? (Ours, in Harlem, was a squat red-headed gorilla of a black fellow, called Andy, with a broad nose and freckles.) Where is the milkman, with his wire baskets of bottled milk, with the bulbs at the top for the cream to separate out? (In Montclair, New Jersey, my aunt's was a very blond white man, in a white, white uniform, with whom she was in steady conflict over his leaving the milk outside the milk door. [Do any of these houses in Lorain have milk cabinets, those little closets at waist level in the house's back wall, with an outside and an inside door, a general feature on houses built between the wars?] Because he was delivering to a black family, he wanted to get out of there as fast as possible and frequently left the milk sitting outside on the ground.) Who's got electricity and who lights the cabin with kerosene lanterns? Who has an indoor bathroom and who has an outhouse in the back? (In the forties, while indoor plumbing's luxuries were available to my family in the city, the more primitive facilities marked country life and defined the difference between urban and rural, throughout the country, for most blacks—light-skinned or dark-skinned, even those who were comparatively middle-class.) We had only kerosene lanterns in our country house, no hot water, and an outdoor water pump. One of my uncles—a judge—had an outhouse at his summer home, until, around 1948, he got indoor plumbing. Is there a radio that the kids gather around at seven o'clock, with their parents, to hear *Baby Snooks, Fibber McGee and Molly, The Lone Ranger, Superman, The* ("weed of crime bears bitter fruit. Who knows? The Shadow knows!") *Shadow,* and ("tipping the scale at three hundred pounds") *The Fat Man?* Black kids listened to these shows just as much as white kids. If you were too poor to own a radio, you went to a better-off friend's house to listen . . .

Mr. Henry has "girly magazines." That's post–World War II (the explosion of pin-ups and girly magazines was a response to the aggregation of male soldiers), not prewar. The point is that Morrison was a girl in Lorain, Ohio, in 1941. But though she's half a dozen years my senior and thus should have even more memories of pre–World War II black life than I do (and there's always research), she hasn't used the texture and materiality of that life to enrich this particular novel. Rather, what's happened is, because we all know she *was* there, few of us question the accuracy of her portrait.

To picture the past as a direct and uninflected extension of the present is a conservative move that erases historical difference—which is to say, it erases history itself.

It's a sad fact, but no work is popular in its own time because of its radical achievement. Popularity is always a conservative phenomenon. Black Nobel Prize–winning authors do not escape that. A sadly similar argument can be leveled at both Soyinka and Walcott.

Morrison's novel aligns itself with the Fantasy Police. Reading it, I find myself asking: What's *wrong* with wanting to be different from what you are? The assumption that wanting to be other than you are means that you hate yourself is pathological and patently absurd. A much clearer and more articulate argument might be posed that to desire effectively to be different, actually to expend energy to bring that difference about (to become surgically a woman if you are born a man; to become surgically a man if you are born a woman; to reconstruct your foreskin if you were circumcised before you could consent to it; to straighten your hair if you don't like it kinky; to wear blue contact lenses if you have brown eyes and dark skin; to wear dreadlocks if you were born with straight blond hair; to pierce, or tattoo, or decorate your body in any way at all; to exercise or diet or contour your body toward whatever ideal you set yourself) requires much *more* self-confidence and a clear sense of who you are than those who never question or wish to adjust their bodily reality at all.

They are wrong if you feel socially compelled to do any of them when you hate the idea and it is *not* your bent. But Pecola *wants* blue eyes. It is not a case of everyone *else* telling her she would be better off with them or more beautiful with them or would go further socially if she had them. (Because blue eyes and dark skin are, at this moment, a relatively rare combination —though certainly such combinations occur—she would look rather unusual. She might well have a *more* difficult time socially because of them than she might have without them. Pecola wants them anyway. But this—and the fact that her particular knowledge of blue eyes is seen to originate in objects of "white" culture—is why the novel demonizes them. To have them would, of course, conjoin Pecola to all the villains in the book. Again and again the novel runs us into a value template where racial purity and cultural purity are seen to be valuable and the same—when, in my humble opinion, such notions are [one] an impossible pipe dream and [two] the source of all the problems rather than an element of any sort of desirable or even conceivable solution.) But it is Pecola's desire itself that Morrison equates with self-destructive madness.

The accusation of self-hatred, whether racial or sexual (and notice, it is *only* blacks, *only* gays, *only* Jews, *only* women who are ever accused of hating themselves—never straight white Protestant males . . .), once we are attuned to it, always carries clear and persistent overtones of sour grapes from the accusers. And it does all through *The Bluest Eye* as well. This has a common name in discussions of liberationist political analysis: blaming the victim. In *The Bluest Eye*, Pecola's desire for blue eyes is presented as a small spot of madness in an otherwise weak and beleaguered personality. As that desire grows, since it is one with madness, the madness grows—finally (once she has been raped by her father and has a baby that dies, in spite of the futile wishing and magic making of Claudia and Frieda) it (the madness) becomes indistinguishable from the punishment for the unacceptable/impossible desire.

Because she is a black girl who wants blue eyes, she goes mad; her desire for blue eyes *is* the madness.

But this is to reduce the novel beyond the social to the political; and a novel is still (since Flaubert, since Joyce, since Woolf) primarily an aesthetic, that is to say a formal, object.

The greatest aesthetic—read: formal—fault of *The Bluest Eye*, and the one that is so characteristic of so much of the fiction in our times, is this: short stories do not make good sections of novels.

The cobbling together of the shorter pieces to make *The Bluest Eye* finally absorbs (that is, explains) the failure represented by the aesthetically redundant (and *ergo* politically unhappy) choice of villains-all-from-the-same-microclass. A single such choice made in one work does not necessarily tarnish that choice if it occurs in another. But although these villains may (or may not) have all started out in different stories, now they inhabit the one tale.

In 1970 when *The Bluest Eye* appeared, MFA programs were nowhere near as widespread as they are now. But what was an interesting flaw in an indisputably talented book by a new black woman writer in 1970 is today (and we know the book comes out of the writer's group to which Morrison belonged) *the* endemic flaw over the range of contemporary academic fiction. The fallout from so many MFA programs, many too many of those novels are groups of short stories lumped together in a single volume, more or less carefully, largely unsuccessfully.

Short stories do not sit well in novels. They don't make good opening chapters. They don't make good closing chapters. (The short story that forms the last chapter of Flannery O'Connor's novel *Wise Blood* [1952] simply flops off the end of her book and refuses to cohere with the rest, even though clearly it inspired her to write it. Its information is at a different density. The structure and form of its material has nothing to do with anything that, after the fact, O'Connor went and placed before it, even though it continues and more or less resolves the novel's "story." The same is true for the short story that forms the last chapter [and obviously inspired the rest of the book] of Ian McEwan's *Black Dogs* [1992]. Short stories don't make good middle sections.)

Today, as they tumble out of our country's MFA programs, these literary gabbols speak largely to the fear on the part of the writers of committing themselves to the problems of the larger and more ambitious forms(s; for the novel is not a single form: it is many—many still to be invented), or, even more quixotically, the hope of placing sections of the "novel" as separate pieces in journals. (Damn it, Q—, when I was sixteen, seventeen, eighteen, that's *how* I used to write novels. I remember that fear, the niggling suspicion that I couldn't possibly do it, that I couldn't write a coherent 250-, 350-page text and keep the material under control. [I wrote nine of them before I was nineteen!] Well, if you're going to write novels, that fear has got to be overcome.) Today a *serious* novel that is conceived, written, and finished *as* a complete novel is so rare that such works register on most readers *as* formal experiments. At least they do on me. At this point, by and large the only writers to do so regularly are genre or commercial writers—or writers with strong genre sympathies.

But I'm getting away from Morrison.

Once Pecola begins to menstruate, all the passages having to do with her are thin and, finally, fake. Critics interested in images of women in fiction have been discussing this problem since Beauvoir's *Le Deuxième Sexe* (1949). In our society, because of the social constraints on women after puberty, while it is relatively easy to make a believable prepubescent girl into a vivid character (Alice in Lewis Carroll, Emily in *A High Wind in Jamaica* [1929], the young Jane in *Jane Eyre* [1847], Scout in *To Kill a Mockingbird* [1960]—or, indeed, Claudia in *The Bluest Eye*), it's difficult to continue that sense of believable humanity for postpubescent young women. Well, the Brontës, Austen, and George Eliot (not to mention George Sand) solved just those problems—as did Louis Bromfield and Jean Rhys. In her or his own way, the contemporary novelist must solve them too—indeed, as long as we live in a patriarchal society, we cannot escape them. (And every writer who solves the problem for his or her own novel comes a step closer to dismantling the patriarchy.) But to give in to them, then say, "See, I'm dramatizing these problems," doesn't cut it.

The passages dealing with Pecola beyond the first chapter of "Autumn" are simply thin. They clink like the hollow, tinny parables they are. The more and more condensed and vertiginous prologue from the elementary reading text is obvious and affected. A scene in a black schoolroom with children *learning* from the same text would have been much richer, more telling—and more difficult to write.

In the first chapter of "Spring," when Frieda is molested by Mr. Henry, Claudia and Frieda search out Pecola to get some whiskey from Pecola's father, which they believe necessary to "cure" Frieda. At the white woman's house where Mrs. Breedlove, Pecola's mother, works, when Pecola knocks over the berry cobbler on the white woman's floor, the two girls see Mrs. Breedlove savage her daughter. The black mother upbraids her daughter, then turns to comfort the little white girl; and the incident ends—

The didactic purpose of the scene having been accomplished, the major dramatic questions (Frieda's molestation, the whiskey they believe they need to "cure" it) are dropped and never mentioned again. What this forgetting of the major drama makes us realize, however, is what a fake it was all along: the cobbler incident was only a set-up, and a silly one at that (whiskey . . . ?), for a narrative sermon as contrived as the one that ended "Autumn" with (mixed-blood) Geraldine shouting at Pecola over the cat she doesn't realize her own son Junior has injured.

I wonder if Morrison could have written such a clumsily thought-out novel if, by the time she was ready to write it, she had read George Schuyler's satire from 1931, *Black No More*, in which Schuyler (a conservative black critic who wrote largely in the twenties, thirties, and forties) posits a process that, indeed, turns black people white. The cutting point Schuyler makes— and the insight wholly repressed from Morrison's novel—is that the group who is *truly* threatened by such a transformation of black to white is *whites*—not other blacks. (In her novel *Passing* [1929], Nella Larsen makes the corollary point that the person goaded to the point of murdering a black woman who she knows is passing for white is *another* black woman light enough to pass, who has chosen *not* to. From my own experience as a relatively light-skinned black, this seems to cleave far closer to psychological reality.)* To analyze the internecine conflicts and complicities of microclasses within the larger group is one of the glories of narrative fiction. But to write a novel set fifteen years before the desegregation battle was won in the Supreme Court by black activists and black leaders, light and dark, that suggests somehow that all the problems of darker-skinned blacks can be attributed to the active selfishness of lighter-skinned blacks is only a step or two away from aligning oneself with George Lincoln Rockwell and the Klan. In Morrison's novel, the traditional view of (white) beauty functions as a singular aspect connected directly to morals as morals connect directly to psychology. (At least for her darker-skinned characters: Pecola and her family.) Morrison fails to show that glamour—be it the glamour of a fireman's helmet, the glamour of a western sheriff's tin star, or the glamour of the blue eyes of the insistently middle-class characters, which, in near cartoon form, illustrate these black children's first-grade readers—is glamorous precisely *because* it is a symbol of power. The blue eyes have been informed with desire *because* of the absence of power—of economic, political, and personal options, of social pleasures ranging from parental approval to friendship to sex, that is to say, personal freedoms, personal power—in Pecola's own life, and because of her perception, however misty, of these options, pleasures, and exercised powers in the storybook lives surrounding the blue-eyed dolls

* A further irony of Larsen's tale is that the murder is committed on the roof of an apartment building on Edgecombe Avenue in Harlem, where a group of men, black and white, each with different relationships to the two women, all stand there and watch the murder occur. Because the two women look so much alike, however—again, they are both light-skinned blacks—the men cannot conceive of the difference between them, so that, within moments of the murder, though all have all seen it happen, all have reread the moment of eruptive psychological and political rage into an accident. It is all too easy to see Morrison herself, among the socially blind witnesses, on that Edgecombe Avenue roof. But this is why the writer must know her or his own tradition.

and the blue-eyed illustrations she's encountered in books and advertisements (as well as the glamour of representation itself), and because of their lack in the lives of the other black children around her, light and dark.

The way that Austen and George Sand and George Eliot and all *three* of the Brontës (not to mention Balzac, Thackeray, Stendhal, and Dickens) got their heroines over puberty and through adulthood was to allow them to know/learn of the material powers they lack that inform and constitute these girlhood desires. (It's called growing up.) Sometimes after they grow up, like Maggie Tulliver, they Die in the End. Sometimes, like Dorothea Brooke, they marry unhappily but stick it out. Rarely, like Sand's Laliá or Sade's Juliette, they live alone to a ripe and joyous old age with the odd lover, male and/or female, off on the side; and sometimes, like Elizabeth Bennet, they Marry and Live Happily Ever After. But more important than the ending chosen for a given life, these writers allow their characters, during the duration of their portrayed lives, to work their butts off at whatever social level they have access to, to achieve that material power, whether that work—because of the pressures from the greater system—is finally a success or not.

These *are* the novelists from the nineteenth century who made it possible for Lukács and Wittgenstein to have their insights at the beginning of the twentieth.

The novel is a great, great form (to write the words—"I am a novelist; my life has been committed to it"—makes my eyes tear) because, *as* a form, it says that evil (like good) is a manifestation of social systems, not individuals, and thus individuals, both the good ones and the bad ones, if they move into new social systems they are unused to, can be changed by them if they stay there. Some of the greatest (and most terrifying) novels, like Flaubert's *L'Éducation sentimentale,* show how already weakened people, even when they appear to have all the advantages, can be made even coarser and more limited by such systems.

These novels take place in the darkest and most severe margins of the novel-as-form. But even they do not contravene it. Now the novel can be about many, many things. Within that larger form it can take up and take on many, many microforms. But if you find your particular novel saying anything that directly contravenes the above, nine times out of ten—if not ninety-nine times out of a hundred—it's a sign of an aesthetic and specifically novelistic *flaw* in your chosen structure—rather than a new and wonderful structural/aesthetic development or recomplication.

A stylistic dictum against redundancy commands us never to use the same word twice for the same object in the same phrase, or even the same few sentences—one of the first stylistic rules the young writer will likely lift from the masters of nineteenth-century novelistic prose. (One of my favorite utterances in English: "This sentence is filled with redundancies, tautologies, pleonasms, and unnecessary repetitions.") The informal rule against redundancy is a dramatic operationalization of the insight poststructuralist critics have been articulating for more than twenty years: nothing is—or can be (*pace*, O ghost of Ayn Rand)—absolutely identical to itself, so that the very act of naming an object, as it allows us to consider certain aspects of it, forces us to consider other aspects the very moment we believe ourselves to be (re-)naming it . . .

After all my grumblings above, the opening pages of Morrison's novel (that is to say, a step beyond the tacked-on silly prologue from the presumed school reader and the sensational evocation of what will turn out to be a pretty strained "plot"), with Frieda, Claudia, Claudia's cold, and their mother, the initial pages of "Autumn," are brilliant.

They inspire the most conservative critic within us to cry out, "They're authentic. They're real. They're wonderful writing"— and to cry it without trammels grown from any liberal embarrassments. Once we pass the scene with Pecola's sudden and frightening onset of menstruation, and Pecola's return to her own house, however, the book loses focus. From there on, it oscillates between unconnected portraits and narrative preachments that do not cohere.

The whole first half of the book would have been stronger if (explains Ms. Sand, before going off to a meeting in her role as minister of culture, her actual title for a while during the Revolution of 1848), after the menstruation scene, Morrison had returned, with authority, directly to the story of Pecola's parents and written the rest of the tale in chronological order.

By the book's end, Morrison's "love" for those characters, who perform some of the more repellent actions in the book, strikes me as lunatic—or, at any rate, morally imbecile.

(An author expressing a stupid, sentimental opinion about a reprehensible character does *not* redeem that character!)

I said that everything about Pecola feels thin. That includes her rape by her father.

Two of the strongest sections of writing in the novel are, first, the one that presents Pecola's mother Pauline's life story up through Cholly's encounter with his own estranged father and its emotional aftermath and, second, the section that presents Cholly's own life story. But when, a page or two later, Cholly leaps on his twelve-year-old daughter as she washes dishes at the sink, scratching her calf with her toe (as her mother had scratched hers, thirteen years before, thus identifying the rape as a distorted reenactment of Cholly's seduction of Pauline), then conveniently disappears, I don't buy it—not from the man Morrison has portrayed, not from the boy she's described him as. It's another fake, done to make something happen—and something socially significant—and by a purely external measure at that.

When I step back from *The Bluest Eye* and survey its weaknesses and, yes, its strengths, what it actually seems to be about is Claudia, a very young, black lesbian, with her older sister Frieda, in the small 1951 Ohio town of Lorain (*not* 1941!), who is more or less in love with the life and sensuality of *all* the women in the community.

This is what the book starts off as—and that start is wonderfully and gloriously rich.

At one point, however (p. 26), Claudia wants to go look at Mr. Henry's girly magazines (a perfectly understandable desire for a young lesbian to have), but her older sister won't let her. Practically from that sentence, the book transforms into a cascade of more or less angry fantasies directed against everyone and everybody around Claudia in the town, because she feels she is being stymied from expressing that awe and wonder directly toward its wonted object. In those fantasies, the love slips out nevertheless—how could it not? Because the anger is never acknowledged as her own, however, it is not aesthetically focused. It is not allowed to cohere with mature observation into the strong form of a novel: Claudia is never allowed to grow up and work at forming the material conditions that will let her desires become real—and thus she is locked in an infantile attack on (or, in the case of the three whores, Cholly, and Soaphead Church, an infantile defense of) the desires of everyone else. Now this is what the text alone (to me) speaks of.

To go and suggest this is because of some imaginary construct to be found nowhere in the text, a presumed authorial conflation of Morrison and Claudia that has internalized too much social fear is the sort of arrogant armchair psychology that should make any critic stand up and shout, "Intentional fallacy! Intentional fallacy!" But had I been in a writers' group with a writer who produced such a work, certainly I think it would be reasonable to ask if such fear was involved—though I would also feel obliged to accept whatever answer I was given. And that includes "No." Which still does not change that complex affect the text goads me toward.

Morrison's "Afterword" makes it clear how much she identified, at least for a time, with the insane Soaphead Church. But what she has succeeded in doing is punishing herself (for her lesbian desire?) by making herself a repressed-male-pedophilic-homosexual-psychotic-nutcase, instead of the full-flowering articulate and intelligent lesbian consciousness that Claudia initially presents in embryo.

When the narrator of the novel then turns around and says that she loves Soaphead—in the same pages as she calls Cholly's feelings for his raped daughter love—it seems nearer to the judgment of an angry child intent on outraging, than to writerly compassion grown from an understanding of the grinding forces of the social systems that produce evil. But can a writer's voice ever achieve either so that, in the reading, there is no interpretive slippage? I suspect not.

The closing dialogue between the split selves inhabiting Pecola's presumably shattered mind reads like another authorial shuck. Again, I don't believe either voice is Pecola's. Both are, rather, versions of Claudia's—the shattered voice of a literate woman who has not been allowed *by the author* to speak as a coherent subject. Neither voice is mad. Neither voice is particularly poor. Neither voice is illiterate. The split between them registers as (another authorial) self-protective device, so that we will not recognize it as Morrison's/Claudia's and will rather *attribute* it to Pecola. (Pecola is mad; this voice is "schizophrenic"; therefore this is Pecola talking to herself)—although, because of tone, diction, and rhythm, I cannot fit it with Pecola as the novel has presented her. Well, literature is a game played naked—so that we can receive the wounds it deals us. It cannot take refuge in such self-protective moves.

The Bluest Eye is a talented but radically underachieved novel. When it sings, who can fail to be lured out over memory's unstable waters? Because it *is* talented, it speaks clearly of half a dozen possibilities of the ideal form(s) for some of its material. But in all cases, to achieve such a form, it would have to have been a different book.

Whether because of white racist tropes (and, yes, some feminist clichés: I do *not* mean feminist concepts; I mean clichés—phrases and images from which the ideas that once made them rich and quick have been drained by repetition, easy emotions —negative or positive—and critical exhaustion), as well as simple aesthetic slovenliness in their presentation (which, again, doesn't mean Morrison didn't work *hard* on what she *did* present), this is not a book in which Morrison comes anywhere near producing a satisfactory (to me) novelistic vision.

In the midst of such a critique, I find myself recalling Randall Jarrell's quip: "A novel is a fiction of a certain length that has something wrong with it." Perhaps such criticism as mine is too easy. It's much harder to write a book. Yet, like the singing of opera, like the writing of poetry, though we are formed by lesser works as much as by greater ones, we are finally only *permanently interested* in what takes place at the highest level of accomplishment.

I begrudge no one his or her enjoyment of Morrison's novel. Still, I feel obliged to say: If a reader thinks this story gives an accurate or even a meaningful portrait either of the subjective lives of dark-skinned blacks or of light-skinned blacks, that reader knows none of us. And that goes for black readers as well as white.

As a black man with a twenty-three-year-old black daughter in racist America (and my daughter had a white mother), I'm bothered by a book that quietly dramatizes notions of "racial purity" (with all but one of its villains neurotic mixed-blood blacks) and quite articulately presents fantasizing about being other than you are as a first step into madness.

As a black father who is also gay, I find the making of Soaphead Church into a repressed homosexual who goes after little girls gratuitous, counterintuitive, and thus, as a narrative move, lunatic.

If any of these faults were idiosyncratic with Morrison alone, they would not be worth mentioning. If, as novelistic strategies, they were original with her, they wouldn't *be* flaws. Quite as much as they mar Morrison's book, they mar Dashiell Hammett's *The Maltese Falcon* and Frank Herbert's *Dune* and Ursula K. Le Guin's *The Dispossessed*—three novels in genres wholly unrelated to Morrison's. They are flaws in Morrison's novel *because* they were already flaws in the novel form when she began to write her own—flaws in the nation's sense of narrative and narration. (If I were criticizing Scott Heim's *Mysterious Skin* or Alice Walker's *The Third Life of Grange Copeland*, much of my critique would sound distressingly the same.) These are the same criticisms I have of the last half-dozen MFA theses I have read in committee.

What makes art good is the ways in which it is new, unique, and exciting. What makes it bad is always a socially shared failing, a socially contoured cleaving to a path of least resistance—in thought, in style, in structure. It is not in its differences from some ideal form that Morrison's novel fails me as a reader, but in the ways it is like so many others—and not those written in 1830 either, but rather those written in the past thirty, fifty, seventy years.

If I speak of an "ideal form" for the material, it's a form originality alone might have made manifest.

Well, it's two days later. The snow has retreated. Branches that dipped to join the white ground have now, many of them, broken under the weight. The campus is scattered with fallen limbs. Hedges that were not there a week ago mound the edge of roads and driveways, full of oak leaves rather than nonde-ciduous needles. But we are progressing into the new landscape, which changes slowly about us.

Sitting here in my office, I have to run downstairs and photo-copy a set of handouts for my class (on Hart Crane), get this en-velope in the mail, run home, get in the shower, and get driven to my reading at Shuler Books . . .

Which is precisely where I was in my letter to you when I came from Shuler's after a pleasant postreading dinner (at, I kid you not, the Travelers' Restaurant and Tuba Museum—fifty an-cient tubas, omphiclides, euphoniums, and even the odd double-belled trombone, unpolished and gone dark with a decade's pa-tina, hung over smoky yellow walls) with Tess, Lister, Carry, and Dennis, and wandered into West Yakely Hall (where the East Yakely mailboxes are) to pick up the mail, and found yours of 25 October.

What a fine letter! What a useful letter! And I'm going to tell you exactly how.

First of all, the reminder in your letter that I was stuck at chapter 22 in my own novel here when last I wrote you is won-derfully freeing.

I am now in the midst of chapter 26—and of course feeling just as bogged down as I was before. I was all but overwhelmed with the feeling that I was simply making no progress, no prog-ress, no progress at all.

Your letter reminds me forcefully that I am.

Each of my chapters runs between eight and twelve pages. (I'm taking a lesson from Dickens—one I've resisted for years. But this novel demands it—and I think it's working.) And I am on chapter 26—I really am!

It goes slowly—slowly. But that's because every time I write another two to four pages, I have to go back and rewrite the last four or five chapters.

I'm delighted that you're making progress with your own work. It stands as a beacon that draws me on.

I finally got to and through Pater's *Plato and Platonism*. It was quite as wonderful as Bloom hinted in his essay. In fact it was better. Really, it's the best book I've read about anything in the last three years. For someone with a philosophical bent,

it's a wonderfully clarifying, useful book. (Pater is clearly a polite anti-Platonist and respectfully on the side of Heraclitus. You
can tell that he, too, privileges the desire and myth-drenched
Phaedrus over the systematic and exhaustive *Republic*, though he
spends a whole chapter elucidating the latter.) For the week after
I read it, I kept wandering around and wondering: why didn't
somebody turn me onto this twenty-five years ago? Boy, would
my intellectual life have been easier! All those Platonic terms
—*ousia*, *aporia*, even *pharmakon*—that Derrida and Heidegger
discuss, I now realize, are not terms they lifted out of the text
by themselves. Here's Pater, in 1893, talking about the same terms,
giving me their contexts—in Greek and in English—where they
occur; and you realize this is all part of a tradition, a dialogue
that stretches back well into the nineteenth century and before.
I learned what the traditional difference between "memory" and
"remembrance" is—things that make reading those translations
a lot easier. Indeed, it precipitated a kind of Walter Pater binge.
By now, I've gotten through a couple of biographies, a couple
of modern studies. I just learned that Djuna Barnes might have
taken the title of the fifth chapter of *Nightwood*, "Watchman,
What of the Night," from the title and opening line of a "long
poem" in Spensereans that Pater wrote in the summer of 1858,
just before his nineteenth birthday. It opens, "Watchman, what
of the night? So asks my soul / In whisper'd fear. Watchman,
what of the night?" His "unofficial" biographer Thomas Wright
discusses it (and quotes a niggling few lines) in the seventeenth
chapter of the first book of his two-volume 1907 biography,
The Life of Walter Pater. (More probably, of course, *both* got it
from Isaiah.) I get an enjoyable feeling when, in my reading, I
come across a piece or a passage that I realize some other writer,
whose work I know, *must* have read—a feeling as though, for a
little, I'm part of a community that spans years but that is still
as close as a good friend in the next room. And I've been brows-
ing over Pater's "Imaginary Portraits" and essays in no particular
order.

Well, right now I have to arrange for a ride to the airport
in a couple of days—at some unearthly time like five in the
morning—to fly off to Florida and abandon Dennis for three
weeks (and with a quick weekend-long return on November 15,

to teach a makeup class, then back to Florida the next day), to do a fiction workshop for the Florida Atlantic Center for the Arts.

Also, at this point, I have fifteen brand new papers to mark, *Beloved* to (re)read (at) for a class I'm visiting tomorrow morning (Friday) at nine—and the rest of chapter 26 to finish. Picture a breathless, overweight gay man, with a beard and a cane, climbing an endless rocky rise. In the snow . . .

Write lots and lots more.

I so much enjoy it when you do.

> All good thoughts
> For all good things—
>
> (*signed:*) Samuel R. Delany

Dear R—,

I received your letter of February 20, with the enclosed poems, news clippings, biographical statement, photograph, and the opening twenty pages of your novel, *Time of Our Regret*. Your request for help was moving. Your basic question seems, in effect, How does a writer go about achieving a literary reputation? It's a question I've been asked before—a number of times by writers writing me more or less out of the blue, as you have. It's a question that always surprises me, as I don't perceive myself to be a writer who's made a very considerable one on my own. The vast majority of my thirty-odd books have appeared only in the most disposable mass-market paperback editions. When they're reviewed—say, in the *New York Times Book Review*—they're always covered in group reviews devoted to science fiction or other genre writing. (The one exception: in the "Fiction in Brief" section a black reviewer dismissed my recent collection of three long stories as not as good as the *Cosby Show*.) More times than not, when people mention me in print, they misspell my name—as indeed you misspelled it in your letter. Though I've had one book that sold a million copies in paperback over a dozen-odd years in print, I've never had a best seller (which means, at this point, a two-million sale in paperback in eighteen months or under—a sales level reached regularly by any one of a hundred writers, King, Koontz, Ludlum, Sheldon, Plain, Grisham, etc.). And though I have been averaging a book a year for more than thirty years, I can't make anything near a decent living from my writing alone.

Even from the little part of it that shows in the photograph of you that you included, the pleasant and charming apartment in which you sit (I assume it's your own; forgive me if it is not) is *much* nicer than mine. If I may broach the self-evident (and also, perhaps, overstep the bounds of manners into what may well be presumption), I must mention that—again assuming it's yours—clearly such an apartment represents time, effort, attention, concern, and work. One difference between your situation and mine may simply be (and if you are not at least willing to start from this consideration, however unpleasant it is, you will never be able to move on from it to more useful and positive conclusions) that when I was about nineteen years old, I decided in no uncertain terms that all my first energies would henceforth go directly into my writing. Only when whatever piece I was working on was as fine as I could possibly make it, would I put any leftover energy whatsoever (and only that) into living what others might think a decent and reasonable life. Family, friends, lovers, education, and even my health have all taken second place to my writing.

A lover of eight years once demanded of me, "Don't you ever think about *anything* other than writing?" some two months before we finally separated for good.

A platonic roommate who rented a room in my apartment, a young man who himself had already written and published two novels by the time he'd moved in, told me, once he'd moved out, he'd given up writing fiction because, after living in the same apartment with me for two years: "I realized, watching you, just how hard someone had to work if he wanted to be a really *good* writer. I decided I just *didn't* want to work that hard. So I've made up my mind to go do something else with my life." And he did.

I remember my two-and-a-half-year-old daughter, in tears, running up to me at my typewriter, grabbing my leg, and pulling on it, crying: "Daddy! Daddy! Don't *write*! Don't *write*!"

If I'd organized my life in a more reasonable way, with priorities laid out in what most people would assume was a reasonable manner (where, at age fifty-one, I could have had a photograph snapped of me in my apartment with a background that looked like yours—rather than mine: unpainted for more than fifteen years, all the furniture even older, and no square inch not overflowing with books and papers), I would probably have published only half the novels I have and none of the nonfiction. The nine (instead of eighteen) novels I'd have put out would certainly not be any better than my first nine actually were. Possibly they might have been notably worse. Though some of them might have won the same awards that two of those novels won (and, again, I must mention: the several thousand dollars *you've* won for your poetry is far more than I have for my fiction: from the Hugo and the Nebula to [the one I'm proudest of] the William Whitehead Memorial Award for a Lifetime's Contribution to Lesbian and Gay Writing, none of the awards I've ever won has ever carried a penny with it), I suspect my reputation today would be precisely what it was in 1968—which is to say, only if you were the most committed, devoted, and fanatical of science fiction fans would you have ever heard of me. Though it is somewhat arrogant of me to bring all this up, it's still necessary at least to consider the possibility that such decisions, early on, *may* have had something to do with why I am as far along as you perceive me to be—and, indeed, why you are not.

Having said that, it's also possible that I have *no* concept of the sacrifices you have made for your work. For me to assume that mine are any greater than yours *is* a presumption that may well be unforgivable. My only point is that every artist—not to mention you or me—must begin by saying: Is there any more I *could* have done? Is there anymore I must do now, in terms of the work itself?

To repeat myself: your letter moved me, and moved me more than I expect to be moved by such appeals. But many of us at fifty or thereabouts go through . . . well, certainly we cannot call it a "mid-life crisis." It's more a two-thirds life reevaluation. With an increased sense of limited time, with an awareness that we have *perhaps* two decades of functional working time left us (or two-and-a-half if we're *very* lucky—and because we have lived through five of them, we realize just how short a decade is), we find ourselves having to reassess just what our priorities are. If the making of art survives as one of them—or perhaps even the first of them—we decide not only that that is what we must do, but also that we must be recognized for it, socially and broadly.

During the Renaissance, artists were assumed to be ambitious for wealth and renown. The artist who shuns all that and cares only for his work is a modernist invention—and probably, when all is said and done, a figure of sour grapes. Whether we act on it or not, most writers spend a good deal of time pondering the mechanics by which literary reputations grow. (I certainly have.) And, yes, fifty or thereabouts is often the age where our thoughts turn from passing speculation to serious consideration.

I'm enclosing with this letter an interview that I gave not quite a year ago.* Its ostensible topic is the canon and canon formation. But for anyone who can read, it's fairly evident that its real object is the problem of literary reputations. It is very much my own first attempt to organize my thinking on the topic. You might want to read it now, because the rest of this letter will use terms and concepts from the article and will assume you are familiar with them. If the article is my attempt to open the question, the remainder of this letter is, as it were, my attempt to bring it on home.

Basically the problem of the writer's reputation is, How, during your lifetime, do you generate as many and as effective literary markers as possible?

I'm deeply committed—and it goes along with that early nineteen-year-old decision I wrote about—to the idea that the fundamental and most important way to generate such markers is by producing work of such high quality that it impels men and women so inclined to write about it and explain to the general reader why it strikes them as being of such extraordinary merit. This in turn inspires others to read it, among whom are some, again, who, because of its quality, will also write about it, producing more markers—and more readers. This process is helped along by the addition of verbal markers—the word-of-mouth praise that also accompanies fine art as it moves through the audience of concerned readers and viewers. I'm quite sure that this is the *fundamental* process that has produced the titanic reputation of, say, Shakespeare. In the best of all possible worlds, the ordinary practice of book reviewing ought to be enough to initiate it, without any other particular interference.

Anyone with any real experience of the literary world knows, however, that this is an ideal far more often missed than attained. Add advertising and general hype, and more often the

* "Inside and Outside the Canon," see page 337.

process propels mediocre work and worse onto best seller lists and makes a lot of money for the publishers of writers of ordinary talent or less. Again and again this process apparently fails to stabilize the reputations of high-quality fiction and poetry with the general readership.

Is there anything that the writer can actively do about this?

Do you ask the literary acquaintances who've accrued to you over the years to review your work? Do you write begging letters to them with requests for reviews? Do you enclose heartfelt entreaties to understand the work's worth and descriptions of your own deserving state? From time to time, I've been tempted to do all this. (What writer hasn't?) But I've never been able to bring myself actually to do so. This is largely for two reasons. First, I know how much I resent it when people ask the same of me. Second, I know too much about the editorial structure of newspapers and literary journals of any substance that actually print reviews. Precisely to prevent the logrolling that would occur if people made such requests regularly, reviewers are given little or no power to select *what* they review. Rather, the books are assigned by an editor, half of whose job is to stay aloof from such requests and to use some more or less objective method for assigning books to reviewers.

About ten years ago, I got to see a rather sad example of just this. I'd been invited to an East Side party for the Italian critic and novelist Umberto Eco, whom I had met and rather enjoyed on several academic panels in which we had been involved. Among the people at the party was Robert Silver, then editor of the *New York Review of Books*. While I was standing around in a group of people, including Eco and Silver, Silver told Eco: "You know, we'd really like to have you write some reviews for the *New York Review*." And Umberto allowed as how he would greatly enjoy that.

Later, when Umberto and I were alone, he said to me: "You know what I would really like to review for them? Teresa de Lauretis's new book, *Alice Doesn't*. I think it's really brilliant."

Teresa de Lauretis was a mutual friend of ours—indeed, she had first introduced me to Umberto, some years before. Her new book was indeed brilliant. I had read it in manuscript, and it *was* a wonderfully exciting academic performance.

"I've actually already written a review of Teresa's book. I wasn't sure where I'd place it. I think I'm just going to send it to Silver in a couple of days and see if he'll use it."

"Did Teresa ask you to write it?" I asked him.

"No! Of course she didn't," Umberto objected. "She sent me a copy. But she certainly didn't ask me to write anything. I was so impressed when I read it, though, I sat down and wrote off a review straight away!"

Although I didn't say so, the problem I saw immediately with Umberto's reviewing Teresa's book was that, years before, in Italian, Teresa had written the first book *about* Eco—in Italian and published in Italy—and a very praiseful book it had been. If Silver realized this, I knew there wasn't a rat's chance of his accepting a review by Umberto of Teresa!

Europe—with its individual nations—is much smaller than America. Because of that, people don't even try to avoid such interconnections; but that was one of the things that the *New York Review of Books* was started precisely *to* avoid.

Umberto sent his review in. It was rejected.

Teresa's book was never reviewed in the *New York Review*. That's sad, because it *was* a fine book and certainly deserved intelligent consideration. But I suspect there was a greater chance of its being reviewed there if Umberto (with the best intentions in the world) had *not* tried to review it himself—the work of a personal friend and someone who had already written (and at book length!) favorably about him.

Looking at my own career, I note that perhaps three times over my thirty-five-year career and thirty-odd books (which probably average about a dozen reviews apiece), books of mine were—quite accidentally—assigned to personal friends of mine for review. (That's three times out of the c. 324 reviews I've received—less than one out of a hundred.)

Once this produced a perfectly balanced and intelligent review.

Once it produced the *most* embarrassing review of my career, where the reviewer spent the bulk of her (lengthy!) article explaining that we *were* friends and therefore how unqualified she was to review the book at all—which novel had been assigned to her *because* she knew me! By the end of the piece, she'd made herself and me both sound like . . . well, not very interesting writers.

Once, actually, it produced the single most glorious, complimentary, and strongest of reviews I've *ever* had—one I shall be grateful to that friend for writing for the rest of my life.

Still, looking at all three, clearly the outcome was a matter of luck. Luck, I've learned, can be bad as easily as it can be good. The hardest thing to accept about luck is that it *is* out of our control. If it wasn't, it wouldn't *be* luck. The best a writer can do with luck is appreciate it when it runs for you and ignore it when it runs against you. Both happen in the course of every career.

About a decade ago, I received a letter and a package of poems about the same thickness as the one you sent—from a man who was also in his early fifties. I suspect he was inspired by many of the same concerns that inspired you to write me and that, indeed, urged me to write the interview I've sent you and that now impel me to continue writing about the topic in more personal terms, in this letter. The man was an academic, and, through a decade of readings by writers visiting his own university, visits which he had often been involved in setting up, he'd amassed an impressive mailing list.

His letter announced (the only word for it) that, at age fifty-two, he had completed his aesthetic apprenticeship, paid his artistic dues, and was now going to spend the next three years establishing his reputation as the Major American Poet he knew himself to be. Included was a sheaf of his mature poetic work. He was mailing this letter and copies of his poems to a hundred well-known writers. We were all instructed (believe me, there was no "request" involved) to read his work, write about it in major periodicals, and pass it on to others with instructions to write about it, explaining that this was the finest poetry being written in the country, for reasons which would surely be self-evident to anyone looking it over.

The letter's simple arrogance was extremely off-putting. I'm sure more than ninety-five percent of the recipients tossed it into the garbage without a further look. That's what I did. But an hour later, my curiosity got the better of me. "Well," I thought, "writers have been madmen before. I wonder what he's actually writing." As well, beneath the arrogance, I detected the real concern that hits all of us at that age to inscribe our positions in the world with real and readable strokes—though certainly the accents in which he presented himself sounded crazed.

I pulled his envelope from the trash basket under my word processor and ferreted out the sheaf of poems.

I started reading—but, after a few lines, stopped: *because,* I realized, I was reading with the foregone conclusion I would find his poems as pretentious and laughable as his letter.

I got up, walked up and down the hall a few times, and tried to clear my mind of preconceptions: "If you're going to bother to read them at all," I told myself, "you must ignore the context entirely and read the poems as if they were on the pages of some book in your local bookstore. That's only sensible. Otherwise, it's not worth the effort."

After five minutes in which I tried to clear my mind of any *parti pris,* I sat down and again began to read.

They were not terrible.

The five years I'd spent as a poetry editor for *The Little Magazine* came back to me. Two or three of the poems I could actually see us as having published, had they come in an ordinary submission. Most of them, however, seemed painfully thin. The cumulative effect, after twenty or thirty pages, was not that of an exciting and articulated vision, but rather a lack of verbal invention and a fairly weak technique in the service of no particularly interesting ideas, images, or esthetic concerns. I say, during the time I'd been a poetry editor, I might have published perhaps three of them. But I also suspect that in the month after I'd printed them, I would have forgotten them.

There are currently many contemporary poets today whose work I find repeatedly and richly exciting. Many come from completely opposing schools. I select specifically a handful from those I've only read but never met or heard read: Mark Doty, Philip Levine, Eleanor Lehrman, Ron Silliman, Jay Wright, Lyn Hejinian . . .

I think I was as open to poetic excitement as a reader in such a situation could be. But I simply didn't find it in this man's work. I (and ninety-nine other writers) received that letter and package about a decade ago. Needless to say, the man has published *very* little since—and has *not* become a major American poet. I doubt seriously whether you'll find him on most concerned readers' lists of the five or six hundred most interesting *minor* poets around—a list on which you might find several readers placing you!

Finally, I just don't think there's any way for a writer to *compel* literary markers into being—other than by refining the quality of (and increasing the energy within) his or her own work. Once, for whatever reasons, literary markers start to arrive in numbers beyond the usual array of reviews, there *may* be things one should do (or not do) that might help them along (or, indeed, hinder them). But here, if only because the situation is as rare as it is, there's probably even more argument about what, exactly, those things are.

Because I am a critic as well as a creative writer, when another critic (or a Ph.D. student, or what-have-you) approaches me and says she or he is interested in writing about me, I try to be as gracious and as helpful as I can. At the same time, I try not to get in the way of the project with my own opinions. I believe in absolute critical freedom. Though I want to be helpful, I don't want to be intimidating—or to let my helpfulness *become* intimidating for a writer who wants to express negative judgments. Many of the great High Modernist writers—Pound, Joyce,* Beckett, Wyndham Lewis, and Djuna Barnes—were famous for rigorously having nothing to do with their critics. They refused to speak to them or help them in any way. And the writers of the fifties and sixties (notably J. D. Salinger and Thomas Pynchon) have as famously followed in their footsteps. In some cases, for example Pynchon's, this makes the writer an even greater object of interest and curiosity. But Salinger, to take an opposing case, while he might have dominated the sixties, though he's certainly still in print, has been more and more reduced to a single novel about a single disaffected upper-middle-class adolescent male, *Catcher in the Rye*, which, skillful as it is, many working-class high school students still forced to

---

* Joyce made a famous exception for Stuart Gilbert's *Ulysses, A Study* (1930).

read it find harder and harder to relate to with each passing year, in the age of gay rights, the Internet, AIDS, and crack.

Myself, I've always wondered which stance—helpful cooperation or aloof withdrawal—is, in the long run, likely to produce more (and better quality) markers. But finally, I think it's a matter of a given writer's personal temperament. Were I not a critic myself, easily I might have followed the aloof isolationist road; but, because I am, I identify with my critics and try to be as helpful to them as I would want someone I was writing about to be to me.

Over the past decade-and-a-half some eight people have approached me, claiming to want to write about my work at book-length. I've been cordial and welcoming to them all, offering to answer questions, provide copies of difficult-to-find material, and even to suggest interpretations (if they're asked for). Five of these eight books—often after I'd put in quite a bit of effort from my side—simply never materialized.

Three of them have indeed come out. Two others have also appeared, where the writers did *not* contact me or solicit my help in any way.

By far the worst of the whole bunch, by all general accounts, is Seth McEvoy's *Samuel R. Delany* (New York: Ungar, 1986). McEvoy's book was once reviewed in a Vancouver literary supplement under the headline "Sub-Literate Sludge." Because, as I said, I believe in absolute critical freedom, I refuse to read the final draft of—or comment on—any work about me until it appears. To repeat: I feel the critic must be free to say whatever he or she believes without any intimidation from me. But in this case, I've been smarting for my principles ever since. Sadly, McEvoy is the single writer writing about me to whom I offered the *most* help.

George Slusser's *The Delany Intersection* and Douglas Barbour's *Worlds Out of Words: The SF Novels of S. R. Delany* were the two books written without consulting me at all. Until they were published, I didn't know they existed. Both are basically praiseful. Slusser's—done completely without my help—is probably the best of the five that has appeared. But there are errors of fact, date, and (yes, even) interpretation (of the "Delany intends" sort) in both Slusser and Barbour—errors that might have been corrected by a half-hour phone call just to check. As a critic myself, I find that sad.

Until very recently I have always wondered if I weren't doing myself more harm than not by being so accommodating to my critics. But I have a writer friend who does biographies—and, in my own opinion, they are first-rate. A couple of years ago, she was commissioned by her publisher to do a biography of South African–born writer Doris Lessing. My friend was a great admirer of Lessing's work and looked forward to the project. But when she wrote to Lessing that she was undertaking it, Lessing wrote back—in typical High Modernist fashion—that she would not cooperate in any way, would answer no questions, and had already asked all her personal friends not to speak to my friend or offer any help. My friend's publisher was perfectly happy to have an "unauthorized" biography appear. But two years later, after several false starts, my friend has gotten nowhere with her book. She is seriously considering abandoning the project. Had Ms. Lessing cooperated, I suspect, she would have had a finely written and sympathetic biography about her—and certainly one that would not have hurt her literary reputation and that might even have helped reaffirm it.

Being friendly to one's critics or being hostile to them can both inspire *and* discourage the production of markers, so that finally it's the writer's own temperament and personal sense of tact that must determine how the situation is to be dealt with.

At this point, it's necessary to note that there are different types of markers. And different types of markers produce different effects.

There are at least three orders of marker I can locate.

The first order is the verbal order produced by readers, at all levels of sophistication, low and high, speaking to one another: "I really liked this book. It was truly extraordinary . . . !" We can call these Marker Ones.

The second order of marker is the written marker that analyzes the excellences of the work somewhere in print where others may read it. We can call those Marker Twos.

The third order of literary marker is the publicity-oriented marker: the personality piece, the newspaper or magazine profile, or what have you. These we'll call Marker Threes. Marker

Threes might even be said to extend as far as any further publicity, even unto the newspaper reports of movie deals or TV versions of one's work. Fundamentally, however, all these markers work in the same way, though certainly some—like having a movie made from your novel—are quite a bit stronger than the simple paragraph about writer X or poet Y that appears in your local neighborhood give-away sheet. But, for our purposes, I don't see any need to distinguish them with a new number. With the application of great amounts of money (far more than the advertising budget any book of *mine* has ever commanded), you can, indeed, move directly into Marker Threes; but while such markers can be used to create/promote substantial money-making properties (the Sidney Sheldons, the Belva Plains, the John Grishams), they don't produce *literary* reputations unless the Marker Twos come along. Once the Sheldons/Plains/Grishams have retired with their millions, no one will ever speak of their novels again, save as economic or sociological phenomena. With all the millions of copies sold, they simply haven't produced a high enough proportion of pleasure-to-time-spent-in-reading among literate readers to generate the necessary density of Marker Twos that preserve a book for the next generation of readers.

The lesson this leaves us with is, once again, that the only thing we can be reasonably sure will enhance our reputation is to write as best we can; anything else is provisional, secondary, and will depend purely on personal temperament—most likely filtered through the idiosyncratic butterfly effects of chaos theory, where the negative attempt to avoid fame is as likely to be as effective in producing some positive results as trying to achieve it directly, when, as is so rarely the case, either one has *any* effect in that direction at all.

With such a situation, the only advice anyone can give is to be true to your work in every way possible—and true to yourself as the worker who has produced it.

From time to time, as I've already noted, all of us covet the effects of Marker Threes, deciding however momentarily that, if we could get them, the Marker Ones and Marker Twos would take care of themselves. But there really *is* a strain of naïveté in this notion. I give you an example from my own recent experience.

A month ago on February 11, the *New York Times*'s "Metro" section ran a front-page profile of me—indeed, I first assumed your own letter had begun as a response to that article. Only on rereading did I realize you hadn't mentioned seeing it; so that there was a chance you hadn't run across it. Such markers by themselves produce fairly large—but fairly soon forgotten—effects. Many of us are aware that among those effects is a kind of general energy field that may linger for some time, which, in itself, can magnify the effect of other markers—say written Marker Twos—if they come into being soon enough and register on the same people who encountered the Marker Three.

Despite this additive strength of Marker Threes, I'm still convinced that, without those Marker Twos, there's nothing one could call *literary* in the reputation produced. In literary terms, the strongest and most long-lasting effect comes from those Marker Twos (I say once again) *written* by sensitive men and women analyzing for the general reader the excellences of the work as they see them.

I first heard that the *Times* profile was to be done through a phone call from a young publicist named Stephanie, who worked for the paperback publisher of my most recent novel. She told me: "I've spoken to a reporter, and she's interested in doing a profile on you for the *Times* . . ."

I'd just assumed that, in her job as publisher's publicist, Stephanie had called the *Times* and managed to set it up. A week later I went through the entire interview and photo session under that impression. Once the article came out, I called Stephanie to thank her for arranging the whole thing. But in the midst of my effusions, she said: "Oh, no! I didn't call them. They called *me*—about *you*!" She laughed. "No, I couldn't have swung that for one of our authors if they hadn't approached me about you first."

Later that same morning, I called the reporter to convey my thanks to her: "By the way," I asked, "what decided you folks there at the *Times* to do the piece? The day you were here interviewing me, I'd just assumed it was because Stephanie had been goading you. But she tells me *you* came to *her* . . ."

"Well," the reporter said, "I just kept running into people who really liked your work; and running into interesting articles about your books. I was considering the piece, along with a number of others, when I went to visit an old friend of mine I hadn't seen in years. It seems you were the favorite author of her very bright younger brother. He talked quite intelligently to us for half an hour, one evening, about what he thought you were doing in your work that no one else was. That, I guess, was finally what pushed me over the edge."

What the reporter made me realize articulately is something that I suppose I've known all along. In literary terms, Marker Ones produce Marker Twos; and Marker Ones and Marker Twos can produce Marker Threes (e.g., her article on me in the *Times*). But while the field effect of Marker Threes can stabilize the effects of Marker Ones and Marker Twos, it can't *produce* them.

Another example more immediate: The young man at the end of the table in the student health food cafeteria of the Union at the University of Massachusetts, where I am drafting this letter right now in my notebook, is reading a copy of John Kennedy O'Toole's 1980 Pulitzer Prize–winning novel, *A Confederacy of Dunces*. I just looked up and noticed, because a moment ago, in his reading, suddenly he laughed out loud!

I've never read O'Toole's book myself, though it was a favorite novel of a friend of mine back in the early eighties. The Pulitzer the novel won (fundamentally an order Three Marker) is certainly what has stabilized the book in the social landscape (if not my own memory), so that copies are still available, and the book has remained in print for sixteen years, etc. But that spontaneous laugh from the young man at the end of the table a minute ago while reading it (the simplest sort of *pre*verbal Marker One! And he has no idea I'm writing this) is what's likely to push me, after sixteen years, over the brink actually to purchase a copy myself and read it. Should my delight in it be equal to his (or to my friend's of a decade back), I *might* just produce a Marker Two, that is, an essay on the book or a mention of it in an essay on something else; that is, if I don't produce some more verbal Marker Ones in the course of it: mentions to friends or students of the fine book I just read. But this, again, is how the process works. Higher level (i.e., more publicity-laden) markers can produce a field in which lower-level markers can operate more effectively over longer periods of time. But only lower-order markers can generally lead to higher-level markers—over whatever period—in any way that stabilizes the work's literary worth.

If real and considerable aesthetic pleasure is not regularly produced by the encounter of reader with text, the process I described above grinds to a halt the moment the publisher ceases to pour $75,000 a year into advertising (Marker Threes)—which, in most cases, is after the book has been out a single season.

This brings me to the most painful part of this exercise, where I must give my response to the work you've sent me. (Grit your teeth; I am not going to be kind.) Your poems show talent. They are clearly written and strongly felt. But I do not see much of the specific verbal invention and energy that make me want to chew them over, that make me walk around for days repeating lines to myself, or that warm me with the glow of a set of virtuoso performances carried out with soaring ease and linguistic panache. And this is what the best poetry demands. There is always the possibility that I am not your ideal reader. But I give you my judgment of their achievement, rather than waffle on about their promise (which *is* real, I assure you: but you know that) and potential. At fifty, we don't want to know what we *might* be doing, twenty years down the track. We want to know how the work strikes people now.

The novel opening displays perhaps the two most common faults for young writers that I know of—and *you* are not that young! It's structured in what I often call "a false flashback." The example of this I usually give for my creative writing classes is the following:

> The sun was shining through the leaves. Little Red Riding walked through the woods, carrying her basket happily. And as she walked, she remembered her mother, in the kitchen of their little cottage that morning, handing her the basket and telling her to take it to her grandmother.
>
> "Now don't stop in the woods to talk with anyone, especially wolves," her mother had said.

"Oh, no," Little Red Riding Hood had assured her mother. "I will go straight to grandmother's and not stop at all."

"Very good," her mother told her. "I hope you do. Otherwise you may get eaten."

Little Red Riding Hood was a little girl who lived in a cottage with her mother. She loved to play among the flowers. She loved to walk in the woods. Her Aunt Evelyn had first made the Riding Hood out of scarlet-dyed burlap one summer when a traveling Turkish peddler had brought through the village a load of Spanish saffron, which, combined with powdered copper, produced the most amazing reds in linens and cambrics . . .

This is the *most* awkward way possible (and the *least* effective way) to tell this story. The story does *not begin* in the woods. It begins *with the advent of the Turkish peddler*, proceeds to the kitchen of the cottage, and only *then* moves on to the woods.

Similarly, *your* narrator's story does not begin in the car on his way to his aunt's. It begins sometime in his childhood, possibly when he first had to spend any considerable time with his cousin Bone, or when he first starts going to the pool hall. Right now, however, in fragment after fragment, you're simply hunting around for your story's start. You must figure out where your story begins—then *tell* it from the beginning. Whether you are in first draft or in third, right now that's what militates most against your novel's ever getting published. There is a substantial rise in verbal energy once you start to write about the pool hall—for that reason alone, I'd begin there. (Always lead from your strength!) Tell us the story of Bone, Philly, and Leroy. Then—I assume it comes later—go on to Ali and Hiram. In the course of all this, we should learn what Hiram has done so that he can no longer face his aunt. His going home to see her (and stopping his car because he is unable to face her) is the *end* of your story. *Put* it at the end—where, having seen the causes, we will understand it and find it moving. Placed at the beginning where it is now, it's empty and merely confusing.

Stylistically, there's too much dull language—too many sentences like, "I kept turning left and right, looking through the windshield, the windows, peering to see how much of my old neighborhood was still recognizable to me at night"—sentences that tell what happened but don't manage to do anything else *but* that. It would work much better if you stated *what* he saw— what he recognized and what he didn't. Then we would have a picture of the neighborhood itself. Your sentences must tell about both the world *and* the character *at the same time*.

Writing in the twenties, the French poet Paul Valéry once said that he couldn't bear the idea of spending his life writing stories that were filled with sentences like "The Marquis went out at five o'clock." Your narrator's "turning left and right" is the modern equivalent of that dull, dull approach to language.

On the other hand, every once and a while you have a sentence which approaches true writerly life: "I was as scared as a cat in a room full of rocking chairs." Well, you need more of that and less of the other.

If the above is brutal, forgive me. Be aware that I could always be wrong. I am only one reader. Keep that in mind, too.

But even if I *did* find the work vivid, exciting, executed with narrative skill and authority, the final question is: What *could* I possibly do for you? Were you writing science fiction, pornography, or literary criticism (the three genres I write in), I could pass your work on to my own editors, each of whom specializes. But since you are writing poetry and general fiction—fields in which my own publication is nonexistent or minimal—there's nothing practical I can do for you, except tell you what I think is wrong with it, whatever my response.

You might do better to write to someone producing in your own genre or genres.

I have not mentioned the topic of racism, which you ask about in your letter, until now because—like homophobia—it's one of the most difficult to talk about objectively in terms of the part it plays in holding back the development of literary reputations. Certainly—like homophobia—it's real. Certainly its effects are devastating and ugly, when not outright criminal. But the fact over which the reality of racism must be inscribed is a simple and devastating truth: Among writers, everyone does not make it. Black or white, *most* people who write do not make it. Black or white, most people who are talented do not make it. Black or white, most people who are highly skilled do not make it. (W. H. Auden once observed, with great insight I think, "Most successful writers overvalue their intelligence and undervalue their talent.")

Art (to quote Valéry again) is a disproportionate act.

First, the time it takes to create a work of art is always disproportionate to the time it takes to perceive it. Consider the three months it took to paint a portrait that we look at for thirty seconds on the gallery wall. Think of the year and a half it took to write the novel we read in an evening or two.

Second, because the rewards that exist to be doled out are always based *on* the perception (and not the work), such rewards tend to be disproportionately small *to* the work that went into it.

This means that *every* artistic reputation that manages to come into being at all is going to be a highly idiosyncratic affair. Artistic reputations are *rare even among artists*—and, as such, are always complex and highly individual. There's no such thing as a general one. They do not have a common form. Thus the part racism will have played in the hindering (or development) of any given reputation is going to be idiosyncratic as well. To seek for an overall pattern to its effect is hopeless, other than to say that it is there—and is malevolent.

In 1967, the manuscript of a novel of mine was rejected for serialization in a science fiction magazine by a white editor because he did not think his readership "was ready for" a black protagonist. (The letter to my agent still exists.) Two years later, the same novel was sold to Bantam Books for a record price—the highest price to date ever paid for a paperback science fiction novel. But one could reasonably ask, *Would* the novel have commanded the price it did had it gone the ordinary route of so many science fiction novels, with serialization, hardcover, then paperback? Books that followed this standard path also got very standard prices. Was the fact that it came to the paperback publisher, Bantam Books, at a wholly different trajectory from the usual science fiction novel, responsible for the high price paid?

Was the overt and documentable racism of the editor a factor in the eventual greater monetary success of the novel?

Who knows? I certainly don't.

In order to combat racism, I've tried—whenever I am called on to judge a contest or officiate in any position where talent is to be judged (such as applicants to writing workshops I have been hired to teach)—to make a real pest of myself, finding out if blacks have been specifically encouraged to submit, if information about the contest or workshop has specifically been disseminated in black schools, black neighborhoods, black churches, places where aspiring black writers, men and women, can learn of it. If this has not been done, I hound folks to see that it is. (Or do it myself.) As I keep telling people, there's no pile of manuscripts on any desk in America that shouldn't be authored by *at least* twenty percent black writers. Anything less than that is your *guarantee* that, on some level, overt or covert, racism is at work. Having made myself a pest—and having tried to up the percentage of black submissions—I feel equally obliged to be scrupulously fair in any subsequent judgment I'm called on to make. I've read broadly over the range of black American writing, and, having grown up in Harlem and lived my life as a black American, I am open to and appreciative of both the rhetoric and the concerns often specific to the best black American writing—so that when black (or, indeed, other) writers turn to those concerns and employ that rhetoric, I don't feel I am in any way excluded from the readership.

The fact that you are writing, submitting, and winning awards means that, through whatever combination of luck, energy, enthusiasm (the early German Romantics thought inspired enthusiasm—*Begeisterung* ["be-spiritedness"]—was the sine qua non of the artist, even more than imagination or intelligence), talent, bravery, and ambition, you have already crashed through the greatest and most destructive hurdle racism sets in our way: the one that gives so many of us a self-image that says, "Who am I to think I could ever write anything worth reading, that I have something worth saying; or that anyone else might take joy in hearing it; how dare I think I have the right to speak, write, or be read." That's the general hurdle we all must face—our people more than most. (Although it is not the only effect of racism, certainly its largest effect today is that the black writer is often unable to find out about the contest, the new publishing program, the journal.) But that is the *only* general hurdle, I would hazard. From there on, every black writer's encounter with racism, though unavoidable, also tends to be idiosyncratic—which makes it particularly difficult to talk about in general terms, in the same way that each literary reputation is, beyond a certain point, idiosyncratic. Once we reach the idiosyncratic stage, you and I are still left with the responsibility to make our work, word by word, phrase by phrase, sentence by sentence, paragraph by paragraph, page by page, as finely wrought, as meticulously honest, as humanly felt as possible. Whether we begin a new piece as a writer with a reputation or without one, whether we are tyro or aging-pro, when we fail in this even the least bit, our work joins that slough of verbiage, much of which is published, most of which is not—and none of which matters.

I hope these reflections have not been too long to be of use or too painful to prompt you to either positive thought or action.

With all good wishes for all the best in all your future endeavors, I am

Sincerely yours,

(signed:) Samuel R. Delany

New York City
July 26, 1996

Dear S—,

Thank you for your letter.

I've read through the poems you sent and your story, "Dark Finale." It's rather unclear from your letter what sort of response you want. But since you've sent them, I must say, what first and most strongly strikes me about the pieces is that they are all from so long ago. When I teach creative writing, today I'm rather strict about not allowing students to submit old work at all. The only work we consider is what they are currently working on. The older the student, the stricter I am about this rule. But I'll get back to the reasons for that at the end of this letter.

The sad truth is, S—, most people are not writers.

This has nothing to do with literacy—or intelligence, or general culture.

There are people who can correct the grammar, spelling, diction, and style of a college English paper with the best of them —who are *still* not writers.

Indeed, most of what gets published in books, magazines, and newspapers is not written by real writers—which is one reason why so much of it is so bad.

What marks the writer—and we are still not talking about good writers versus bad writers—is that he or she writes. You say "Dark Finale"—from 1973—is your last completed fiction. My take on the tale is that it's not really a story at all: it's an essay or sermon (Nate's speech) embedded in an account of the prevalent black nationalistic ideas of the late sixties/early seventies. In short, it's two position papers put together. My suspicion is that it helped you, back at the time you wrote it or just after, to straighten out a lot of thoughts you were having about the difficult and uneasy relation between "high" culture, "white" culture, and "black" culture. Since you've sent me the piece, I will tell you the thoughts it evokes: I think the best thing the writer of that story could now do is to let the story lie, and take whatever understanding you have reached through it (whatever it is: it doesn't have to be the position either of your narrator *or* of Nate), and move on in the world to new situations where you can apply that knowledge. Because you once wrote that tale, if you are called on to explain yourself today, you'll probably be much more articulate about it than if, twenty-three years ago, you had *not* written it.

The poems come off a little better, but they still veer now and again into pompousness and sentimentality. There is talent there. There is even more intelligence. But from the quality of what you have sent me—and the fact that the most recent (dated) piece is eleven years old—I would suggest that you are not a writer.

(Were you to tell me that you had thousands of pages of journals on store, in which you had been keeping a detailed and daily account of your life, then there might be reason for me to revise the above.)

Writers are people who write. By and large, they are not happy people. They're not good at relationships. Often they're drunks. And writing—good writing—does not get easier and easier with practice. It gets harder and harder—so that eventually the writer *must* stall out into silence. The silence that waits for every writer and that, inevitably, if only with death (if we're *lucky,* the two may happen at the same time: but they *are* still two, and their coincidence is rare), the writer *must* fall into is angst-ridden and terrifying—and often drives us mad. (In a letter to Allen Tate, the poet Hart Crane once described writing as "dancing on dynamite.") So if you're not a writer, consider yourself fortunate.

You say that there are things in you that you want deeply to communicate. Fine. Through a job or through volunteer work, you should put yourself in a position where you are around the people, young or old or both, who need to hear what you have to say. You should work with them, demonstrate what you have to show them, *and* tell them—when they need to hear it.

I suspect that's what will give you the most satisfaction.

You also write that there are "not fully resolved" problems having to do with racism and attitudes toward sexuality in this society that still, today, impede you. Let me be blunt: I distrust such claims when people write to me using such phrases—and they often do. It's not that such problems don't exist. On the contrary. They are real and huge and oppressive conditions in this nation, and every black (not to mention gay) man and woman must deal with them, and deal with them from childhood on. Racism or homophobia may well have injured you or deflected you from where you tried to get to. How could it not have, if you are black and gay? But you should know it—know how they did it, and why. There should be nothing unresolved about them. To have a *not fully resolved* problem with racism or with homophobia strikes me about the same as having a not fully resolved problem with air or with gravity. These are total surrounds. We've known them too long and too well.

But let me get back to the writing. In brief, if you'd asked for my advice, it would be: Do it when it strikes you as something that will help you think through whatever you're involved in. When you have finished, put it aside and get on with your life. (I've been writing poetry like that for years. But, though, yes, it has helped me to work a few things out, I wouldn't dream of showing it to anyone. Certainly I wouldn't think of publishing it! When people ask me do I write poetry, I simply say no. And if you now went and told someone that I was "really a poet," then you'd be majorly misreading *and* misunderstanding what I am saying here. Which is to say: *All* civilized people write poetry from time to time. Both its reading and its writing are necessary to a civilized mind. But, in most cases, we should be civilized *enough* to keep it—at least the writing part—to ourselves.) Of course it's possible I'm completely wrong in what I've been telling you. If that's the case, you must also remember: Writers—real writers and real poets—are constantly being told by high-sounding authoritative figures (teachers, parents, good friends, other writers) that they are *not* real writers, that what they're doing *isn't* any good, that it's silly, and that they should cut it out and do something socially useful. The real writer *must* learn to hear that again and again—and ignore it and go on in spite of it.

You of course are the only person who can tell whether what

I'm saying is reasonable advice—or if it's advice you should laugh at, ball up, and toss into the trash. But I have been as honest as I can.

I close with a couple of brief tales—the first of which I find distressing, and the second of which I think is quite wonderful.

First tale:

I've taught writing workshops all over the country for the last thirty years: in Seattle and New Orleans and Cambridge and Ann Arbor and Wisconsin and East Lansing and Cincinnati . . .

But about ten or twelve years ago I became aware of a phenomenon that has become more and more prevalent as time has gone on.

A new workshop will meet—and there will be two, or five, or seven older students. Often they're extremely social and pleasant individuals, easy for me as a teacher to like and to feel a kind of instant friendship with. Frequently the stories that they have submitted ahead of time show some marked talent as well—which only inclines me to like them the more.

But, on the second or third day, when we are all, say, having lunch together, I'll overhear snatches of conversation among them: "Yes, three years ago my story was workshopped by John Wideman. He had some very encouraging things to say about it . . . Anthony Burgess, back when he was teaching Creative Writing at Columbia in the late seventies, workshopped that story once and said some very nice things . . . You know, it's funny, what Judy said about the climax this morning was just what Robertson Davies said about it when I handed it in twelve years ago when he was up at Wesleyan . . . When Edmund White read it, back at the Haverford Workshop—I think that was '84—he didn't like the way I handled the setting at *all* . . . "

Finally I asked: "When did you *write* that story we went over this morning?" With a big smile, the man or woman will tell me: "Oh, this is just about the last story I wrote. I did it back in 1977 . . ."

And I'll realize that this person has been going from workshop to workshop, often for as much as twenty-five years, handing in the same tale—which, by now, he or she knows will get a fair amount of praise. The "student" hasn't changed or rewritten a word of it, however, over that same time. The game is that of a gunslinger, collecting notches in the handle of his gun. *This story has been workshopped by Ernest Gaines and John Yates and Marge Piercy and John Updike and Lorrie Moore . . . And they all said I had talent.*

I've done workshops where I had *more* "students" of this sort than I had of working, producing writers (however talented or not).

These people are workshop junkies. They are incapable of reworking or improving the story, whatever you tell them about it. They want your praise. They're very polite in listening to your criticism—often, they even take careful notes. Frequently they're very good at critiquing other students' stories. But that is the price they pay to get the praise that is the all-important commodity for them. But they're not writers because they don't write —and haven't written for years; though they desperately yearn for the approval that sometimes comes with having written.

I think there's something fundamentally wrong—and rather creepy—about what they're doing. If they do have something inside them that they want to express—now, today, then and there—it never comes out. Because all they are doing is maneuvering themselves into position to receive pats on the head for work that, fifteen, twenty, or twenty-five years ago, was not in any way accomplished but that simply showed they once skirted the possibility of pleasing through one verbal skill or another.

But this is the reason, as I said at the start of this letter, I try to exclude old work from the workshops I do. Most of the people who lean on these terribly old stories, by now, have convinced themselves that there is nothing wrong with what they're doing. Perhaps there isn't. But to me it seems that it can't be very fulfilling. And it takes places in the workshop away from students who are working, growing, perhaps developing and who *might* move on to refine their talent—as these folks have completely given up on ever doing.

I tell you this tale because I believe you when you write that you do have something to say, something to communicate, something to contribute.

I would hate to see that urge stifled and the simple search for praise at any cost grow to take its place. But this is what, more and more frequently these days, I see among people who once wrote or who once wanted to be (or, alas, still want to be) writers.

Another anecdote, however, that you may find more salutary.

Second tale:

Margaret Walker wrote three hundred pages of her novel of black life during and after the civil war, *Jubilee*, when she was nineteen years old, in 1939. But she could not finish it, nor was she satisfied with what she'd actually done. Though she was doing research for it constantly after that, it was not until 1954, when she was taking a creative writing workshop with Norman Holmes Pearson, as a Ford Fellow at Yale, that she first realized what she had to do with it: and it was not till seven years after that, at Iowa in 1961, that she was able to sit down and, in Verlin Cassill's fiction writing workshop, actually *do* it. Doing it required her to rethink and rewrite every sentence, every paragraph, every chapter of that original three hundred pages and, indeed, keep going: —after more than twenty years!

Jubilee is a lively book that speaks to many, many people.

I don't know which of the two tales above speaks to *you* more. The one you need to hear may well be one *I* haven't heard yet and thus can't tell you. But when you find it, pay attention to it—and forget all others.

And please accept

All my best wishes,

(*signed:*) Samuel R. Delany

Part III FIVE INTERVIEWS

A Para•doxa *Interview*

Experimental Writing/
Texts & Questions

Questions by Lance Olsen

SAMUEL R. DELANY: I'd like to use your questions as an opportunity to talk about some ideas—and some texts. The texts
come from among the alternative, or experimental, pieces I've
read and reread over the last forty years that have given me
much readerly pleasure. I don't put them forward as any sort
of history. They come from different genres; and freely I admit
I've had some sort of personal relation with most of the writers,
in some cases as fleeting as attending the birthday dinner of my
friend Bruce Benderson, where I met Ursule Molinaro, whose
birthday it also was; and in others, warm relationships of long
standing, as with Richard Kostelanetz—we went to the same
summer camp as boys, though we didn't become friends till
twenty-five years later. I might mention too that, in at least half
the cases (Disch, Keene, Abish . . .), I knew the writing before
I knew the writer. With a couple of these, I'd been impressed
enough with the writing to seek the writer out after reading him
or her.

The ideas have to do with writing and its renovations, its
innovations, and its fundamental graphic energies—about how
those energies shake the body itself and how, through some astonishing butterfly effects, those rumblings eventually work to
erect the very structures of culture. With that as prologue, let's
look at your first question.

LANCE OLSEN: *Why do you write, and, more interestingly, why do
you choose to write alternative (that is, experimental) fiction?*

DELANY: Once we get beyond the rich and intricate Bloomian answer to your question's first half (artists create in rebellion against the failure to create), we're faced with a more limited field in which to look for answers, a limitation already suggested by your question's second half—really a form of "Why do you create *what* you do in the *way* that you do?"

As I worked through them, some of my science fiction novels presented problems I thought might be solved by appropriating techniques from across various genre boundaries over in the literary and experimental precincts. Only two of my novels started out, however, as experimental *per se*. The first was *The Tale of Plagues and Carnivals*, which began as a response to the AIDS situation, back in 1983. That is, it grew out of a sense of crisis.

The second was my short novel, *Atlantis: Model 1924* (1995). We'll return to that one. Paradoxically, when I was a kid, I associated certain sorts of writerly experiments with heightened readability. As a fourteen-year-old, when I first read Alfred Bester's *The Stars My Destination* (1956) over the summer issues of *Galaxy Magazine* in which it was first serialized, I soon knew I was reading something very different—and clearly it was far more readable than anything else in the magazine. As a seventeen-year-old immersed in Faulkner, I found *The Sound and the Fury* (1929) certainly an easier and—for me—more intense read than the more ponderous (and traditional) *Light in August* (1932), both extraordinary novels. When, as a thirty-three-year-old, I read Joanna Russ's *The Female Man* (1975), I realized that I was reading a novel conceived in an entirely different way from most. It went down far faster and more energetically than most novels—not to mention that it made its points with greater intensity.

When, in the midst of her strange and unusual rhetorical ploys, straining so hard—and so frequently managing—to say things I'd never heard before about a world I'd certainly known and lived in and looked at, Russ wrote:

> This book is written in blood.
> Is it written entirely in blood?
> No, some of it is written in tears.
> Are the blood and the tears all mine?

Yes, they have been in the past. But the future is a different matter. As the bear swore in *Pogo* after having endured a pot shoved on her head, being turned upside down while still in the pot, a discussion about her edibility, the lawnmowering of her behind, and a fistful of ground pepper in the snoot, she then swore a mighty oath on the ashes of her mothers (i.e., her forebears) grimly but quietly while the apples shaken from the apple tree above dropped bang thud on her head: OH SOMEBODY ASIDES ME IS GONNA RUE THIS HERE PARTICULAR DAY. (95)

—well, I was, as they put it, blown away. All the passage's rhetorical artifice—the use of the comic to distance the violence beneath it, so that, of a sudden, you see that violence in its actual light, positioned in a garden rich with both Edenic and Newtonian resonances—all of this *worked*, just the way it was supposed to, on the body of this particular reader. And I heard, no, I *felt* and was deeply shaken by, truth's bong, peel, and clang.

(Russ's next novel, *We Who Are About to . . .* [1976], is an even more subtle and more devastatingly successful experiment; though what's experimental about it is a bit harder to detect.)

No, I have never been quite the same.

Now, back in the sixties, I'd also read Dalton Trumbo's *Johnny Got His Gun* (1939), another novel of crisis—and an effective one it is. But Russ's novel was the first *experimental* novel of crisis I'd read. And it was, for me, so much *more* effective than Trumbo's that, when AIDS precipitated the time for me to write my own novel of crisis, it never even occurred to me to put it in, say, the fairly traditional narrative form Trumbo used. With Harlan Ellison's extraordinary mosaic story "Deathbird" (1975) in pursuit, I went right for the experimental.

Because of the topicality and the urgency of my own undertaking, I felt it was worth the risk to hoist up on my own shaky shoulders the burden of the experimental, when I decided to take on AIDS, life, and death in a novel started in '83 and finished in June '84.

That judgment of the crisis was *not*: I must reach as many people as possible. Rather, it was: The people I reach, I must reach as *intensely* as possible. I wanted to create a reading experience at least as intense as the ones I'd had—the ones given me by Ellison, Russ, Faulkner, Bester . . .

My publisher was bewildered by the manuscript—and, through a kind of self-fulfilling prophecy, *Flight from Nevèrÿon* (1985), which contained *The Tale of Plagues and Carnivals*, over two printings sold only 85,000 copies. At the time, my other books were selling in the 150,000 to 250,000 range. I'm still convinced that if my publishers had dared to print the book in the same numbers in which they had printed my others, it would have sold equally well, if not better. But I'm also convinced that, among those readers who read it, it got the effect I wanted: AIDS was fixed in their attention as something important, so that when new information arrived, it could and would be dealt with—rather than sloughed off and ignored. That was 85,000 readers, back when there were only some eight thousand cases of the disease. However local the accomplishment, I felt I'd done what I set out to.

But to write that book, I said: Even if I don't use it all, I've got to have the full range of the contemporary aesthetic armamentarium from which to choose. Later in the eighties, Julian Barnes's *Flaubert's Parrot* (1986) benefited from the same sense of increased readability that came simply from its greater rhetorical range. For many readers this and Barnes's next book, *The History of the World in Ten-and-a-Half Chapters* (1990), were also a departure from what most readers think of as traditional plot and traditional storytelling.

My book—indeed, the entire series of texts in which *The Tale of Plagues and Carnivals* falls out as the ninth, novel-length tale—was moderately controversial (as, half a dozen years before, Russ's had been). Today, that controversy is fourteen years in the past. It's been chronicled elsewhere. But my sense from readers is certainly that *The Tale of Plagues and Carnivals* remains the most readable text in the Nevèrÿon series—if not among the most readable I've produced. The strongest motivation behind the experiment was simple: "I've got things to say that are too important and that will not fit within the structures of narrative fiction as it is usually handed to us." But for such motivation to produce other than chaos, it presumes in the writer a history of reading and a sense of what can be done outside those strictures, of what's to be won by *going* outside. Here I want to anticipate by a bit your upcoming questions on heuristics: Though we live in an age bound by a formalist aesthetic, I still tell my writing students—and I still believe—it certainly doesn't hurt them to have something *they* believe is important to write about in order to goose themselves into thinking about particularly effective ways to write it.

There's a danger, let me add, in too quickly equating the rhetorical variety of the experimental with readability. Indeed, the experimental is often doing precisely its most interesting work when it retards readability. Addressing a readership appreciative of what is to be gained from the "difficult discourse" of Lacan and Derrida, however, certainly I shouldn't have to mount any defense, or interrogate the fallacies and political dangers, of a "transparent" language on that front.

I said we'd return to *Atlantis: Model 1924*, from my collection *Atlantis: Three Tales*. That short novel began almost entirely as a critical consideration: *Ulysses*, *The Waste Land*, and the *Cantos* are, for better or worse, our waning century's paradigmatic literary works. Each is presumed, as a text, to stand before an all-but-endless intellectual armamentarium that, in its range, is said to encompass the entire history and tradition of European art, to which these texts are connected by an all-but-endless number of allusions and references. In 1993 I decided to write the short novel that became *Atlantis: Model 1924*, to see what it felt like to have the experience of writing such a work.

Joyce's novel is organized around Homer's *Odyssey.* In much the same way, I decided to organize mine around Hart Crane's *The Bridge* (1933). In *Ulysses*, Stephen's boss at the school, Mr. Deasy, represents an ironic Nestor, a character from Homer's epic; in *Atlantis: Model 1924*, Sam's Raleigh friends, Lewey and John, represent ironic portrayals of Luis de San Angel and Juan Perez, historical characters who appear in Crane's poem.

Ulysses is packed with allusions. Before I started (and while I was actually) writing, I filled pages and pages with phrases, most of them from books about Crane and studies of the period, to work them into my text.

When a piece is conceived so cerebrally, at a certain point

something has to ground it. I was sure the work would be auto-biographical—but where in my own life I would find the particular passage to interrogate, I didn't know.

In 1992 I was invited by the Dark Room, the Harvard University Black Students' Collective, to give a reading for them in Boston—I believe it was November. That evening I was scheduled to read with a young writer I'd never heard of before and whose work I did not know, John Keene. Keene read an extraordinary piece about his childhood in St. Louis, among the black middle classes of the city. Though I grew up in New York, it was a social stratum I knew well—and, hearing Keene, I realized that was the social stratum from which I wanted to mine my own material.

When I returned home next day to Amherst, I broke out my copy of Crane's *The Bridge* and reread it for perhaps the tenth time in three weeks; but now, as I was going over the closing movement, "Atlantis," something snagged my attention and came together with a memory of a tale my father had told me several times during my adolescence—one that I'd not thought of for years.

The youngest of ten children, Dad had come to New York City when he was seventeen from a small black college campus in Raleigh, North Carolina, on which he'd been born. By his own admission, his abiding motivation for the trip was to see New York City's skyscrapers. On his arrival his brother Hubert met him at Grand Central Terminal and took him directly up to Harlem, so that Dad's first view of the city, once they came up out of the subway, was pretty disappointing. Still in quest of skyscrapers, at the suggestion of a friend of his brother's, a few months on, that spring my father took a walk across the Brooklyn Bridge. What Dad recalled from that walk, more than the view of the city (which, as I'd taken it many times myself, I knew was quite wonderful), was that the Brooklyn side of the bridge was nowhere near as built up as it is today. The highway decanted into farm land, the road running by some cornfields, practically as if (the metaphor had been my father's) it led back into North Carolina.

My dad was born May 6, 1906. He came to New York in 1923. I envisioned his walk across to Brooklyn and back as occurring toward the end of April or the beginning of May, 1924, just before his eighteenth birthday: April 1924 was the month Hart Crane moved into his Brooklyn residence at 110 Columbia Heights, with Emile Opffer, just on the far side of the bridge. And there, in "Atlantis," which Crane had already written several drafts of, about his own time on the bridge, were the lines:

> Pacific here at time's end, bearing corn,—
> Eyes stammer through the pangs of dust and steel.
> (lines 51–52)

And—

> With white escarpments swinging into light,
> Sustained in tears the cities are endowed
> And justified conclament with ripe fields
> Revolving through their harvests in sweet torment.
> (lines 69–72)

Suddenly I was as sure as I have ever been of anything that there, within Crane's famously dense lines, nestled references to the same corn and cornfields my dad remembered, when he'd told me the story from more than thirty years before, cornfields now gone beneath the concrete of Borough Hall and Brooklyn Heights, even as Crane's own house (once owned by Opffer's father) had, by the time the poet Alfred Corn went to search it out, already been torn down years ago. There's an insightful comment by Robert Musil (whose novel *Der Mann ohne Eigenshaften* [1932] I'd taught in a modernist novel seminar the previous spring). Wrote Musil: There's a period between your father's twentieth year and your own twentieth year that you can never fully understand from a historical perspective. You will never understand the first part, because you weren't there. You will never understand the second, because you *were*—but you were there without the tools of logic and analysis honed to negotiate it intellectually.

Suppose, I wondered, on the Saturday before his eighteenth birthday in 1924, my father had gone down to the Brooklyn Bridge, and suppose he had actually run into Hart Crane (who would have been twenty-four at that point) on the bridge . . .

Somehow all this came together for me, with Keene's piece

as catalyst. With my notebook full of jottings and quotes that I wanted to work into it, I began writing the actual text that afternoon.

I dedicated my novella—that is to say, the book it appeared in—to Keene. I think he was rather surprised by it. But since then, we've become friends.

If the key to the experimental surface of *Plagues and Carnivals* is the social crisis it grew out of, the key to the experimental surface of *Atlantis* is in the Flaubertian subtitle, *Three Tales.* I had just turned fifty and I wanted to strut my stuff, show what I could do.

My reason for undertaking this experiment was, however, not for the results—though, I confess, I'm happy enough with them—but rather to see what it *felt* like to be on the inside of such a conscientious writing process. To repeat and expand, *Ulysses* is the paradigmatic art work for our century as Wagner's *Ring* was paradigmatic for the half-century before Joyce. I wanted to know what, subjectively, it felt like to write a text at that level of allusional density, with that much research, with those particular organizational constraints, dependent on that particular mode of personal material.

We can all read Joyce and appreciate him as a meticulous observer of the world around him. Still, a lot of people wonder if he did all the things *organizationally* in *Ulysses* that critics are always finding in it—at the level of allusion and structure. Indeed, the question is, for most of us, is it even *possible* for a writer to do all that?

Well, when I started *Atlantis: Model 1924*, that's what I wanted to find out. (My novella is a kind of literary Kon-tiki— you know, *could* the natives actually cross the sea on their handmade raft?) Any observational elegance the piece did or did not display was, for my purposes, secondary. Having finished it, I can answer the question "Is it possible for someone to do all that?" with an unreserved yes.

I can answer yes, because I tried it myself. It was an interesting, obsessive, and, in many ways, unpleasant experience. (Three years after writing it, while I can remember many of the allusions, I *can't* remember most of them and would have to check my notebooks to confirm the majority—as there were literally hundreds.) Also it was a very different experience from the one I've had writing most of my other books. Critically, however, the experience of writing *Atlantis: Model 1924* was invaluable.

The only thing I can say that strikes me as slightly odd about Joyce's enterprise in the light of my own experience is the following:

Atlantis: Model 1924 took me ten months of arduous work. (That's the same amount of time it took me to write *Trouble on Triton* [1976], a book four times as long, far more traditionally structured, and requiring much less labor.) Most of that work, as it was for Joyce at the deposit library in Zurich when he was writing *Ulysses*, meant I was buried in other books.

The moment I finished *Atlantis: Model 1924*, because of all the research and the organizational work I'd put into it, a nonfiction work on Crane's poem and his times virtually erupted from me, all but spontaneously—subsequently entitled "Atlantis Rose . . ." It's almost the same length. (Though it took much less time to draft.)

Because of what I went through in the writing of *Atlantis*, there's no *way* I could *not* have written that essay. So—I'm a *little* surprised that, given what Joyce is presumed to have gone through in the writing of *Ulysses*, he has no major nonfiction work either on Dublin at the turn of the century and/or on the *Odyssey*. But, again, this just may be a temperamental difference (there's no nonfiction work on turn-of-the-century Paris from Proust, either . . . though Proust died, of course, *before* he finished his great novel), or, once again, it might even be the result of the change in the class structure between what Joyce's novel represents and whatever, at the social level, my novella responds to.

Now, the question arises, of course: Are the 112 pages of *Atlantis: Model 1924* in any way, shape, or form alternative fiction? The answer, I assume, is a matter of deciding what exactly it might be alternative to.

My personal sense is that the conscientious experiment that impelled *Atlantis: Model 1924* makes it feel, at least to me, closer to "alternative fiction" than, say, *Dhalgren*, which, whatever *its* failings, was basically an attempt to write a more or less interesting novel, as I happened to conceive "interesting" at the time.

(But then, the French experimental writer Raymond Roussel [1877–1933] was not *trying* to write experimental fiction either. He sincerely believed the homophonic sentences with which he began and ended his tales and novels were simply a method for generating more interesting fiction than that which was being written around him—and, when you compare his fiction to some of what was being written around him, he was right!)

Ulysses was certainly alternative fiction at the time it was published in book form in 1922. For practically two decades it was illegal in this country and occasioned a famous court battle. Though hindsight makes its canonization look inevitable, we know it was a long, slow, and gradual process.

Atlantis: Model 1924 was written in 1992 and 1993. By 1997 its most difficult and least accessible section had got itself included in the *Norton Anthology of African American Literature*—without my knowing about it till it was a *fait accompli.* To the extent the Norton anthologies represent for some people a certain degree of canonization, *that's* fast enough to make your head spin! (If only for the speed of its acceptance, I suspect it'll be forgotten equally quickly, or remain as the most eccentric and marginal occurrence, of interest only to whoever collects such marginal and eccentric literary experiments.) But all this only suggests once more that the structure of the world to which the various practices of writing respond has . . . well, changed.

Once more, I feel obliged to point out that, however brief my text, the sheer monumentality of the project again marks the conservative aesthetic behind it—to which its inclusion in the Norton only adds its terminal period. Thus, if it *is* "alternative or experimental fiction," it's a pretty conservative and tame experiment. But, as I keep reiterating, as a writer that's who I am.

In 1995 with New Directions, John Keene published an extraordinary experimental novella, *Annotations.* It's worth looking at, I suspect, in some detail. What is *Annotations* about? I would call its topic the gallery of middle-class black impressions of life in St. Louis and environs from the late sixties through the early eighties.

First, there is a modulating subject: you/he/we/and I are all given as modalities of a single consciousness.

The book's eighteen brief chapters (recalling *Ulysses*'s eighteen constitutive hourly novellas; personally, for some years I've felt that, in *Ulysses*'s case, it's better to look at the book as a progression of eighteen experimental novellas than as one novel of eighteen chapters . . .) are divided up into three major groups of, respectively, five, six, and seven chapters each. The nature of Keene's experiment here is that he has significantly turned away from literature's traditional focus on metaphor and allowed, rather, metonymy to extend itself vastly in its associative range. This is not to say that there aren't metaphors aplenty throughout the actual writing. But they are not asked to do the organizing job we are familiar with in much "normative literary fiction."

"What memory is not a 'gripping' thought?" Keene quotes, in a page of mottoes from Lyn Hejinian's *My Life* (1980, 1987). In Hejinian's experimental "autobiography," you recall, sentences accrete within severe mathematical limitations. When Hejinian was thirty-seven, *My Life* consisted of thirty-seven chapters of thirty-seven sentences each. For the second edition, published eight years later, Hejinian added eight more chapters *and* eight more sentences *to* each chapter. As we grow older, we forget more and more of our lives. This sentential accretion is a bodily way of fighting the brain-body's own irrevocable deterioration. The field in which Hejinian produced her sentential accretions, like the one in which Ron Silliman worked both in his *Ketjak* (1978: here a geometric doubling controls the intratextual accretion of sentences, in what is certainly the single most gorgeously written book of nonlinear prose in English, as beautiful as *Nightwood* [1936] or *Omensetter's Luck* [1966], each of its twelve longer and longer sections beginning with the sumptuously seductive euphony, "Revolving door"—the door to the Bank of America across the street from where Silliman was having lunch on the afternoon he began the poem in San Francisco) and his poetic series The Alphabet (*ABC* [1983], to *Xing* [1996]), was one in which the narrative topics of the individual sentences were largely discontinuous. This produced a new kind of "verbal animal" that one could pursue and enjoy, as it were, through the text: the points of discontinuity within sentence N + 1 where, with the discourse of continuity pulling us along, the narrative breaks with sentence N actually register.

Keene is nowhere near as strict as either Silliman or Hejinian in his antinarrativity. Again and again two, three, or four sentences may revolve around one topic, even sharing a grammatical subject: two consecutive sentences about a pet dog in chapter 1, three consecutive sentences about what people wore in chapter 7, seven consecutive sentences about sexual attitudes at the head of chapter 8. Rarely in *Annotations* does traditional narrativity sustain itself, however, much longer than this. Constantly the writing tries to see how far it can leap over those associative metonymic bridges. Thus we have a text peopled with those strange associational beasts, banned from the traditional writing arena by writers as early as Horace, in his *Ars Poetica*. Those "unbelievable" creatures with "the body of a lion and the head of an eagle," those griffins, chimeras, and sphinxes are still the ones, after two thousand years, that we continue to sit at the feet of, fascinated, attending to their riddles.

Keene's is writing that locates itself at the most serene point in the tradition of the novel, at the very opposite of crisis. The experiment in focused meditation becomes precisely an experiment in beauty. And—beautifully—it works on us.

OLSEN: *How has the marketplace changed since 1962 when you began to publish?*

DELANY: First of all, not many writers like Keene are fortunate enough to make their way into print. Only a handful of months ago, a young writer came to me, with a manuscript of very impressive stories, and a handful of rejection letters from commercial publishing houses (one *actually* said, "This is too well-written for us"!), and a proposal to self-publish. Even ten years ago, I wouldn't have given much energy to his project. The fact is that in '79 some eighty independent publishers flourished in New York City. Today, depending on how you count, there are only nine. Some all-but-catastrophic changes have reshaped the general matrix of American publishing in the last twenty years.

But if we're going to talk about markets, let me start with another case, a limit case that, I think, bears on your question.

James Keilty was a San Francisco city planner on the edge of a circle of fifties, sixties, and seventies writers that included Robert Duncan and Richard Brautigan, many of whom were of an experimental bent. A frighteningly literate, gay aesthete, he died of lung cancer in the early nineties. More obsessive than most, however, Keilty went so far as to invent his own language, complete with its own grammar and vocabulary, as well as an imaginary country and a culture to go with it. He wrote stories and folk plays in his invented language, Prashad. He began a lengthy novel in the language. He even went so far as to translate classic works of world literature into Prashad, such as Shakespeare's *Hamlet* and Proust's *Du Côté de chez Swann*. In the early seventies, I got a chance to attend a performance of three of Keilty's one-act plays in Prashad, where the actors were rehearsed and schooled in the meaning of the somewhat Slavic-sounding lines. Prashad had been constructed with euphony uppermost in Keilty's mind. It was quite an experience—and quite beautiful! I reproduce here one of the few published pieces Keilty left us, "An Informal Introduction to the Language of Prashad." (There is at least one full story, "The People of Prashad," *Quark/2*, ed. Samuel R. Delany and Marilyn Hacker, New York: Paperback Library, 1971.) I am fairly sure that Keilty devoted at least a couple of decades to this project, if not more.

An Informal Introduction to the Language of Prashad
A short conversation:

—*Nyod dai bli?*	"What do you want?" (1)
—*Dai fi antulitel forfai-id?*	"Do you have something to drink?" (2)
—*Kai menida an faisil sishilisio.*	"Here is a glass of water." (3)
—*Sha bal irda nyod ablijhamum.*	"That's not what I meant." (4)

(1) The peculiar English "do" does not, of course, translate. *Nyod dai bli'n* would be more polite but that's for a later lesson. *Nyod dai'l blin* would be used if more than one person were being spoken to. (' is pronounced like the "u" in "dull.")

(2) In asking a question, the subject and the verb are never reversed. If the question is not preceded by an asking word such as *nyod* (what) or *sili* (why), the question is implied by a rising tone on the final word.

(3) *Menid* is a root word meaning "being in a place, rest, remain-

Character	Romanization	Pronunciation	Character	Romanization	Pronunciation
∽	a	f<u>a</u>ther	ص	th	<u>th</u>in
ϐ	'	m<u>o</u>ther	ϐ	v	<u>v</u>an
◆	o	d<u>o</u>g	ϐ	f	<u>f</u>an
◞	e	ch<u>ao</u>s	ϲ	m	<u>m</u>an
ϐ	e	b<u>e</u>d	ϲ	n	<u>n</u>et
ϐ	i	f<u>ee</u>	ϲ	ng	ri<u>ng</u>
ϐ	i	t<u>i</u>p	ϲ	d	<u>d</u>ot
◥	ai	h<u>igh</u>	ϋ	l	<u>l</u>ot
ϟ	oi	b<u>oy</u>	ϳ	r	<u>r</u>ag
◣	ei	s<u>ay</u>	―	w	<u>w</u>ill
ϟ	o	n<u>o</u>te	ϒ	y	<u>y</u>et
ϊ	u	s<u>ue</u>	ϯ	yu	<u>u</u>se
ϊ	au	h<u>ow</u>	ǀ	h	<u>h</u>at
ϊ	iu	n<u>ew</u>	ϯ	kh	Ba<u>ch</u> (Ger.)
)	s	<u>s</u>o			
)	sh	<u>sh</u>am			
ϯ	z	<u>z</u>eal			
ϯ	ch	<u>ch</u>ain			
ϯ	jh	plea<u>s</u>ure			
ϟ	k	<u>k</u>id			
ϟ	g	<u>g</u>od			
ϙ	j	<u>j</u>ob			
ϲ	b	<u>b</u>ad			
ϟ	p	<u>p</u>ad			
ϲ	t	<u>t</u>an			

PLATE I

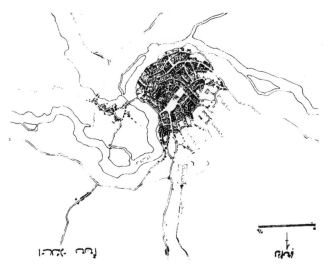

PLATE 2

ing." *Faisil* means something to drink out of, not the material glass, which is *bailkam*. *Sio* means "of" or "from" and, like most positional words, is added as a suffix to the noun it refers to. Thus, the sentence reads literally: Here is a glass water-of.

(4) The final sentence reads literally: That not is what I meant. The root *ir* means, for one thing, being in a state or condition as contrasted with *menid*, being in a place. The verb *irid*, to be, as is often the case with this verb in other languages, is slightly irregular, but *ir* also means "god" or "wrong" (for reasons best known to the Prashadsim); *sha ira* would mean "that is wrong" or "that is god." This also illustrates that any root word can be made into a verb. *Sha irtumia* means "that is difficult," or literally "that difficults." The pronoun *a*, meaning "I," is never separated from the verb, thus *ablijhamum* means "I meant," *Al* or "me" is used where there is no verb to support the *a*.

The normal conjugation of a verb in the present tense goes as follows:

akhebilo	—	I give
dai khebili	—	you give
si, se, su khebila	—	he, she, it gives

ami khebilon	—	we give
dai'l khebilin	—	you give (plural)
sei khebilan	—	they give

This pattern of *o, i, a, on, in, an* endings carries through all but the imperative and the past tenses, thus: *akhebilvo*, I am giving; *akhebilo'*, I will give; *akhebilo'n*, I would give; *akhebilido*, I may, might give; but *khebilami*, let us give. *Akhebilum* is "I gave" and the *um* ending is the same for all persons. The same applies for *akhebilu'm*, I was giving, used to give; *akhebilum'*, I will have given; *akhebilu'n*, I would have given; *akhebilum'n*, I had given; *akhebilidum*, I may, might have given.

The root word (*drukhpadi*), as distinguished from the auxiliary or helping word (*kthirpadi*), has a very versatile character. By itself it is always a noun or word idea; *goimi* sight, scene; *goimidam* is the noun gerund, seeing; *goim'l*, sights, scenes; *goimid*, to see (the root serves as the stem for all verb endings); *semgoimid*, to be seen; *goimin*, a person who sees; *goimida*, a place where one sees; *goimsim*, an extrinsic quality, seen; *goimsum*, an intrinsic quality, "the seeing eye"; *goimibi*, a capability or potential quality visible; the adverbs *goimsimi* and *goimsumi* have no exact equivalents in English, but *goimbai* means "visibly"; *goimo*, more seeing (*mo* is the comparative ending); *goimul,* most seeing (*mul* is the superlative ending).

In writing the Prashadsim alphabet (see plates 1 and 3), the vowels are placed between the consonants close to their tops and linked with them where possible or, in printed form, above and separate from the consonants.

The short poem that ends our introduction to the language is typical of the somewhat ironic little messages the people of Prashad write each other:

Esram,	Young man,
tam so tali so tudam	do you choose
dai telpilshami?	art or life or both?
Atelpilshamo dil,	I choose you,
diliam.	little Mister.

—James Keilty

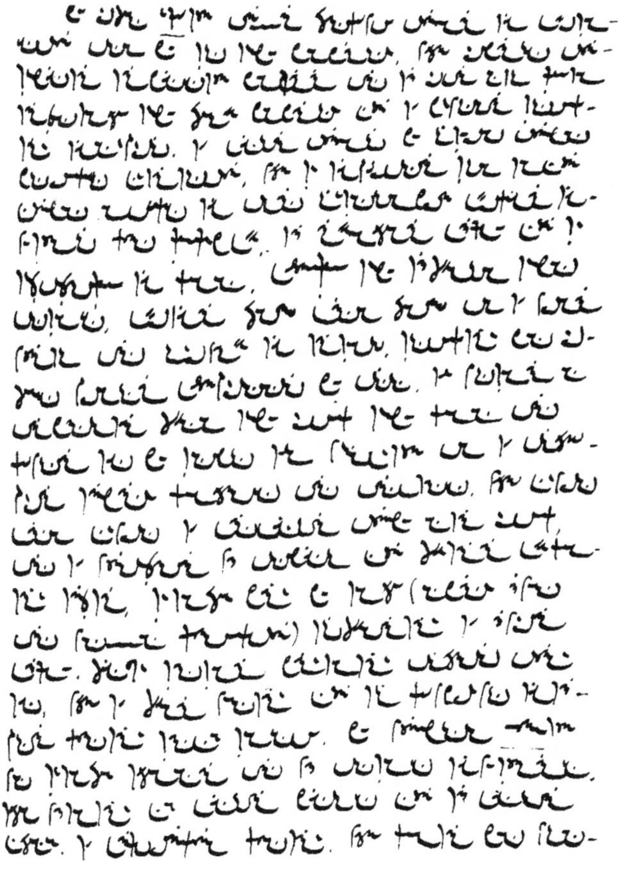

PLATE 3

Half a dozen years after his death, Keilty's papers, preserved by Bill Moore—including the massive Prashad work—were acquired by the library at SUNY Buffalo.

As soon as we run Keilty's Prashad writings—and how can the concept not fascinate any of us?—up against any marketing questions whatsoever, it strikes a blank wall. And in our society, it's a-marketability—as it defines an arena of dedication, invention, and obsession—is where its fascination lies. This is the contradiction that, for better or worse, all experimental writers have to deal with, one way or the other.

At the 1994 OutWrite convention of gay writers in Boston, I sat in the audience of a well-attended panel of young, published authors. The four panel members were all under thirty-five. So was most of the audience—I had been given a seat because I came in with a cane. But many others were standing in the back and sitting on the floor in the front.

After the presentations, and during the question session, the moderator asked the panelists, "What do you think of experimental writing for gay writers?"

Norman Wong, one of the more articulate panel members, immediately declared, "No experimentation! Experimental writing is just bad writing." He said it, by the bye, with all the conviction of someone who had said it many times before. He teaches creative writing at The Writer's Voices in New York City and—in my own judgment—is a talented and interesting author in his own right. Wong went on: "It mutes and muddies your ideas, makes for dull reading, and loses you your audience. So don't do it."

Immediately, someone else on the panel added, "Most 'experimental writing' is just a lot of subjective gushing in the present tense—and the stuff that isn't is just a cascade of unrelated sentences and sentence fragments. It seems to me that's the last thing that gay writers—or any writer with something to say—would want to get involved in."

Responsive applause swelled from the enthusiastic audience around me.

Now, the first thing this means to me is that Wong's reading experience has certainly been different from mine. But I wonder if it also means that the publishing mentality, which I always thought was largely a bunch of ideas that flew in the face of my most profound experiences as a reader, has on some level been triumphant. That strikes me as bad—not to mention naive. But if writers are going to turn to the experimental today, they'd best be aware that not only do publishers distrust experimental writing, but many writers who have just the sense of crisis that, a decade and a half ago I had (when I decided I had to write a novel about AIDS), no longer see experimental writing as a way to deal with it aesthetically. Might the codification of it in textbooks on how to write experimental fiction and poetry and academic considerations, even such as this one, have something to do with that, however indirectly?

OLSEN: *In what sense do you think writing can be taught?*

DELANY: My question to you, in answer to your question to me, is simply, How do you go about teaching people to invent their own language—as James Keilty did? How do you teach people to want to make up their own language in the first place? Some of us, yes, do it naturally. Well before I knew Keilty existed, that's what Marilyn Hacker and I spent the bus trip doing, the weekend we ran off to Detroit to get married. Four years later, that same language became the topic of an SF novel. But the exhortation "Come up with your own ideas" is one that can only be followed in a very limited way—and the more people who try, the more limitations tend to fall into place.

I don't know if writing on the level we are speaking about *can* be taught.

The mechanics of grammar and various rules of organization and style can be. Frankly, I would like to see them taught far more thoroughly than they are.

On the level we're discussing, however, when we speak of creative writing, writing presupposes a certain kind of reading. Now reading can be taught. When I teach reading, and point out various patterns in the text, be it at the level of the phrase, the sentence, the scene, or some larger structure, I feel I'm much closer to teaching writing than I am when I actually run a workshop and people hand in their attempts at stories, essays, or poems.

In one important respect, all there is to learn about writing is a number of patterns, on all those levels (phrase, sentence, scene . . .), that writing can conform to. New levels of observation and organization make us violate (or, indeed, conform to) some of those patterns. The existence of those previous patterns alone is what makes the new patterns (of alternative fiction, say) signify.

In terms of teaching, in terms of reading (and as someone who spent five years on the editorial board of a literary magazine reading between thirty and forty submissions a week), I think, yes, there are certain things that writers should be discouraged from doing. That takes teaching. Many critics have noted: the number of ways writing can be fine, fecund, and inventive are as uncountable as wheat grains across the windy field. The ways it can be bad, however, are limited. Though it's harder than it sounds to follow such advice, half of good writing consists merely in avoiding the bad. (Unfortunately it's only half—and probably not the more important half.) Pretty much all my exhortations come under the rubric "When, as an artist, you're doing what *most* other artists are doing, chances run high you're doing something wrong." The first bunch of rules I won't dwell on: ninety percent of all bad writing is either too cluttered, too thin, or cliché. I could expand on each of these. Here, probably I don't need to.

Assuming I am dealing with writers who have left the incoherent pastures of pure illiteracy and, having come to terms with these ideas, are thus working within the range of (dare we call it) professional literacy, usually I urge my students—especially those interested in experimentation—to avoid present tense narration; that's quite apart from the sadly accurate (at least in terms of what's done in classes) observation of Wong's fellow panelist. If you've been a literary editor, I needn't say more. But circa seventy percent of all literary fiction submissions these days are written in the present tense—eighty-five percent of the awful ones. Today, the present tense has become *the easy sign of the literary.* It functions the way "thee," "thou," rhyme, meter, and grammatical inversions functioned in poetry in the first half of the twentieth century. The simple present is the quick way, requiring no necessary thought, to announce, "Hoo-ha! I'm bein' literary!" (The writers who write such stories well do it, of course, with a great *deal* of thought—as do a number of formalist poets today.)

As Wordsworth notes at the beginning of romanticism in his "Preface" of 1798, an inexhaustible fount of poetic energy is the "language really used by men." Over the last twenty-five years, the present tense has clogged the drain on that fountain and rusted closed the spigot. It's a purely artificial tense. Such sentences as, "George goes into the room," or "Mary takes the paper clip from the manuscript corner and holds it in her hand awhile," exist only on paper. It's all but impossible to come up with actual life situations where such sentences can be normally uttered. The various narrative past tenses (as well as the *continuous present* ["George *is going* into the room"], in which ordinarily we narrate what's going on around us to someone who can't see it—a very different matter from the simple present) are associated with innumerable tones of voice and specific experiences, which enrich them as we write and which the writer must learn to work with and modulate. The simple present has only a single, distanced tone. Thus, writing in the simple present cuts out three-quarters of your writerly material. Like anything else, this is not a hard-and-fast rule applicable in all situations. But if, when presented with the question "Why use the present tense?" the writer's first impulse is to blurt, "It makes things more immediate," then you know the writer misunderstands the present's use and effects and is almost certainly employing it poorly.

Because it's an unspoken and artificial tense, the present puts things at a distance and makes them seem thin, colorless, and voiceless. That's all. (And sometimes muting the voice *is* a valid effect.) These are the only effects it should be used to achieve.

It's the equivalent of taking an ordinary photograph and hanging a piece of gauze before it to make it look misty. If that's the effect you want, fine. But how often can it be used before it becomes an affectation? As well, the interesting works that employ the technique (Allison Lurie's *War Between the Tates* [1976], Thomas Pynchon's *Gravity's Rainbow* [1974], and various stories by Barthelme) are products of the sixties and seventies; it's not new.

Another thing I try to discourage is ironizing into an unrealistic mode presentations of all heterosexual activity in excess of the bourgeois monogamous norm. This is a purely political beef—and I present it as such. The nature of the beef is that such ironic representations fall directly into the discourse that ends up supporting the artificial heterosexual scarcity at the center of heterosexism and homophobia—and that makes the lives of the straight male writers who favor it as a rhetorical trope pretty miserable too. Again, it's not a hard-and-fast rule. But it doesn't hurt to remind the largely young, mostly male writers who are drawn—in droves—to play with this particular sort of very tired irony, of just what all these comic rapes and nobody-could-believe-'em orgies are actually about. There are so many other ways to write about sex (not to say violence), I like to encourage those writers so inclined to explore them—and, again, stay away from what is, after all, a hopelessly cliché way of dealing with what I'm sure the writers (almost always straight) think is just the cleverest and most imaginative thing in the world, because they've read one or two others who've done it and think they're doing something no one or only one other person has done before. What their choice really signals is, of course, the trope's ubiquity and their own naïveté as readers.

The last thing I try to make students aware of: experimental or otherwise, shorter or longer, works have their own forms. A collection of shorter works does not make a longer work: put a bunch of short stories together and they don't automatically turn into chapters in a novel—even if the main characters all have the same names, like Martin and . . . John. The inclusion of one or more short stories in a novel is almost always a flaw; it's a flaw in *Wise Blood* (1952), where the previously written short story that forms the final chapter and that has clearly inspired the whole enterprise simply hangs off the tale's end like a weirdly out-of-tune coda; it is a flaw in *Omensetter's Luck* (1966), where the opening two chapters, while providing all sorts of data, just don't connect with the Reverend Furber's malevolent meditation that forms the actual novel; and, yes, it's a flaw in Dale Peck's *Martin and John* (1993). Fortunately, other things are going on in all these texts that add compensatory excellences. But the separate stories *still* register as flaws—and flaws easy enough to avoid.

Don't put them in there.

One thing experimental fiction can do, if pursued properly, is develop a feeling for various possible and potential fictive structures. A shortcoming of most MFA programs is that there is little or no intelligent discussion of the novel's internal (*or* overall!) structures. Neither scenes within chapters nor chapters themselves are structured like short stories. (Scenes within novels just don't end with the kind of structural closure that short stories, experimental or traditional, have when most satisfying.) A sense of this is valuable, if not imperative, for the novel writer. As well, in certain paraliterary genres, science fiction and/or sword and sorcery, there already exists at least one macrostructure for the story series, that is, where the solution to story "N" becomes the problem for story "N + 1." Needless to say, this is absolutely *not* the traditional structural relation of novel chapters except in a few very clunky mysteries. One welcomes structural experiments of all lengths. The easy way out is rarely, however, the most interesting choice aesthetically. The last dozen MFA theses I've read have all been series of short stories that the writers kind of hoped would stand as (maybe, almost) novels. (For what it's worth, so were two of my late adolescent novels that I could never get published.) The fact that I've read twelve in a row *should* condemn it as a formal decision without further comment.

Undertaking a real novel is scary. If you have no idea what you're about, you probably shouldn't try it. The best idea, if you're going to write one and you feel you haven't already got a sense of the novel as structure, is to read some good ones with an analytical eye and see if you can figure out how they work. By all means include some with more or less successful experimental aspects, *Nest of Ninnies* (1975), *The Female Man* (1975), *Flaubert's Parrot* (1984), and *Readers' Block* (1996). But don't shirk the traditional biggies either—*Emma* (1816), *The Red and the Black* (1830), *Lost Illusions* (1837–43), *Jane Eyre* (1847), *David Copperfield* (1850), *Bleak House* (1853), *Great Expectations* (1861), *Sentimental Education* (1869), *Middlemarch* (1872), *Tess of the D'Urbervilles* (1891), *Under the Volcano* (1947), *Lolita* (1955), *The Sot Weed Factor* (1960) . . . Like a lot of readers, personally I don't think there's *anything* that you can't learn about novel writing from *Sentimental Education,* if you read it carefully enough—with *Trois contes* (1877) thrown in, perhaps, to wind up loose ends. Nor should you be afraid of the truly grand ones, *War and Peace* (1868) or *Les Misérables* (1962). Another thing it's important to remember: *The Brothers Karamozov* (1881), *À la Recherche du temps perdu* (1913–27), and *Der Mann ohne Eigenschaften* (1932) are all *unfinished* novels. They can tell you little about the largest novelistic structures. They never get to manifest them. Really long novels are structured very differently from novels the length of *The Great Gatsby* (1925), *Mrs. Dalloway* (1925), or *The Sun Also Rises* (1926). Generally speaking, the bigger the novel, the simpler the overall structure.

But with all these caveats and warnings in the name of heuristics, I'd like to spend just a moment looking at a work by an extraordinarily fine writer, Ursule Molinaro. *Fat Skeletons* (London: Serif, 1993) is a beautifully wrought metafictive novella that develops on a classical novelistic trope. Some critics claim to trace this trope as far back as *Don Quixote* (1605–15). The don, you recall, was inspired to his erring quest by reading in the adventures of Montalvo's *Amadis de Gaul,* Ariosto's *Orlando Furioso* (1515), and other literary heroes. First published in 1605, volume 1 of *Don Quixote* was soon even more popular than its nonironic models, inspiring at least one unauthorized sequel by Alonzo Avellaneda, in 1614—which probably prompted Cervantes to get to work and complete his own second volume (published a year after the phony sequel, in 1615). Taking advantage of the popularity of his own work, when he wrote volume 2 Cervantes has his mad old gentleman meet characters who have read volume 1 (as well as those who had encountered Avellaneda's bogus sequel!), so that both Cervantes's volume 1 *and* Avellaneda's bogus volume 2 become, in effect, objects in the world of Cervantes's novel. The place where the trope catches fire and burns, as it were, with metafictive luminosity is, however, in the early German romantic poet Novalis's hauntingly eccentric novel from the end of the 1790s, *Heinrich von Ofterdingen.* In *Ofterdingen's* fifth chapter, on a sumptuous moonlit night with a bunch of local farmers, Heinrich enters a legendary cave and, after noting some dinosaur fossils in his torch's light, finds, deep in the cavern, an old duke reading a book on a stone table.

A little later, Heinrich gets a chance to look through the book, only to realize it is a Provençal history of a poet whose life story is almost indistinguishable from Heinrich's own adventures so far. It appears to be a historically earlier version of the very book we are now reading!

In brief, the novel contains itself—or a book uncannily close to itself. This trope surfaces repeatedly through the course of modernist writing. Gide's *Les Faux-Monnayeurs* (1927) is an example. Joyce's *Portrait of the Artist as a Young Man* (1915) is a slightly more oblique version, in simply being the book to be written. And so, quite elegantly, is Molinaro's *Fat Skeletons.*

A forty-two-year-old Czech translator, Mara Pandara, has come to the United States twenty years before the story starts.

Her recently deceased mother is a now forgotten Czech novelist, only one of whose many novels Mara has actually read (and translated). This book is her mother's attempt to write about Mara's childhood and young adulthood. Mara has always felt that she herself should have written a novel about her relationship with that strange and difficult artist who bore her. Over the years, however, translation has displaced Mara's own creative work.

One day Mara's publisher sends her, for translation, a novel by a new, young Czech novelist. Though the protagonist is a young man, the story has uncanny parallels with Mara's own life. At the same time, through a number of friends, she begins to learn something about her mother's final years. A decade before her death, her mother picked up a young, homeless man and took him into her house. He nursed the aging woman through her last years and listened to all of her stories, including all her regrets about her life with her long-gone daughter. Then, in Czechoslovakia he became a novelist—

Of course, he is the author of the new book. How it all resolves is a minuet of the major and minor characters, with plots and schemes and schemes backfiring, which I leave the reader to learn for him- or herself.

Such a précis, however, elides (one of) Molinaro's major strength(s) as a writer of experimental fiction. The first thing anyone who starts one of Molinaro's texts sees is that her approach to punctuation is most unusual. She employs lines of white space liberally.

She also uses extra-length spaces between words   such as the ones on either side of this phrase   to set her phrases apart. & she uses ampersands preceded by periods, such as begins this sentence, regularly.

The elongated space between words is a punctuation mark that has an interesting history. I first came across it in the poetry of Robert Duncan back in the 1950s. The one piece of prose still generally read that employs it is William Gass's Faulkneresque novella of a midwestern winter, "The Pedersen Kid." The story first appeared in a 1961 issue of the literary journal *MSS*. When it was reprinted in Martha Foley and David Barnett's *Best Ameri-*

can Short Stories 1962 (Boston: Houghton Mifflin, Dolphin Edition), the typesetter simply omitted the careful spacings and ran the text all together. It had to wait for Gass's own 1968 story collection *In the Heart of the Heart of the Country* before he could reinsert them. But there are always forces at work to exclude the odd, the eccentric, and the idiosyncratic from the text—even if that oddness is an elegance, a nuance, or a truth.

In my own mind, the comma is a mark controlling inflection and logic, while the space between words is, rather   an actual suspension of sound.

Because Molinaro also uses all the traditional punctuation marks, and because obviously she is an extremely careful writer, the many more possible stops that she employs soon take on an individual weight. We must virtually learn *how* to read Molinaro's prose. When, after a dozen or so pages, we begin to do so, we become aware—in the reading body, in the lungs and the tongue and the teeth struggling to remain silent before her rich prose—of a more subtly voiced and paced English than we are used to in the ordinary ranges of fiction.

Molinaro commits us to a strict education of the silent ear.

I can't imagine a serious reader who would not feel she or he benefits from it.

Others of her beautifully crafted tales include *The New Moon with the Old Moon in Her Arms* (1990) and *The Autobiography of Cassandra, Princess and Prophetess of Troy* (1979), both published by McPherson, a publisher who brings out some fine alternative fiction.

OLSEN: *Is there a difference between teaching how to write mainstream fiction and teaching how to write alternative fiction? If so, can you articulate the difference?*

DELANY: The general assumption—though I don't know how good an assumption it is—is that, somehow, "everybody" has a "natural feel" for the structures that control normative fiction, while the structures that control experimental or alternative fiction have to be hit on more consciously and need to be more conscientiously manipulated.

One of the great problems with experimental writing is that

most young writers would rather write it than read it. But to stay on top of any practice of writing, you have to read in it—preferably widely.

The kinds of things that are assigned in other classes (write about such-and-such a topic, the paper organized in such-and-such a way) in a class in experimental writing *become* the assignments: come up with something to write about (which could be, of course, an assignment in any creative writing class) and think of an interesting way to organize it.

I recently read an interesting short story by Eric Belgum, called "Star Fiction" (in *Star Fiction*, St. Paul: Detour Press, 1996). The title piece in this elegant booklet consists of a series of more or less surreal anecdotes labeled STORY, each followed by a brief ANALYSIS of the anecdote's truth claims, or, as the piece continues, other aspects, punctuated now and again by a set of meditations, each labeled INTERMISSION. It kind of wakes you up; and during the course of it, it calls up an intense awareness of the fact that the way truth and falsity stitch and sew together the rhapsody of our lives is a far more intricate process than most of us take for granted.

As you might imagine, long ago I put together a theoretical construct to obviate any fundamental difference between the normative and the alternative. It's the theoretical bridge, I suppose, over which I and how-many-other writers make our appropriations, in whatever directions, among whatever genres.

Alternative fiction might be seen as fiction in which the pressure of observation and the complexity of organization are simply at a different level, or pitch, from where they're set in more normative endeavors. But (or, better, therefore), save on the most contingent, provisional level, *I* don't see the fundamental enterprise of, say, Dickens, Joyce, Kathy Acker, or Eric Belgum to be particularly, meaningfully different from one another's.

The variables (in all of these cases, for example) are variables in observation and organization. In the work of each writer, observation is aimed in one direction or another, then adjusted up or down as one moves along through the text. Organization of the textual material in each case is either complex, or formal, or simple, or informal.

In all this, the aesthetic is the specific meaning unique to a given set of signs, in the sense that, as with *any* set of signs, the aesthetic is what is in excess of any and every other possible set that we can agree functions as a paraphrase or that means more or less "the same thing." Content comes apart from style (in a rich semiotic field) when we start to ask ourselves, "What does it mean to contemplate just this, with signs of this particular materiality, with this particular history?"

Richard Kostelanetz graduated from Brown University in 1962. In the midst of his four years at Columbia Graduate School, he began his literary career. Since 1967, he's been committed to writing experimental fiction. When I asked him what my theory of the relation between normative fiction and alternative fiction leaves out, he burst out laughing and declared:

"Everything that's central!"

The rest of the evening's lively conversation revolved around notions of parasitism—that is, all those possible relations between texts not covered by such benignly neutral terms as "inter-textuality" and "allusion," those relations where the parasitic writer ("For me," says Kostelanetz, "'parasite' is not a bad word") is highly critical of the host text—or outright contemptuous of the host text.

Kostelanetz: "Alternative fiction is about extremes."

If you look for a characteristic text among Kostelanetz's more than a hundred books, there simply isn't one. There are (more or less) ordinary commercially published volumes of nonfiction, such as *The End of Intelligent Writing* (1973) and *The Old Poetries and the New* (1981). He has edited numerous perceptive anthologies of essays, such as *On Contemporary Literature* (1964, 1969), *The Avant-Garde Tradition in Literature* (1982), and the two-volume compilation on *American Writing Today* (1982). He has edited anthologies of experimental poetry, such as *Text-Sound Texts* (1980), even anthologies of experimental criticism—*Younger Critics of North America* (1975)—and several anthologies of work by major American artists put together with the specific goal of revising the current critical view of them: John Cage, Gertrude Stein, and E. E. Cummings.

Kostelanetz's own fiction/poetry/art tends to break down the generic barriers of just such executive departmentalizations as those that allow me to catalogue his nonfiction productions for you.

One Night Stood (1977) is a Kostelanetz short story, published in a single four-inch-by-five-and-a-half-inch volume of some 172 unnumbered pages, each with only two, three, or sometimes only one word taken from the beginning (most of them) of sentences of dialogue, which, in sequence, narrate the pick-up of a young woman student by an older male painter:

Like drink

Scotch sour

Actress

Then modeling

Oh, where

Down south

That's south

Like it

You're pretty

If quick

Same

Not yet

No school

Sweet Briar

Virginia

Sure is

Sorta dull

(13–29)

Because each pair of phrases occurs on recto and verso with the paper page between, the isolation of the "characters" is redramatized in the structure of the work as object.

The pick-up leads to a sexual encounter between them, but this soon becomes a fiasco, and after rather crassly throwing the young woman out (when she has grown derisive at his impotence), after a blank page, the painter's last words are "Work now." Both characters seem rather limited people—a limitation dramatized in the truncation of the phrases that limn their encounter. But it remains undecidable whether that limitation is actually there or is simply an effect of the clipped style. *One Night Stood* takes about four minutes to read through. Rereading it, however, you notice a great many suggestions have been crammed into its microtext, having to do with the way the painter offers his friendship with a well-known theatrical personality to entice the young woman up to his studio, and she mentions an art critic she knows to impress him.

The story is entirely in these dialogue snippets.

At the start of the text, the male speaker's words are high on the rectos.

The female speaker's are low on the versos.

But toward the three-quarter point of the story, in the midst of sex, he tells her:

Turn

over
(144–145)

These words are on facing pages—the first time the words of one speaker persist over two pages. With this displacement of each other's textual position (the distance between them figuring the weight of the body that, in the diegesis, responds with a roll: for me, the most *bodily* moment in the text), their positions of psychological power in the encounter also reverse (as do the two characters' positions on odd and even pages)—or, at least, as readers we are alerted to pay attention to any such signs of reversal in the tale's remainder. Though the story seems somewhat schematic and almost artificially symmetrical over a first reading, with multiple perusals it gains in nuances and richnesses of the sort characteristic of the best fiction. In the thirty or forty times I have read it over the years, rarely have I failed to notice something that had escaped me on previous perusals. That's quite an accomplishment, considering the tale's brevity.

One of my personal favorites of Richard's pieces is a story? poem? art work? called *Modulations* (1975), published in Brooklyn, New York, by Assembling Press. I have "read" and "reread" it many times over the years. But what occasions both question marks and quotation marks is, however, simply that there are no words, other than the title, in this work.

Modulations is one of six constructivist fictions Kostelanetz "built" in the middle seventies. Two, *Modulations* and *Extrapolate* (Brooklyn and Des Moines: Assembling Cookie, 1975), occupy their own small volumes. Four others (CF 1, CF 2, CF 3, CF 4) exist in a photocopied edition, at 8.5 by 11 inches, published together with an introductory untitled manifesto (*Constructs, Stories* by Richard Kostelanetz). The volume bears no date or place of publication. Indeed, the author's name does not appear on it, save as patterned letters—material for the final page). Here are the manifesto's opening paragraphs from its first page:

> Constructivist fictions are built, rather than expressed; they originate, to a greater degree than other art, in those parts of the writer's mind that are, in Mondrian's phrase, "unconditioned by subjective feeling and conception."

> Constructivist fictions exist in space and time—the space of a printed page and the time it takes a reader to turn from one page to the next.

> Conceived before they are executed, such fictions customarily reflect premeditated principles that are articulated within the work itself: the relevance and meaning of each detail are initially intrinsic . . .

> The materials within a particular fiction constitute its predominant language, and how they change within the space and time of printed pages is the principal method of "story telling."

As I turn to write about *Modulations* itself, however, I pause . . . and the pause has gone on for several days. That is critical resistance. In this case, that resistance might articulate itself: How does one meaningfully analyze a narrative that has neither figures (human, animal, vegetative) nor ground? But as easily the critical question might be, How do I analyze meaningfully this piece of art that I have lived with, now, since the early eighties, have read and reread—and have even written about, *en passant* (*The Tale of Plagues and Carnivals* [1985], §8.55, p. 249). I began by measuring the object with the rule on the edge of a plastic draughtsman's triangle, by counting the unnumbered pages. (From my notebook: "Over the course of its 28 pages, *Modulations* presents a set of geometrical patterns that shift, subtly, page by page . . . ") But when I glanced at that list of figures (8 by 8.75 centimeters . . .), I realized it told little I felt to be meaningful about the work. I looked around for common household objects to compare it to in size, and was surprised how long it took me to find one.

Virtually square, *Modulations* is a smidge smaller than an old-fashioned square plastic computer disk. It's a bit thicker than an old wooden match box and is made up of three strips of yellow cardstock, rubber-cemented one to the other and accordion-folded into a twenty-eight-page pamphlet or volume—counting back and front cover.

When I was in high school, for my birthday a young woman named Ana gave me a copy of the Japanese artist Sesshu's classical work, *The Long Scroll*. In a format only a breath bigger than *Modulations,* within two wooden covers of carefully blocked sandalwood and unfolding to a length of about two-and-a-half feet, a strip of white paper opened to reveal a black-and-gray-inked Japanese landscape that modulated through an entire twelve-month cycle, with hills, mountains, streams, bridges, trees, and a few minuscule monks in the distance walking with parasols. It pictured its annual cycle without calling particular attention to itself and without displaying any signs as obvious as leafless branches, snow, or the sharp shadows of leaf-loaded trees in summer. It accomplished its temporal narrative by no more telltale signs than presenting the plants on the hillsides and dells that were out in the various months of the year. The original of *The Long Scroll* is, if I remember aright from the information on the back, some three or four feet high and correspondingly long. But my copy was, for many years, this simple handheld miniature. Having identified a harmonic resonance, I must go on to say that nothing in *Modulations* looks like *anything* in *The Long Scroll*. They bear far fewer correspondences than do, say, Norman Maclean's *A River Runs through It* (1976) and Richard Brautigan's *Trout Fishing in America* (1967). Having broken through my initial critical resistance, my next comment is simply that *Modulations* is not an elegantly produced work. The copy of *The Long Scroll* that I'd been given had been made (for tourists) in Japan and had a precision and neatness about it characteristic of much *japanoiserie*. Contrastingly, *Modulations* is a messy little American text. The pages do not all line up properly. When folded together and held by its rubber band, it does not make a precise rectilinear solid, but rather lists to one side and the other, its pages folded not entirely at the proper lines.

This is not only part of its charm.

It is part of its meaning.

Cast in a decidedly urban mode that recalls Mondrian's *Broadway Boogie Woogie* and the urban fantasias of Joseph Stella from the teens and twenties, Kostelanetz's little book seems to tell its story with much the same structure as Sesshu's, though it has suppressed almost all recognizable referential content, spatial or temporal.

Once beyond the title page, the remaining twenty-seven pages of *Modulations* each shows a grid of seven horizontal lines and seven vertical lines, producing a veritable eight-by-eight checkerboard.

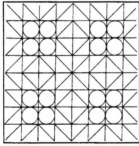

MODULATIONS
RICHARD
KOSTELANETZ

Assembling
Press
c 1975
300 copies
26 signed
& numbered

Fig. 1: Opening page (i.e., the cover) of *Modulations*, by Richard Kostelanetz.

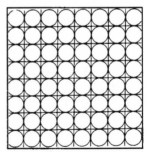

Fig. 2: Page two (verso): the initial page of "text."

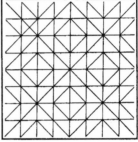

Fig. 3: Page ten (verso): the first page on which circles appear.

Fig. 4: Page twenty-eight (verso), the final page of *Modulations*.

The pages above are given at about 70 percent of the area of the originals. The edges of the pages have been sketched in.

In the original, however, each page runs directly into the next without a separating black line: between them is only a fold of the cardstock. On page 2 and most of the pages following it, a series of diagonals produces a highly symmetrical pattern. Indeed, from page 3 onward, all the eight-by-eight checkerboards are symmetrical around four axes: A–A′ through D–D′:

Because of a single diagonal on page 2, however, the pattern on that page alone is *only* symmetrical around axis A–A′. In figure 2, examine the upper left-hand corner. The symmetry-destroying line crosses the A–A′ axis, producing a box containing not *one* diagonal but, rather, a box Xed with *two*—the only square on the page (indeed, in the entire text) containing an "X." If we number the grid from top to bottom and left to right, the box with the X is at position 2/2 (two down/two across).

Is it an error? Is it an intended anomaly?

Either way, once we have read through the whole work and gone back to reread it, this initial restriction of symmetry, opening out into the greater symmetrical freedom of the remaining twenty-six pages, registers in the body of the reader, and—even more than the modulations in the other, more richly symmetrical pages—becomes the first modulation I become aware of, playing against more homogeneous rhythmic changes across the yellow and black surface.

As we turn over page 9, Kostelanetz introduces the first circles into his pattern—on page 10 (fig. 3). Indeed, if we go back to compare page 2 with the terminal page 28 (figs. 2 and 4), we see that overall the text moves between a state defined wholly by horizontals, verticals, and diagonals to a state where all possible diagonals have been replaced with circles. The algorithm that transforms page 2 into page 28 is simple. Regardless of which direction it runs (i.e., regardless of its slant), each diagonal is replaced with a circle. But because of that anomalous square at position 2/2 on page 2 (and because beginnings and endings are such powerful positions in the discourse of Western aesthetics), that moment of bodily awareness is recalled, in a concentration on square 2/2 on the final page.

Square 2/2 remains privileged. Is there one circle or are there two circles in that particular square? Another way to ask this: "Is the symmetry that has so freed the modulations among the various pages maintained between the text's first page and its last?" Concentric circles of the same diameter being congruent, there's no way to tell. (In the current rhetoric of literary criticism, it's "undecidable"—and, for this reader, that undecidability registers as an uncertainty in the body.) Now we begin to appreciate the placement of that circular eruption at page 10—specifically it is *not* at the story's center (i.e., *not* on page 13). The circles in Kostelanetz's text (and the circle is the geometrically *most* symmetrical of forms) function specifically to *destroy* the temporal symmetry of the textual progression. Even while, on any given page, their placement is a model of spatial symmetry, their progressions always violate temporal symmetry and express rather a progression of domination: information-erasing circles (their infinite symmetry makes no distinctions) encroach on and take over the spaces defined by information-producing diagonals (they can slant either left or right, producing an asymmetrical distinction). If *Modulations* is "about" anything, it would seem to be a dramatization of the way asymmetries can insert themselves into the most symmetrical and ordered of presentations.

Because *Modulations* is so purely a visual work, without quoting (i.e., reproducing) the entire piece it is almost impossible to discuss the wonderfully lyric transformations that turn—that modulate—page into page, or the reframings that, with the reader's eye, slip across the double pages (another method by which the reader finds the various symmetries disrupted) in either direction—for, without being palindromal, the narrative runs either way—that make the harmonic experience so much like a visual music. The structural care of *Modulations* organizes the chaos of the object's specific materiality. But because of the messiness of the object itself, that organization registers much like music coming from a tiny speaker in an old-fashioned three-transistor radio. I have several places written that there is a level of storytelling that seems to me entirely structural, topological even, and that has nothing to do with reference. I feel that—in an aesthetic which holds that formal recomplication lends art its interest and even its greatness—*Modulations*, as much as any piece of fiction I have ever read, plunges directly to this level and dances and leaps about there with a purity and richness that is, in a word, wonder-filled.

Before we leave Kostelanetz, I want to return to his comment about—or rather his laughter at—my theory concerning observation and organization, as in the case of *Modulations*, as the shared centers of all writing (even when what is being observed and organized is the signifier, rather than the signified): perhaps what is needed for experimental writing is a more experimental theory—where what is at the center is not the conceptual anchor for this untroubling and homogenizing bridge that smooths away all differences as it soars between the experimental and the normative. Perhaps what is needed is a theory that centers instead on experimental writing's specific differences, its pricklinesses, its problems . . .

OLSEN: *You wrote a number of sentences in* Dhalgren, *the novel many (including myself) consider your magnum opus, on individual cards before inserting them into the text. Why craft so carefully when so few will notice?*

DELANY: Somewhere in my adolescence I encountered Emily Dickinson's observation, "Nothing survives except fine execution." Well, I bought it. Again, to rephrase something I've already said, taking pains with your language results in a more intense experience *for the reader.* I take pains with my language for the same reason, from time to time, I experiment with it. To play with a dictum by the Big F: the reader, *c'est moi.*

When we read a marvelous passage by Nabokov and, in the muscles of our throat and tongue we experience the passage of its language, we also experience the discrepancy at the level of mind between Nabokov's sensuous thinking, his wonderfully witty observation, and the kind of thinking and observation—both the observation and the organization of it—we are used to in the daily language around us.

We read over the equally marvelous, but very different, sentences in Walter Abish's alternative fiction work *Alphabetical Africa* (New York: New Directions, 1974) and, once again, as we perceive the linguistic constraints Abish has placed on himself, we experience it as an energetic discrepancy with the language of normative prose. All the words in *Alphabetical Africa*'s opening chapter "A" begin with the letter *a*:

> Ages ago, Alex, Allen, and Alva arrived at Antibes, and Alva allowing all, allowing anyone, against Alex's admonitions, against Alex's angry assertions: another African amusement . . . anyhow, as all argued, an awesome African army assembled and arduously advanced against African anthill, assiduously annihilating ant after ant, and afterward, Alex astonishingly accuses Albert as also accepting Africa's antipodal ant annexation. (1; ellipsis Abish's)

The chapter goes on:

> As alien airforce attacks Angola, Albert asks, are anthills anywhere about, agreeing as Alex asserts, all Angolans are absolute asses. (2)

In chapter "B," all the words begin with *a* or *b*:

> By and by Butoni buys an Anglican bishop a beer (4).

In chapter "C," all the words begin with *a*, *b*, or *c*:

> As always, Chester amuses Alva by continuously casting aspersions against Alex and corpulent Allen, and also casting Corinthian carvings against Alva's bedroom ceiling. (5)

This continues up through the twenty-sixth chapter, "Z," in which, finally, words are allowed to begin with any of the alphabet's twenty-six letters. Then, over the concluding twenty-six chapters, the process reverses, each chapter subtracting a letter from the possible letters with which words can begin, till, in the penultimate chapter (again designated as "B"), Alex and his lady friend Alva finally get together. ("Baby, admits Alva, as bus and buros arrive at airport, authors aren't such bad advisors after all. Afterwards Alex and Alva announce a betrothal. Ahh Alva.

Am anticipating April blossoms" [150].) In the final chapter, "A," again all the words begin with *a*—this time a single cascade of a sentence in which (almost) every other word is "another":

> . . . another autumn another available average another avalanche another avenue another aversion another aviary another avoidance another avocation another avid avowal another awareness another awakening another awesome age another axis another Alva another Alex another Allen another Alfred another Africa another Alphabet. (152)

(Is the *other* Alphabet hailed at the end of Abish's tumultuous anaphor, finally, the ideal and all-but-private one of Keilty's Prashad . . . ?)

Today, two dozen years after it was first published, most people who read *Alphabetical Africa* will read it aware of the constraints it sets itself. (Certainly that will be any reader who turns to it after learning of it in this essay.) To turn to the novel, curious as to how its text will negotiate those constraints, is to turn with a certain resistance. In matters artistic, curiosity is resistance tamed and contained.

Tristram Shandy (1760), *War and Peace* (1868), *Ulysses* (1922) . . . If we know anything at all about the first of these, we know that the narrator is conceived in chapter 1, and, though the midwife is summoned to his birthing in chapter 5, he does not manage actually to get born till well beyond that large novel's midpoint. If we know anything at all about the last of this trio, we know that its seven-hundred-eighty-odd pages covers the waking eighteen hours in an ordinary day in Dublin in June of 1904. In both cases the awed question that fixes our necessary resistance is "How do the writers manage to write so much about so little . . . ?" But isn't this question remarkably close to the one with which we turn to Tolstoy's 1,450-page tapestry of early nineteenth-century Russian life? The writer is going to write about war *and* peace. Here, prompted by the bulk of the text, the question becomes simply "How will the writer manage to write—and write about—so *much*, period?"

To describe the restraints within which the prose of Abish's novel situates itself is to locate another sense of resistance. Meanings there are aplenty—and even plot. But, because of the constraints and limitations, certain kinds of verbal events and expectations end up occupying far more important places in our attention than they would in a normative work:

The first time the word *the* appears in Abish's novel, on page 51, and the last time it appears, on page 97, forty-five pages from the end, are such events.

Will the word *genital* appear in chapter "G" or not becomes one of our questions. (It doesn't.)

In both chapters "X," the only *x* word to occur is "Xenephon." Is there any significance to the fact that the childhood and adolescent favorites "xylophone" and "xenophobia" are skipped over?

In the first chapter "Z," a single three-quarter page paragraph, only three words occur beginning with *z* (*Zambia*, *zigzag*, and *zapping*) and no words at all with *u*, *v*, *x*, or *y*; while in the second chapter "Z," nine pages long, only one word begins with *v* (*vandals*, 67) in the entire section, by far the longest in the book. This lets us know—and know forcefully—that the constraint is that words beginning with certain letters *can* appear, but not that they *must* appear.

The first chapter "W" allows the words "we" and "would" into the novel's vocabulary, but "will" (along with the whole concept of futurity) and "what" stay outside it. (The word *will* occurs, in the phrase "if you will," only once in the novel [66], the word *what* not at all.)

The arrival and vanishing of the possibility of various words in the text (and whether or not those possibilities are realized within their various embedded windows of possibility) become major textual events during our reading, just as important as, or even more important than, such questions as whether Alva and Alex will make love or what the outcome of the various ant attacks will be, or how Queen Quat will be received at her press conference.

We experience the writing as occurring at the greater level of energy it took to assemble and limit these words into such a pattern. Even as the central chapters gather toward a more and more normative prose, surface events still admit of a certain pleasing discontinuity, so that certain kinds of linguistically self-referential moments leap out as the most effective form of humor.

Chapter "V" begins:

> Veiled threats. Prior to my departure, my hasty and un-
> planned-for departure from Antibes, I kept receiving
> veiled threats. Sometimes I also received muffled threats.
> (57)

Which sends the reader back to check in the previous chapter,
"T," for any "muffled threats"—the earliest *they* could have
shown up. (There are none.)

At one point, after little Alfred has not yet gotten food poi-
soning and Alva is staring out of the window, Alfred asks Alva
where she has been.

> I have been staring out of the window, she replies.
> It must be the zucchini, Alva tells Alfred whose face
> has turned a deathly white.
> I'll never touch the stuff again, he says.
> It must be the zucchini.
> Promise me, he says, that you'll never mention the
> word again.
> What word, she asks innocently. (69)

But since we are in the second chapter "Z," beyond which, according to the rules the novel has set up, no more words beginning with *z can* appear, it is the form of the novel as much as it is
the will of the character that vouchsafes the obeying of Alfred's
injunction.

These and many like occurrences become the novel's memorable moments.

OLSEN: *You recently shared with me your caveat about putting together an issue such as this* [the special *Para•doxa* issue "The Future of Narrative"] *by telling me the story of how various groups,
in need of knowing the future of anything from mobile homes to
metallurgy, will call up a science fiction writer and query him or
her about these things . . . as if she or he has some sort of privileged
position upon tomorrow. But your sense is that SF proves nothing if
not that the future can't be forecast. As a genre, then, what is SF's
special relationship to time, narratological and phenomenal?*

DELANY: It doesn't have one.

The relationship of *writing*—more specifically narrative, if you prefer—to time is that writing is *always* a message from the past. It is always interpreted by someone—a reader—with a more recent set of past experiences than the writer's; unto the limit case where the reader is reading his own writing the instant after he or she puts it down.

Thus writing is always historically bounded; at the same time, through the nature of reading, it always escapes the historical specificity of the moment of writing and begins to partake of a historically interpretive excess—in excess of the time it was written—that relates it to (makes it a commentary on) the time it is read. This, of course, is the relationship of all writing to time. The point to be made is that this relation is just as true for science fiction as it is for any other practice of writing. At this particular level, science fiction doesn't *have* a "special" relationship to time—more special than any other narrative genre. One even suspects some sort of category/concept mistake lingers somewhere in the question's very articulation.

Your question has the same form—and embodies the same misconception—as the question one might pose to a painter whose sunsets you particularly admire: "What is the special relation that exists between paint and sunset?"

Well, the relation between paint and sunset is no different from the relation between paint and a wheatfield with black crows swooping above it, or the relation between paint and a mysteriously smiling sixteenth-century merchant's wife, or the relation between paint and a swamped raft full of sailors shouting after a ship retreating at the horizon. That is to say, the specialness of the painted sunset does not inhere *in the paint*—as the specialness of science fiction does not inhere in a specific relation of narrativity per se to one or even a handful of generic rhetorical features. Rather, the specific knowledge with which a particular painter uses his or her paint to implement the various suggestions of the rocky shore, the sea beside it, the sun through the copper clouds above it makes *that* specific painting of a sunset special in its special way; it is how the writer employs the range of narrative rhetoric that makes a given SF text special.

Naive viewers that we all, on some level, are, we *want* the specialness to inhere in the medium, in the genre—rather than in the artist. But that is simply hoping for the easy way out. And there isn't any.

For a couple of pages, now, I want to talk about two texts I consider special; as well, I want to show the way they address one another. One is a piece of science fiction. One is a piece of experimental fiction.

Part of the resistance we bring to Pamela Zoline's superb and lyrical sixty-seven-page experimental novella "Sheep" (*Likely Stories: A Collection of Untraditional Fiction,* ed. Bruce McPherson [New Paltz: Treacle Press, 1981]) is the simple and bewildering "What is it going to be—or to be about?" This question—which is often the mark of the resistance that identifies alternative fiction as a genre—is often the hardest resistance to overcome. (This is why alternative fiction tends to be read only by readers who are interested in the genre as a force effective on the arts.) In the first half dozen pages, however, "Sheep" establishes its organizing conceit. A woman is having trouble sleeping. (The decision as to whether she is "real," or a textual construct to facilitate the organizing of the text, or a metaphor for something else is left to the reader entirely.) To overcome her insomnia, she resorts to the tried and true practice of counting sheep jumping over a fence. In the course of the text, by means of scientific accounts, quotations from agricultural manuals, as well as wonderfully fresh and lyric writing, we get a compositionally satisfying embraiding of meditations on sleep, sheep, and dreams, as well as cowboy movies, wolves, a full-fledged pastoral, several recipes for the preparation of lambs (forestière, roasted . . .), instructions for—and descriptions of—their castration and slaughter, and various fantasias on meadow fencing and breeding, as sheep after sheep leaps across Zoline's fence.

Many moments in the story are highly moving, such as when, menaced by the Wolf, who is wreaking havoc on the pastoral landscape, the sheep become hysterical, with as many jumping back over the fence in the *wrong* direction as are jumping over in the right one—or when one sheep tries to crawl under the fence and becomes hopelessly stuck.

The text's associations range as far afield as "The Wiffenpoof

Song," which is presented as a fill-in form for the reader, who is urged to write in the lyrics in the blanks provided.

> We are poor little lambs who have lost our way.
> Ba-ba-ba!
> We are little black sheep who have gone astray.
> Ba-ba-ba!
> Gentlemen, songsters, off on a spree,
> Damned from here to eternity.
> Lord, have mercy on such as we.
> Ba-ba-ba!

At another point, we are given the text from a sampler describing the advantages of wool, from which moths have eaten all the vowels.

By taking our own associations much further than we are likely to, by concretizing them so beautifully, "Sheep" invites the reader to continue this metaphorical exploration. ("Sheep" is an extraordinarily suggestive text to read alongside some of Foucault's late examinations of "pastoral power" and governmentality.) Through it we pursue our own associations with sheep and the body politic, into the political or the aesthetic, however we might like.

We've mentioned parasitism already, and there is a parasitic aspect to "Sheep" that may eventually bring us to something important about alternative fiction. With all the texts that "Sheep" is parasitic upon (cookbooks, farming manuals . . .), there is one line of parasitism/intertextuality that is not immediately apparent from the text.

In 1968, I published a science fiction novel called *Nova*. A couple of years later, Thomas Disch wrote a brilliant satire/ critique of the novel in the form of a short story, first published in Marilyn Hacker's and my *Quark/3* as "The Planet Arcadia" and, in other venues, as "Et in Arcadia Ego." Taking off from a notion put forward by William Empson in *Some Versions of Pastoral* (1974), the fundamental conceit of Disch's story is that all adventure fictions, such as *Nova* or, indeed, *Moby-Dick*, are basically versions of the archetypal pastoral story. (With only the faintest irony, my space-captain hero was named "Lorq Von Ray." With a much larger ironic smear, Disch named his minion of death and the empire "Captain Garst Flame.") Disch's story bodies forth the conflict between the "Empire" and the "Arcadians." After reading Disch's tale, his longtime friend Pamela Zoline clearly felt that there was a great deal more you could do with the Arcadian notion—and "Sheep" was the result.

Let's compare Disch's science-fictional "Wolf" with Zoline's. We'll look at Disch's first, as it emerges from the Arcadian temple where the Abba Damon has kept it in hiding, as a weapon with which to attack the Imperial Invaders, in the person of Captain Garst:

Concerning the Wolf.

Though not larger than a double sleeping-space and almost noiseless in its operation, the Wolf was expressive, in every detail of its construction, of a sublime rapaciousness, a thirst for dominion so profound as to make our Empire, universal as it is, seem (for the moment we watched it) as insubstantial as the architectures shaped by the successive phrases of a Bach chorale, which fade as swiftly as they rise. Here, incarnate in chrome-vanadium steel, was the Word that our lips had always hesitated to speak; the orphic secret that had been sealed, eons past, in the cornerstone of the human heart, suspected but never seen; the last, unwritten chapter of the book.

Busy swarms of perceptual organs encircled its crenellated head to form a glittering metal annulet; its jaws were the toothy scoops of old steam shovels; it was gray as a glass of breakfast juice is gray, and beautiful as only a machine can be beautiful . . .

Dinosaurs quarreling; the customs of pirates, of the Iroquois, of carnivorous apes; the great superbowl between the Packers and the Jets; the annihilation of Andromeda III; Norse berserkers hacking Saxons and their horses to bits; the hashish-inspired contretemps of the Assassins of Alamut; the duels of Romeo and Tybalt, of Tancred and Clorinda; killer-dwarves of the Roman arenas; John L. Lewis smashing the skulls of company scabs with his mammoth jackhammer; Apollo flaying Marsyas, slaying the Delphian Python at the very brink of the sacred abyss;

bloodbaths, bullfights, drunken mayhem, battle hymns, Schutzstaffel death-camps, missiles programmed to reproduce themselves in midflight; Germans galloping across the ice of Lake Peipus; Juggernauts and abattoirs; Alexander's delirium at *Arbela*; *Bull Run*; the Romans slaughtered at *Cannae* and slaughtering at *Chaeronea*; *Droghedea* defeated and depopulated; Panzers swarming across the sand toward *El Alamain*; the Carolingian empire dissolving at *Fontenay*; the French victorious at *Fontenoy*; images that can only begin to suggest the weight and excitement of the drama our cameras recorded that day, as nine and a half feet of red-haired, blue-eyed human fury matched its strength and wits against six tons of super-charged, kill-crazy engineering. (318–21)

If we herd together some of the references to the Wolf in Zoline's tale (omitting those that turn on the notion of "A wolf in sheep's clothing," with which, several times, Zoline plays brilliantly), we get a rather different effect—or, indeed, set of effects:

The old gray Wolf pads along through the brush, keeping a set distance between himself and the flock, keeping downwind of them, not in a hurry. He sees three more silly sheep leap over the fence, Number 34, Number 35, Number 36. (109)

And the flock could smell the Wolf's scent, which was sharp, and they could hear the Wolf's voice, which was loud, and they could see the Wolf's markings, which were subtle, and they became afraid. Agitated, they ran this way and that, a group of them leaped over the fence, Number 111, Number 112 . . . (124)

The Wolf's menu, à la carte, includes grouse, insects, rabbit, deer, salmon, mice, and mutton. (126)

The Wolf is hungry. Traveling behind the flock he has come to know them, their individual scents, their tracks, their habits. And now the winds are cutting cold, and the casual bounty of summer and early autumn is gone, and it's getting to be time to risk the dogs and the humans and their weapons and go after the sweet, tame meat of the flock. In the Wolf's mind is a map of his territory in which every tree, bush, stream, ditch, hill, pathway is featured and remembered.

He sought out the ridges and the high slopes where the scents were clearest. Since he had become separated from the rest of the wolf pack, he had been forced to develop his strategy and learn to hunt alone.

He located the flock again, half a mile down wind of him and moving at a slow pace Northwards. He set out to follow them, circling, moving at the tireless trot which he could keep up all day. The ravens, his friends, followed after him waiting for their share in the kill.

the selection of the victim

the eye contact, the contract

the pursuit, separation from the flock

a movement through the landscape, thriller/western/pastoral/bed

The sleeper cannot sleep, the mind's computer processes the alphabet soup.

Like an anti-sheep, he looks with great knowledge over the flock. Like a shepherd selecting a sheep for special care, he turns his great eye on her. He chooses the old balding ewe, Limpfoot, will you dance? His gaze is like a lover's, and she is required to return his gaze. And, like lovers, they exchange a pledge.

He edges her out of the flock, she is solitary, she is on her own, she is running. She is running, alone, the panic of pursuit makes her drunk, it anesthetizes her, she runs and runs.

The sheep runs and the Wolf runs after her, through the area of the Border Control, past the edges of the herd of grazing cattle, upwind from Phoebe's dog, past the unsleeping Sleeper who is dreaming of a drowning mermaid, the sheep tries for one more chance at safety, she jumps the fence, Number 126.

Lamb, How to Roast

1) Season with salt and pepper, if desired
2) Place fat-side-up on rack in an open roasting pan
3) Insert meat thermometer
4) Roast in a pre-heated oven at 300° F
5) Do not add water, nor cover, nor baste
6) Roast until the meat thermometer registers rare, medium, or well done as desired. (128–29)

And Limpfoot is running and running, and the Wolf is after her.

Limpfoot is still running with tremendous effort but her flickering feet are not covering much ground, her breath is painful, it does not nourish her, she smells the Wolf, she hears the Wolf, she sees the Wolf, she feels his breath, his teeth on her leg, his teeth on her shoulder, she sighs, she falls. She switches from subject to object. She is switched. The Wolf ends her life with a bite to her throat, he sets about his supper. (130)

And in a raw panic, scenting the blood, the flock goes mad and rushes at the fence, and then: four sheep jump over the fence; six sheep get down on their bellies and wriggle under the fence; a frenzied ewe throws herself at the fence again and again, and finally bursts the wood and pushes through, eleven sheep follow her through the gap. Number 141, Number 142, Number 143 . . . (132)

And the Wolf lies in his cave, belly distended, licking his chops, asleep, dreaming already of his next meal. (133)

There is a fundamental difference between Disch's Wolf and Zoline's Wolf that is only touched on in the quote from Disch. Disch's Wolf is an agent *of* Arcadia, hidden in the temple, and released by the druidic Abba Damon to battle the agent of Empire, Garst Flame—"nine and a half feet of red-haired, blue-eyed human fury." Though, like death (the traditional speaker of the Latin tag that titles Disch's story), it too is in Arcadia, by contrast Zoline's Wolf, because it preys *on* her Arcadians—and by extension, on their sheep—soon becomes a symbol (the "anti-sheep" Zoline describes it as) of all that menaces Zoline's Arcadia from without.

From "Sheep":

> The poet in the garden extemporizes on the politics of the pastoral. "Removing themselves from the appetite for wealth and fame, and turning aside from the pungent variety of city life—also denying the claims of family, the shepherd and shepherdess give themselves over to the celebration of the beauties of the natural world, and of love. After a space, that world is breached and broken by those energies forbidden to it." (147)

In Zoline, the Wolf plays the paradoxical role of that which is both ("Et in Arcadia Ego") in Arcadia and the energies forbidden there from without that menace, subvert, and destroy it.

Disch's Wolf inhabits, however, another paradox. Disch's Wolf belongs wholly *to* his Arcadia but exists entirely as a rhetorical fusillade *from* the Imperial tradition. Both the breakfast juice and the machine, whose antipodal distances define the range of its beauty, are objects of the Empire—*not* of Arcadia. The existence of the Wolf (which, finally, both castrates and kills, not sheep, but the Empire's implacable hero, Garst) in Disch's tale functions as the Empire's excuse to incinerate the planet—and move on to other conquests, other destructions. It is not the symbol of any breaching by those energies. It is what causes those energies to breach Arcadia in order to destroy it.

Compared to Disch's Wolf, Zoline's would seem somewhat naive. Is there any recomplicated hint of Disch's Wolf in Zoline's world? There is, and it rings out clearly and conscientiously.

As Zoline's pastoral shepherds mourn the death of the Great God Pan with a traditional drunken revel, one of them, Bion, shouts: "'We begin!' in a voice like a wolf" (122). (Note the small letter.) For the first time, one of the Arcadians is, indeed, identified with the Wolf itself. Later in the scene, as they fall to drunken lovemaking, we read:

> Another wolf scare in the flock.
> At the top of the arc of these drunken revels, they come upon a track in the grass, unlike any track they have ever

seen before. The ground shakes, it is something completely new. Ordinary heroics do not serve, and they tremble at the altogether frightening and disorienting sight of a great machine, an engine of destruction. The sheep are frightened, as much by the spectacle of their guardians' terror as by the thing itself, a Debouillet jumps over the fence, Number 106, a Corriedale jumps over the fence, Number 107, a Karakul jumps over the Fence, Number 108, a Targhee jumps over the fence, Number 109, a Panama jumps over the fence, Number 110. (123)

No other mention is made of these strange tracks nor of the great machine, the engine of destruction, that left them—and, presumably, the "wolf scare." But it is here, along that track in the grass, that Zoline welcomes the rhetorical energies of the non-Arcadian into her pastoral in the form of Disch's mechanical "Wolf." I think she meant for a few readers to be aware that Disch's Wolf was there in Arcadia as well. This boundary crossing —to which we shall return—is perhaps the strongest technique and most subversive move either the artists committed to experimental fiction or its critics can make.

Disch himself has written some fine experimental tales, by the bye, including "The Squirrel Cage," "The Master of the Milford Altarpiece," and the eponymous novella in his superb story series *334* (1974).

OLSEN: *Many of your characters—Hogg, for instance—are less than likable, even frightening and repulsive. Why choose to write about such social pariahs, and how do you ease the reader into coming along for the narratological ride? In other words, what can be learned about the nature of characterization from your choices?*

DELANY: I'm not comfortable with the rhetoric of easing the reader into anything in fiction, normative or experimental. It sounds more like somebody talking about marketing. There are expositional techniques, and there are developmental ones, and there are recapitulations and closures in writing. But making things easy is only a provisional task, not a central one. (Nor do I believe in making things unnecessarily hard, either.) Rather than talk more than I've done already about my own texts, however, I'd rather use your question as a take-off to make two brief points.

First: unpleasant (or unusual) characters or unpleasant (or unusual) situations are *not* what make experimental fiction. That's a point worth stressing. Experimental fiction is precisely that genre where it is perfectly reasonable to ask, why does fiction need characters at all? There've been times, certainly, when I've felt that any writer writing a novel in a "classical" or normative form, regardless of subject matter, is de facto an experimentalist because so few people do it well. It presumes a concern *with* form itself that for me is what characterizes the experimental. But of course this is only an extension of my theory that, I think we've already seen, is inadequate.

Second: in my criticism of science fiction, I've written repeatedly about the tyranny of the subject. This, if you'll recall, is not a problem of science fiction but is rather a problem of literature's that, among other things, keeps it blind to the worth of extra-literary genres such as science fiction, even as it restricts what literature can say about society. Experimental writing is the one literary generic area where there's the possibility of sedimenting a body of texts that interrogates and even moves to remedy this problem from within the literary boundaries.

OLSEN: *Is it possible to frame a question about the future of narrative in a way that would yield illuminating results about what's worthwhile to contemplate and why?*

DELANY: Not without speaking about its past.

I have felt for some time now that generic boundaries—boundaries which are constituted of discourse in its most pure form—are the real object of any disciplined history of the various practices of writing; and thus, if you will (and in passing), the key to the future of the literary.

The point of course is that alternative fiction is a genre *within* the literary precincts. Among the solidly literary genres, experimental fiction is arguably the least powerful. The only literary genre less powerful as a whole is experimental poetry (as distinguished from traditional poetry).

Theoretically, by the same theory that connects experimental fiction to normative literature, the genre that experimental fiction is closest to on the absolute scale is comic books: its reliance on the visual and its intermingling of words, meaning, and image put them cheek-a-jowl. But there is a discursive palisade separating them, a granite incline with experimental fiction at the cultural height and comics at the cultural nadir. (One reason, doubtless, I'm so fond of *Modulations* is because I'm also a comics lover.) From the bottom of the decline, Scott McCloud (in *Understanding Comics* [Northampton, Mass.: Tundra, 1993]) has written brilliantly about the literary anxiety, as it appears from the paraliterary side of the border, over the literary mixing of words and images.

Part of that literary anxiety exists entirely to maintain (indeed, constitutes) the boundary itself—it is the bodily manifestation *of* the boundary—between alternative fiction and comics, between alternative fiction and advertising. Comics and advertising are, of course, two practices of writing on the paraliterary side where words meld with pictures all but seamlessly.

(In his lovely *Star Fiction*, Eric Belgum attacks the literature/advertising border directly. Recalling the first anonymous 1798 edition of Wordsworth and Coleridge's *Lyrical Ballads*, which, you remember, began with an "ADVERTISEMENT" ["The majority of the following poems are to be considered as experiments"], Belgum's text carries no clear demarcation between itself and its advertising, promotional copy, and titles.)

Those boundaries lend endless complexities to the task of ecrival historiography through their rich and rugged erections of bodily resistances separating various genres one from the other, which fix these cultural boundaries' relationships.

Within each specific subgenre of literature and paraliterature, there are, indeed, far more informed judgments in circulation about what is being done *there* than in the genre of normative literature across the way.

I don't say there will necessarily be agreement. But the conversations within given genre boundaries will at least address the same landscape, will agree, if only ostensibly, on what objects are within it. Problems arise at the borders when there's interest within one genre (say, normative literature) in receiving delegates from another. Rarely if ever is the chosen delegate an artist whom even a plurality of those who work and live their lives within a given genre would judge among the greatest or the most influential. Usually the chosen one will be, rather, somebody who is definitely middle of the scale, possibly with some topical tag—and a great deal of chance configuration of nonliterary factors. This is especially true of emissaries from the paraliterary genres to the literary.

I don't believe any notable number of people working within the comics field, for example, think Art Spiegelman's *Maus* represents any kind of pinnacle or high point in contemporary comics art. By that, I mean Spiegelman is a talented guy, certainly. His work is interesting and worthy of being read. His work on *Raw*, the comics magazine he did in the eighties, was undoubtedly important and influential. But the idea that, as a comics writer/artist, his work is better or more talented or has done as much to influence and shake up the genre than, among his contemporaries, say, Alan Moore, Neil Gaiman, Harvey Pekar, or the artists they work with, Dave Gibbons, Dave McKean, and Eddie Campbell, not to mention Mobius, the Hernandez brothers, Kyle Baker, or any one of a dozen others, including, in another area of comics, Neal Adams or Frank Miller, is cause not even for argument but for uproarious laughter at the absurdity of the universe. Nevertheless, outside the boundaries, supported by his Pulitzer Prize, Spiegelman's name is known, while generally these other, far more important names, are not.

Within science fiction, for forty years, the giants have been Heinlein, Bester, and Sturgeon—not necessarily in that order. Outside the field, the giants have been assumed to be Heinlein, Asimov, and Clarke—which is not to put down Asimov or Clarke, but only to draw attention to the absurdity of the systems of the world. In fact, at this point, the inner and outer judgments have so melded that they can no longer be really distinguished.

As to the boundaries themselves, some are large and clear, such as the one between the literary genres on one side and the paraliterary genres on the other: the boundary that separates novels, short stories, poetry, and drama as they are usually conceived from mysteries, westerns, science fiction, comic books, and pornography. But, at various places at various times, even that boundary had a very different grade from the one it exhibits today. Between the twenties and the forties, it grew permeable enough for literary maven G. K. Chesterton to write his Father Brown mystery stories and for Dante scholar Dorothy Sayers and serious novelist Graham Greene to write their own mysteries; and, indeed, for William Faulkner to pen his Gavin Stevens tales and novels—and, conversely, to allow the novels of Chandler and Hammett to end up, by the sixties, as Modern Library volumes and James M. Cain to be eventually republished by Vintage Books. In no case, however, was the breaching of these borders—at least from the weaker field to the stronger—a simple shoo-in. Writers as diverse as W. H. Auden, André Gide, and Albert Camus were lobbying, as it were, for Hammett, just after his death—while others worked just as hard to keep those borders intact, claiming that mysteries were just *not* literature, no matter how you sliced it.

Some of the texts I've already spoken about (e.g., Zoline, Disch) were generated specifically in the breaching, during the 1960s, of that same long-established literary/paraliterary border —but at another location. In the history of science fiction, this breach was known as the "New Wave." When, in London, twenty-six-year-old Michael Moorcock took over *New Worlds Magazine* in 1965 and, a year later, received a London Arts Council Grant, he opened his magazine to experimental fiction as well as the science fiction it had traditionally published. The cross-pollination was wonderfully exciting and kept writers and critics on two continents buzzing for the next two decades.

But the same problems—at least the same *kinds* of problems —exist on the literary side, between, say, the genres of experimental writing and the genres of normative literature.

Living entirely within the normative precincts is an official history of experimental fiction that remains wholly unaware of such boundary breachings, such histories. Indeed, it is based on a view that assumes there *are* no genres, much less boundaries between them, but only an undifferentiated mass of texts, for which an anonymous synod is always in session, egalitarianly perusing them all, in order to bring the finest ones to light. We can pick this history up with Gertrude Stein's *Three Lives* (1909) and move right on past World War I (as though it never happened, at least in this history) and sweep through the twenties, the decade that was ushered in with *Ulysses* (1922) and tolled out with *The Sound and the Fury* (1929), while, after trying her hand at two normative novels, Virginia Woolf turned to a new sort of fiction with *Jacob's Room* (1922), which she developed through *Mrs. Dalloway* (1925) and *To the Lighthouse* (1927), unto *The Waves* (1931). Recent attempts to read cultural diversity back into this history will point out, as a kind of footnote to it, Jean Toomer's *Cane* (1923). The most contemporary version of this history even notes that Stein's *The Making of Americans* was published—at her own expense—in 1925. (Back in 1913, Proust had published at *his* own expense *Du Côté de chez Swann*—and, in the same year in Chicago, Edgar Rice Burroughs had published, at his own expense, *Under the Moons of Mars*, the only one of the three self-published endeavors to be financially successful.) At the same time, fascinated with the work of Jules Verne, the wealthy French eccentric Raymond Roussel was attempting to operationalize, through homophonics and other linguistic methods, the creation of eccentric fictive objects and wacky incidental developments in a series of novels, poems, and plays, also self-published: *Impressions d'Afrique* (1910, novel), *Locus Solus* (1914, novel), *L'Étoile au front* (1925, play), and *Nouvelles Impressions d'Afrique* (1932, a poem in four cantos). Roussel is, incidentally, the topic of Michel Foucault's least read book (and one of his most interesting), *Death and the Labyrinth: The World of Raymond Roussel* (trans. Charles Ruas [Galimard, 1963; University of California Press, 1986]). Those of a more leftist leaning might include in this history poet Kenneth Patchen's perennially popular *The Journal of Albion Moonlight* (1941). Though I have not seen anyone refer to it in print in more than twenty years, it is still regularly stocked on the shelves of Barnes & Noble, even as we speak. Those familiar with Russian writing will rush to include the works of Velimir Klebnikov (some of which are available in a brilliantly inventive translation by Gary Kern, *Snake Train* [Ann Arbor: Ardis, 1976]; a more recent anthology of Klebnikov's work is *The King of Time: Poems, Fictions, Visions of the Future*, translated by Paul Schmidt [Cambridge: Harvard University Press, 1985]). "Around 1948" (I am quoting Hugh

Kenner's *Samuel Beckett, A Critical Study*) in France, Joyce's one-time secretary wrote his trilogy, *Molloy, Malone Dies*, and *The Unnamable*, which first appeared between 1950 and 1952. The advocates of this "history" already have a place for the French writers of the "new novel," Robbe-Grillet, Nathalie Saurat, Claude Simon (who, after Beckett, would go on to win the Nobel Prize), and Philippe Sollers; while in 1957, on the same Saturday the Russians announced Sputnik's circling of the globe and U.S. newspapers were filled with stories and pictures of the white demonstrations against black students in Little Rock, Arkansas, attempting to integrate the schools, the *New York Times* carried Gilbert Milstein's praiseful review of Jack Kerouac's (1922–69) "spontaneous prose" novel *On the Road*. A decade and a half after his normative *Beetlecreek* (1950), William Demby published his austere experiment *The Catacombs* (1965). The same folk who might want to include Patchen might want to include, from 1963, French jazz-maven Boris Vian's wonderfully playful *L'Écume du jour*. During my first trip to Europe in '65, every French-speaking youngster I met carried a copy of it in his or her back pocket. Two years later, Richard Brautigan's *Trout Fishing in America* (1967) would go on to a similar sort of popularity in the States as Vian's in France, in the decade that saw *The New Yorker* flog the work of Donald Barthelme to unmitigated popularity and John Ashbery and James Schuyler write their delightful *A Nest of Ninnies* (1969), while more adventurous readers were becoming excited over the new work of Robert Coover, especially his story collection *Pricksongs and Descants* (1962), following on his normative novel *The Origin of the Brunists* (1960). Meanwhile the French Oulipo Group, with Raymond Queneau at its center and Georges Perec its most dazzling younger member, were producing, alongside Harry Mathews in English, their various works in France, while Kathy Acker celebrated *Great Expectations* (1982) and looked forward to *Blood and Guts in High School* (1984). Joseph McElroy published *Plus* (1987) and *Women and Men* (1993), and David Markson, inspired by the dedication of the Dalkey, produced *Reader's Block* (1996). If one is looking for loose schools or groups, one might even continue this tale with the prose works of the L=A=N=G=U=A=G=E poets, particularly Lyn Hejinian's *My*

Life (1980, 1987), up through the avant-pop writers and today's New York–based Unbearables . . .

I hope we can all agree that what I have traced out here is in no way a history of alternative writing. It is simply and wholly a myth—a myth based entirely on normative popularity. And while popularity must certainly be *a* factor in any such history, just as certainly it cannot supply the only criteria *for* history and still produce a historical narrative worthy of the name. It is neither comprehensive nor does it chronicle the best work being done—nor the most interesting work in alternative writing at any moment it purports to cover. To say that it does is tantamount to saying that the history of American literature in the last quarter of the twentieth century is exhausted by the romances of Rosemary Rogers and the horror novels of Stephen King—since these two writers have easily sold as many books between them as any ten other writers one can name and are more widely read than *anyone* else, often by a factor of hundreds, of thousands . . .

Along the boundary that separates commercial fiction from alternative fiction, commercial fiction occupies the stronger side and alternative fiction the weaker. Thus, when a writer from the strong side invades the weaker side and brings back rhetorical and aesthetic trophies to display in her or his next work, the general society celebrates. When, however, artists from the weak side invade the strong side to retrieve like rhetorical trophies and incorporate them in *their* work, it is not that the thefts are ignored: they may well be celebrated in the weaker precincts. But the stronger side does everything in its power to bruit it about that no raid even took place.

Without in any way denying that he was an often brilliant writer, I feel I must point out that Donald Barthelme (and, indeed, most of the other figures in the list above) functioned, during the decades of his ascendancy, mostly as a kind of dam *against* further interest in literary experimentation per se. Even though critics like you (Lance Olsen), Larry McCaffery, and Jerome Klinkowitz were celebrating in normative venues his specific linguistic energies and incisions, outside that circle, readers who encountered his tales would take it that now they knew all there was of interest to know about things experimental; and certainly the people who published Barthelme felt, "We've already got one. We don't need any more." Many people, especially younger writers with an experimental bent, hoped that they were involved in some sort of trickle-down intellectual economics. But it doesn't work that way—neither in economics nor in art.

Even discussions of Joyce, which relate him to everything under the sun, from Irish mythology to Wagnerian dramatistic inspiration for stream-of-consciousness, rarely discuss him today against the rich French avant-garde tradition from the 1890s on, without which the specifically *textual* strategies in both *Ulysses* and *Finnegans Wake* would be unthinkable. In his famous study, Stuart Gilbert tries to sever Joyce from that tradition: "There could be no greater error than to confuse the work of James Joyce with the harum-scarum school or the *surréaliste* group (to whom some of the most brilliant of the younger French writers belong, or once belonged) whose particular *trouvaille* was a sort of automatic writing, no revision allowed" (31). While objectively all Gilbert is saying here is that Joyce revised his work, his choice of a way to say it makes the overall suggestion clear. Today, Joyce is practically anything *but* an experimental writer. Rather he has become a kind of hypernormative "innovator." That too is a matter of discursive boundary shifts that could be usefully historified.

Having said that, I don't believe in this society anyone can come to alternative fiction by any other route than through this "myth." But to accept it, to let it stand there, not to question it, not to interrogate it, not to revise it constantly and rewrite it continually in the light of new readings, new researches, is to declare oneself an enemy of alternative fiction—and, indeed, to reveal oneself a Philistine and enemy of art itself. The only use for such a myth is as something always to look beyond, always to search behind. To the extent you ever accept it, you become its victim—and one with the border problem, by *becoming* the border.

Such lists don't go away. They are a discourse in themselves.

You ask for predictions.

The most usual (the most predictable) prediction—I have heard it put forth from the very first days of the New Wave in 1965 to the most recent reading of the Unbearables, in the basement of the Spiritual Body Piercing Emporium on Canal Street—is that, imminently, all boundaries will dissolve and that potential mass of undifferentiated texts will arrive/return, and the field of writing will aspire to/fall into a prelapsarian state of undifferentiated genreless bliss, in which every artist will be given a fair hearing, a fresh start, as that all-powerful, wholly responsible, and magnanimous synod turns to constitute a fresh and ultimately fair canon.

Don't even think about it.

That's just not the way social boundaries—discourses, if you will—work. Squeezed in by their boundaries, genres are obliterated by the force of other genres. *No* one writes eighteenth-century physiologies any more. They did *not* turn into short stories. They really *were* ousted by the novel. "The arts are produced," William Empson reminds us in his book *Some Versions of Pastoral* (1935; New Directions: New York, 1974), "by overcrowding" (6). Those boundaries inch along into new territories. They erupt in existing genres to sunder them all but completely, in response to infrastructural economic differentiation. Not Stephen King and Rosemary Rogers as writerly forces, but the economics *around* King and Rogers have created immense genres within our time. As a check on the bookstore shelves will show, Rogers *herself*—by far the most widely read writer in the English language of all times, and of the seventies and eighties in particular, which is to say she beats out Shakespeare, the Bible, *and* Stephen King (her something like sixty million sales make the success of *Gone with the Wind* [c. twelve million all-time] look piddling)—has even fallen out of the picture. Even though her books created the largest *category* of commercial fiction of all times, the contemporary "bodice-buster romance," she did it wholly without critical support. When I say that genre boundaries are power boundaries, I mean that they are self-replicating barriers, composed of socioeconomic conditions that are stabilized through being interpreted in a particular way by an existing set of rhetorical expectations. (The fact that most English professors don't even know Rogers's name is proof of the impermeability of such boundaries.) Such is an understanding, a discourse. The power of such discourses is manifested and replicated precisely in such enterprises as this one, of which, let's face it, journals and books such as this are, more often than not, intricately entailed—unless someone is prepared radically to seize the traditional rhetoric by its neck and strangle it. We become accomplices in their mystificational processes precisely by not talking about the material forces that create them and not analyzing the discourses that stabilize them. We sabotage understanding by constantly moving the discussion entirely to the aesthetic plane and downplaying its political/economic realities.

If you want to talk about the future of any practice of writing, with the broadest synchronic view available, that's what you have to look to.

OLSEN: *The novel's death is news every three weeks. But can you imagine the novel's continuing to exist in its present forms and with its present concerns very far into the next century? If so, what will the mechanism of its survival look like? If not, what might account for its mutations, and what shape might they take?*

DELANY: The fact is, *nothing* continues in its present form. Things only continue with their present names—sometimes. Even as discourse preserves (and discourse is the mechanism by which anything that appears to remain stable coheres—including various words with various objects), it does so by fixing a name to an ever-changing field of incidents, material events, and interpretive codes. Western art is an enterprise that values originality; that is to say, as a discourse change is built into it. No one is ever going to write a novel like Longus's *Daphnis and Chloë* (c. 200 CE) again. No one is ever going to write a novel like *Notre Dame de Paris* (1830) or *Ulysses* (1922) or *Infinite Jest* (1996) ever again, either.

In that sense, the notion that the novel *has* a present form is an illusion. (The structures behind all music, Susan Langer told us, ape the developments of human emotion. And my own observation: the structures behind the novel limn the movements of social power. Often they are the same structures, though they point at different things.) It has many past forms and many future forms—and they are always . . . modulating. Given that it's been around as long as it has, given that it's as flexible as it is, given the shots of life it's received from books such as *Gargantua* and *Pantagruel* (1532, 1534), *Tristram Shandy*, and *Ulysses*, not to mention *Sheep*, *Fat Skeletons*, and *Annotations*, I think the novel will probably stay around awhile longer—which is merely to say the name will endure, affixed to *something* . . . because, actually, that's all the novel has ever been. The rest is discourse.

OLSEN: *At a more local level, what is the future of your own narratives? I mean this in several ways. Do you sense, for instance, a deep structural change in the way you've been telling stories from the first time you began to publish, and, if so, what sort of forces besides the obvious ones of artistic maturation have impinged upon them? Where would you be interested in that narrative trajectory carrying you in the future?*

DELANY: Do I sense a deep structural change? No, I don't. At least not at the level we're discussing things.

A novel is a structured arrangement of different modes of rhetoric. That was the awareness that allowed me to write my first published novel thirty-five years ago. It's what's allowed me to write my traditional novels *and* my more experimental ones—however little they deserve the "experimental" label. The traditional novel is not, of course, one structure. It's thousands of possible structures. And experimental work encompasses thousands on thousands—indeed, limitless numbers—more.

As with your question about the relationship between narrativity and the future, I sense a fundamental confusion, in the way it's been put, between, if you will, variables and verities. The former far outnumber the latter—which are only relative and provisional, anyway.

Where is my narrative trajectory going?

On my side of fifty, well, I have four or five more projects that I've had in mind for some time that I hope I'll get to and finish. I hope as well that, somewhere as I move between them, one or two new ones may spring to mind—inspired by whatever shift of leaf light, or gas-in-the-gut, or history—and strike with the force necessary to carry them to completion. Should these be wildly new and experimental, I shall be very happy and will revel in the prospects. Should they be pastiches of the wholly classical, I shall revel equally. Both, to me, represent formal challenges. But—at least to me—as long as they are recognizable *as* fiction, they fall within the theoretical purview I've laid out. My theory is, after all, a theory of the object. Perhaps I shall discover that I have, indeed, described it inadequately, improperly, and that it needs to be retheorized. Certainly *that* would be exciting!

Perhaps what is needed is a more experimental theory—one that can regard my own merely as a particular fiction, a specific text, of no more interest than its difference from an ideal elaboration which it merely ironizes. Perhaps what we need in the theoretical elaboration of alternative fiction is an active suppression of any fixed and sedimented canon. Eco's reading of Alphonse Allais ("Lector in Fabula," 1979) must learn to consort happily with the meditations of Marjorie Perloff—which is to say, we must relearn how to reread our critics.

The forces that vary the production of fiction I see as the swing and interbraided mechanics of life (which, yes, contains art; as, yes—*pace* Wilde, *pace* Artaud—art contains life), which are—still—no more predictable than what I shall be doing at 4:15 PM next Tuesday: eating, napping, wandering through the apartment with a new twenty-foot cord talking on the phone, working at my word processor, strolling along a rainy sidewalk in the East Village, picking through the ruins of what's left of my apartment building after a terrorist bombing, having a major philosophical revelation by the Hudson River, or watching some children play beyond the park fence from the sixth-floor window of Beth Israel North Hospital, waiting for the results of an emergency cardiac stress test, or gazing at the back of Dennis's shaved head while he sits on the rug in front of me and together we look at a tape of TNT wrestling, him with a Bud and me with a Diet Snapple. The future is precisely as circumscribed as that (some possibilities are certainly more probable than others) and as unpredictable (none can be ruled out entirely till we get there).

Whatever art I may be lucky (or unlucky) enough to make is part of that unpredictability.

For me (and again I remind you that basically I speak as an

aesthetic cannibalizer), experimental fiction is the privileged genre in which one finds the pyrotechnical and virtuoso aesthetic cadenzas that feed the range of the written arts.

Certainly, one loves it for itself. But it is so exquisitely useful in the bodily shattering and reforging of formal possibilities for other genres that I find that aspect impossible not to remark—and to remark constantly.

—New York City
1998

The Situation of American Writing Today

1. No matter how strict your sense of career as an individual endeavor, do you also find that your writing reveals a connection to any group—political, religious, cultural, national, international, racial, class, gender, sexual, or other? Do you see your development as a writer as contiguous with the interests of any such larger group? Do you see this development as linked in any way to the socioeconomic circumstances of your upbringing?

2. What has been the public mandate of American writing in the last twenty years? How has contemporary writing responded to the political and economic contexts of the late twentieth century? How have you met this invitation or challenge?

3. How would you characterize your readership today? For whom do you write and why?

4. How would you describe your relation to an American literary past? Do you see yourself as belonging to a specific tradition or generation of American writers?

5. How has your sense of a subject changed in the last twenty years? What pressures have stimulated a change?

6. Has the quality of editing changed during your career? How would you describe the ideal relationship between editors and writers?

7. What value do you place on the way your work has been reviewed? Has the quality of reviewing changed over the course of your career? What has been its effect on the growth of your generation of American writers? On your peers? On yourself?

8. What value do you place on scholarly assessments of contemporary writing? Do you believe that academic critics have something important to say to you? How would you character-

ize the current state of relations between academic criticism and creative writing? How would you envision profitable exchanges among scholars, critics, and writers?

[Questions are by the *American Literary History* editors.]

SAMUEL R. DELANY: This somewhat lengthy overview of your eight questions in general will allow me to answer them later briefly and individually. In their positivity the questions suggest an author—authoritative, intentions wholly present to himself, centered in the current of some mainstream society—who possibly (and comfortably!) *could* answer them directly: "These are my social, group, and political allegiances. This group and that are for whom I write. Once I wrote about topic X, but (because of this or that historical occurrence—the defeat of the Equal Rights Amendment, the Stonewall riots of June 1969 in New York City [from which dates the modern leg of the Gay Liberation Movement], AIDS, the fall of the Berlin Wall, the reign of Reaganomics, Tiananmen Square, the horrors of Bosnia and its unending continuation, the attacks on abortion clinics, the beating of Rodney King, the reinstatement of the death penalty, Clinton's failure to effect a health plan, his failure over gays in the military, the homeless situation in America) now I write of topic Y." Let me risk a certain reductive romanticism: *I* think of writers as seekers, specifically seekers after questions, questions that are dramatized by what Nabokov once called "sensuous thought," for him a description of art.

Your questions suggest, however, an author as finder of answers —and answers of a particularly hard-edge nature—which, to the extent they imply a process that has something to do with writing as a social practice as I have known it, I just don't recognize—the implied writing practice that stands behind your questions, that is. Understand, then, I shall not be able to answer them directly, but will rather slide and slip and fall askew among them.

Human beings are constituted of just the political alliances suggested by your categorical, and my more historical, paradigm (in the sense of "list"). The profession of the writer is, however, not. That is to say, no member of any group your list suggests (party member, church member, class member . . .) nor any individual who survived or was affected by any event on mine is, by belonging to the category, *categorically excluded* from writing.

This is not to deny, in any way, that what *is* required to write is a certain familiarity with one or another "technology of communication" and that such familiarities are likely to lie more readily among the middle classes than not, or that the various class, religious, and cultural enclaves look at writing *very* differently. But this in turn is only one handful among the endless topics the writer can interrogate, castigate if he or she so chooses, and organize an educational and material movement to change: the place where the writer intersects the political citizen, be it Byron or Yeats in Parliament; Grace Paley's or Norman Mailer's (often mutually contentious) antiwar activities; whether it is Kenneth Koch's teaching poetry in the schools or Ron Silliman's teaching poetry in the prisons; whether it is any number of writers' struggles with their families or against whatever social bonds to *be* writers; or even the relative day-to-day isolation required to write at all.

But by the same token writing as a practice is not in any *necessary* way allied to any of these categories.

This salvo against the political presuppositions of your questions I launch as someone who believes passionately (perhaps it seems paradoxical) that *all art is political*. In keeping with a view of the perceivable world as an economic arrangement (that economy is called "discourse" or "discursive structure," and cuts the metaphysically untenable up into the reality seized up among and by our limited mediate faculties) of an endless and unlimited play of differences, I add this antiessentialist note: all art is political not because the politics is *in* the artwork, but because the relevant manifestation of politics, in the area of art as we more or less understand it, is a set of questions that can be asked of pretty much anything—and no one should be able to stop anyone from asking any questions he or she wants.

It seems to me art is interesting in our society precisely because it is a human activity that commands, by tradition (since Wagner, since Flaubert), a level of attention at which we are more likely to hear richer answers about those most disturbing tripartite aspects of *reality/politics*, truth, beauty, and form—answers more interesting than we are likely to hear in any other field save history (with which, of course, it—art—is inextricably allied). For the first—truth—appears the fount of all science and morality, and the second—beauty—the inescapable perception accompanying any new form/relation taken from the cosmos, which is how it segues into, becomes one with, and finally appropriates the third—form *per se*—the enjoyment and employment of which, today, is art.

As well, I write as someone who believes that "reality" and the "political" are one. (Reality is, if you will, the questions you can't avoid asking ["If I jump out this window, will I live or die?"]: reality, a.k.a. the political, is what you *have* to deal with, one way or the other.) But the manner in which total surrounds are of limited interest ("I am not interested in God," wrote Whitman, because as far as he could see God was everywhere), I wonder just how interesting some of your questions are politically as part of an attempt to interrogate writing.

I am a black, gay man who hails from the petite bourgeoisie. Born a slave in Georgia, my paternal grandfather became eventually a bishop and a vice principal of an Episcopalian college in North Carolina. My paternal grandmother was born an issue-free Negro, and after her marriage became dean of women at the same school. The youngest son in this family of black educators, my father came to New York at seventeen and eventually became a Harlem undertaker during the Depression. Born in Virginia, my maternal grandmother followed her mother (a fancy pastry cook) to New York in 1898 to work at age eighteen as a maid. My maternal grandfather, her childhood sweetheart back in Petersburg, after some traveling around the country during which he worked as an elevator boy in Dayton, Ohio, came to New York, where he shortly became chief red-cap at Grand Central Station. They were married in 1904. Both were born free; both their parents were born slaves. Youngest daughter of these black working-class parents, born at home in the Bronx on Morris Avenue, my mother before her marriage worked for the WPA and after that became a stenotypist and later a clerk in the New York Public Library system. Born in New York, raised in Harlem, I began as a freelance novelist and critic and today am a professor of comparative literature, whose politics are (as were my parents') farther to the left than not on a host of issues—African American rights, women's rights, gay rights—and whose writing time is divided between criticism and fiction. I was married for thirteen years. I have a twenty-four-year-old daughter. My life-partner Dennis and I have been together, in an open relationship, for going on nine years.

While your questions suggest to me a healthy vigilance toward all the ways in which writers might write out of self-interest, what I don't hear among them is any acknowledgment that writers write out of desire. Pygmalion spends endless months making notes and observations on the realest of real (again, read: the most political of political) women around him, noting their wants, their behavior, their oppressions and their triumphs, their specificities, their fears, fancies, foibles, and strengths, which preparation alone will, once he begins to revel in the sensuous thoughts asleep within his marble, wake Galatea, with her beauty, into life. Today we'd like to think his observations would have taught him, as well, that he can never speak *for* those women, because the desire that impels him means he is, radically, not one of them. (You can never be identical with what you desire. The bodily apperception of that is what desire *is*.) But that is a matter of political good manners today—not some universal mandate of correct politics.

If you will introduce this "opening of the field" (as the poet Robert Duncan called it: I am now looking at your question 5, on the change among writerly "subjects") into your image of the writer, then I doubt any of my writerly topics, given my briefest and most telegraphic of self-characterizations two paragraphs above, would *surprise* you, whether you looked at my earliest handful of science fiction novels from the sixties, or my recent work, pornographic and historical, from the nineties. Here I've written about a poet, there about a novelist, both in futures envisioned to highlight the substance of their art. There I've written about a would-be poet, here about a would-be scholar in a world that poses some of the mysteries that ensnare, distract, and finally suspend "the truth."

At the same time, however, I doubt anyone could *predict* my topics (and certainly not their genres), especially at any greater specificity, only from knowing my class or classic ties (or even my aesthetic allegiances). Like many writers who dare a far less overt political espousal, what interests me is what I *don't* know.

I say my topics would not surprise. Yet the only things I wrote those books for, any one of them, *was* to surprise, to surprise with every sentence, scene, chapter—which is to say the books are not reducible to their topics, their synopses.

I am, if you will, the opposite of a mystic. I feel myself radically broken off from the Universe, and I know the ragged and intricate edges of that break in the same bodily way in which the mystic knows his oneness with the cosmos. Nevertheless (call it political, if you like) *that* knowledge is denied me and (call it sour grapes, if you will) seems, in most of the manifestations that I've encountered it, somewhat cheap and tawdry.

I enjoy Whitman, Simone Weil, Pascal, René Dumal . . . but more for their intellect, rage, and passion, their commitment to their struggle with belief—than for any particular belief any one of them holds. (In Whitman this struggle is entirely in the language: the battle metaphor for states of peace, the violences of verbal juxtaposition, the self out of the self apostrophized by the self. Whitman the pure celebrant is as much a bore as any other priest of uplift; Whitman the poet who struggles to create a celebration is an interesting writer. In Weil it is all intellectual articulation. Both require historical insight.) I enjoy Fanon, Césaire, the writers associated with the Black Arts movement, Larry Neal, Sonia Sanchez, Amiri Baraka . . . and, on another front, Paul Goodman. The writers I read *as* mystics, that I feel I can trust, are probably Robert Duncan and Helen Adam, Jack Spicer and Robin Blaser, and the rough, tumultuous mountain of Charles Olson's *Maximus* and, even more, his poetics. My political writers are likely to be my fellow science fiction writers. And for the pleasure that occasionally can dupe us into calling it "pure," I read and reread Guy Davenport, Ethan Canin, Frank O'Hara, Hart Crane; Alan Moore and Neal Gaiman among comics writers; Martin Scorsese and Katherine Bigelow among movie directors. And all this changes.

From such an idiosyncratic reading list (but today can there be any other kind?), I turn to your second question about the public mandate for American writing over the last twenty years.

Immediately it prompts me to ask, who *is* this public who can or should mandate what writing might be? Is it the educational panels that declare, "These are the books students have been repeatedly shown to be able to relate to—though, for myself, I find them all but without appeal or interest." Is it the students who pay five or ten dollars for faded Xeroxes of some other student's "A" paper written on the same book five years ago, so that *they* don't have to read it either? Is it some TV- or advertisement-driven "general readership," flogged by the media into driving this or that book up the best seller list?

But, if any one of those is the case, why bother?

To speak about a *public* mandate to the writer about writing is, on whatever level, not to address the process of reading (whether of the learner, the journeyman, the fan, the addict, the critic, or any of their overlaps) but rather to articulate a program based on various notions from many, many men and women old and young, from illiterate Philistine to *haute* theorist, who are all articulably in one state or another of "not reading"—or of not reading *now*.

That is to say, the dialogue you want to interrogate is just not between a public and a writer, however much it may first look as if it is. Rather, your topic is always a private relation between a reader and a text. Our best critics overhear the resultant dialogue in themselves and transcribe it—for a very small public indeed. If we so care, among their audience we listen and enjoy because we recognize it for our own, or are troubled and contest it, because we do not.

Trust to the agglomeration, rather, of private mandates that each reader makes for what writing would be to her, to him. (Ask your students. Trade yours with theirs, back and forth. That's how we learn to teach. That's how we learn to read.) At any economic station, the agglomeration may sustain an articulate critique from whomever, and may be adjudged by anyone who hears that critique; and, after whatever necessary winnowing of concepts, agglomeration begins anew.

But you choose the final, eviscerated, and devolved product of this long, long process (which finally manifests itself in some reduction of the concept of the "current best seller," whether in the bookstore or in the textbook annex) no more than I. While the choice you do make—where, personally, you choose to lift out your own view of aesthetic necessity—is wholly social and controlled by a complex notion of what is good for various sectors of the democratic society, there's no more pandering to some "public" with only a statistical reality one with some majority opinion (a concept that, I would hazard, constitutes the concept of "the public" quite adequately for certain questions of "public good") in that choice for you no more than there is for me.

Most public mandates that I am aware of for writing—for accessibility, teachability, relevance, uplift, or (even worse!) the *negative* of any one of these (for those mandates exist too)—are, all of them, simply the parameters of aesthetic abuse. The writer's focus must be elsewhere: that difficult spot where clarity and simplicity do not in any way contradict richness and complexity; the hard rift where structure and form in no way contradict mystery, chaos, beauty, insight, desire, and horror. They, in their noncontradiction, it would seem, mark out the difficult realm of the aesthetic. Like the cruelty of Artaud's theater, that difficulty/cruelty, rather than the passions that manifest it, is the identificatory aesthetic mark. Small, *local* mandates occur: for greater invention, coherence, logic, truthfulness to life, sincerity, wit, originality, sensitivity to the tradition, complexity, simplicity, decorativeness, austerity, suggestiveness, seductiveness, wackiness, allusivity, autonomy, intellectual daring, relevance, mystery, more awareness of popular culture, more awareness of high culture—and, for our local projects, we individual writers take them up or ignore them. We make them every day.

Popularity/publicity in the market of art or ideas is only a political indicator, however. Anyone who confuses an indicator for a mandate in that market has got Big Problems and is, at best, doomed to serve up kitsch.

Your question about changes in editorial and reviewing practices seem, if anything, closer to the mark than questions about public mandates or political allegiances because they refer to material practices that concern what writers *do* (submit manuscripts, have them rejected or accepted, proofread, publish, read and write reviews) rather than some essentialized notion of what writers *are* (a Man of Certain Political Allegiances; a Responsible Auditor of a Public Mandate . . .).

Today we have reached the point where editing is two all-but-unrelated practices. The first is the job of the professional editor: acquisitions.

The second is that job which, in moments of hope, some of us still like to imagine an editor is going to do: reading, responding, making suggestions, trying to help the writer move the text as close as possible toward its own ideal form. The latter requires sensitivity and readerly intelligence. In more than thirty-six years of professional writing, at well over fifteen publishers in America and England, and probably twice that number of editors, I've only had one such professional editor for fiction (Ron Drummond, of Incunabula Press) and only three such for nonfiction (David Hartwell, Victoria Schockett, and Patrick Merla)—that is, where the editing wasn't just cutting, pasting, and patching for some benighted notion of the commercial (e.g., "Cut 750 lines. It's too long for our format." "Cut your mention of this store Ferrara's you say is at the corner on 42nd Street at 7th Avenue. Our fact checker can't find it in the phone book. We don't want to be accused of error.").

When, in 1962, I began to publish, I didn't receive any helpful line editing from the professionals because the novels I was publishing weren't considered important enough for anyone to bother. Today I suspect I've become (in the tiny pool in which I splash about) such a fat, warty toad that no one cares to or dares to edit me. Both, however, amount to the same thing, and are not necessarily good—either for the tyro or the oldest pro.

The twin reasons acquisitions editors don't do much in the line of line editing are (one) because it's easier not to and (two) because the type of marathon reading acquisition editors *do* tends to blunt just those finer sensibilities needed to get inside a text and take it apart from within in order to make useful suggestions for improvement that the writer can hear and respond to. In short, most acquisitions editors don't line edit very well. After leaving two or three frustrated, sputtering writers behind, usually they learn they can't (even if they blame it *on* the writers) and stop trying.

This means the writer, neophyte or established, must set up his or her own editorial-critical networks. I've tried to keep such a network in place since my teens: two or three readers who will read my texts and respond, "Cut that word, that phrase, that sentence, that paragraph." As every teacher knows, you have to read far more carefully to understand why something *doesn't* work than to respond to the places it does. That's why bad papers take so much longer to mark than good ones. "It's unclear *just here* what you're saying: rethink, reorganize, rewrite . . ." As often as not, these people were not writers themselves, and rarely writers in the same genre I was working in.

The history of the novel, from the Brontës with Branwell and each other, to Djuna Barnes with Emily Coleman, to Eliot with Pound, to Joyce with Frank Budgen, bears it out: fortunately one such reader is adequate. Two such are a garden of critical delights. Three such are an overabundance of riches. I cannot imagine how I would negotiate four.

Paradoxically, the hardest time I have had establishing such critical relations was when my social situation was closest to that of (or sometimes was) a writing workshop. The reason, I suspect, is the same one that tends to make acquisitions editors poor line editors. Everyone in the workshop situation is reading too much, too critically, to couch criticism constantly in the textually specific mode that the writer can hear. Because of the amount read, the criticism must, over any range, list toward the generalized and effect-oriented, rather than toward the specific and causally sensitive. Criticism such as "The ending is too slow" (*where* does the ending begin?), "I don't really understand this character's motivation" (among *which words* on the page is the character manifesting or not manifesting his or her motivation?), or "This all goes too fast" (what *is* "this" in term of the textual elements?), while they may be accurate and honest reader responses, are often all but useless to the writer. They refer to a *memory* of the text, not the actual *experience of reading* the text—which is what the writer, writing, is always more or less skillfully modulating and manipulating.

The problem segues directly into the question of reviewing. If not for thirty-five years, then certainly for the last twenty-five, from the *New York Times Book Review* to the local review column in your regional newspaper, our national fiction reviewing practices have been plagued by a shared awareness that serious fiction is seriously menaced, unto its very existence, by the power of the commercially popular genres: horror, techno-thriller, espionage, Ninja epic, romances from historical bodice buster to contemporary social melodrama, even science fiction, as well as all sorts of nonfiction (all the genres that have had, at least till recently, their own bookstore paperback sections in mass market or trade) and, so much more as to make the menace from other *books* a joke, by movies and television.

Thus, almost anyone who loves that amorphous beast "good fiction" finds himself or herself in the position where, if a new book, especially by a new author, in any way reads like "good, serious fiction," to attack it in print is tantamount to aligning oneself with the totally Philistine and savaging the good, the true, and the beautiful—unless, of course, the book deploys the wrong political allegiances . . .

It's probably directly related to the practice from, say, the 1830s and 1840s, that at first so astonishes anyone who does research on the world of American journalism, in which writers like Poe and Hawthorne moved. There it was a given that the reviewer would simply hack and slash at any new work, usually because it wasn't as good as some fancied European model. You *had* to throw the kid into the icy stream. Otherwise, he'd grow up to be a sissy and a weakling. Both in its older form and its newer, one has to learn to read through it. Though it's a different smokescreen, that's still what we try to do today.

Perhaps half a dozen times now I've been retained by the *New York Times Book Review* to review one book or another. Like all who have written for the *Book Review,* I have my bouquet of anecdotes:

The time I was told, "Well, if you didn't like the novel, we'll only publish a 750-word review. Why spend a thousand words on a book you don't like?" (Well, I can think of all *sorts* of reasons . . .)

The time I was told, "We don't believe in quoting bad prose and telling people what's wrong with it. We assume that everybody *knows* what bad writing is already." (Oh, I don't think so . . .)

The time I spent an hour-and-twenty-minute editorial phone conversation about the first paragraph of a review, bewildered by what the editor was trying to get me to understand/change, until, finally, I was told by that highly frustrated man: "Look, the *Book Review* does not have any one formal way it wants to make you write your review. But we *prefer* you to mention the author by name in the first three sentences. *You* don't mention him till your *fifth*!"

(I said, "You mean *that's* what all this has been about? Please, move the fifth sentence to the head of the article!" and, somehow still cordial, we said good-bye and hung up.)

It only takes a little imagination to see, however, that all three, to the extent that they delineate a policy, conscious or unconscious, militate to suppress any heuristic aspect to the reviewing practice. (Even the last of the three makes much harder the review that begins with an abstract point, then uses an aspect of the book under consideration to demonstrate it.) Without such heuristics, however, reviewing must lean closer and closer to advertising.

Despite the *Book Review*, reviewing must constantly take it upon itself to teach people what the individual reviewer thinks is bad prose (or good prose, for that matter) and tell a good deal more than whether a book is good or bad—as though these were universally acknowledged categories, circulating free of just the political considerations you began your questions with and that I cited at the beginning of this answer. It has to tell why the critic thinks so—and *that*, to be meaningful, involves educating the reader: we educate the reader by reminding ourselves.

It's odd. I read the *Book Review* most regularly when I was a teenager. Certainly that's when it had the greatest effect on me. When I say, as I shall, that I write for myself, one of the things I mean is that much of the general readership journalism I write—reviews or articles—I write for smart, verbally adventurous kids such as I was.

And, no, it wouldn't have hurt to tell me a little about bad prose back then. The afternoon when I was sixteen that I got my first real handle on it, stretched out alone on my bed in the third floor, above the rumble of Seventh Avenue's traffic outside, when I first read and reread Orwell's essay "Politics and the English Language," remains with me as one of the most exciting days of my life.

Don't we all realize it by now? What is wrong with "politically free" criticism (that can name and delimit the political in such positivist terms as you do) is not its apolitical slant, but only the presumption to be outside of politics and looking in; by never stating *its* politics, by never calling the political into question, it becomes the locus for *every* sort of concealed political abuse.

When I read through the essay collections of modernist writers—from Virginia Woolf and Yvor Winters to R. P. Blackmur and Edmund Wilson—there is usually an interesting admixture of criticism of the tradition and of the contemporary.

I much enjoyed the fascinating collection of writers Edmund White deals with in his energetic and intelligent collection *The Burning Library* (1994).

What I miss is (granted we are generally within the field of the criticism of matters gay) the serious consideration of a contemporary novelist such as Robert Glück (*Marjorie Kemp*, *Jack the Modernist*, two extraordinarily interesting gay novels) followed by a consideration of, in the next essay, say, Pater's *Marius the Epicurian* (the most important nineteenth-century gay novel and the model for Yourcenar's *Memoirs of Hadrian*—not to mention its immense influence on both Joyce's *Ulysses* and Woolf's *To the Lighthouse* and *The Waves:* and White *does* review Yourcenar's 1993 biography by Josyane Savigneau). The earliest writers White takes on as writers of specific texts are James Jones, Christina Stead, and Tennessee Williams. Indeed, the suggestion of White's whole book is that there is so much of the contemporary to chronicle before, unsung, it slips away (the David Kalstones, the Coleman Dowells, the James Merrills—and Merrill he embraids with Proust in a rich Homeric comparison) that there is no time to take the leisurely look at Melville, Whitman, Pater, or Shakespeare, or any of the other gay (or straight) writers from the tradition whom one might examine for the profit of a contemporary audience. The suggestion goes further: only a certain political prescience (demonstrated by the opening arc of essays, starting with the 1969 piece, "The Gay Philosopher") has allowed White the range to do the job of preserving *his* present (his library before it burns) as well as he has.

Well—some months ago I had what I considered a consoling thought. When someone dies, it is *not* a library that burns.

It's only a card catalog. The library is still there for other young minds to enter, to begin to read, to write out his or her own cards and begin his or her own catalog—or to bring, who knows, an entirely different technology of organization to the task. I think we can relax a bit and dare a few more interesting juxtapositions—which juxtapositions, possibly more than the content (as long as content is vouchsafed), mark culture's generosity, civilization's range.

Does this sound like a criticism of White? It's not intended as a condemnation. Rather it's a symptom that I see in essay collections all about me, my own not excepted. As I see it, the problem is *purely* literary, *purely* educational, *purely* a matter of a historically educated sensibility. (I would suggest all three are, politically speaking, synonyms: White's essays are largely occasional—and these are the occasions that came up. Call that the aesthetic field. Call it the political field. It's the analysis of that field which is important, not the term it's lumbered with.) It appears as a problem, however, when my gay graduate students under thirty pick up White's book, read the first half dozen pages of the opening essay, and declare, "But how can you like a piece like 'The Gay Philosopher' or, indeed, take seriously anyone who would write such a piece today? Politically, it's troglodytic! The problem is White's politics!" Most don't even reach its resonant concluding peals—more sonorous now than when they were written, because we have come as far as we have.

If it's a choice between having students who can read a text intelligently by the political schemas of their own day and those who can't, then certainly one chooses the former. To develop the ability to read with political sophistication takes work—work one can be proud of. Those who can read in this way *may* learn to reconstruct the historical contexts to read more intelligently the texts of another time. Those who can't, won't.

To those who want to gain some understanding into that earlier context, I find myself saying, "Consider, 'The Gay Philosopher' was *not* written today, but in 1969—the year of Stonewall—at which time it was so radical as to be unpublishable. Consider the problems of writing a piece that logical, that thinks against the current grain as concertedly as this one thinks against the grain of 1969 without sinking wholly into fascism.

That *you* think the problem *is* political *is* the political problem." But the fact is, this is (again) the point beyond which it doesn't matter whether we call the problem political (ethical) or literary (aesthetic), because once more we are at the place where (to quote Wittgenstein, who first wrote it in a notebook in Norway in 1916, before I, White, and any of our graduate students were born) "ethics *is* aesthetics"; that is to say, we are at the place where knowledge of the tradition, of the context, of the history of the language, the law, and the land alone will tell you what, in any given text, the language is *doing.* In a 1990s essay, White comes down very hard on the cartoons from the 1950s and 1960s of Richard Prince, which he calls "empty shells, long since abandoned by the wit that once inhabited them." But so are many of the political writings specifically on the Left from the 1960s and 1970s. It's a fate politics and comedy share.

To approach such students as a politico-aesthetic educator, one suggests, first, that they put Judith Butler and Eve Sedgwick out of their minds. Now (I have to say), try to imagine a time, call it 1969, where (I go on), if you sent in the same application to graduate school you sent to us, here, two years back and on the strength of which you were so welcomed as a teacher and a potential scholar ("I'm interested in the place of sexuality in culture, in the representations of gender, gay and straight, and would like to approach this material from the position of contemporary queer studies and gender studies"), not only would you *not* have been admitted, but anxious phone calls would have been placed discreetly to your parents and/or advisors suggesting that someone think—very seriously—about having you committed.

The straight faculty would want you committed because they were afraid you were a step away from exploding in the street and running around killing people.

The secretly gay faculty would want you committed because they were afraid you would probably be killed fairly soon and they might think your being in a hospital was safer for you than not.

And the fact is, if you could *write* that to a university at twenty-two or twenty-three, you probably *would* want to kill a lot of people because you'd have a lot of scars and broken bones already, been jeered at in the street, taken into back rooms and beaten up—and, assuming you were still alive, would have been called sick and a criminal so often you couldn't even *hear* the words any more.

Now, holding that in mind, go back and reread White's essay.

Am I overstating the case? No. Am I giving them any of the complexities of the time that allowed people to live, sometimes in and sometimes out of the closet, during the period between the close of World War II, say, and Stonewall? No. Through the lack of those complexities, are there notable awkwardnesses constructed into my argument? Yes: in 1969, terms like "queer studies" and "gender studies" would have been construed as parodic or more likely nonsensical. Still, the slang term "queer," even in a nonsense phrase, would have likely raised, by a process of contagion, the same suspicion, prompted the same intervention. You have to start somewhere.

The problem, as anyone over forty can attest, is that because so many under thirty have so little idea of how the world was put together even twenty-five and thirty-five years ago, they would seem to have little armament against those people who would move the world as catastrophically in a repressive direction over the next twenty-five to thirty. Call it a political education that's needed to understand the era; call it an aesthetic education that's needed to read with understanding the texts from that era. I don't really care.

Your final question asks us to assess scholarly assessments of contemporary writing. Well, if I miss the range that considers the present and the past by a single educated sensibility among contemporary fiction writers, I miss that range just as much in academic writers—who tend to err on the other side.

Helen Vendler, finally taking on Jorie Graham (after a MacArthur) and Rita Dove (after a Pulitzer) and Seamus Heaney (after a Nobel Prize), won't do, because, in her rush to treat the poems as aesthetic objects, she staggers into the same slough of political positivity in which your opening questions were mired:

Vendler begins her examination of Rita Dove's work with the statement, "The primary given for the black poet Rita Dove has to be—as for other black writers in America—the fact of her blackness." Now try to imagine my writing an account of Vendler's critical enterprise over the years that began: "The primary given for the female critic Helen Vendler has to be—as for other female American critics—the fact of her femininity." The point is, there may indeed be some interesting things to say about Vendler's criticism in relation to her position as a woman in the intellectual pantheon of American criticism, as there are many relevant things to say about Dove as a black poet, but *that* isn't one of them!

It is not the blackness (or the feminine)—the politically focusing agent—that has to be gotten rid of. Rather it is the notion of the transcendentalizing, totalizing, absolute "primary given" that needs to be jettisoned if the criticism is to reach any level of sophistication—by which I mean that place where aesthetic sophistication and political sophistication are, yes, one. That, two pages on, Vendler can write, seemingly defusing her opening totalization, "No black has blackness as sole identity," gets entirely absorbed by what Derrida analyzed as the logic of the supplement.

About one of Dove's dramatic monologues by a slave, Belinda, petitioning in 1782 to be set free—

> I am Belinda, an African,
> since the age of twelve a Slave.
> I will not take too much of your Time,
> but to plead and place my pitiable Life
> unto the Fathers of this Nation.

—Vendler comments, "Belinda has only two identity markers: she is female and she is a slave," before she goes on to consider other poems with other slave narrative stories. I think here we can see where such political positivity breaks down on the heuristic, the aesthetic, and the political level all at once. There are many more identity markers here than two, but they lie directly *in* the language: "I am Belinda, an African," "I will not take too much of your Time," "[I] plead and place my pitiable Life / unto the Fathers of this Nation." Were this spoken by someone today, it would be stilted beyond belief. Nor is it the speech of slaves during, say, the last days of the American Civil War. Should someone read Dove's lines either as contemporary English *or* mid-nineteenth-century American, that reader will be reading a poor poem indeed. As an attempt to ventriloquize eighteenth-century English, that marks and identifies the speaker as a cousin to Wheatley, Equiano, and, yes, even a distaff descendant of white Mistress Bradstreet or a contrasting collateral with Pope's satiric heroine of the same name in *The Rape of the Lock*, Dove's poem starts to become an interesting piece of language. (And *we've* entered Pierre Menard territory . . .) But the political positivities and the marginalizing of everything (dare I say) aesthetic (I could just as easily say, *specifically* political: a slave *in 1782*) go together. The fact that Vendler is specifically not interested in any of this and the fact that she is presenting what she is interested in (historical poetry as diegesis without specific language, where the lyricism doesn't fit, leaving the tales "stagy" and the poems—her final judgment—"relatively unsuccessful historical excursions in a lyric time-machine") under the rubric of a political positivism are *not* an accidental political/critical alliance, if you will.

Now perhaps Vendler wants the reader to assume (not unrelated to the *Book Review*'s assumption that everyone knows what bad prose is) that, in the same way as the *Book Review*, everyone knows the intellectual fine points of eighteenth-century rhetoric, so that the critic need not mention them, designate them as among Belinda's markers of identity, or analyze them. But you wouldn't have to go too far afield to find critics who would agree that, by fairly ordinary standards, it is the consideration of what most poetry readers would designate the poetry (i.e., the linguistic materiality, the artifacting of that material, historical and contemporary) that is being "repressed" in Vendler's consideration of Dove as a poet under the rubric of, not the political per se, but rather of a positivistic politics (which I wouldn't be surprised if, at least for the course of her writing the piece, Vendler mistook for the political itself), a politics (Vendler's, that is), which, while it may well have a place in activism and out on the barricades, just doesn't yield much of interest when applied so grossly to the arts.

A page later, Vendler abandons these poems of blackness to cite what she judges "the best poem" in Dove's first volume, "a poem of perfect wonder, showing Dove as a young girl in her parents' house doing her lessons, mastering geometry, seeing for the first time the coherence and beauty of the logical principles of spatial form." This poem, Vendler has already remarked, "has not a word to say about the fraught subject of blackness." Vendler quotes the whole three-stanza poem, whose title and opening tercet I give here:

Geometry
I prove a theorem and the house expands,
the windows jerk free to hover near the ceiling,
the ceiling floats away with a sigh.

Again, while she quotes it and analyzes much in between, she does not mention the strongest semantic contrast in the poem, that between the first line and the last, where *prove* is held up against *unproven*. Dove writes of the expanding walls, the departing scent of carnations, the rising windows flapping on their hinges like butterflies in the last line of her poem:

They are going to some point true and unproven.

As an amateur math-lover, I hear (in the juxtaposition of "true" and "unproven") a suggestion of Kurt Gödel's great undecidability proof of 1931, concerning the existence of a possibly infinite number of true arithmetic theorems that are nevertheless not susceptible to proof *within* an arithmetic system. Thus, for me, it is not a poem of perfect wonder so much as it is about the most human sort of curiosity about the coherence of the wonderfully incoherent universe. But no matter.

The rhetoric is Dove's, but its meaning is manifested through Vendler's contextualization: one would have to be culturally deaf not to hear, beneath Vendler's explicit argument, that, somehow, in this poem, as it's placed not in Dove's book but in Vendler's exegesis, after the "stagy" and "unsuccessful" historical poems about blackness that don't quite work, an implied contention that, by writing a poem that "has not a word to say about the fraught subject," Dove has herself, like her house, expanded, expanded *beyond* blackness into the realm of pure poetry by writing a poem that is, rather than about blackness, "about what Geometry and poetic form have to say about one another." And, to put it gently, I just don't think this is the case. I don't think this is how blackness figures either in the lives of black men and women, nor in the art of most black writers, nor in *this* poem: a primary given that, somehow, the writer must expand beyond (impossible, however, because it *is* a primary given) to achieve a poetry of perfect wonder. Indeed, this is much closer to how blackness functions in the *white* sensibility (a primary given that must be gotten beyond), when the goal is not poetry but civility, fairness, and tolerance. And that is really (i.e., politically) basically what I see Vendler's attempt to interrogate this particular black poet finally being about. History remains the villain—not, we begin to suspect, because the poet's lyricism fits it awkwardly, but because history itself is just ugly and unpoetic.

After praising a poem about Rafael Leonidas Trujillo Molina's massacre of 20,000 Haitians (because they could not pronounce the letter *r* in the Spanish word *perejil* [parsley]), because Dove displays sympathy for both the "white dictator" and the black victims, the final poem Vendler chooses to analyze in some detail is, significantly, a poem lifted out of its poetic context, from the Pulitzer Prize–winning collection *Thomas and Beulah*, in which Vendler again notes approvingly, in the poem she has chosen to analyze from the sequence, "The things that make Thomas unhappy are not his blackness and his oppression by whites—not at all." (Who in the *world* is Vendler talking down to like that?) The fact is, the critic cannot just recognize the eighteenth-century diction and walk wisely beyond it without falling back into a less sophisticated mode that sees poems only as plots. Critics must be able to hear the cultural tales implicit in their own rhetoric and, if that is not what they mean to say, first articulate it and then say, "But I mean something else"—just as the critic should be able to hear Thomas's perception of his relation with the other women in the airplane factory as emblematic of many black men's feelings about their social relations to black women over the years, whether the word "black" appears or not. One wants the critic, more than other readers, to pay attention to the words themselves—as well as, historically, what the words suggest.

I hope it's clear. Whether I disagree or not with Vendler's

particular judgments on particular poems, my point is that by placing those judgments at particular points in her argument, by placing them in relation to her particular rhetoric (which I have scattered about mine here, some in quotation marks, some, yes, implied), she tells a story other than the one she seems to be telling—one that undercuts what, I hope I will in no way sound patronizing when I say, are probably laudable intentions. Well, I think critics have to pay attention to those stories (subtexts, if you will) too. At the risk of being disingenuous, I only say that criticism is writing too, and to do it well you have to pay attention to what you're doing on several levels.

The problem that most younger critics would hear, here, I hope, however, is simply one of critical tact. The question that needs to be addressed and which Vendler's own rhetorical choices excise from her inquiry as unseemly is why she, as a white critic, needs to use, needs to exploit Dove as a black poet, needs to neglect "for the most part the handsome poems Dove has written that do not take blackness as one of their themes." Is this supposed to be purely altruistic intellectual generosity? Or is there another cultural project involved, and if so, why not articulate what it is? (Is it possibly only a strategy to place the black poet in the patronizing double bind of deigning to teach her why the "poetry of wonder" is only attainable once she or he has expanded beyond blackness—after having categorically declared such to be an impossibility because "the fact of . . . blackness" *is* a "primary given," i.e., inescapable?) And who does this project belong to? Black Dove? White Vendler? What are *its* political-aesthetic allegiances, if you will? The project may, indeed, be quite interesting. Or it may just be a critic declaring: I am only interested in using this art work as my other—as a place to project into it my own lacks, what a repressive culture constrains *me* from doing (whether that is: I am not supposed to sing and dance wildly; or is: I am not supposed to write about the politics of my situation directly. That's not good art. So I will use this, that, or the other poet to do it for me). I think critical readers today want their critics to be a bit more self-aware of what the critic him- or herself is doing—as opposed to making absolute pronouncements about the proper concerns of blacks, women, gays, or even poets and writers in general.

The critic's job is not to see language and history as some sort of annoying hindrance that stands in the way of the poet getting at some sort of, oh, I don't know, "perfect wonder." I do not mean to say that everything in Vendler's analysis of Dove is either useless or tainted. That would be to acquiesce to her positivistic presuppositions, to say that those suppositions were somehow a "primary given" for her, when my point is, precisely, that I don't believe they are, any more than femininity is for women in general, or blackness is for blacks in particular. (Vendler's schematization of the poem from *Thomas and Beulah* is, for example, accurate and interesting. But at almost every point she would be intriguingly suggestive, that intrigue turns out to be all politics.) This is not to say that, from time to time, for one or a whole series of local projects, these may *not* be of central or even of obsessive importance, for white or black, male or female, gay or straight. But Vendler's analysis of Dove is sunk in the same positivistic politics your questions demonstrate—and thus both require a lot of fancy footwork for someone who does not share them to tease out the aesthetically interesting from the, yes, vulgar political projection. What I've been trying to do is tease out what Vendler's allying blackness absolutely as a "primary given" to Dove in particular and black poets in general accomplishes in *Vendler's* analysis. Certainly it seems to ally Dove absolutely to her flaws (as Vendler sees them), so that they do not have to be considered any further. Because they are awkward, ugly stories, there is no need to treat them like poetry, like history.

Understand that, when I say I want to see academic critics approach the new and the old, I do not want to see Pater's *Marius* (1885), Barnes's *Nightwood* (1936), and John Keene's *Annotations* (1995) all judged by the same "objective" standards. I want to learn, rather, what kind of education is necessary to form an aesthetic sensibility (or, what kind of political savvy it requires, should you be more comfortable with that idea: as I said, on the level I'm speaking about, they're all but the same thing) that can appreciate, enjoy, and be deeply moved by all three. I think, today, I'm *probably* more likely than not to find this from a writer who has had *some* affiliation with the academy. As a reader, I'm probably going to be able to hear it a bit more easily from a writer who feels at least somewhat comfortable with the ideas, if not the rhetoric, of the theoretical developments in criticism since (arbitrarily) 1968 broadly called critical theory. But the fact is, I *don't* find it with any regularity. And the academics who *never* sharpen their analytical teeth on a current work that speaks to them seem to me somehow to be shirking the full employment of the sheer power (constituted as largely by disinterest as by bias; by both blindness and insight) their position and their concomitant educations bestow.

Having said all that, let me turn from this garrulous generality (the *most* general of it my characterization of me and my family) to a particularity that I can at last feel—here, now—won't be betrayed by lack of context.

1. More or less since the middle or late sixties (the beginning of my career), the writers with whom I have felt I formed some nebulous group were Joanna Russ, Thomas M. Disch, and the late Roger Zelazny, with his earlier work, up through, say, his superb *Doorways in the Sand* (1976). Let me say as well, I don't know if any of them felt the same way about me—or, indeed, about any of the others. But these were and are the writers I return to regularly. They are writers who, the ones that remain, when they publish something new I drop everything to purchase it and read it immediately. My experience of their work is far more invigorating than competitive. Their successes still split my face with a pumpkin-hack of a grin.

Currently none of us are, today, personally particularly close. But they are the contemporaries who make your question—to me—answerable.

If your question means merely, however, am I interested in blacks because I'm black, gays because I'm gay, males because I'm male, and Christians because I was brought up Christian and am now an atheist (i.e., what are my primary givens); if, because I have a long white beard I feel some camaraderie with other bearded men; if, because I'm a hundred pounds overweight, I have noticed the way the fat in America are often discriminated against; if, because I'm a science fiction writer, I have noticed that my status as a writer is, as is that of all commercial writers, regularly denigrated (but the list of power differentials I sit on one side of or the other is endless, and my sympathies cross them, more or less strongly, less or more effectively, as often as not), my answer is: Of course—and so what? While some of these may even be among the many primary givens of my *life*, they are not the primary givens of writing: they are, all of them, at best provisional material *for* writing.

When, either in fiction or nonfiction, I plumb them for material, I try to use them the best I can.

To say what I said in my overview in another way: It is not your question that bothers me, as I hope I have shown by answering it. It is the implication *in* the question that there exists a position outside the political from which such a question can be asked about a dense political interior, and that someone answering "no" to it would be somehow joining you in that neutral spot on some sort of uncommitted political high ground, when in reality all you are asking is, Are you a specific human being, or are you some sort of generalized abstraction without a body and of wholly homogenized catholic sympathies—a nonquestion, I hope we would all agree, which invokes my analysis as much as my disingenuousness above.

2. I have a private view of writing, gotten entirely from reading (I might add) and looking and listening to life and the other arts, that relates writing to observational truths as much as it does to those inventions which occur only with the eyes squeezed tightly against the "real," a view that encompasses both clarity and richness. It was pretty well in place by the time I was twenty. But it is only as private as language functions can be; many writers share it.

Over time it's grown crisper, firmer, and has been tested against a series of personal and aesthetic . . . events. For better or worse it remains in place.

The various provisional comments you can make about art (I want this work to be fun, light, and disposable; I might want another—or, indeed, the same—to be dark, beautiful, and transparent) are all relevant only as they are couched in the gut complexities of the above.

There have been challenges, of course, but they are local and dull and only concern me when I am sitting at my word processor—or thinking about the same.

3. I write for myself—because it's all I know how to do. Statements such as this are, of course, polemical. That is, they are only meaningful as they are read as attempts to correct the abuses inherent in the opposite position.

To continue with my polemic, however: I write for an audience who is interested in what I'm interested in. And I don't write for one that couldn't care less about those things—nor do I feel any constraint on me *to* write for those who care nothing about what I care about. What's important here is, however, that I am talking of a conjunctive field, not a disjunctive one. Some are going to share some concerns and not others. Thus they are likely to argue with me—which is good, so says my personal view. In a megalithic republic of circa 281 million people, I feel this is a reasonable position for a writer. The only manipulative move I will allow myself is the reticence not to tell you what those things are. You can find them only by allowing yourself to collide with one or another of my texts—even this one, perhaps.

For all we talk about freedom of speech, students *are* forced to write and forced to read.

But I think there's an important adult component to reading and writing that's one with the democratic freedoms, even as it denies the democratic tenet of majority rule.

Readers don't like to be bullied. Nor do I like using a forum such as this to bully them. That is to say nothing more than:

If you are curious to find out what sort of writer I am, read me. If you are not—please—read somewhere else.

I do think the reader *must* be allowed the first move.

4. A child of intertextual studies, I think one could argue that the writer has no existence without a relationship to the literary past. It's only a matter of how aware or unaware of it he or she is.

I've mentioned the three other writers I feel closest to. If some critic felt we were important enough and the relationship between us interesting enough to give the group a name, I'd only smile—even as the others might frown; or loudly balk.

5. As a gay man in America, who was twenty-seven at the time of (to pick an arbitrary date) Stonewall, I spent half my life

before it and half my life after it. During that time, what we roughly designate as "sex," both before and after, has marked out for me a rich and wonderfully educational imbrication of experiences, even as that imbrication has produced its pains and disappointments.

Nothing that Flaubert said about it in *Sentimental Education* or that Proust said about it in *Remembrance of Things Past* strikes me as fundamentally false. Yet the social field in which my education occurred was so different from that in which theirs occurred, I've felt I have had to reinhabit their position and view to tell my own tales, so different from theirs—even unto their outcomes.

My topics have changed as both position and view have changed.

If you're really asking me to comment, however, on "early Delany" versus "late Delany" with any specificity, I must once more take refuge in that reticence I spoke of two questions up.

6. My best editorial experiences have usually been (with some notable exceptions) from "amateur" editors rather than professional ones—usually in terms of friendly relationships. That has not changed. But the systems in which both professional editors and amateur editors are entailed has, over the years, changed mightily. Again, the specific answers I'd risk to that in a piece of this length are to be found above.

7. One is happy for attention. When that attention is intelligent, one is happier. In that strange, ironic, and highly comic construct called a reputation, at least at the level mine circulates at, reviews are probably the most important element—followed, I would hazard, by in-print appearances such as this one.

Because the serial venues in which most reviews appear consider reviewing commercial and disposable, that and the "genre guilt" I've written about above create a situation in which, often, you have to fight to get much of substance into a review.

I think the fight's worth it, though.

But, Lord knows, I wouldn't want to have to make my living that way.

When you add to the general fear of putting forth constructive criticism, all the problems of coteries, cabals, and logrolling that people are always intuiting just under the surface of all this terrified *Gemütlichkeit,* I think we now have an institution that, by and large, writers have grown pretty distrustful of, even as they feel they are still trapped by it, both as reviewers and writers.

The various webs, from electronic to social, that contour all of this are always changing shape. You probably need a sociologist here rather than a writer to get more specific.

8. Because I'm a critic as well as a fiction writer, I have all the sympathy in the world for critics. (Do I have something important to say? I should hope so.) At the same time, I know the anxiety of writing about pieces that nobody else has written about before: it's the true exercise of critical power—and power is scary.

Editors are scared by it just as much as are the critics themselves.

But power yearns to link itself with power, so that putting concerted effort into the new often seems like throwing power away. Well, remember that you've put your critical powers out there. People will want to link up with it.

How might I envision a more profitable exchange among scholarly critics and writers? (I realize that's not exactly what you asked.) First of all, there needs to be much *more* scholarly consideration of contemporary writing—preferably passionately felt.

That's for openers.

—New York City
1998

A Silent Interview

ST. MARKS POETRY PROJECT: *What form/shape will writing of the twenty-first century take?*

SAMUEL R. DELANY: I can't believe you're really frivolous enough to think that, because I'm a science fiction writer, I have some privileged, informed, or even interesting take on the future, more than do ditch diggers, dry cleaners, insurance salesmen —or, indeed, the run-of-the-mill poet or novelist. The only thing SF writers are apt to know about the future that the ordinary woman or man on the street does not is that it's *really* unpredictable.

That alone is what allows our genre to be.

Once, about twenty-five years ago, some people in Missoula, Montana, flew SF writers Frank Herbert (*Dune*), Frederik Pohl (*Gateway*), and me out to their city to take part in an audience-packed, Saturday-night panel that addressed the question "What is the future of Montana geological study and mining?" They were incredibly impressed with their own cleverness and originality in inviting some science fiction writers along with the geologists and mining engineers who were the program's other participants. The organizers were quite convinced no one had ever done such a thing before. We were each paid five hundred dollars for our appearance.

But I'm doing *this* interview for free. Therefore, you have to compensate me with intelligent and reasonable questions about which it's possible to say something interesting, based on something I might conceivably know.

POETRY PROJECT: *How does the creating and making (or unmaking) of myth function in your work? Or how might this function in our postmillennial writing?*

DELANY: For me, myths are what we tend to believe when there's no direct sensory proof of that belief available. Thus, when I'm in New York, Paris functions in my life largely as a myth. When I'm in London, New York functions for me as a myth. And, of course, there's all of what we take as history. The myths that concern me, of course, are the ones we believe, the ones we hold true. Since the evidence for most of our modern beliefs about the universe is not immediately available, most of contemporary life is fundamentally mythic. (Heidegger calls this the "inauthentic," but I'm not so sure that's the best term for it—at least in English.)

Because of the myriad ways and the multiple trajectories through which they are communally enforced, myths are very similar to discourses on the one hand and to ideologies on the other.

A communal task that art accomplishes—particularly the verbal arts of fiction, poetry, and criticism—is to help with the all-important shifts in discourse that must occur for there to be meaningful historical change.

Because it *is* a communal task, because no *single* work of art can accomplish such a discursive shift by itself, the artist (responsible only for her or his own work) *doesn't* have to worry about preaching. It does no good; don't waste your time. It's far more effective to look at a situation and dramatize, in however complex allegorical terms you'd like, what it is you've seen.

Science fiction's karygma contains a story about SF editor H. L. Gold and the great SF writer Theodore Sturgeon, during the early fifties—the McCarthy period. Sturgeon found himself so upset about what was happening to people all around him, the lives and livelihoods of his friends that had been destroyed, that he could no longer write. When Gold asked him for a story, Sturgeon told him, in despair, "Unless I let everybody know what that evil demagogue is doing to the country, writing fiction doesn't seem worth it."

Gold told him: "Look. You write me a story about a man who, unbeknownst to his wife, goes to meet her at the bus station when she's returning from a visit to her mother's. He sees a strange man meet her, and follows them through the city . . . and I *promise* you: By the end of that story, *everyone* who reads it will know what you feel about that demagogue there in Washington." Well, that's how writing works—and it works because what validates a McCarthy (or a Hitler, for that matter) is a *discourse* that says such behavior is or is not acceptable. That same discourse controls how A treats B when they meet in a store on opposite sides of a counter and one tries to buy something from the other.

For the same reason that poets and artists don't have to worry about preaching, the general public doesn't need to worry about imposing censorship. "For poetry makes nothing happen," W. H. Auden wrote in his elegy for Yeats. That privileged lack of power of the single work of art—the single poem, say—is precisely what, I feel, Auden was getting at.

Many works of art taken together, however, through the very process by which we learn to read them, establish discourses—discourses of the possible, discourses of the probable, discourses of desire. Discourses are the conceptual tools with which we socially construct our world, materially and imaginatively. That's what I think the late-Victorian poet Arthur William Edgar O'Shaughnessey (1844–81) was getting at when *he* wrote in his poem "Ode":

> We are the music makers,
>   We are the dreamers of dreams,
> Wandering by lone sea-breakers,
>   Sitting by desolate streams . . .
> World losers and world forsakers,
>   On whom the cold moon gleams:
> But we are the movers and shakers
>   Of the world forever, it seems.

Both Auden and O'Shaughnessey are true at the same time. But one was referring to art as an individual enterprise of powerless separate works. The other was referring to art as a collective enterprise facilitating social mentation. The two function differently in two different conceptual spaces: the space of individual appreciation and the space of shared discourse.

POETRY PROJECT: *List your favorite utopias.*

DELANY: I don't very much like utopias as a form. I much prefer science fiction—which, as a genre, is fundamentally antiutopian (and equally antidystopian) in the thinking it supports. I suspect, indeed, that's why science fiction has largely displaced utopian fiction as a genre. Again, Auden is the one who spelled out the explanation for us, in "Vespers," from his poetic sequence *Horae Canonicae*, and again in some of his essays in *The Dyer's Hand*.

For city lovers, the city is New Jerusalem—the site of knowledge, sophistication, freedom of action, as well as of all true learning and culture. For the urban-oriented temperament the country, the rural landscape, is the location of the superstition-, disease-, fire-, flood-, and earthquake-ridden Land of the Flies. There life is harsh and brutal and all society is bound by the chains of gossip and village opinion.

For country lovers, the rural world is Arcadia, and the city is, rather, the dirty, shabby, mechanized, and inhuman place where everyone wears the same uniform and does the same repetitious and meaningless tasks in quintessentially boring settings: Brave New World. As Auden points out, the decision as to whether you are more comfortable in the city or the country is largely a matter of temperament and/or habitation.

It is not a matter of objective facts. You pay for the culture, variety, and freedom of cities by having to toil in Brave New World. You pay for the beauties of nature by having to live in a relatively small-minded and oppressive township.

Science fiction—unlike utopia/dystopia—has traditionally taken its images from all four forms and integrated them into single visions of a rich and complex world. (After all, temperaments change, sometimes hour by hour.) The best and most characteristic SF novels (Bester's *The Stars My Destination*, Pangborn's *Mirror for Observers*, Harness's *The Paradox Men*, Sturgeon's *More Than Human . . .*) allegorize complex possible relations among all four. More recently, since cyberpunk, two more image clusters have added themselves to the mix: both Techno-Junk City and the Empire of the Afternoon have joined with New Jerusalem, Brave New World, Arcadia, and the Land of the Flies. But such complexity—the hallmark of science-fictional thinking—leaves the simplistic templates of "utopia (good)/dystopia (bad)" far behind.

If only because of their insufferable and insulting arrogance, time-hogging utopian monologists don't command much of a place anymore. Rather we need to encourage a polyvocalic politics, through dialogue and an appreciation of multiple prospectives, which is what science fiction as a genre does—and by science fiction I specifically do *not* mean "speculative fiction," which is, at least today, a monologic imposition by which one or another academic tries to privilege the particular science fiction he or she most prefers (cyberpunk, social, feminist, or what have you), at the expense of the overall genre's range and richness, a range and richness that make the individual novels and stories in any or all of those parenthetical subcategories signify in a dialogic and polyvocalic process.

POETRY PROJECT: *In your autobiography you state that you are "neither black nor white . . . male nor female. And [you] are that most ambiguous of citizens, the writer." Explain. What roles does or will that most ambiguous of citizens play in our public or private culture(s), or in our potential utopias?*

DELANY: I've always found it interesting the way people misread that passage, the way they pull it out of context. You'll remember, in *The Motion of Light in Water*, my autobiography, I present that as an *error* in my thinking that I got trapped into when I was at an emotional nadir—and on my way to a nervous breakdown that eventually landed me in a mental hospital.

Only when I began to get it back together and was in the midst of the kind of thinking that got me *out* of the hospital and, at twenty-three, back into the world—and that started me writing again—did I realize that I *was* a "black man, a gay man, a writer"; that these were specific, if complex, categories. As categories, they were social impositions—not essences. They were what had always already *given* me my identity; and an identity was something to be examined, interrogated, analyzed: vigilance and, often, resistance were the *conditions* of being able to function.

Now people desperately love all that wonderful-sounding ambiguity—just as I desperately desired it when I was beaten and confused and exhausted by life and overwork. "I belong to no category; I straddle them all . . . " It sounds romantic—decadent, but somehow still transcendent. When we pursue such ambiguity, mistakenly we feel it's a way to escape social accountability. That we crave such ambiguity *is* the sign of just how wounding the categories can be or have been. Still, espousing that ambiguity was and is a way of saying: "Not me . . . I'm above all that, outside of it, not a part of it."

What I learned is that precisely when one says, "I'm not a part," one is most trapped by one's identity, most paralyzed and most limited by the greater society, and that is the sign one has given up, given in; that one is precisely *not* in a condition of freedom—but of entrapment. Saying, "I am not a part" is *very* different from saying, "Because I *am* a part, I will not participate in *that* manner." The first is delusion. The second is power—which is inimical to the cry of powerlessness that you quote—and is the other way discourses are changed.

POETRY PROJECT: *In your collection of essays,* Longer Views, *you name a dozen poets whose work you have enjoyed over the last few years. How has poetry influenced your work? What is the connection, for you, between, say, poetry and science fiction writing?*

DELANY: You'll have to excuse me. Auden's on my mind, because only yesterday someone sent me an audiotape of two TV programs that featured him, which I first watched in 1953 when I was eleven years old. The second one in particular—in which Auden was interviewed—made a great impression on me as a child. One of my best friends in elementary school was a boy named Johnny Kronenberger, whose father, Louis Kronenberger, had collaborated with Auden on *The Oxford Book of Aphorisms.* From time to time Auden babysat for Johnny and his sister Liza. So, by the time I was eleven, I already knew of

Auden and knew he was a famous poet—that, indeed, he was queer and lived with Chester Kallman. (The kids at my New York private school were *quite* a bunch of gossips.) With great glee, Johnny had described to me Chester's imitations of Diana Trilling at his parents' annual Christmas party.

I'd mentioned seeing the *Camera Three* program in my autobiography. Involved in collecting all the extant Auden interviews, Auden scholar Jacek Niecko had recently read my book, phoned me up, and offered to send a copy of the programs to me.

I listened to the sound track of the programs just last night —for the first time in forty-five years. Hearing the voice of Jim McAndrew, the *Camera Three* spokesperson (in the 1950s McAndrew was the poor man's Alistair Cooke), for the first time since before I entered puberty, last night I was most aware of how people use poetry for their own purposes—which may or may not have anything to do with what the poet is interested in, writing his or her poem.

Camera Three was a wonderful show. There I saw my first modern dance. There I first heard the poetry—in both English and Spanish—of Federico García Lorca. There I first saw Balanchine's choreography. But it was, I also realized last night (as are so many attempts to "bring Art to the People," of which *Camera Three* was a classic example), in many ways an aesthetically conservative program.

In 1953, McAndrew was probably somewhere between thirty-eight and forty-two. He'd graduated from college just before World War II—in that age when *not* everybody went to college and when the mark of intelligence was merely having a high school diploma. He'd missed out, doubtless, on the New Criticism and probably regarded it as a suspicious order of recent academic nonsense—the way someone who'd graduated from college in the fifties might have regarded poststructuralist literary theory ten or fifteen years ago. When, during the second program devoted to the poet, he got around to interviewing Auden in person, clearly he had an intellectual agenda already in place. What I realized last night, however, which needless to say had completely escaped me at eleven, was that his only interest in Auden was in how Auden was going to validate that agenda.

Moreover, equally clearly, he couldn't imagine Auden himself having any other interest *than* to validate it. With every "question/statement" McAndrew poses, his point is that the historical purpose of the poet has been to provide images of heroes for the nation. Clearly that's what Homer did. Clearly that's what Shakespeare did. Thus, that's what Auden must be doing, too. ("The poet must speak from a position of strength," he begins by declaring.) "Okay, Mr. Auden, tell our audience just how *you* go about doing this." And whenever Auden tries, however politely, to move the conversation toward something that might actually be interesting about poetry (at one point, while describing how technology changes the structure of the personal act, Auden explains that pressing a button to drop a bomb is far different from Achilles fighting a one-to-one combat with Hector), McAndrew diligently takes it back to this narrow and straited notion: "Of course the people *must* find a hero in the midst of something technological. They might pick the tail gunner of the plane that dropped the bomb on Japan twelve years ago. But the poet wouldn't be interested in the tail gunner, of course."

Realizing he's been completely misunderstood, Auden declares: "Oh, he *might . . .* "

McAndrew's tail gunner was certainly a not-so-veiled dig at a then much-discussed World War II poem by Randall Jarrell, "The Death of the Ball Turret Gunner," about an insistently *un*-heroic death (Jarrell's poem ends, "When I died they washed me out of the turret with a hose"), but I was eleven and oblivious.

McAndrew reminds us, however, how relatively new and troubling for the modern critic the poetic task of protesting the ironic futility of so much modern life—not to mention modern death—actually was; it was as new and difficult to deal with as, a hundred years before, Browning's celebration of the barren and ugly and insistently unbeautiful landscape in "Childe Roland to the Dark Tower Came" (1855) had once been. I don't believe McAndrew would have been able then to conceive of the flowering of such a poetic task in a poem, from only a handful of years later, such as Allen Ginsberg's *Howl* (1956), a protest Auden's own poems had taken on in works such as *For the Time Being* (1942): "If, on account of the political situation, / There are quite a number of houses without roofs, and men / Lying about in the landscape neither drunk nor asleep . . . ")—and "The Shield of Achilles" (1952), which he read that same morning on the show.

Today McAndrew sounds unbelievable clunky, dated—and incredibly dictatorial: he knows what poetry is for, and that's all he's interested in hearing about. At the time (to repeat), the establishment critical position was that the purpose of poets was to write great poems about great political leaders; and the fact that no poet whom anyone actually wanted to read was even vaguely interested in doing anything like this was a sign of the decadent times in which we lived.

Against this, Auden tries to maintain a demeanor that is at once light, conversational, erudite, and not *too* appalled. Within the margins of civility, he protests all this strait-laced intellectual flapdoodle. At one point, when McAndrew is going on piously about Shakespeare, and says, "Henry the fifth was a popular hero—"

Auden interrupts: "And rather a bore!"—and McAndrew, you can hear it, is actually shocked!

If you are familiar with the history of criticism, you realize that McAndrew's thematic dogmatism is precisely what the New Critics of the late forties and early fifties were—really—just then in rebellion against.

(The earlier program, in which half a dozen actors *declaimed* Auden's poems like a bunch nineteenth-century Shakespearean hams, ranges between the comic and the pathetic. But this is what people thought poetry was, back then. Even recordings of Sylvia Plath, reading her own poems in that decade, fall into that same mode. Auden's great love lyric to Chester Kallman, "Lay your sleeping head my love . . . ," was read out by a woman to a snoozing man: the directors probably thought they were being quite daring, if not revolutionary. Auden, as he reads "The Shield of Achilles" and "In Memory of William Butler Yeats," alone comes anywhere *near* the tone of intelligent conversation in which the vast majority of his poems are actually written. And, forty-five years later, *that* was what I remembered.)

While there are *more* poets today, and people have become *somewhat* more comfortable with them, conversing with them, hearing them read, and perhaps a little more polite to them, I don't know whether the fundamental situation has changed. We find lines that we love and quote them out of context—only to reread the entire poem a decade later and discover that the poet was telling us that is something we must *never* do or think!

The very brilliance of expression was the poet's attempt to allegorize its seductiveness as a dangerous idea.

In his essay "Writing," Auden tells us: "The English-speaking peoples have always felt that the difference between poetic speech and the conventional speech of everyday should be kept very small, and, whenever poets have felt that the gap between poetic and ordinary speech was growing too wide, there has been a stylistic revolution to bring them closer again." Auden was writing this—and I first read it—during the ascendancy of Dylan Thomas. Auden's poetry was, of course, insistently a poetry of highly intelligent conversation, whereas Thomas was a surreal and flashy ranter. But with observations such as the one I quote above, by the time (a shy decade after watching him on *Camera Three*) I had begun to publish, Auden's work was there to help make me aware that the language labors that produce poetry were not very different from those necessary for prose.

That fundamental closeness between poetry and prose in English is what allowed me to see poets laboring over their poems and to put like labor into my prose. What differentiates the two is the discourses that control the way in which the two are read. Though there's some, of course, there's much *less* difference in the way the two are *written* than it would otherwise seem.

INTERVIEWER: *Define silence.*

DELANY: I won't try to define it, because silence—at least in the way it interests me—is one of those objects that resists definition. But I can certainly make some descriptive statements about it so that we might more likely recognize it the next time we encounter it in one of its many forms.

Today silence is a rather beleaguered state.

And silence is the necessary context in which, alone, information can signify—in short, it's the opposite of "noise."

As such, it's seldom, if ever, neutral. It's pervaded by assumptions, by expectations, by discourses—what the Russian poet Osip Mandelstam (born the same year as our Zora Neale Hurston, 1891) called *shum vremeni*, "the hubbub [or *buzz*; or *swoosh*] of time." As such, silence is the only state in which the *shum* that pervades it can be studied.

Since Wagner at least, silence has been considered the proper mode in which to appreciate the work of art: Wagner was the first major artist to forbid talking in the theater during his concerts and operas. He began the custom of not applauding between movements of a symphony, sonata, concerto, suite, or string quartet. Also, he was the first person, during performances of his operas at Bayreuth, to turn off the house lights in the theater and have illumination only on the stage.

Silence.

Darkness.

For better or worse, this aligns art more closely with death: it moves us formally toward a merger with the unknown.

Carnival, circus, and social festival are the lively arts that fight the morbidity of that early modernism/late romanticism. They are the arts around which one is expected to make noise, point, cry out, "Oh, look!," then buy cotton candy from a passing vendor, and generally have a life, while the artists satirize it in simultaneous distortion, as clown, acrobat, and animal trainer —with silly prizes to the people for random effort and skill.

But, whether one is looking at comic books or construing philosophy, silence is still the state in which the best reading takes place; not to mention the writing—or revising—of a story or a poem.

—New York City
January 1999

A Black Clock *Interview*

Questions by Steve Erickson

STEVE ERICKSON: *A lot of your work, particularly in the late six-ties and going into the seventies, seemed intended both to transcend the conventions of science fiction and at the same time to embrace science fiction as a kind of outlaw genre, relative to what we'll call, for lack of something better, the "mainstream." But as your biog-raphies have it, you grew up not necessarily reading a lot of science fiction but a lot of more classical literature.*

SAMUEL R. DELANY: I read both. I was an avid science-fiction reader. I read it morning, noon, and night. But I read everything morning, noon, and night. I read lots of literature. And I read lots of science fiction. Paradoxically, the most emotional things that happened to me as a reader tended to come from the sci-ence fiction. When I was about ten or eleven, the first piece of writing to make me cry was Robert Heinlein's young-adult SF novel *Farmer in the Sky*, in which an ordinary American family emigrates from Earth to a moon of Jupiter. That's a father, a mother, their son, along with a pesky kid sister. Well, I had a fa-ther, a mother, and a pesky kid sister. And when the family gets out to Jupiter's moon, everybody else adjusts to the new world, but the younger sister just can't. She has allergies; the inert gases used to extend the artificial atmosphere make her ill; the hydro-ponic vegetables don't agree with her; she's the only one in the colony who needs to go around with special breathing equip-ment. Nor does she take any of this with good grace. She didn't want to come, and she's a natural whiner—what we would call today "high maintenance." Then they have a moonquake. The air dome breaks.

When, looking for the survivors, they manage to get back into the compound, the sister is dead . . .

Under the covers, hunched over with my flashlight, I turned the page and . . . sobbed, while I resolved to let my own sister play with my Gilbert Space Station with the little space-suited figures any time she wanted. I would even play with her, too. I would never tease her about being a slow, picky eater again. How awful it must be, I thought as I knuckled my nose, to have an always busy older brother, who you really wanted to play with but who never had any time for you, because you were two years younger—which, after all, wasn't her fault.

And for three whole days, all that I'd resolved to do I did.

Heinlein had pulled a number on me.

Still, it was the first time I realized words on paper could do that—to me. But because, when I was so young, some of my most emotional reading experiences came from science fiction, probably that's why, years later, I considered writing it.

I never thought I was going to write science fiction until I actually started doing it. I just wanted to write novels. I made stabs at writing novels all through my adolescence—wholly unreadable! Eventually, though, I wrote one and it sold. Since it happened to be science fiction, I kept on writing the kind my editor would buy. Once I'd published three and was half-way through a fourth, it struck me: "I must *be* a science-fiction writer." But I never made a decision. It was something that just happened.

ERICKSON: *Well, it sounds like—and this may be an impossible question to answer . . .*

DELANY: My favorite kind.

ERICKSON: *My favorite kind to ask as well. But it sounds as if there was a lot of random chance in what attracted you to science fiction; which is to say you might have read a mainstream novel where the pesky sister died and had the same response—rather than something in the genre itself that was attracting you.*

DELANY: Probably you're right. But I didn't. Also, the fact is, other than your normal *True Confessions* magazine writers, at the time most writers of "realistic" fiction were, I think, afraid of attacking emotions directly. Emblematic of the feelings you *could* portray—and the limits on the techniques you could use to portray them with—is the famous last sentence of Hemingway's *A Farewell to Arms*: Lieutenant Henry's newborn son has just strangled at birth in its own umbilical cord. Henry has pleaded with God to let Catherine Barkley, the love of his life, live; but, with hemorrhage after hemorrhage, Catherine dies, while he sits with her unconscious body. Out in the hospital corridor the nurses let him know she's really dead. Then, stoically, he tells us: "After a while I went out and left the hospital and walked back to the hotel in the rain." And the novel is over.

Now adolescent boys loved this kind of thing. It reassured us. No matter what happens to you, don't worry: You'll *look* okay. Nobody's going to laugh at you in the street. That fitted with the postwar mentality—though the book is about World War I, the forties and fifties, post–World War II, were the real heyday of Hemingway's popularity—and its mania for conformity and security, where nothing was ever supposed to look out of the ordinary or odd.

Aestheticized politics is the hallmark of fascism, Benjamin tells us. Well, aestheticized living often has its fascist current, too.

Then we grew up a little. One thing growing up entails is learning that once, twice, three times in your life you *will* experience some passion—jealousy, love, lust, hate, grief—to the point where you lose it. If you happen to be in public, it doesn't matter. You may collapse beside the park path and lie there five hours, unable to move, or you'll stagger, wailing, through the traffic, or even go screaming after someone along the waterfront for an hour and a half.

It doesn't happen often. If it occurs with any frequency, probably you need help—if not medication. If it doesn't happen a *couple* of times, however, you're not human.

At sixty-one, I've gotten off with three.

With that Hemingway line, yes, emotion lies *under* it. But it's all implied. None of it shows. For some reason, while writers in the literary precincts were extolling this notion of great emotions never expressed, science fiction was willing to take on, relatively speaking, the emotions full force. You'd think it would be the other way around. Possibly it was the distancing effect of all that technology, which made (some) SF writers more willing to chance the grand emotional move.

Think of what the great American SF short-story writer Theodore Sturgeon would have done with Hemingway's ending. We would have felt the fist clamping the lower part of Henry's intestines, so that, as he went stiff-legged down the hospital stairs, he was almost nauseated. We would hear how, every eight or nine steps he stopped and dragged in some great breath that had an ugly sound hooked to it he hardly heard, though it made someone else in the street glance at him. Believe me, no matter what he said, until he was more than halfway to the hotel, Henry didn't even *know* it was raining!

ERICKSON: *I've always thought Hemingway's best work was his short stories—that the only novel that came close to sustaining that highly distinctive self-repression was* The Sun Also Rises.

DELANY: Yes, I'm with you there. Certainly that distanced, deadly cold style—Mérimée (as Wyndham Lewis noted) out of Gertrude Stein—can achieve some spectacular effects. I suppose it's not fair to belittle the end of *A Farewell to Arms*. It's knocked people's socks off for seventy-five years, now. But after the Victorian melodramas of the nineteenth century, when Oscar Wilde noted that only a heart of stone could fail to giggle at the death of Little Nell, and the Edwardian beginning of the twentieth, yes, there *was* a reaction among fiction writers. It ran through realistic narrative—from high art to low, from Hemingway and Stein to Hammett and Chandler. The worst thing you could be accused of was sentimentality. One thing that makes Sturgeon such a great writer—as it helps make Fitzgerald, Hemingway's rival, a great writer—is that he's not afraid to risk sentimentality. He's not *afraid* of that big emotional gesture. Yes, sometimes it doesn't work; then it can be as mawkish in Sturgeon as it can be laughable in the Victorians. (With "A Diamond as Big as the Ritz," Fitzgerald could at least giggle at himself.) But when it works, it's powerful. Sentimentality is the flaw of the great storytellers. It's not a little flaw. Small writers don't risk it. They want everything perfect.

Auden felt that raising the sexual urges in a piece of fiction distorted the reader's aesthetic judgment. (This is why he felt pornography couldn't be art, even though he wrote a very good example himself, "The Platonic Blow.") But over the history of Western art, many have felt that raising even the emotional responses beyond a certain point is equally distorting or damaging to the aesthetic. This is the argument that favored—and in some precincts still favors—Mozart over Beethoven. Is the mark of great art high sensation—to make us cry or laugh or yearn—or simply intense beauty? There's no way we can deny that on some level, the two *can* get in each other's way. But Beethoven and Bruckner and Mahler try for both. So do the Balzacs, the Dickenses, the Sturgeons—as do Tolstoy and Shakespeare.

ERICKSON: *Well, if a writer isn't willing to risk sentimentality, then he or she isn't likely to be emotionally engaged with the work, or to emotionally engage anyone else.*

DELANY: Again, agreed. Of course there *are* other ways to be involved in a work besides emotionally. Still, it's paradoxical to find this willingness to engage readers emotionally in the paraliterary genres, those genres outside the literary precincts. You've probably figured out: I think of science fiction, including my own, as very much a paraliterary genre. The fact that it lives—and has lived—on the margin is important to its history. If you remove it from that margin, you remove it from its historical context; I don't think that's such a good thing. Genre boundaries are real power boundaries. Bringing all the genres together into what, following Roland Barthes, Susan Sontag called "the great democracy of texts" has endless problems—quite as many as trying to mete equality out among classes, races, and religions. "Let's get all the races together and we'll have no problems"—starting tomorrow.

Sure. Tell me another one.

History—which is what those races, those classes, those religions, and, by extension, those genres *are*—is too strong. Which is to say, as in a society aesthetic democracy must be sensitive to history. Democracy that is not historically sensitive is no democracy at all. If SF were to lose its history, it would become unreadable, just as literature would become unreadable without its own history.

ERICKSON: *So you didn't feel caught up by a dual impulse to transcend the genre on the one hand and embrace it on the other.*

DELANY: For some reason, I've never felt that way. The arts, yes, even the paraliterary arts, value originality. Thus, when you say "transcend," you only mean doing something new *in* the genre. You decide to write a literary novel, and you want it to do something new, something different, something unusual. Transcending the genre? At best it's a conventional—*and* somewhat hyperbolic—way to refer to the writer's unusual contribution to the genre itself. But the SF novelist who wants to do something really good and new is no more trying to *transcend* the SF genre than the literary novelist who wants to write a really good and new literary novel is trying to transcend literature. In both cases it's a matter of trying to live up to the potential of the genre.

To use such rhetoric—the rhetoric of transcending the genre —about the SF novelist is just a way of announcing you don't think most SF is very good, so that *any* SF novel that *is* good must be something *more* than SF.

Most people who attempt to write literary novels, let's face it, do a pretty piss-poor job. As Sturgeon himself put it, in what came to be known in the SF field as Sturgeon's law, when someone once asked him how he could defend science fiction when ninety percent of it was crap: "Ninety percent of *everything* is crap." No one uses the myriad failed literary attempts to demean the whole category of literature. "Since ninety percent of most literary novels are finally pretty terrible—that is, the hundreds and hundreds published every year—this must mean that the occasional really good one actually *transcends* literature." I think you can hear, just from that, that your claim of transcendence for good SF is, at its worst, an equally conventional way of insulting the overall SF genre in a way most of us simply wouldn't consider for insulting literature.

ERICKSON: *Well, let's give this dead horse one more whack. It doesn't seem such a coincidence that* Dhalgren *and* Gravity's Rainbow *were written pretty much during the same period of time. We could say the line between "science fiction" and "mainstream" was being attacked from different sides by both books.*

DELANY: Yes, I think it was. But, to repeat myself, genre distinctions are fundamentally power boundaries. The one between literature and paraliterature is a palisade, with the "high" arts (poetry, essay, fiction, drama) up there and the "low" arts (comic books, science fiction, pornography, mysteries) down here. When a literary writer strikes out to bring back rhetorical figures from the marginal, low, or folk arts for use in his or her literary work, everybody says, "Wow! Isn't that great!" The writer is using the marginal, the naive, the all-but-folk forms to replenish and revitalize the oversophisticated and overrefined literary precincts. When a marginal—or paraliterary—writer appropriates literary rhetoric, however, and carries it back across the border to his or her side of the boundary, to hear most people talk about it in the literary precincts, you'd think a native had broken through the fence into the farmyard and swiped a chicken.

I use these extreme metaphors to talk about this kind of thing because those exclusionary attitudes are part of the history of science fiction and the other paraliterary genres. I think that history is important. Those exclusionary forces rigorously shaped the space in which the rhetorical richness, invention, and genius of SF was forced to flower.

ERICKSON: *Well, though I don't mean to exclude anything here, including a sense of genre, when a writer is working on a novel sometimes there's a breakthrough—maybe the work takes a turn to some place it's never gone before, or maybe a lot of things that were going on in earlier novels come together in a way they never have—and it seems like* Babel-17, *written and published in the mid-sixties, might have been that kind of book for you. The space ship is called the* Rimbaud, *suggesting the metaphorical vocabulary of your fiction was now symbolic, hallucinatory, rather than just futuristic.* Babel-17 *dealt with language as a kind of human tech-*

nology of its own, or some synthesis of technology and psychology that's always held secrets from us even as we invented it. In a way Babel-17 *anticipates not only* Dhalgren, *where language becomes a city, but a book like DeLillo's* The Names *that came almost twenty years later. Whether you were conscious of it at the time, do you now look back and see that you were going through something, or that something was happening then in what you were doing or thinking, that would account for the creative leap of* Babel-17?

DELANY: A writer talking seriously about his or her own break-throughs is a guarantee of arrogance, pomposity, and aesthetic clownishness. I'm afraid I've listened to too many writers talk about their breakthroughs, then gone and read the book, only to scratch my head and ask, "Breakthrough into what?" Cordwainer Smith wrote "Drunkboat," his homage to Rimbaud, a decade before I wrote *Babel-17.* And I have pointed out to class after class, year after year, Alfred Bester's *The Stars My Destination* begins with a challenge to Joyce's *Portrait of the Artist as a Young Man* in precisely that playful way that writers do such things! When last I read it, *Babel-17* struck me as a thin adventure story dramatizing an idea—the "Sapir-Whorf hypothesis" —that is, among other things, wildly wrong. Now the twenty-two-, twenty-three-year-old kid who wrote it had never heard of the Sapir-Whorf hypothesis, but he had picked the notion up indirectly from a couple of very poor books by linguistics popularizers of the day—and not very good popularizers at that.

Having said that, some things do feel like breakthroughs—to the author, that is. But, more and more I suspect, rarely do they leave as big an effect on the textual surface as the writer who experienced them imagines. Wagner had a famous breakthrough after he wrote his fourth opera *Rienzi*—till then his most successful bid for popularity. His post-*Rienzi* breakthrough was important enough so that, when he went on to write *Lohengrin*, *Tannhäuser*, *The Flying Dutchman*, and the *Ring* cycle, he discouraged performances of *Rienzi* or any of his other three previous operatic works. Well, a few years back, Carnegie Hall hosted a very good full-orchestra concert production of *Rienzi*. A friend and I, who the year before had gone to the Met to hear Hildegard Behrens in the *Ring* cycle, went to hear *Rienzi*. From the way Wagner had carried on about it—not to mention a good number of Wagner critics—I expected something as different from his mature operas as Mozart is different from Beethoven.

You know what *Rienzi* sounds like? Another Wagner opera. And a rousing and relatively accessible one at that, which builds nicely to a very satisfying musical climax.

Every once in a while, one of Wagner's first three operas—*The Ferries*, *The Wedding*, or *Love Denied*—gets a laboratory production somewhere, and someone invariably writes, "Hey, you know, they're not bad!," though Wagner himself left strict instructions that none of the first four was ever to be played at his own theater, the Festspielhaus at Bayreuth (with the result that many people don't even know the first *three* exist). Most "breakthroughs" are a matter of some new philosophical position the artist arrives at; it may or may not be accompanied by a relatively small technical change. From inside, it feels like the earth moved. From outside, however, often it looks relatively small—and, as time goes on, even smaller. Even the most historically sensitive poetry reader will probably not be able to spot, unassisted, why Auden so passionately wanted to drop "September 1, 1939" or "Spain" from his collected works. Today's readers find *The Voyage Out*, if not *Night and Day*, a pretty good Virginia Woolf novel—both books Woolf was ready to disown; Cather's first book, *Alexander's Bridge*, strikes me as far better than her second, *O, Pioneers!* (which, frankly, is a mess), even though it shares a "theme" and location with her brilliant and exquisite third, *My Ántonia*. All of us, even artists themselves, want to map the reality of the shift in our own interests and movements among various techniques against the model in which the ignorance and innocence of the child give way to the maturity and wisdom of the adult, which, in turn, eventually grow weak and feeble with age. But while physical energy does change (as a sixty-one-year-old diabetic with a two-and-two teaching load, graduate and undergraduate, I can't write as much as I could at twenty-one), I think we would do well to bear in mind Goethe's wise observation: "A man of fifty knows no more than a man of twenty. They just know different things."

Babel-17 certainly *didn't* feel like a breakthrough to me. What did feel like one, however (though, again, I don't believe it was anywhere near as large or as important as it felt), was the change between *The Towers of Toron*, the second volume of my early trilogy, and its third volume, *City of a Thousand Suns*. That second volume was the hardest book I've ever written, before or since. Getting it down on paper was like pulling three of your own abscessed teeth at four on a February morning with nothing but a pair of pliers, a hammer, an ice pick, and a flashlight, using a shard of mirror nailed to an outhouse wall behind a barn. Even taking time out to write the short novel *The Ballad of Beta-2*, to which at one point I turned in despair over volume 2, didn't make it any easier. In terms of the psychology of the "breakthrough," however (rather than in terms of any notable difference in the text; that's a judgment and a topic left wholly to the reader), there may be some interesting things to say about it. First, there was no time lag between the ending of volume 2 and the beginning of volume 3. I finished book 2—kicking and screaming. I got up, probably went to the bathroom. Then, in great excitement and with boundless enthusiasm, I returned to my notebook and started the first chapter of volume 3 not ten minutes later: it was a hawk flight over mountain, lake, and trees.

The nature of the breakthrough was, you see, wholly intellectual. In my first four novels, written over the previous two or two-and-a-half years, what I was mainly—all but exclusively—interested in was saying—carefully, precisely—exactly what I wanted to say. To that end, I did a lot of rewriting. I cut lots of extraneous words and dead phrases, pared away anything that stuck me as cliché or verbal clutter. I was ruthless about getting rid of passive constructions. Clarity. Simplicity. Economy. These were my intellectual benchmarks. Reading over my first drafts, the phrases that went through my head most frequently were: "That doesn't mean anything. That doesn't say anything. That's not even English. Get rid of it. Say it again, only more simply, directly, accurately."

My newer version was invariably shorter than the older.

That was my working method. It remained my working method *over* the breakthrough. For what it's worth, it's still my working method. It's what persisted *across* the disruption I'll now go on to describe:

Till the end of that second volume—that is, during the thirty or forty pages I had to write in order to end it—I wanted to write down and get correct the things I had needed up till then to tell the story, to manifest the plan I had in my head. In writing those pages, however, another enterprise, another notion of what I might do as a writer had formed and grown vivid in my mind, something I could only take up directly once I'd gotten this volume out of the way.

The trilogy's third volume had been outlined—at least in my head. I knew how it was going to begin. I knew how it was going to end. A clear picture of the last chapter had come, a year-and-a-half before, with my picture for the first volume's opening chapter. The last would simply replay the first in reverse. But instead of writing about *only* the story's incidents in an attempt to dramatize them, wouldn't it be more interesting, wouldn't it be more fun, wouldn't it make a more vivid read, I decided, to write not only about the direct actions that made up the story but, as well, cram the novel—the surface texture of the writing itself—with the excesses of sensory and emotional experience the characters might have perceived while living through them? I could give much more of the life, pulse, and texture of the experiences that made up the story than I had been. Phrases like "describe the setting" and "show what the characters did" and "make clear their motivations" pretty much covered what I had been trying to do in books 1 and 2. Now I started to think about what I wanted to do as "cramming my narrative with verbal tags suggesting the sensory and emotional richness to the texture of those experiences, of those settings, of those actions, those motivations." I'd been playing with bits of this in volume 2's last thirty or forty pages. But I couldn't do it as much as I wanted to, there, because the effect on the reader would have jarred too much with what had gone before.

The last chapter of the second volume took me about a *week and a half* to draft. It took me a day to draft the first chapter of the third and rewrite half of it. Another two days, and I did two more retypings. When I finished that first chapter of the new volume, I read it over. To me it felt like something written by a different person. I suspect that was a private experience; I have no way to know if any of it got onto the page. I don't think you can hold up any individual sentence and say, "There, this is the difference between the writing in books 1 and 2, and the writing in book 3." I would *like* to think at the end of an incident, a chapter, a whole section, however, it produced a greater sense of vividness, of immediacy. I repeat: One can make too much of such a "breakthrough." (All I have to do is go back and read any of the early books that came after it.) Still, at the time, it felt like an upward leap of miles.

Perhaps it lifted me an inch.

ERICKSON: *So your "breakthrough"—I know you're resisting the word, but bear with me—didn't have so much to do with "vision" or "concept" or whichever one of those words we're not using, as it did with the process or method of communicating the story to the reader. Although of course at some point "process" or "method" becomes integral to the vision, is a part of it.*

DELANY: You've got it. I think my method of writing, clarification, and revision—what was in place before this development and remained in place after it—restrained a certain excessiveness to the process. I was sure I might do what I wanted to in book 3 only *because* of my method. Without it, those tags and indicators would have sunk into the general wash of inaccurate and unclear nonarticulation all my writing starts out as. It felt like a whole reconceiving of what writing—what narrative—could be.

Regularly I've written that cliché, clutter, and thinness are the cardinal crimes of writing. But that's where I learned my own writing was thin. I've tried to make it less so since. But I'm painfully aware how inadequate many if not most of the things I've done to improve it have actually been.

Years later, however, in reading Walter Pater's wonderfully fecund *Plato and Platonism*, I was warmed to find Pater felt Plato's genius was not in his intricate argumentation or any "universal" truth he arrived at. Often those arguments, in parts of *The Republic*, are rather stodgy and conservative, when not, as in *The Laws*, terrifyingly repressive, and can only really be appreciated in terms of Plato's response to long vanished traditions and social realities all but irrecoverable for the modern world. What Pater praises Plato for is, rather, that excess, that richness of life and experience in which the portraits of his debaters and the world around them are picked out—all the things that make one think Plato would have made a fine novelist, if the novel had, indeed, existed when he wrote. It's a richness Plato communicates through the texture and generosity of his own linguistic attentions, his various ironies conveyed by use of commonplace reality to make or highlight—even more often to undercut or qualify—a point. Let's turn from Pater to Virginia Woolf. She was tutored in classics by Pater's sister, Clara, and on her father Leslie Stephens's death, took the first installment of her inheritance and bought the ten volumes of Pater's complete works (Stephens had written vehemently against Pater in the 1870s and would not have his works in the family library), which she went on to devour. There, in *A Room of One's Own*, I find that same richness in the pointed descriptions of her exclusion from the lawns and libraries of Pater's own "Oxbridge," of the sumptuous luncheons at the male colleges and the impoverished camaraderie at "Fernham" ("prunes and custard") in the shadow of the great "J— H—" (Jane Harrison). She drenches them with the same richness of texture to the experience that makes Plato's own work worthwhile.

I've always sympathized with Pater. If pure reworking into precision, economy, elegance, and balance could create readability, his single completed novel *Marius the Epicurean, His Sensations and Ideas*, would be the late nineteenth century's most accessible work. Instead, it's the first great modernist unreadable work—the forerunner of Stein and Proust, Woolf herself, Joyce, and Beckett. When I say "unreadable," I mean, of course, the work of fiction that can be read only as a project. Because of declining literacy, it's a road we all find ourselves, I suspect, more or less further along. I've read *Marius* three times and taught it twice. Woolf herself read it five times and revered it—and in its shadow had her own "breakthrough" into modernism; as did "vulgar" (Woolf's assessment) Joyce. Says shaving Buck, incapable of remembering his offense to Kinch the Knifeblade, "I remember only ideas and sensations." In 1904 Dublin's students were still deeply under the influence of Pater, Wilde, and the Oxford aesthetic movement of the 1870s and 1880s, and by inverting Pater's subtitle Joyce memorialized it.

ERICKSON: *You've written that "science fiction is science fiction because various bits of technological discourse . . . are used to redeem various other sentences from the merely metaphorical, or even the meaningless, for denotive description/presentation of incident." This suggests that one of the things that makes science fiction what it is, is the way technology informs not so much the themes of the genre but the language of it.*

DELANY: Yes—in the sense that, say, the neurological discourse of synesthesia makes sense out of all those otherwise surrealistic sentences in the *dérèglement des touts les senses* that climaxes *The Stars My Destination* (Bester's own homage to Rimbaud, in the burning cathedral's ruin): "Hot stone smelled like velvet caressing his cheek, almost the feel of wet canvas. Molten metal smelled like blows hammering his heart, and the ionization of the PyrE explosion filled the air with ozone that smelled like water trickling through his fingers . . . Smoke and ash were harsh tweed rasping his skin. It was cold again, and vacuum raked his skin with unspeakable talons."

We might back up a bit, though, and just say that science fiction acknowledges that technology exists, that technological change has some kind of influence on how people live their lives. A lot of literary fiction takes place as though technology wasn't a part of the world. You could go through the entire works of Henry James and not find a mention of technology. But literature exists by means of vast areas of experience not talked of. It's one of the things that makes it literature. You could read all the novels in Leavis's "Great Tradition" and not learn that human beings were biological creatures who took a leak three times a day, what exactly sex entailed, or that from time to time people went to the bathroom and took a shit. From the moment Aristotle declared that tragedy could only be about kings and queens—people whose fates affected hundreds or thousands, thus excluding the whole working class as fit topics for literature—narrative has abided by one set or another of such constraints. Every era's art is constrained by that era's concept of vulgarity. The artistic is precisely what is not vulgar. (Until Dante, the language the people actually spoke was outside the precinct of art.) Vast areas of experience always remain outside the literary precincts. People don't question it. Of course, in some of my science fiction people *do* go to the bathroom—in *Dhalgren* in particular.

More accurately, literature (in its largest meaning) might be seen as the battle of the unsaid to enter the precincts of the articulate. For the whole of the world's many practices of writing, this is the importance of that which, for many, first entered our awareness under the rubric of feminism—in science fiction one thinks preeminently of the novels and stories of Joanna Russ, *We Who Are About To . . .* , "Souls," *The Female Man*, along with, of course, the work of Carol Emshwiller, Ursula K. Le Guin, Octavia E. Butler, and more recently L. Timmel Duchamp as well as Karen Joy Fowler, Nicola Griffith, Nalo Hopkinson, Kelly Link, Mary Anne Mohanraj, and Vonda N. McIntyre with her fine novels *Dreamsnake* and *The Moon and the Sun.* These writers draw much human experience into the light of the richest and most exciting articulation—experiences often excluded previously because they *were* women's, or black or Asian women's, or working-class women's.

ERICKSON: *Well, picking up on that a little bit, much of your fiction—and this is also where technology sometimes comes into play—is about the "other." That is, people who have been, say, sexually neutered by radiation, or have been locked out of themselves by the flight of their own memories. Or, as in the case of the short story "Driftglass," amphibian beings who've been scarred by accidents where technology came into conflict with nature. And while I realize there may be no way for you to know this, do you think it was easier to create this literature of the other, and to work as, if you will, a gay African American writer, within the ghetto of science fiction, particularly since that fiction was already outcast by "mainstream" fiction?*

DELANY: Actually, no. The analogy that comes so readily to most intelligent people's minds (that it might be easier to write about marginal people, especially for a marginal writer, in a marginal genre) is too easy. It hinges on a misunderstanding of just how powerful the power boundaries that organize the various practices of writing into genres are—as it helps mystify those boundaries' workings. We all have a general desire—I think it's part of why we read in whatever genres we do—for the genre itself to take care of some political problem or other. And of course it never does. The assumption that it might is the same order of category-concept mistake as someone makes who says, "Well, you painted this wonderful picture of a sunset and it was so colorful. Is there a special relationship between sunset and paint?" No. It's only the skill and sensibility of the artist that solve these problems. Somebody who can paint well will paint a good sunset; somebody who can't, won't. Because the genre happens to be a marginal genre won't make the stories more sympathetic to, understanding of, or insightful into the problems of the other. Now, genres have a tradition of dealing with certain groups in certain ways—as I said, for SF, women in particular—that you can historify. Women's treatment in SF goes back to the character of the rancher's competent daughter in the western, the woman who can ride and shoot like a man. That's because, in the West, an awful lot of women were raised that way. The stories reflected some of what was there. But when the "western" metamorphosed into this perfectly artificial genre, science fiction, the rancher's daughter became the scientist's daughter—of which there were two kinds. One could fix the spaceship, when it had a problem; the other simply sat around and listened to explanations or got rescued. Alas, this *doesn't* make the range of SF in the fifties any less sexist than the concomitant range of mainstream literature.

A woman named Louise White noted back in the middle seventies that during the thirties, forties, and fifties, however, a number of extraordinarily powerful women characters had emerged in science fiction. They tended to work for men who had power, she noted. Either they worked for the state or they worked for men who had enough power to topple states. From these grew Joanna Russ's Jael and Janet, and in reaction, Jeanine and Joanna (the other daughter); Le Guin's Takvar, as well as Gibson's Molly Millions; and in Alfred Bester you have Olivia

Presteign, Jisbella McQueen, and Robin Wednesbury . . . one novel with *three* extraordinary women characters, one of whom is even black. And *it's* a novel from 1956. Not that Bester anticipates the feminist thinking of the next fifty years. But just for color, liveliness, and general interest, it's a lot better than, let's say, Philip Roth's *Letting Go* from ten years later, or any number of other literary novels, in terms of the character templates.

ERICKSON: *The temporal consciousness of your work is pretty breathtaking, meaning the novels often seem aware of All Time, from past to future, but most particularly the times in which they're written. That might not sound revolutionary to someone who doesn't know much science fiction, but the way the sixties books were informed by that era even as it was unfolding, and by the way the era was mythologizing itself even as it was happening, was different from not only a lot of the science fiction being written then but "mainstream" work as well. The Beatles show up in 1967's* Einstein Intersection *as a kind of fabulist memory, for instance, which means you had to have been thinking about them as early as 1965 or so, a year before songs like "Strawberry Fields Forever" and "A Day in the Life" and "Tomorrow Never Knows," when it still wasn't clear to some people how important they were going to be artistically beyond the ongoing mania of the day.*

DELANY: My own interest in the Beatles started with the *Meet the Beatles* album, about a year before intellectuals began to pay serious attention to pop music. As a kid I played the violin. At fourteen I even wrote and orchestrated a violin concerto for a young violinist (much better on the instrument than I was), Peter Solaff—which is tantamount to saying I had the usual dismissive attitude, ubiquitous at the time, with which almost everyone with any intellectual pretensions denigrated pop music. In high school, however, I also had a friend—a slightly pudgy, blond-and-rose young man, Joe Weintraub—who was obsessed with Buddy Holly. "And this is *really* good music!" he insisted, as he played me one album after the other, then played them all again. He played me a song called "Sheila" ten times; even I could hear—because I wrote music—that the chords behind it were not the usual C, A-minor, F, G-7 "heart and soul" progression that underlay most rock music. "Even my brother-in-law, Leon, says it's musically interesting—and *he* teaches at the Juilliard School of Music!" Juilliard was then on Broadway, a block and a half from where I lived in Morningside Gardens, and every other day I walked past their practice rooms behind the gray cement wall, with the cacophony of pianos and trombones and violins coming from the windows. Leon was a jazz musician and had just made an album. There, in his blue bedroom, Joe got it out to show me—there was a picture of Leon on the back: he was black.

The fact that Joe—and his family—were *so* white, and that his twenty-three-year-old sister had a black husband who taught at Juilliard (this was 1957 or 1958, remember), rather startled this quintessentially conservative black kid from Harlem. But it also shook loose some of those entrenched cultural dogmas of the decade (that popular music and film were the most tertiary of arts that only ignoramuses and illiterate fans paid any attention to at all), which—in the sixties—would wholly topple. I've written in my autobiography, *The Motion of Light in Water* (1988), how, issuing from a radio on the sill of a first-floor apartment on West Fourth Street one July afternoon, Martha and the Vandellas' "Heat Wave" began the whole of the sixties for me. After hearing that song and its unusual music structure (the musical introduction takes up half the record), I knew something had changed in the society. From then on in, I had only to wait and watch for further manifestations.

One Friday or Saturday evening, Marilyn and I went to visit my Aunt Dorothy and Uncle Myles in Brooklyn for dinner. My young cousin Karen Randal lived with them and was about eleven at the time. She had just gotten her copy of *Meet the Beatles*. (I have an image of eleven-year-old Karen coming down the blue carpeted stairs from the second floor, dangling their Siamese cat, with its chocolate paws and ears and eye-mask and tail tip, by its foreleg over the heavy mahogany banister, the black-and-white album cover under her other arm.) I recall Karen's mother, a young doctor, dismissing the whole phenomenon as kids' noise. But, primed by Joe and Buddy Holly and Martha and Vandellas' Motown rhythms and harmonies, I said, "Hey, let's listen to it." So we did. Aunt Dorothy allowed as how one or two of the songs were actually rather nice. Barbara (the doctor) and her father (Karen's grandfather, my Uncle Myles, the judge) both agreed that, as far as they were concerned, it was just noise. Marilyn and I walked back to the subway later that night, however, pretty much in agreement that we'd found the whole thing musically quite rich.

"I Want to Hold Your Hand" had already rocketed to number 1 on the charts, and the "British Invasion" was under way. Marilyn and I were both in line at the Eighth Street Cinema for the first day's opening of *A Hard Day's Night.* We left the theater feeling that we had seen some aspects of a phenomenon that was really going to change notable factors in the cultural world. And we were right. Later I ran into a statement by composer Aaron Copeland: "Anyone wanting to know what the decade of the sixties sounded like must listen to the Beatles." With some incursions by others, yes, he's right. We listen to the Beatles today, and they sound very restrained. They're upbeat, "good-timey" music. But there's not a lot of distinct emotional articulation throughout the songs, changing from beginning to end. They are much more allied to, say, a Willie Nelson than to a Celine Dion, a Julio Iglesias, a Bonnie Tyler. Melodic change, yes; but emotional change came only with Richard Harris's version of Jimmy Webb's "MacArthur Park" and eventually Bonnie Tyler's performance of "Total Eclipse of the Heart," as pop music appropriated the affective variety found in more serious show music and in mini–folk cantatas like Woody Guthrie's "Song of My Hands." But, yes, the Beatles were the medium through which the audience was prepared for that enrichment.

We've already talked about that austere aesthetic of repressed emotion uppermost in the decades *before* the sixties. Have you ever listened to recordings of the way, say, Sylvia Plath reads her poems? The point is, everyone read their poems like that, back then—even Dylan Thomas. His voice was theatrically richer; that's all. (This whole *aesthetic* question about the expression of emotions leads directly into questions of performativity in general.) Both T. S. Eliot and W. H. Auden were notoriously bad public readers of their own poetry. Their public inaccessibility was a notable factor of their greatness.

It was Beaumarchais, speaking of opera, who wrote, "Anything too silly to be said can always be sung." Well, recently, going to a number of successful literary readings, I've thought: "Anything too silly to be read to oneself can always be made to sound good by reading it out loud." That represents a major cultural change—post-sixties variety.

ERICKSON: *After the breakthrough at the end of* The Towers of Toron, *you continued to incorporate into its more "literary" concerns the pulp motifs that people love about science fiction—in* Nova *for instance, which may reveal the Alfred Bester influence as much as any of your novels, and later in the Nevèrÿon books, which sometimes read like Godard and de Sade collaborating on a film adaptation of one of Edgar Rice Burroughs's Mars novels.*

DELANY: When, in the summer of 1957, as a fifteen-year-old, I first read Bester's *The Stars My Destination,* I thought it the most wonderful and original novel I had ever read. (When I was thirteen, I'd stayed up thirty-six hours in a row to read the last eight hundred pages of *War and Peace.* They were pretty wonderful, too.) Those adventures were the most real experiences of my childhood.

In 1965, when as a twenty-three-old I picked Bester up and re-read it, I realized, however, though was an extraordinary little novel, here and there in it things had been done rather quickly; sections had been dashed off without much thought. An uneven quality in the execution marred its finish. The energy, color, and velocity were there. But it was not the aesthetically perfect work the fifteen-year-old had seen. Immediately, the question became: Could *I* write a book with that much color and energy but with a higher surface polish—a book that a twenty-five-year-old could read and have the same order of experience that *Stars* had produced in the fifteen-year-old? That's what I aspired to do in *Nova.*

The Stars My Destination is inarguably the better novel—not *only* was it written first, but its breadth of vision is notably greater. Still, Bester's are the shoulders on which, shakily, I tried to stand. Any purchase I held there was all from the writer who was my model and base.

The Nevèrÿon series, Return to Nevèrÿon, was a different enterprise, however. With relative frequency readers say my claim to fame is that I write with both literary techniques *and* plot interest. I'm not sure, personally, what either of them is. But that's just not what the eleven Nevèrÿon stories and novels are trying for. What "keeps the reader reading" in the Nevèrÿon stories is, if it exists, closer to what keeps someone reading to the end of an essay. Certainly it's not to find out what happens in the sense of who-done-it or what prize lies at the quest's end. Perhaps there's a little of that in the novel *Neveryóna*. But in the other ten tales, nothing pulls the reader on that can be posed as a question at the story's beginning that its end will answer. There are only sentence rhythms, the color of the experiences described, and—at the end—the patterns they form to keep you interested. En route, reversals occur. Expectations are subverted, and unquestioned things are revealed to be quite different from what the reader might have assumed up until a certain moment they were. But these are all in the service of those narrative patterns: incidents from the past replayed out in occurrences in the present; patterns writ small repeated in much larger form, when characters enter situations similar to those other characters have entered and forces constrain them to make choices similar to choices made by those who were there before. Still, no plot occurs in the standard paraliterary sense of the term—the kind that controls a mystery or a western or an SF or traditional sword-and-sorcery tale.

That is to say, these are untraditional sword-and-sorcery tales, though they're sword and sorcery nevertheless. They don't transcend the genre. They do something within it that's a bit unusual. That's all. Anyone who begins those books looking for a traditional story will be pretty unhappy with what he or she finds. You say Godard and the Marquis de Sade—and I am complimented. But, as Bester is the model storyteller underlying *Nova*, Isak Dinesen and Marguerite Yourcenar are the model storytellers underlying the Nevèrÿon tales—both, I note, were *New York Times* best-selling authors now and again in their lengthy writing careers. Both were also Nobel Prize nominees: the year he won his, Hemingway said, perhaps with more honesty than gallantry, that it should have gone to Dinesen. Though no one would call either of them adventure writers, again and again both turned to material that other writers have written about in traditional adventure forms. Well, *my* material comes directly from Robert E. Howard: what was it like at civilization's beginning? I don't think you can address that question without some irony—irony is the atalette which skewers the Nevèrÿon stories, an irony I hope is similar to that which suffuses all those mid-century French dramatic retellings of Greek myths, from Cocteau's *Orphée* and *La Machine infernale*, to Gide's *Le Roi Candaules* and *Oedipe*, to Giraudoux and Anouilh, to Sartre's *Les Mouches*. In that sense, the Nevèrÿon project is to give someone who finds of interest the material associated with the earliest moments of civilization a new kind of read—and, I would hope, new pleasures.

ERICKSON: *Well, to pursue the matter of motifs and themes that run throughout all your work, including the science fiction and the stuff in the last twenty years that's been outside science fiction, I've noticed two things in particular that characterize it. One is the motif of the city as a colossal psychic construct, to the point that the very text of* Dhalgren *forms a kind of urban schematic. The other is the growing exploration of sex, which in your novels became prominently explicit at least as early as* Trouble on Triton *and has become more daring and outspoken in recent books like* The Mad Man *and* Times Square Red, Times Square Blue. *On the one hand, in the city you have what may be the grandest expression of human artifice, and in sex you have the most basic of human drives, the artistic expression of which, various aesthetic establishments still resist—no matter how much sex dominates our day-to-day thinking. The collision between the grand artifice of the city and the fundamental inevitability of sex suggests a kind of fetishized urbanism . . .*

DELANY: Do you mean I love the city? I do! Yes, and reasons to love it, to seek it out, to leave the provinces and refashion your life among its squares and courtyards include the fact that sex in particular and satisfying relationships in general are more generously available there than among the forests, in the deserts, and on the plains—not to mention in the suburbs. Cities are the site of theater and art, which challenge God in their representation of complex worlds. That's why (Plato suspected and William Gaddis knew) they are fundamentally evil and godless—thank God! I was born in New York, in Harlem, in Harlem Hospital at 138th and Lenox Avenue. I lived in Harlem but went to a Park Avenue private school that was mostly white. As I have repeatedly written, my daily trip between these two cityscapes was a journey of near-ballistic violence, though carried out in perfect silence, as though it were the most ordinary trip in the world. It taught me about the range of ways people live in cities. Once you get that template down, you learn wonderful things—the widely different lifestyles that can exist cheek-a-jowl in cities. It makes for good novel material—science fiction or any other kind.

At the same time, as a black gay man, just over half my life was pre-Stonewall. *Almost* half has been post-Stonewall. My gay graduate students are frequently between twenty-four and thirty-five. They have a difficult time understanding what the world was like forty or fifty years ago. They really can't grok—to use a science-fiction term—why or how, in 1950, F. O. Matthiessen, a famous and respected literary critic at Harvard, leapt from a window and killed himself when it was discovered that he was gay. Or, in 1960, when it was discovered that Newton Arvin—a well-known critic and teacher at Smith College—was gay (someone reported to the police that he had a cache of gay pornographic magazines—stuff *far* milder than things sold openly at any big city news kiosk or most small-town newspaper stores today; the police broke into his apartment—illegally—and broadcast it to the world: today, such magazines have done articles about me and run interviews with me not unlike this one), he had a mental breakdown and spent the rest of his life in an institution, his career at an end.

At the last three universities I've worked at, I was hired *because* I was gay.

Which is to say they wanted somebody to do queer theory, gay studies, and things like that. That's quite a change. I was alive when Matthiessen and Arvin made headlines. Those scary tales were part of my life. But it's hard for people to understand the nature of that change, how you can go from a situation where to be outed is practically to lose your life, to the situation we have now.

A lot of the early thinking about putting gay material into public narrative—let's call it "public narrative," rather than literature *or* paraliterature—was about trying to win a certain kind of acceptance for things gay. The point is, the word "gay" is an inadequate indicator for a bunch of historical trajectories. It covers, among many other things, institutions that are historically sedimented and have been there a long time.

What interests me—and has interested me for twenty-five or thirty years—is how these institutions differ from heterosexual institutions, not how they're the same. I'm interested in showing people the fine points of that difference. The similarities that we can construct between these straight and gay institutions are an initial field on which further differences can be teased out —a notion courtesy of Gayatri Chakravorty Spivak. They have some good points and they have some bad points. And the good points are well worth touting and celebrating. I scandalize my straight graduate students regularly: when they turn in another story about the guy whose girlfriend goes and cheats on him, and he walks back to that hotel in the rain, I say, "You know, monogamy is not the only game in town. And you don't get points just by pushing the monogamy button. There are different kinds of relationships. There are open relationships that really work. They require thought, intelligence, responsibility to the other person, and you really have to think through how these things are done." Deeply I question—dare I call it?—the *Jerry Springer* approach to life, which holds that somehow any time someone has sex with more than one person, it's got to be fundamentally a bad thing. I've lost friends over this. People have stopped talking to me, because I've suggested that maybe there *are* other games in town. I have a great deal of respect for the monogamy game. Still, it's *only* a game. Choosing to play it (or not to play it) doesn't give you any privileged or fundamental superiority or mental or moral health. Faithfulness is a symbol. But like all symbols, it's a symbol that either you do use or you don't use. Lots of very intelligent and sensitive people, straight and gay, will tell you today they're just not really into it: they're actively trying to come up with other social forms. And I've been interested in exploring this in fiction. Most of the fiction in which I've tried to explore it is closer to pornography (another paraliterary genre with a venerable history) than science fiction. Something is to be gained by taking the despised form and working with it and doing the best you can. You do a lot better, anyway, if you take on a marginal form and write it so well that people say, "Hey, you know, this is really literature," than you do if you write literature so badly that people say, "This isn't any better than science fiction—or pornography."

In any case, I prefer that route.

—Los Angeles,
Philadelphia
2003–2004

A Para•doxa *Interview*

Inside and Outside the Canon

PARA•DOXA: *What is the canon? How does it get formed? Does it have value?*

SAMUEL R. DELANY: The *Oxford English Dictionary* devotes two and a quarter columns to some fourteen definitions of the word —from "canon" as rule (from the Greek κανών), through "canon" as "a standard of judgment or authority; a test, a criterion, a means of discrimination," through "canon law," the biblical "canon," and the "canon" of the saints, to—finally—"canon" as "the metal loop or 'ear' at the top of a bell." But not one of these definitions corresponds to the "canon of English literature," much less to the "canon of Western literature."

The use of the word "canon" that has excited so many of us to so much polemic recently is a metaphorical extension of the notion of canon as the list of books approved as part of the Bible or the list of saints approved of and canonized by the church. As Foucault reminded us, in his ovular essay "What Is an Author?" (1969), the controlling concepts of historical, stylistic, ideational, and qualitative unity holding stable the notions of "author" and "authority" are themselves religious holdovers, as is the concept of the canon: the canon is a list of approved books, that is, books that have been verified to have come from God.

If we are to make any headway in such a discussion, we have to start with a few reasonable statements, however, about what the canon is *not*.

First, the canon is not a natural object. That is to say, if the canon is any sort of object at all, it is purely a *social object.* To use an example from the late Lucien Goldmann, the canon is not an object like a wooden table weighing three hundred pounds.

Rather it is a *social object* like the strength required to move a table that is too heavy for one, two, or even three strong men to move without help from a fourth. Largely because they are notoriously unlocalized in space, social objects do not lend themselves to rigorous definitions, with necessary and sufficient conditions. (Does it matter which four men move the table? Does it matter if one, two, or three of the movers are women . . . ?) At best, social objects can be functionally described (in many different ways, depending on the task the particular description is needed for, i.e., depending on its required function). But functional descriptions are *not* definitions. To speak of them as if they were is to broach terminological chaos and confusion. Along with many forms of power, social objects include meanings, genres, traditions, and discourses.

Second, the canon is not a conspiracy. That is to say, while the forces that constitute it are often mystified and frequently move to heal the breaches inflicted on it, there is no synod, no panel, no authoritative council, actually or in effect, that confers canonicity on works or establishes their canonical rank. While the history of the canon is full of campaigns, mostly unsuccessful, to bring writers or works into it—or often, to exclude writers and works from it—and while there are often elements of the conspiratorial *in* those campaigns, the canon itself is not one with them.

Third, the canon is not a list. Though from time to time the canon presents itself as a paradigm, this is merely a flattened representation of a complex system, of a rhizome, of a syntagm, or simply of an abstract set of interrelations, too rich to be mappable with any sophistication in less than three—and more likely four—dimensions. The canon's self-presentation *as* a paradigm —or ranked list of works (or more accurately, as a set of contesting ranked lists)—is (1) always partial and (2) part of that complexity. Which is to say, its self-presentation as a paradigm is *part* of the mystification process by which this highly stable syntagm protects itself and heals itself from various attempts to attack it or to change it.

In short, the canon is an object very like a genre. That is to say, it functions (in a way almost too blatant to be interesting, but is thus perhaps more easily memorable) as *a way of reading*

—or, more accurately, as a way of organizing reading over the range of what has been written. The astute will realize that, having declared that the canon is not just a ranked list but rather the discursive machinery that produces the many contesting lists involved, we have actually described an object that is nothing less than the historical and material discourse of literature itself.

How is the canon formed? By political forces—in the sense that all social force is political. Traditionally a great many of the forces that we would recognize today as overtly political are also overtly conservative. At this point, one can go back and read the arguments that fulminated over the worth of, say, Edgar Allan Poe—who only just made it into the canon; or James Thomson—who still hasn't, in spite of the campaign launched by Bertram Dobell in the 1890s to have him included; or the various poets of the Rhymers' Club, also from the 1890s, for instance, Ernest Dowson, Lionel Johnson, John Davidson, William Sharp (a.k.a. Fiona McCloud), and Arthur Symons. Or the novel that was, during the nineties, the most talked-about and highly favored work among these same writers: Olive Schreiner's *The Story of an African Farm* (1883). Schreiner's work is as openly feminist a work as James's *Portrait of a Lady* (1881) and, later, D. H. Lawrence's *Sons and Lovers* (1913) were overtly anti-feminist. It is naive to assume this hasn't at least something to do with the reason James and Lawrence *were* canonized while Schreiner was not. But it is equally naive to assume that such ideological forces *exhaust* the politics of the canon. There are too many counterexamples.

A little book called *The Tourist: A New Theory of the Leisure Class*, by Dean McCannell (New York: Schocken Books, 1976), is one I would recommend to anyone interested in the formation of literary reputations in particular—and of any sort of social reputation in general. *The Tourist* professes to present a semiotics of contemporary tourism, but McCannell states in his introduction: "The tourist is an actual person, or real people are tourists. At the same time 'the tourist' is one of the best models for modern-man-in-general. I am equally interested in 'the tourist' in this second, metasocial sense of the term" (1).

Prompted only a bit by a quotation from Baudelaire that precedes it, we can easily locate in McCannell's "tourist" a descendant of Walter Benjamin's *flâneur*—whom Benjamin saw as the privileged subject in Baudelaire's newly urban bourgeois world.

But the strength of McCannell's study is not his meditation on the subject, but rather his astonishingly insightful dissection of the structure of the object: not what goes into making a tourist—but rather what goes into making a *tourist site.*

McCannell states that, naturally, the tourist site must be picturesque, enjoyable, or interesting in itself, and worth visiting in some more or less describable way. (See? You don't *have* to say "define" and "definable" every time you want to specify something. Get used to it. We'll never develop a sophisticated theory of paraliterary studies if we don't.) But basically what makes a tourist site is the "markers" scattered about the landscape pointing it out, directing us to it, more or less available on the well-traveled road—even when the site itself lies off the path. These markers, McCannell points out, can be as ephemeral as a word-of-mouth comment. ("Just before we got to the turnoff on I-66, we stopped at this place that served the most delicious, homemade blueberry muffins! Next time you're up that way, try it!") Or they can be as solid as a three-volume history and guide to *Life, Craft, and Religion among the Pennsylvania Shakers.* They can be as traditional as a brochure in a tourist office or a signboard on the road ("Just Twelve Miles to Howes Cavern"). The markers can generate as advertising by those who have invested in the site itself. Or they can generate spontaneously as writings, photographs, or artworks from those who have simply passed by and been moved to create these more lasting representations, impressions, and interpretations. At larger and more famous tourist sites, the markers can be intricately entwined with the site itself, such as the archways, broadened highways, parking lots, motels, and guided tours that have grown up to accommodate floods of visitors—to the Grand Canyon, say, or to Niagara Falls. Some sites are conceived, created, and built to be nothing *but* tourist sites: Mount Rushmore, Disneyland, the Epcot Center, each functioning more or less as one of its own markers. And there is a whole set of sites—often the spots where historical events took place—that are sites *only* because a marker sits on them, telling of the fact (so that, in effect, the informative marker *becomes* the site: an apartment house on West 84th Street bearing the plaque "In 1844, Edgar Allan Poe lived on a farm on this spot where he completed 'The Raven.'"). Without the marker, these sites would be indistinguishable from the rest of the landscape.

Without markers, even the most beautiful spot on the map becomes one with the baseline of unmarked social reality.

And until someone thinks to emit, erect, and/or stabilize a marker indicating it, no tourist site comes into being.

The accessibility of the markers, McCannell notes wryly, is far more important to the success of the site than the accessibility of the site itself. In the case of some sites (various mountaintops, or the like), their *in*accessibility is precisely part of the allure—often pointed out *in* the markers.

Yes, we're talking about advertising and commodification.

But it requires a very small leap to realize that McCannell's discussion holds just as true for establishing "tourist sites" in the landscape of art and literary production as it does for establishing them in an actual physical landscape. For a complex mapping of those literary sites, with suggestions as to what to see now and what to see next, is what the canon *is*.

The first major demystifying and axiomatic claim we can make, then, about the canon, in light of McCannell's semiotic survey of tourist sites, is that the material from which the canon is made is *not* works of literature (and/or art); rather it is made from works-of-literature-and/or-art-and-their-markers.

The variety of the markers for tourist sites (from word of mouth to the researched historical study) applies to the markers for literary sites.

If the canon *is* made up of literature-and-its-markers (and I believe it is), then to study the canon and canonicity *means* to study literature-and-its-markers. That is the object that controls the discipline. Literature alone will not suffice. The determining relationship of literature-and-its-markers to the canon should be, I suspect, self-evidently clear. If, for example, the major critical markers (or marker sets) associated with *Ulysses* were obliterated and had never existed—*James Joyce's* Ulysses: *A Study* (1930) by Stuart Gilbert, *The Making of* Ulysses (1934) by Frank Budgen, various works on Joyce by Hugh Kenner, and the two biographies by Richard Ellmann—*Ulysses* would occupy a *very* different place in the canon.

Positions in the canon do change: we are currently seeing an attempt at a major reevaluation of Hart Crane—though one could easily argue that Crane has been undergoing "a major reevaluation" at least since 1937 when the first biography by Philip Horton appeared, seven years after Crane's death; and that to be majorly reevaluated is finally Crane's function, persistent and unchanging, within the canon, from his initial consideration period until today. The high modernists launched a fairly strenuous effort to dethrone Milton from his place beside Shakespeare and Chaucer—and failed—while the conflict of values that has continually raged about Walt Whitman since his acceptance into the canon has stabilized his canonical position as firmly as any writer in the history of American canonicity. (A similar conflict of values has kept Robinson Jeffers from being finally and ultimately excluded.) The canon keeps alive what might be called "the Keats or Wordsworth problem," which memorializes a moment when poetry might be seen to bifurcate into two different sorts of (and possibly even mutually exclusive) verbal objects—as different, indeed, as the work of Crane and Auden; at the same time, through its stabilizing forces, the canon is what keeps us calling both "poetry."

One of the most fascinating and informative examples of canonization is the "invention" of Stephen Crane—by Thomas Beer in 1923. In terms both of the literary texts involved and their markers, at least two aspects of this "invention" are particularly worth discussing: one concerns the young man who wrote the novels *Maggie: A Girl of the Streets* (1893), *The Red Badge of Courage* (1895), and *The Third Violet* (1896–7), and the various poems and stories; the other concerns the texts themselves.

Between the two—and the markers associated with both—we have an extraordinarily informative tutorial case in canonical appropriation.

Allow me to review it:

Crane became a popular—even a best-selling—author, first with the newspaper syndication in 1893 of *The Red Badge of Courage* (written a year before, when he was twenty-one) and then, a bit over a year later, with its release as a novel by Appleton in 1895. Crane's experiences on the *Commodore* in December of 1896 returned him briefly to national attention in January of 1897—and produced both his newspaper account of the ship's sinking and his short story "The Open Boat." But the most interesting literary document to endure from the days of his initial popularity is probably Frank Norris's parody of Crane's impressionistic style, "The Green Stone of Unrest" (1897): "The day was seal brown. There was a vermilion valley containing a church. The church's steeple aspired strenuously in a direction tangent to the earth's center. A pale wind mentioned tremendous facts under its breath with certain effort at concealment to seven not-dwarfed poplars on an un-distant mauve hilltop . . . "

By the time he was twenty-eight, however, Crane was dead in Europe of tuberculosis. And while, in his last years in England, a number of writers, including Edward Garnett, H. G. Wells, Henry James, and Joseph Conrad, had befriended him and his common-law wife Cora and felt that his narrative artistry was well above the ordinary (and in this country, Elbert ["A Message to Garcia"] Hubbard, James Gibbons Huneker, and Willa Cather all wrote notes on his passing), twenty years after his death Crane was as forgotten as any other young writer who had written a best seller once twenty-five years before.

In the July 1920 issue of the *The Sewanee Review,* Vincent Starrett published "Stephen Crane: An Estimate," which, a year later, became the foreword to the Starrett-edited volume of Crane short stories, *Men, Women, and Boats,* the first book of Crane's work to appear for twenty years. Prompted by Starrett's volume and remembering *The Red Badge of Courage,* in 1922, Thomas Beer (1889–1940) suggested a biography of Crane to the Alfred Knopf publishing company. Beer's biography, *Stephen Crane: A Study in American Letters* (1923), became, in its turn, a best seller. From its publication we date the rise in Crane's reputation as the father of American poetic realism. Willa Cather, whose novel *One of Ours* (1922) had just won the Pulitzer Prize, had known Crane briefly (i.e., for some four or five days) when, in 1896, the twenty-three-year-old author had come through Lincoln, Nebraska, and had to wait over for money at the Bacheller-Johnson newspaper office, where the nineteen-year-old Cather then worked. Shortly after Beer's book appeared, Cather wrote an appreciative introduction to another collection of Crane's stories, *Soldiers in the Rain*.

To get some idea of how *unimportant* an author Crane was by the beginning of the twenties, however, one notes that James Gibbons Huneker, a well-thought-of critic at the time, a good friend of Crane's when Crane was in his twenties and Huneker was just thirty, and the source of a number of incidents in Beer's book, gives the young writer only the two briefest of mentions (one in each volume, in the second subordinated to Conrad, in the first to Howells) and cites none of his works in his two-volume autobiography *Steeplejack*, which became a best seller upon its publication in 1920 (three years before Beer, following Starrett, began the resuscitation of Crane), and remained widely read through several editions over the next decade.

Even with the success of Beer's biography, the growth of interest in Crane was slow. But by 1925, a complete works of Crane began to appear in ten volumes (the final volume of the set appeared in 1927), and by 1936 discussions of the development of the American novel now mentioned Crane regularly. Starting at the end of the forties and blossoming at the beginning of the fifties, what had been a slow-growing interest became a major explosion of scholarly attention. But, with Beer's 1923 biography at its origin, one might argue that a solidly canonical writerly reputation would not be more the product of a single volume until Max Brod's 1937 biography of Franz Kafka.

Almost from the beginning of this surge of interest, however, scholars began to find problems with Beer's account of Crane's life. But, then, Beer's book had not been presented as a scholarly biography; the general trend was to forgive him any small mistakes he had made. As a graduate student with access to Beer's papers during the late forties, the poet John Berryman published his own biography of Crane in 1950, ten years after Beer's death. This attitude persisted up to Berryman's 1962 revision of his book.

The Crane letters Beer's biography quotes were the first indication that something major was amiss. Throughout the fifties, working together to collect Crane's letters, R. W. Stallman and Lillian Gilkes found some 230 for their 1960 edition, but *none* of the originals of the letters Beer had quoted in his biography turned up—anywhere!

Finally, thanks to the work of scholars Stanley Wortheim, Paul Sorrentino, and John Clendenning, it is fairly clear:

(1) All but two of the letters Beer quoted in his biography are fabrications. Among Beer's papers are several sets of vastly differing versions of what are obviously, in each case, the "same" letter—all but conclusively suggesting a novelist inventing and rewriting the "letters" for effect.

(2) The romance between Crane and one Helen Trent that forms the centerpiece for the first half of Beer's biography is a fabrication. Neither the beautiful Miss Trent nor her guardian existed. A few incidents—including a night Crane spent mooning outside "Miss Trent's" window in the street—*may* have been borrowed from some several other much less intense relations Crane had with a number of other young women, generally beefed up, and attributed to his passion for the wholly fictive beauty. But even that is bending over backward to be kind to Beer.

(3) In an appendix to his biography, Beer claimed that a Mr. Willis Clarke had preceded him in his attempt at a biography of Crane—and that Clarke had even interviewed Crane in England, taking his words down in shorthand, shortly before Crane's death. Eventually Clarke had abandoned his biography (states Beer's book) but turned over his notes and his interview to Beer. Beer quotes several times from the Clarke interview. But, as far as we can tell, (a) Clarke never existed, (b) no biography was ever begun, and (c) the quoted interview is as bogus as the quoted letters.

(4) Finally, Beer refers—once in his book, and once among his papers—to two unpublished stories Crane is supposed to have written, "Vashti in the Dark" and "Flowers of Asphalt," the manuscripts of which were supposedly lost or destroyed. "Vashti in the Dark" was supposed to have been about a minister whose wife was raped by a Negro, who then dies of grief.

The story around "Flowers of Asphalt" is interesting enough to merit greater detail in its recounting because it offers a possible explanation for Beer's imaginative flights. As well, it poses an all but unsolvable enigma. The details around the writing of "Flowers of Asphalt" were found among Beer's papers by the young poet John Berryman, after Beer's death, and utilized for his own 1950 biography of Crane.

Here is a transcription of an unsigned page, quoted in Berryman and presumed by him to be by the music and art critic James Gibbons Huneker (1860–1921), an older acquaintance of Crane's as well as a fellow journalist during the nineties—before the extent of Beer's fictionalizing had been assessed.

One night in April or May of 1894, I ran into Crane on Broadway and we started over to the Everett House together [a hotel on the north face of Union Square, whose bar was popular with reporters in the 1890s; recently the hotel's old shell was converted into a Barnes & Noble]. I'd been at a theater with [Edgar] Saltus and was in evening dress. In the Square [Union Square] a kid came up and begged from us. I was drunk enough to give him a quarter. He followed along and I saw he was really soliciting. Crane was damned innocent about everything but women and didn't see what the boy's game was. We got to the Everett House and we could see that the kid was painted. He was very handsome—looked like a Rossetti angel— big violet eyes—probably full of belladonna—Crane was disgusted. Thought he'd vomit. Then he got interested. He took the kid in and fed him supper. Got him to talk. The kid had syphilis, of course—most of that type do— and wanted money to have himself treated. Crane rang up Irving Bacheller and borrowed fifty dollars.

He prompted a mass of details out of the boy whose name was something like Coolan and began a novel about a boy prostitute. I made him read [Joris-Karl Huysmans's] À Rebours [Against the Grain] which he didn't like very much. Thought it stilted. This novel began with a scene in a railroad station. Probably the best passage of prose that Crane ever wrote. Boy from the country running off to see New York. He read the thing to Garland who was horrified and begged him to stop. I don't know that he ever finished the book. He was going to call it Flowers of Asphalt.

Written to Garland shortly after Crane moved from the old Arts Students' League building at 143 East 23rd Street into a studio rented by Corwin Knapp Linson (1864–1960) at 111 West 33rd Street, an extant letter (May 9, 1894, *Correspondence* I-68) declares: "I am working on a new novel which is a bird." Berryman took this as possibly referring to "Flowers." In Wortheim and Sorrentino's 1988 two-volume edition of the letters, the editors footnote this, however, as Crane's novella "George's Mother."

Without a signature, the status of the "Huneker" passage is problematic enough; throw on it the light of Beer's other fictionalizing, and it becomes even more so.

This is not a typical letter from Huneker: it has neither salutation nor closing. Edited by his wife, two volumes of Huneker's letters were posthumously published. Graceful and lapidary communications, they are neither blustery nor telegraphic. It could, of course, be a hastily dashed-off note. But it could also be Beer's reconstruction of an anecdote remembered from a previous conversation or from an early research session with the moribund music critic. But it could also be Beer's attempt—safely after Huneker's death in Brooklyn from diabetic complications in 1921—to ventriloquize Huneker toward a fictionalized Crane that, later, Beer abandoned for whatever reasons of believability or appropriateness.

The editors of the magisterial *Crane Log* (Wortheim and Sorrentino again; Boston: G. K. Hall, 1996), from which I've transcribed the page, in their notes to *this* passage mention a 1923 statement by Starrett of Huneker's account of "Flowers of Asphalt," in which Starrett says that the work was composed in October of 1898 and was about "a boy prostitute." They note as well that Crane's relationship with newspaper publisher Irving Bacheller in the spring of 1894 was just not the sort that made either the request for or the granting of such a loan likely; as well, they note that the date Starrett gives is between unlikely and impossible, as Crane was in Havana at the time. What we can't know is if Starrett's account came directly from Huneker (with the date simply misremembered)—or if it came to Starrett *after* Huneker's death by way of Beer.

A year or so later, once he became famous after the publication of *The Red Badge of Courage* by the Bacheller syndicate of newspapers around the country, Crane *is* known to have borrowed fifty dollars from Bacheller himself in order to help out a young woman accused of prostitution—a scandalous incident reported in the newspapers, which Beer certainly knew about. Perhaps Beer—who was himself gay—was for a while considering introducing evidence into his biography to suggest that Crane was gay . . . or at least bisexual, or at least sexually adventurous.

Circumstantial as it is, there is other evidence to suggest a gay Crane. First, there is Crane's close friendships with a number of the young men living and studying at the former site of the Art Students' League on East 23rd Street of New York City. During his twenty-first and twenty-second year, Crane spent nights there—crashed there, as the sixties would have put it—for weeks at a time. The building rented to young artists. *Some* of the young men who lived and studied at the 23rd Street institution were—probably—straight. Corwin Knapp Linson, the art student seven years older than Crane who befriended the young writer and wrote his own memoir of Crane (*My Stephen Crane* [Syracuse: Syracuse University Press, 1958]), *may* have been one such. But there is at least one photograph surviving from the period—a joke photograph taken by some of the boys—that shows Crane, in bed, under the covers, with another boy, asleep with his head on his bearded friend's shoulder. The prankster photographers have filled up the foreground of the room with old shoes and boots—the classical sign for marriage (this is why we still tie old shoes to the back of the honeymoon car today). The usual way the photograph has been read is that Crane, innocently asleep in his friend's bed (we know the boys sometimes slept three in a bed), just happened to snuggle up against his sleeping friend, and some passing art students, looking in on the scene, ran off to get a camera, lights, set them all up, filled the room with shoes, and "snapped" the picture—which, when it was developed, they all had a good laugh over.

The difficulty of taking a picture in the 1890s (there *were* no Kodak moments back then!) simply militates against this interpretation—or of Crane and his friend actually *sleeping* through all the preparation. The question here is, What exactly *was* the prank's nature? Was it some straight young men, Crane among them, parodying the relations of the many gay young men around them? Or was it some gay young men parodying themselves—or, perhaps, documenting a love relationship with heterosexual marriage symbolism? Or was it something in between or just other? The blanket in the photograph looks very much as if it has been painted in later: perhaps the two boys were originally photographed naked with each other, and the picture was doctored. There is no way to tell for sure. But if Beer knew of the photograph, it may well have prompted him, however briefly, to elaborate on the notion of a gay Crane.

Of course the "Flowers of Asphalt" account might be one area where Beer actually had the truth and was simply suppressing it; while Berryman, later, revealed it.

The only hint of deviant sexuality that Beer finally allows into his biography comes in the appendix:

> It was suggested to me by Mr. Huneker that Crane's picturesque exterior offered a field for the imagination of some contemporaries and that "they turned a little Flaubert into a big Verlaine." The injustice of that romancing was great, however, and inevitably I have concluded that a great spite followed him after his success. Else why did three unsigned letters reach me when Mr. Christopher Morley printed my wish for correspondence in the New York *Evening Post*? All three votaries of romantic love had charges to make and the charges were couched in excellent English.
>
> Some of Crane's friends erred in their mention of him after death. Elbert Hubbard's paper in *The Philistine* contained equivocal statements and Robert Barr's "qualities that lent themselves to misapprehension" is not a fortunate phrase. (244–45)

After Oscar Wilde and Alfred Douglas, Verlaine and Rimbaud represent perhaps the most notorious gay relationship in the annals of nineteenth-century literature. It is odd to think of somebody like Berryman missing the reference. But in his own biography, Berryman writes: "Homosexuality was the only thing

Crane was never accused of." Apparently in the late forties the young Berryman was just not privy to the coded manner in which such accusations were made among twenties literati.

Among Huneker's last publications before his death in 1921 (two years before Beer's book appeared) was a novel, *Painted Veils*, written in six weeks in 1919, published in 1920, and initially available only through subscription from Simon and Schuster. (Liveright reprinted it in 1942—two years after Beer died a destitute alcoholic at the Albert Hotel in Greenwich Village—with an interesting and informative introduction by Benjamin DeCasseres. For some years it was on the list of Modern Library volumes.) Set in the last decades of the nineteenth century, *Painted Veils* details, among other things, a lesbian affair/ fascination between a younger woman musician and an older woman, assumed to be a scandalous exposé of the American classical music scene: that is to say, by the time Beer was putting together *his* book, Huneker was known among cognoscenti to be the author of an elegant and immoral gay novel—*and* he was recently dead. He was known to have known Crane. Thus, if Beer had decided to go with a Crane with gay interests, Huneker was a believable person from whom to invent evidence.

But then, *some* of Beer's biography is accurate.

It's understandable why Beer chose not to include the story behind "Flowers of Asphalt" in a biography for the general public in 1923; and while it's possible that the account Berryman saw and I have transcribed was an early draft *by* Beer of something he was once thinking about including—like the early drafts of the bogus letters—it's equally possible that the gay 1920s critic Beer was protecting the reputation of a young writer with significant gay (or at least bisexual) interests—which would also account for the fictive "Miss Trent."

In an April 12, 1962, letter to E. R. Hageborn, Wilson Follett, who edited the ten-volume *Works of Stephen Crane* that Knopf published between 1925 and 1927, admits—even celebrates— Beer's extraordinary capacity to fabricate practically anything: "Things that never were became real to him, once his mind had conceived them, as the rising moon or a drink at the Yale Club during prohibition era. He could quote pages verbatim from authors who never wrote any such pages; sometimes from authors who never lived. He could rehearse the plots of stories never written by their ostensible authors, or by anybody, repeat pages of dialogue from them, and give you the (nonexistent) places and dates of publication." But Follett goes on to say: "The point that always escapes an assailant of his biography . . . [is that Beer] *loved* Crane, humbly idolized him, and was incapable of setting down a syllable about him prompted by any force except that love and idolatry." If Follett is right, and it has the ring of truth, then the page might have been one of the unsigned letters (either actual—or invented by Beer himself) that he refers to in his appendix. The only way it suggests any homosexual interests by Crane himself is through traditional homophobic contagion: the only person who could be interested in the topic *must* also indulge in it. But what it clearly presents is, whether fictive or factual, the young Crane as an interested champion of gay male prostitutes in New York during the Mauve Decade—a champion turned aside by the exigencies of social convention, represented by Garland's horrified plea to desist.

The fact that the biography that first propelled Crane into the general awareness of the greater literary population turns out to be between thirty and forty percent fiction—and knowingly so by the author—is, however, almost overshadowed by the textual problems that circulate about the text of *The Red Badge of Courage* itself.

For a moment let us discuss the text.

The twenty-one-year-old Crane wrote a truly extraordinary novel—which he called *Henry Fleming, His Various Battles*. Sometime later, possibly during the rather violent editorial process (from fifty-five thousand words to eighteen thousand for serialization), he renamed the book *The Red Badge of Courage*. But to distinguish the book as Crane first drafted it from the eighteen thousand words of it later published by the Bacheller & Johnson syndicate in newspapers in New York, Philadelphia, and other cities around the country, first in December 1894, then again in its almost full form in July of 1895, we will use the *Henry Fleming* title. And the fact is, *Henry Fleming* has never been published—though a book very close to it was published in 1951 by the Folio Society, and then again, by the indefatigable R. W. Stallman in 1952. But even here there were significant differences.

The Red Badge of Courage is a brief novel: in the Library of America Edition its twenty-four chapters run to only 131 pages. *Henry Fleming* is thousands of words and a complete chapter longer.

What makes *Henry Fleming* so astonishing is that it is a novel both of poetically rendered action *and* incisive psychological analysis—an ironic comedy in which we are never allowed to identify fully with any of the characters. Rather, the young writer keeps a cold eye on them all. It is a novel about young soldiers named Jim Conklin and Wilson and Henry Fleming. All its characters are named, not only in dialogue (as they are now), but in the running narrative of the novel itself.

When the possibility of newspaper syndication arose, Crane —from a commercial point of view quite wisely—decided (or was strongly urged) to omit the ironic psychological analysis. In the course of his cutting, he decided to "universalize" his characters by suppressing their proper names—so that Conklin becomes "the tall soldier" and young Wilson becomes "the loud soldier" that today's reader of the book is familiar with. Later in the story a Lieutenant Hasbrouck loses his name and is referred to only by his rank. Fleming retains his name only when he is addressed by others. The overall result of the cutting is a somewhat more readable novel—but a *far* less interesting one.

On completing *Henry Fleming* the reader feels that he or she has just encountered a great novel. Its interplay of ironies and associations is masterful. (One suspects that it simply could *not* have been written by a twenty-one-year-old.) Within the superbly orchestrated progression of events, *Henry Fleming* delineates how the characters—especially Fleming—perceive themselves as *unlimited*, and at the same time shows the precise ways in which that perception *limits* their understanding, their actions, and their futures. This is to play the game of the novel on the fields marked out by Flaubert, Stendhal, James, and Proust.

By comparison, the reaching after some ill-conceived "universality" through the suppression of specific names (not to mention slicing a great psychological novel down to a more or less colorful adventure) is the single thing about the book that strikes me as a pretentious verbal gesture and the mistake of a twenty-one-year-old: the sort that one constantly has to tell enthusiastic young creative writing students *not* to do.

I say *Henry Fleming* has never actually appeared; when Stallman published his version from an uncut manuscript in 1952, he nevertheless changed the names of the characters to the "universal" forms readers of the book were already familiar with (though he indicated the names in notes, so that one can reconstruct the original form). The book as published by Appleton, after its successful newspaper syndication, is an interesting and talented novel. The book as first written (as close as we can get to it is the Henry Binder edition published by W. W. Norton & Co. in 1979) was a great one. But the final and almost inarguable point is that, if the original and better version of the novel had appeared, it would *not* have been anywhere near as popular as it was.

Large, statistical audiences are simply not prepared to do the sort of emotional and moral acrobatics necessary to appreciate an exquisitely crafted book in which there is conscientiously no moral or emotional center of identification. (Slight correction: very occasionally they will do it if the foreground cast of characters is female; but rarely will they do it for a collection of male characters in a tale of war, syndicated in a weekly newspaper.) This brings us to what is certainly one of the most important factors that goes into securing a book a position in the canon— as it deals most directly with the markers:

The Red Badge of Courage contains one of the most discussed (i.e., marked) sentences in the whole of American literature. I mean of course the dazzling concluding sentence to chapter 9 (in which we also have the excruciating description of Jim Conklin's death, "His face turned to a semblance of gray paste . . . [Fleming] now sprang to his feet and, going closer, gazed upon the pastelike face."): "The red sun was pasted in the sky like a wafer."

Because of its power, its originality, and its orchestration into the rest of the passage, few sentences in American literature have sustained as intense an examination as this one. (In an earlier draft, Crane had written "fierce wafer," but at some point he omitted the editorializing adjective.) In a November 1951 article, however, in *American Literature* 23, Scott C. Osborn pointed out that, however inadvertently, the line likely had its source in Kipling's novel *The Light That Failed* (1891), which we know Crane read enthusiastically shortly after publication: "The fog was driven apart for a moment, and the sun shone, a blood-red wafer on the water." In a footnote Osborn went on to point out that the religious overtones of the "wafer" (as in the Eucharist) that had fueled so much of that praiseful discussion of Crane's "symbolism" simply hadn't been available to Crane (or to Kipling) as a writer in the last decade of the nineteenth century. The common use of "wafer" that most certainly controlled the contemporary reading of both lines was the wafer of sealing wax with which letters, at the time, were still commonly fastened. Most eucharistic services before World War I were conducted with locally baked unleavened bread; the "wine and the wafer" did not come into common parlance until after World War I, when, with the gummed envelope, wafers of sealing wax vanished as all but eccentric affectations.

Now if most people had to summarize the elements that militate for entrance into the canon, they would probably produce a list something like the following:

Fame (and/or popularity) . . .

Critical reception . . .

Enduring worth of the work, in terms of its originality, quality, and relevance . . .

More cynical (and/or more conservative) commentators would likely include what the work had to say, that is, its ideological weight . . .

Those of a more psychoanalytic bent might add that certain figures of desire inhere in the biographical reputations of certain artists and keep pulling interest back to the work—Chatterton's suicide at seventeen years and nine months, Georg Trakl's suicide at twenty-three, or Rimbaud's debauched relations with Verlaine between the ages of sixteen and nineteen, culminating in his abandonment of literature for the life of an African adventurer; Nietzsche's or Hölderlin's ultimate insanity, Novalis's, or Keats's, or Poe's, or James Thomson's sexual love of an early-dying (in Keats's case, unresponsive rather than dying) girl-child, the pansexuality of a Catullus or the homosexuality of a Hart Crane coupled with *their* own early deaths . . .

Well, there are cynical comments to be noted about all of these factors from our Crane story.

Crane's own early fame—followed by almost total oblivion afterward—reminds us forcefully that fame alone is no guarantee of acceptance into the canon. What is suggested by the creation of his reputation twenty-five years later through Beer's book is that the fame of the marker (Beer's biography) is finally much more to the point. As far as critical reaction, it is certainly paradoxical that the most recent confirmation of Crane's canonical position comes from the almost total demolition of the credence given to Beer's initial biography/marker. But rather than dislodge Crane, it has only aroused more interest in him—as I would hope *this* marker does, even while it attempts to demystify the mechanics of the marking system itself.

Indeed, this may be the place to articulate a basic principle of canonical self-preservation. Poets and artists have noted for many years that a too-virulent attack is often as great a goad to readerly interest as equally great praise. Heap too much scorn on my grave, said Shelley, and you'll only betray the place I am buried. But once the marker configuration has propelled a literary work *into* the canon, the subsequent complete denigration of a primary marker, even when it is revealed to be nothing but a collage of misstatements, fictions, and outright lies, does not alter the canonical position of the literary work associated with it—because that denigration can only be accomplished by the erection of other markers that are effective only as they exactly replace the effects of the former marker. Indeed all such denigration can do is further the canonical persistence of the work.

Aside from its fabrications, the aspect of Beer's *Stephen Crane* to sustain the most consistent criticism since its publication is its tendency to soft-peddle the various scandals that all but constituted Crane's life once he left Syracuse University. (A handful of years his senior, Crane's common-law wife was Cora Taylor, with whom he lived until he died. Crane had met her within days of his twenty-fifth birthday in 1896, while she was the madam of a Florida brothel—a fact elided by Beer.) Despite Crane's (or Beer's)—possible—interest in matters gay, we must mention that it is not scandal per se that generates markers. Rather, it is scandals that a succession of commentators feel must be re-interpreted (and we may read suppression as the ultimate [de-] interpretation) *because* the topics represent changing social values: divorce, marriage, prostitution, homosexuality . . .

This is why (to anticipate myself) the canon—and all the textual material, primary *and* secondary, that constitutes it—is nothing *but* value.

As to the enduring worth of the work, Osborn's demolition both of the notion of Crane's stylistic originality and the religious value of the "wafer" metaphor happens in a textual marker that largely serves to stabilize our attention *on* the text, even as it displaces certain values in the critical syntagm. (What was discussed for almost twenty years as a religious metaphor is now historified into an epistolary one. What was a sign of originality now becomes an emblem of influence.) But this is the way the canon constantly functions, destabilizing and stabilizing in the same move.

As to the simple attractiveness of the Crane myth, this is the one thing that is not figured directly by our tale so far—unless our simple inability to see Crane through the various inventions and distortions of Beer in itself constitutes a measure of attractiveness that pulls the modern scholar, the contemporary reader, onward to look harder. Crane's two apocryphal stories ("Vashti in the Dark," "Flowers of Asphalt") are certainly enticing points for speculative research. But the fact is, they look more and more, the both of them, like Beer's inventions from the twenties rather than Crane's efforts from the nineties.

The early iconography of Crane, left in this mythic margin, *is* fascinating, however; the most common among the early images of our young writer was a photograph of Crane looking serenely out from among the other players on the Syracuse University baseball team. As were many of the men of letters who presided at Crane's early rise in the canon, Beer was gay. It is a paradox that in the early days of baseball, many of those who wrote about it and memoired it and generally exhorted it into the position of the country's national sport were also articulate gay men; and the image of Crane as the pure, unblemished athlete (dying young) had a lot to do with the homoerotic libidinal charge underlying much of his early popularity. This is a paradox because, by 1962, when John Berryman's revised biography of Crane appeared, the situation had reversed to the point where numerous practicing psychologists by now put a good deal of faith, possibly with some reason, into the general rule of thumb: to determine whether an American male was homosexual or not, simply ask him whether or not he liked baseball.

If he did, he was straight.

If he didn't, he wasn't.

We have already mentioned the clandestinely famous picture of Crane (known to scholars but not printed till 1992)—in bed, asleep, with his head on the shoulder of another boy, in a room at the old Art Students' League. To repeat: many of the male art students who composed Crane's circle were doubtless gay. The Bowery, well known as one of Crane's haunts, was as famous in the 1890s for its gay life as it was for its more traditional vice—in which Crane so famously indulged. The hint of homosexuality and the vice that surrounded Crane (despite Berryman's obtuse statement that homosexuality was the one thing Crane was never accused of; we've cited a blatant account of several such accusations in the appendix of Beer's biography [pp. 244–45]) very possibly drew not only Beer but other gay men of letters to Crane's cause.

But all these factors were at play in the mythology of the "purest" of American writers—"pure" being the epithet used of Crane by both Berryman and the librarian at the University of Syracuse Library, back in the fifties, then in charge of the library's considerable Crane holdings.

This brings us to the last part of your question.

Is the canon of value? The canon is nothing *but* value. It is a complex system of interlocking, stabilizing, and destabilizing— constantly circulating, always shifting—values. The course of that endless circulation alone is what holds the canon stable, is what alone allows it to bend and recover. We think of the canon as a social object that holds things comparatively stable *in the face of* shifting values. But that "in the face of," with its suggestion of opposition, is only more mystification. The canon is not a passive natural object, but an active social object, and it is precisely the shifting of social values that *fuels* the canon and facilitates its stability. (As an extraordinarily important corollary to our basic principle of canonical self-preservation above, it is the value shifts alone that *produce* the new markers.) Without those social shifts, the canon would collapse. But (within the canon) we can only study those shifts by studying the markers and their history, since they alone memorialize the evidence.

Finally, it is necessary to point out no one *knows* the canon. And the assumption that other people do, whether those other people be a high school teacher, a professor emeritus, or Harold Bloom, is to grant power to an Other (and to put into circulation a value)—a power and a value that the canon itself might be seen as exploiting.

At best, we can know *something about some of the works (and their markers)* that make up the canon. We can know something about one part of the canon and/or another. Very few of us would argue, for example, with the assertion that Shakespeare is number one—or, more accurately, in terms of my web model, is at the center—of the canon of English literature. But who is number two?

Chaucer?

Spenser?

Milton?

I have graduate students (under thirty years old) who would be surprised to see Spenser even in the running for that still titanic secondary slot. But, by the same token, anyone over forty who has spent a life in the field of letters would probably be distressed that the same students should *not* know this. Does that mean that Spenser's place in the canon has changed or is changing? No, but it may (or may not) mark a social value shift that will soon begin to emit some stabilizing markers.

PARA•DOXA: *One common criticism of the term "paraliterature" is that it implies a generically constant body of writing that lurks around outside the library of serious or authentic literature, but, in fact, new works—in whatever genre—constantly enter into the "upper" ranks. How would you define—or, perhaps, describe "paraliterature"? (By the way, are there nonfiction paraliterary genres?)*

DELANY: The initial criticism you speak of arrives because *literature* implies a generically constant body *within* the library. It's the notion of "constant, stable, and fixed" that has to go in both the literary *and* the paraliterary case. Once we establish a clear view of the circulation of values limned by the range and change in literary markers, the circulation of values in the paraliterary follows pretty directly—though the picture of literary discourse above should immediately highlight the first distinction between the literary and the paraliterary: I mean the relative saturation of the literary *with* markers, and the relative *scarcity* of markers in the paraliterary. (Although one *can* study literature without studying paraliterature, one *cannot* do it the other way around.) And, of course, there is the difference among the *kinds* of markers prevalent in both areas.

Because of the differences between literature and paraliterature—that is, the difference between the saturation and scarcity of markers, the kinds of markers on either side, and the way those markers facilitate the circulation of values (in short, paraliterary markers generally facilitate that circulation far less than literary ones)—I have suggested that we adopt a different methodology for studying paraliterature. Because we cannot count on the markers the way we can in literary studies, we must compensate by putting more emphasis on paraliterary genres as material productions of discourse. We need lots of biography, history, reader-response research—and we need to look precisely at how these material situations influenced the way the texts (down to individual rhetorical features) were (and are) read. In short, we need to generate these markers from a *sophisticated* awareness of the values already in circulation among the readership at the time these works entered the public market. Again, let me reiterate: *sophisticated* awareness. If you are going to start with some ridiculous and uncritical move of the nature, "Well, these works were read only for entertainment. They were without any other value," then I throw up my hands and go off to talk with other people. That is simply accepting the literary mystification that still redounds on the paraliterary.

Anyone who has even the vaguest suspicious that "entertainment value" actually covers all that's of interest in the values circulating throughout the paraliterary, I ask them only to bear with me until I can begin to describe some of the behaviors that constitute the paraliterary, below.

First, however, we must talk about a rift.

The abyssal split between literature and paraliterature exists precisely so that some values can circulate across it and others can be stopped by it. The split between them constitutes literature as much as it constitutes paraliterature. Just as (discursively) homosexuality exists largely to delimit heterosexuality and to lend it a false sense of definition, paraliterature exists to delimit literature and provide it with an equally false sense of itself. Indeed, since both were disseminated by the explosion of print technology at the end of the nineteenth century, the two splits are not unrelated.

But that abyssal split—which impedes the circulation of values here, while it promotes it there—is as imperative to the current structure of the canon as is the circulation itself.

Now, to say (as you do) that "new works . . . constantly enter the 'upper' ranks" of the canon is, I think, absurd—or rather, it is to speak with very blinkered eyes from the paraliterary side of the abyss with no understanding or perspective on what is occurring on the literary side.

New literary works are constantly being made the focus of attention for more or less extended periods of time in order, as it were, "to decide" if they can enter the upper canonical ranks. (*There* is that illusory synod, lurking just behind the infinitive.) But the vast majority don't make it. Nor should they. Still, it's arguable that once a work is past the consideration stage and has actually become part of the canon, it is harder to dislodge it than it is to get a new work accepted.

Now the vast majority of works easily locatable as paraliterature do not even have a chance for a consideration period. They are marginalized at the outset. But it is absurd to confuse the—admittedly, sometimes very generous—trying-out period with canonical acceptance itself. Yes, by comparison with the attention paid to paraliterary works, which, generally speaking, cannot get any such trying-out period, no matter how well thought of (that is, without some violent displacement from the context and tradition that makes them signify), it might well *look* as if "new works" are constantly entering the upper ranks. But that's just not what's happening.

If we, say, anthropomorphize it for a moment, the canon "puts great trust in" the most conservative methods. The canon "believes in" the worth of the society that has produced it. Thus, any work that both is presumed to be literature and achieves a notable measure of social fame is tentatively accepted into the canon for such a trying-out period, when various people get a chance to generate the particular sort of markers—critical and otherwise—that may or may not go on to stabilize its position. But while a Pulitzer, National Book Award, or Nobel Prize may well promote canonical *consideration*, none of the three is enough to assure canonical *acceptance*—as unclear as the line might be between them.

Since World War II, one of the greatest—and, I think, most pernicious—factors in canonicity has been the *teachability* of works. Whatever criticisms one has of the ability of the conservative notion of general literary fame to select the best works, the problem of teachability undercuts it. General literary fame is still dependent on the acceptance by a *reading* public— however sophisticated, however unsophisticated. Teachability puts a further filter over the selection process, a filter constituted of the popularity of the works among an essentially very young, *non*reading population—who are presumably in the process of being *taught* to read. But this is a disastrous way to select—or reject—books of aesthetic worth!

We have all heard it many times, from the graduate school T.A., through the junior, the associate, and the tenured faculty: "It was a wonderful book. But my kids just couldn't get it. Oh, a few of them did. But for most of them, it was just confusing." Nor is it a problem confined to the literary. Those of us teaching science fiction or other courses in popular culture find ourselves with the identical problem. Any work that makes its point in pointed dialogue with a tradition—any tradition—is simply lost on inexperienced readers unacquainted with that tradition. Works that are new and exciting are new and exciting precisely because they *are* different from other works. But an "introductory background lecture" cannot substitute for exposure to the dozen to two dozen titles that would make the new work come alive by its play of differences and similarities. I don't wish to imply that the problems—not to mention the insights—of nonreaders must somehow be excluded from culture. On the contrary. And I am also aware that student enthusiasm can be as surprising as what it rejects. I will ponder for years, for example, the upper-level modernist novel class of mine in 1991 that reveled in Robert Musil's *The Man without Qualities*, while finding Julian Barnes's *Flaubert's Parrot* somewhere between boring and pointless—even after reading (and enjoying) *Trois contes* and *Three Lives* as preparation. But young readers who have absorbed only the limited narrative patterns available on prime-time TV simply don't have a grasp of the narrative tradition broad enough to highlight what is of interest in the richest and most sophisticated fictions currently being produced, literary *or* paraliterary.

The discussion (markers, if you like) of people *who read* must generate the canon—not the acceptability of works to people *who don't read*. But that has been more and more the case for the last fifty years. It's worth pointing out that this teachability problem is not new: from the time that it was formulated, the canon was assumed to be a teaching tool. Teaching was precisely what Matthew Arnold and the other nineteenth-century theorists of the uses of culture were concerned with. It was their arguments which promoted the switch from the Greek and Roman classics to works of English literature as the basis for public education. But the difference is, the teachability of works is not being handled today by public discussion but rather by natural selection. And in matters intellectual, natural selection simply doesn't work. (Intelligence would seem to exist primarily as a way to outrun natural selection.) But this is one of the reasons that the canon is undergoing the apparent upheavals that it is. This is directly behind the growing interest in the paraliterary—which interest, by now, at the ontological level, we can recognize as following a very canon-like process. It is the same order of social object. It's easy to describe it in the same terms.

Which brings us to the second part of your question: how would I describe paraliterature?

While you recall the mystificational notion that the paraliterary is "purely entertainment," let me recount some tales.

Here, from an autobiographical essay written for his therapist, Jim Hayes, in 1965, the great American SF writer Theodore Sturgeon tells about his early encounter in the first years of the Depression with his multilingual stepfather (whom the family called Argyll) over the paraliterary genre of science fiction:

> It was about this time that I discovered science fiction; a kid at school sold me a back number (1933 *Astounding*) for a nickel, my lunch money. I was always so unwary! I brought it home naked and open, and Argyll pounced on it as I came in the door. "Not in *my* house!" he said, and scooped it off my schoolbooks and took it straight into the kitchen and put it in the garbage and put the cover on. "That's what we do with garbage," and he sat back at his desk with my mother at the end of it and their drink. (*Argyll, A Memoir*, 36 [The Sturgeon Project: Pullman, Washington, 1993])

At the time, Argyll was giving his stepson such volumes to read as "*The Cloister and the Hearth, The White Company, Anthony Adverse, Vanity Fair, Tess of the D'Urbervilles*, Homer, Aristophanes, Byron (*Childe Harold*), *The Hound of Heaven, War and Peace, Crime and Punishment, Dead Souls*, God knows what all" (*Argyll*, 29). And young Sturgeon devoured them. The family even had a regular "reading aloud" session after dinner.

But Sturgeon also continued to read the forbidden pulp stories. He sought for a way to collect the magazines, and he expended a good deal of ingenuity figuring out a way to read them—in his desk drawer, while he was doing his homework, the sides waxed with a candle to keep them from squeaking when the drawer had to be quickly closed—and to store them: finding a trap in the roof in his closet, young Sturgeon (he described himself then as "twelve or fourteen") placed his magazines, two deep, between the beams—starting five beams away. He even went so far as to replace the dust on the beams after he had crawled across them, and did everything else to cover up the traces.

Some time later, however—

I breezed home from school full of innocence and anticipation, and Argyll looked up briefly and said, "There's a
mess in your room I want you to clean up." It didn't even
sound like a storm warning. He could say that about what
a sharpened pencil might leave behind it.

The room was almost square, three windows opposite
the door, Pete's bed and desk against the left wall, mine
against the right. All the rest, open space, but not now. It
was covered somewhat more than ankle deep by a drift of
small pieces of newsprint, all almost exactly square, few
bigger than four postage stamps. Showing here and there
was a scrap of glossy polychrome from the covers . . . This
must have taken him hours to do, and it was hard to think
of him in a rage doing it, because so few of the pieces were
crumpled. Hours and hours, rip, rip, rip.

It's hard to recapture my feelings at the moment. I
went ahead and cleaned it all up and put it outside; I was
mostly aware of this cold clutch in the solar plexus which
is a compound of anger and fear (one never knew when
one of his punishments was over, or if any specific one was
designed to be complete in itself or part of a sequence) . . .
(*Argyll*, 38–39)

Now *that* describes a room full of paraliterature—and how it
got that way.

But here are some stories of a more recent vintage.

A bit over a dozen years ago, around 1980, in my local bookstore, I came upon a young woman in her early twenties standing next to a dolly full of books, shelving them. At the Ds, she
was putting away copies of Don DeLillo's *Ratner's Star* (1976).
Smiling, I said, "You know, you should shelve some copies of
that with science fiction."

She looked up startled, frowned at me, then smiled. "Oh,
no," she said. "Really, this is a very good book."

I laughed. "It's about three-quarters of a good novel. But at
the end, he just gets tired and takes refuge in a Samuel Beckett-
like fable. It doesn't really work."

"Well, you can't make it science fiction just because of the
ending!"

I laughed again. "The ending is what makes it literature. But the rest of the book is a very believable account of a young mathematician working for the government, trying to decipher messages from a distant star. It could go upstairs in SF."

Her frown now had become permanent. "No," she repeated. "It really *is* a good book. I've read it—it's quite wonderful."

"I've read it too," I said. "I liked it very much. But that's why I'm saying it's science fiction . . . "

The young woman exclaimed, really not to me but to the whole room, "That's just *crazy* . . . !" She turned sharply away and began to shelve once more.

But when, after a few seconds, I glanced at her again, she was still mumbling darkly to herself—and *tears* stood in her eyes!

Now that too is an account of the social forces constituting paraliterature.

In the late seventies, shortly after receiving tenure in the Pratt English Department, a friend of mine, Carol Rosenthal, was teaching a graduate seminar that year called "Literature and Ideas" and invited me out one Wednesday afternoon to address her students.

Suited, tied, and with briefcase under my arm, I arrived at noon. We had a pleasant lunch at a local Chinese restaurant, and returned to the building for the one o'clock seminar. As we were walking down the hall toward the classroom, another woman faculty member in a stylish green suit was coming toward us. Carol hailed her, then turned to make introductions. "Chip, this is my friend—" we'll call her Professor X— "Professor X. Professor X is in economics. And this is Samuel Delany. He's speaking to my Literature and Ideas seminar this afternoon."

Brightly Professor X asked, "And what will you be talking about?"

I said, "I'll be speaking about science fiction."

Professor X got a rather sour look on her face, her shoulders dropped, and she exclaimed, "Science fiction . . . ? Oh, *shit*!" at which point she turned on her heel, and stalked off down the hall, leaving an astonished Carol, who, after a few nonplussed seconds, began to splutter and make excuses—her friend was *very* eccentric, and probably just having a bad day as well—while we made our way to the class where I was to give my talk.

That *too* constitutes paraliterature.

Paraliterature is also the hundreds of people who have said to me, on finding out that I'm a science fiction writer, "Oh, I don't really like science fiction," as though (a) I had asked them, (b) I cared, or (c) I should somehow be pleased by their honesty.

Believe me, *far* fewer people like poetry than like science fiction; but *far* fewer people, on being introduced to poets, respond with, "Oh, I don't really like poetry." They are much more likely to proffer a socially equivocal "Oh, really?" and change the subject. The forces that make the one a commonplace of my life (but promote the other in the lives of poets) are precisely the real (i.e., political) forces that constitute paraliterature (and literature).

Only consider the general layout of most medium-size to large bookstores, with the best sellers in the front, the literature and fiction placed so it is easily available to the entering customers, and the paraliterature—science fiction, mysteries, horror, and romance titles—toward the back (and, yes, sometimes the poetry placed even *further* back!)—for, as countless articles and guides to the running of bookstores have explained, "People who read such books will hunt them out wherever you have them in the store. Thus you need not waste valuable display space on them and can put them in the back, wherever it is most convenient."

That too constitutes paraliterature.

I describe paraliterature by these messy, highly interpretable social tales—rather than by turning to texts to discuss rhetorical features—because, before everything else, paraliterature is *a material practice of social division.* (That's *not* a definition, mind you. But it's a powerful and important functional description.) These tales represent some of the most revealing and informative *social markers* (verbal, informal) that go along with it. And, as we have noted, they are *very* different from literary markers. Paraliterature is a practice of social division that many people are deeply invested in, often at a level of emotional commitment that many others of us have simply forgotten, as we notice more and more that so many texts developing on the paraliterary side of that division display great intelligence, are produced with extraordinary art, and have extremely relevant things to say about the world we live in. The material practice of social division fuels the canonical/noncanonical split. The split fuels the material practice of division.

If paraliterature were really only "pure entertainment," I could not possibly tell such tales about it.

At the rhetorical level, paraliterature is best described as those texts which the most uncritical literary reader would describe as "just not literature": comic books, mysteries, westerns, science fiction, pornography, greeting card verse, newspaper reports, academic criticism, advertising texts, movie and TV scripts, popular song lyrics . . . But if contemporary criticism and theory has told us anything, it is that the rhetorical level—the level of the signifier—is the slipperiest to grasp and hold stable.

That's because, at the level of the signified, things—values, if you will—are *always* in shift.

Are there any nonfiction paraliterary genres? Absolutely. Philosophy has been *trying* to dissociate itself from literature since Plato—and failing. But, for openers, everything in this and any other critical journal is paraliterature. ("Philosophy has no muse," Walter Benjamin comments in "The Task of the Translator." Though Memory's nine daughters who sang on Mount Helicon represent a genre system far older than our current postindustrial one, in general it's not a bad notion to check with them and see who was assigned to what. It explains why history —overseen by Clio—is part of literature and why philosophy has, until recently, felt it might escape.)

The paradox is that the vast majority of literary markers are, themselves, paraliterary. Often they are consulted, but rarely are they studied—which is only another reason why the overall process, which includes the literary/paraliterary rift, is so mystified.

You can easily pick out the parameters of the nonfiction paraliterary genres. First and foremost they include any texts not considered literature. They include any texts considered more or less disposable. They include any texts that, if we go back to consult them, ten, twenty, thirty years after the fact, we do so purely for information. They include any text not considered primarily aesthetic.

Now the assumption of aesthetic worthlessness is nonsense.

Recently I went back to reread Leonard Knights's essay "How Many Children Had Lady Macbeth?" (1933)—in conjunction with Stephen Orgel's "Prospero's Wife" (*Representations*, no, 8, 1984). They are two beautiful pieces, rhetorically balanced and wonderfully rich. But my particular view comes out of an appreciation of the aesthetics of paraliterature—which is, in a word, not supposed to exist.

Paraliterary studies can arise only when we begin to historify how this literary/paraliterary split came about (largely in the 1880s when, thanks to the new printing technology represented by typewriter and linotype, the explosion of printed matter reshaped the informative structure of the world), and examine the absolutely necessary function that rift plays in the persistence of the notion of literature today.

PARA•DOXA: *The focus of the second issue of* Para•doxa *was the mystery genre. In what ways do you think the mystery genre fits into the paraliterary arena? Is there a relationship between paraliterary genres that defines them at the same time that it distinguishes them from nonparaliterary genres? Is there a hierarchy among paraliterary genres? Is there a family tree, a genealogy of genres?*

DELANY: Literature as we know it is born *with* the literary/paraliterary split that arises when the tenets of modernism are employed to make sense out of the simple and overwhelming proliferation of texts that started in the 1800s and that has continued up to the present.

The reason one cannot know the canon is because one cannot know all texts. Because, by the end of the 1880s, there were so many texts, some genres simply had to be put out of the running *tout court.*

The mystery was the privileged paraliterary form up through World War II—when, until the Hollywood "blacklists," it was briefly joined by the film script. It meant that intellectuals like G. K. Chesterton and scholars like Dorothy L. Sayers—who was, after all, first and foremost a translator of Dante—and literary writers like Graham Greene (generally regarded as one of England's great twentieth-century novelists), even our own William Faulkner, with his Gavin Stevens tales, could offer you "entertainments" in the mystery form and be accused of nothing worse than slumming. Respected playwrights like Lillian Hellman could have passionate literary love affairs with folk like Dashiell Hammett, and, in the more liberal drawing rooms of the literary, both could be received.

For the sixties and seventies, SF was the privileged just-sub-literary genre. I think we may be entering a period where that position may soon be filled by pornography.

PARA•DOXA: *"Paraliterature" has become, paradoxically, an academic specialty at many universities in Europe. Is this encouraging or alarming?*

DELANY: Why should it alarm? To return once more to Lucien Goldmann: disciplines are defined by their objects—not by their methodologies. The question that must always be tugged around and chewed over at the beginning of any disciplinary speciation is, "What are the structure and organizing principles of the *object* we are looking at?" A good long wrestle with such questions alone is what lets us know when we are all examining the same object—and when we aren't.

This is just another reason why we must get rid of this incredibly limiting notion of generic definitions. (A discipline is *defined* by its *object*. But disciplinary objects themselves are usually *not* definable. That's why they must be so carefully and repeatedly described.)

We are like the famous blind men with the elephant. If, at trunk, tail, tusk, and toe we keep trying to shout one another down with quintessential elephantine definitions, we won't get anywhere. We have to be willing to engage in dialogue, present our many descriptions humbly, talk about what they do and don't allow us to do, and only then decide whether we are indeed all talking about elephants, the same elephant, or if, in fact, a few of us have inadvertently gotten hold of crocodile tails or hippopotamus ears.

Let me close off this section of your question with the description of the results of social forces that are very similar, if not identical, to canonical ones—indeed if they were at work in the precinct of the literary rather than, where I shall locate them, in the paraliterary, we would have no problem recognizing them *as* canonical.

Let's consider several books that deal directly with contemporary science fiction: Scott Bukatman's *Terminal Identity* (1993), Damien Broderick's *Reading by Starlight* (1996), Mark Dery's *Flame Wars: The Discourse of Cyberculture* (1995), and my own *Silent Interviews: On Language, Race, Sex, Science Fiction and Some Comics* (1994). Now, which SF writer do you think has the greatest number of citations in the indexes of all these books? In all cases, it's William Gibson—which, today, I doubt should surprise anyone. I can't speak for the other three writers, but I can tell you that, for me, the realization that Gibson was, indeed, going to be the most cited writer in my book was an occasion for some concern.

I think Gibson is a fine writer. I don't begrudge him one iota of his fame. What becomes problematic is when we get to (a) the markers that have brought this situation about and (b) the "worth of the work" vis-à-vis his fellow science fiction writers.

The major markers propelling him into this position were, first, an extraordinarily uninformed article in a mid-eighties issue of *Rolling Stone* that made the first spurious connection between Gibson's work and computers—a connection Gibson himself began by balking at, until, with his fourth novel, in collaboration with his friend Bruce Sterling (*The Difference Engine* [1991]), he decided to exploit it, however ironically. The second (really a marker set) was a series of Big Movie Deals, starting with the proposed film of *Neuromancer* (1984), going on to his scripting an early version of the third *Aliens* film, and finally the $30 million Longo film released in June 1995, from Gibson's fine short story "Johnny Mnemonic" (1981), for which Gibson himself has screen credit. Add to that the extraordinary teachability of his first and best known novel (*Neuromancer* [1984]), and you have the complex of reasons for his prevalence in the indexes of all four books.

Yet these are *not* the markers the books discuss. These are *not* the markers whose values the writers of any of the books in question are interested in either contesting *or* supporting. Indeed, they're hardly even mentioned. Actually, when we step back from it, the whole process looks more than anything like a race to obliterate the first set of markers and replace them by a far more acceptable academic set that, indeed, *does* put into circulation values far more in keeping with what we might find appropriate for a literary text.

Now—do I find Gibson's work of great social and aesthetic value?

Yes. I have taught it before. And I hope to teach it again.

Do I think it is the *most* valuable work being produced in the science fiction field at the moment?

At this point, *I* balk—at the whole concept that assumes such a question could (or should) be answered!

What I pose against both the question and the assumptions one must make to answer it either yes *or* no is the incontrovertible and blatant fact that there are more than half a dozen contemporary writers, from the same science fiction and fantasy field that produced Gibson, who are doing extraordinary work, work of at least as *much* social and aesthetic weight as Gibson's: Gene Wolfe, Octavia E. Butler, Michael Swanwick, Kim Stanley Robinson, Lucius Shepherd, Karen Joy Fowler, Greg Bear . . . Along with Gibson, all have produced work of a very high order. (And this is only to look at the generation after mine, completely ignoring my contemporaries Russ, Disch, Zelazny, Crowley, and Le Guin.) Without any one of them, the current SF field, and our potential for reading pleasure and enlightenment, would be greatly impoverished. They simply lack these all-but-accidental-in-literary-terms markers: *Rolling Stone* and the movies! (The strength that the *concept* of "the movies" has in the realms of the literary is quite astonishing. Sometime in the middle eighties, a novel of mine—*Dhalgren*—was optioned by a movie company. The people involved sent someone out to buy seven copies of the book—to the same bookstore, as a matter of fact, where the young woman had been so upset about my suggesting DeLillo's *Ratner's Star* might be science fiction—and when one of the clerks asked him why he needed seven copies, he answered, "We're going to make a major picture out of the novel." The next day, when I came into the store, all the copies had been pulled out of the SF section and reshelved as "Literature"—where they stayed for the next four months! The project, as is the case with so many such, never came to anything. But I can assure you, if it had, and the bookstore people had encountered further markers to stabilize their reconception, the novel might well have jumped genres in bookstores all over the country.) To read Gibson with these writers makes Gibson's work much richer. To read any of these writers along with Gibson is to make their work more significant.

Well, with all that in mind, prior to publication, I went through my book and everywhere I could, wherever I'd used Gibson as an example, if it was at all possible I substituted work by another writer. And do you know what the results were?

Gibson was *still* the most frequently cited SF writer in my book.

Why?

Because my book is a series of *dialogues.* And my interlocutors ask more questions *about* Gibson than any other writer!

Well, the fact is, any set of critical essays is, on one level, part of a critical dialogue—only the questions are not necessarily articulated as such nor are their attributions always given. But as long as the dialogic process is implicit in intellectual work, it functions to hold the position of various writers stable—even in the face of an active attempt, however local, to dislodge them from that position, such as the one I've just described.

Now—we must make it clear—what's being afforded Gibson in this dialogical process is *not* canonical acceptance. By no means. What is being afforded him is that trying-out period, so rare as to be otherwise all but nonexistent in paraliterature, that may or may not *lead* to such acceptance in ten, fifteen, or twenty years.

But the same forces that work at the canon's edge to stabilize that trying-out period also work—once a piece of writing (through the course of its markers) has been moved deeper within the canon toward the canonical center—to stabilize its position within the canon itself.

Would I like to see similar periods of serious consideration offered to other writers of paraliterary texts? Would I like to see writers chosen for reasons that have nothing to do with *Rolling Stone* and the movies? In the long run, when social values and aesthetic values are somewhat further teased apart, at this particular point of seeming canonical upheaval, that's the *only* lasting justification I can think of *for* paraliterary studies.

But again: the canon "believes in" the society that produces it. Thus the canon can only be the canon *of* that society. If we want to displace *Rolling Stone* and the movies as significant and powerful social markers promoting canonical (or precanonical) literary (or paraliterary) consideration, we must start producing our own. We must produce social and critical markers that put in circulation values *we* think are important—and we must do that with works (literary or paraliterary) that *we* think are worthy of critical attention. However contestatorily, we must join in our society. We must become (to borrow a term from Bloom) *strong readers* of the paraliterary.

If we do not, then *Rolling Stone*, the movies, and equally extraliterary forces alone will decide what scholars (literary or paraliterary) pay attention to.

PARA•DOXA: *Could you say something about the impulse (either in general, or as regards your particular impulse) to choose to write in a particular genre—whether SF, literary criticism, fantasy, or something else? Where do you begin to conceive a piece of writing? (This is not a thinly disguised version of "Why do you write SF?")*

DELANY: Well, first of all, it's not an impulse. It's not a decision. It's not a choice per se. It's far more like giving in to a habit. When, for a moment, the barrier between what one has been reading and what one might write breaks down, discourse sweeps one up, and somehow absorption becomes emission; and what is emitted is simply going to be controlled by that discourse.

I read criticism; I write criticism.

I read SF; I write SF.

I read sword and sorcery; I write sword and sorcery.

I read pornography; I write pornography.

I read fiction; I write it, too.

Now in my case there's also a desire formally to criticize the genre in which I'm reading—an urge that has something very important to do with obliterating the barrier between absorption and emission. However politely articulated, there's always some element of an oppositional stance. But how that critical desire functions specifically in the process would be difficult to specify.

PARA•DOXA: *You have written that all genres—literary and para-literary—are "ways of reading." Could you elaborate?*

DELANY: I'm afraid I must sigh and say, "No. Not here." But that's exhaustion speaking.

Still, anyone interested in such an elaboration as you ask for should, for an introductory view, read the "K. Leslie Steiner Interview" in my recent collection from Wesleyan, *Silent Interviews*. And anyone who wants to see the process elaborated even more fully should read *Starboard Wine* and, finally, *The American Shore*.

The ideas you are asking me to elaborate are counterintuitive ones; thus, to grasp them, they require repeated exposure. Encapsulating them in a single paragraph, no matter how pithy or aphoristic, only betrays them. They require looking at the language in a different way from the one most of us are used to—and they require a constant vigilance against slipping back into looking at it in the old way. Rather than giving a reassuring little summary that sends the reader off with the feeling that the idea has been rendered summarizable, consumable, and that it has (therefore) *been* consumed, internalized, mastered, I would leave your readers with an exhortation to pursue the notion through others of my texts, through some other writerly labor.

For people who are always ready to read another book, literary *or* paraliterary, the canon becomes a far less intimidating concept than it first appears. And the literary/paraliterary split, while real (i.e., political) and important, *can* be negotiated.

—New York City
July 1995

Nits, Nips, Tucks, and Tips

Name, Date, Place

Whenever I start a manuscript—any manuscript, story, essay, or novel, rough draft or final—in the upper right-hand corner of the first page I put my name and address, always.

Whenever I conclude a manuscript, I finish with the city or town I'm in and the date I completed the most recent major draft. (Sometimes this is called the "place-date subscription.") In this age of word processors, it is, of course, up to you to decide when changes are major and substantive and require a new place-date, or when they are merely cosmetic.

I began both these practices as a teenager. Again and again I have been glad I did. Because of them, people have returned manuscripts I've misplaced, lost, or left behind. Manuscripts I've loaned to friends have sold because the friend showed them in turn to someone else, who happened to be (or to know) an editor, who could then get in touch with me.

Perhaps you only started writing a few months ago. Before you know it, however, you will have been writing for years, if you haven't been already. It's surprising how quickly you forget when it was or where it was that you wrote a story, an article, even a novel, especially once it's three, seven, or fifteen years old. It's useful to know whether a story or a story idea is seven years old or twelve years old. Believe me, you'll forget. You'll be grateful for the reminder.

Once every year or two, I go through my apartment and clean out the manuscripts people have given me over the intervening months. Frequently these will amount to fifty or sixty manuscripts in a year, novels or short stories. Rarely have I read them all, but often I've read a handful. In a number of cases,

I've rather liked the tale and would have liked to tell the writer so before I dumped it. More and more, however, manuscripts arrive without names or addresses. Someone hands me one at a reading or a conference. Someone leaves one in my university mailbox. (Always I say: "Even if I take it, I can't promise you I'll read it. Should I have time, I'll try.") But after a year or so, since I no longer remember the writer's name or under what circumstances I received it, it must go into the garbage. Those who did not put a name and address on it will never know what I thought.

Twice now in thirty-five years I've found myself with a surprise anthology contract from a major publisher and gone hunting through a pile of old stories people have left with me for one I remembered that would have been perfect for the proposed book. I *found* the story—but because the writer had not put a name and address on it, I had no way to know who the story was by or how to get in touch with him or her. Thus I couldn't publish it. (To quote the British comedian Anna Russell: "I'm not making this up, you know.") Putting your name, address, place, and date on all your manuscripts seems so simple and obvious that I'm astonished how many would-be writers still don't do it. In terms of advancing your career, there's no better way than leaving your name off the manuscript to make *sure* you remain a would-be writer.

It's not my job (or an editor's) to copy names and return addresses from envelopes onto manuscripts when the writer was too lazy or too thoughtless to do so him- or herself. I get far too many. I assume the lack of a name and address, phone number, or e-mail means "I want you to see this, but I don't want to hear what you have to say"—to which my response is "If you *don't* want to hear what I have to say, I don't have time to look at it."

Today, when I receive an envelope in the mail, open it, and remove a manuscript with no name on it, I throw it away immediately—to avoid the frustration, weeks or months down the road, of not knowing who wrote it.

I've said before that all suggestions in this book are guidelines, not rules. But if there is one that should be considered as a rule unbreakable, this is it: Treat all your manuscripts as if you expect them to be read *and* you expect someone to get back to you about them. Put your name, address, and the date on them all.

Don't let a copy, hard or electronic, get six inches away from your keyboard, without containing your name and address, snail-mail and e-mail. Make this a habit. You'll be happier you did—and unhappier if you don't. It doesn't *guarantee* people will get back to you. But if you don't put them there, then they can't—even when they want to.

And finish with the place-date subscription. That's for you.

Read Widely

Paradoxically, the most important thing a fiction writer can do is read. Read widely in contemporary fiction. Read good stuff. Read bad stuff. Think about what makes the good stories good. Analyze why the bad stuff is bad. Keep a journal. Write down your thoughts about what you read. Discuss how *you* might have done it better. Read at least one contemporary novel and one contemporary short story collection every month. Read at least one classic novel every other month. You'll learn more from your reading than from all the books about writing (including this one) and writing workshops you attend put together.

The ideas in this (or any other) writing text will most likely strike you as useful when they resonate with something dramatized in a work of good fiction you've read recently.

Grammar and Parts of Speech

Every profession has it own specialized language. That goes for writing, too. For writing, grammatical terms make up one part of that specialized language. Learn the names of different kinds of words and groups of words: noun (ordinary noun [*chair, woman, pencil . . .*], proper noun [*William, Audrey, Rover . . .*]); article (definite [*the*], indefinite [*a, an*]); verb (simple [*fell*], compound [*would have tried to stop falling*]); adjective (simple [modifying], demonstrative, substantive, possessive); adverb (of time, of place, instrumental; remember, adverbs modify not only verbs; they modify adjectives and other adverbs too); pronoun (subjective, objective, demonstrative, relative, possessive); preposition; conjunction (coordinating [*and, or, but*], subordinating [*than, as, while, because . . .*]); participle (present, past); gerund; as well, learn what a clause is, a noun absolute, a periphrastic ("She is more dear to me than life itself" is the periphrastic version of "She is dearer to me than life itself." Unless you are trying for a historical effect, periphrastics are to be avoided. That said, a historical work whose style is speckled with brilliantly used periphrastics is Ford Madox Ford's trilogy *The Fifth Queen* [1906].) Learn the difference between a direct object (accusative) and an indirect object (dative). All this will help you with Latin, Greek, Hebrew, Russian, German, Sanskrit, Finnish . . . It's not a long list. Look them up. Google them. Remember them. You don't have to learn them all by this evening. But you can certainly know them by the time the weather turns.

Some six months ago, on the line for the Greyhound Bus from Philadelphia to New York, an accountant in a gray silk suit standing in front of me started up a conversation. When he learned I was an English professor, he said: "I'll give you a dollar if you can name the ten major parts of speech. You give me a dollar if you can't. You know, I've won this bet with a dozen English professors over the last few years. They can name nine—but they can't name all ten."

I won my dollar—not because I'm a professor, but because I'm a writer. The tenth one that so many people miss is "gerund"—because it's so easily mistaken for a present participle. Both are verb forms ending in "ing," and they're only distinguished by their use. (A present participle is an "ing" verb used as an adjective: "The man walking through the streets looked quite happy." There *walking* describes—or modifies—*the man*. Or, as it is more likely to appear: "Walking through the streets, the man looked quite happy." It tells what he's doing. (Because "walking" modifies "man," a few pundits, and more than a few computer grammar checks, omit the comma; there's no logical reason to separate the modifying phrase from the noun it modifies—other than the fact that, for the last three hundred years, most writers have put one there.) The participial form is also part of the progressive present tense. ("I am walking into the room." "She is closing the door.") Introductory adverbial clauses—those beginning with (subordinating conjunctions)

When, If, Because, While, and the like—are also followed by a comma because they modify the verb of the main clause, which almost invariably falls further along in the sentence, rather than the subject noun. Thus, with adverbial material, there's more justification for the comma. But personally, I'm on the side of tradition.) The gerund is an "ing" verb form used as a noun. "In busy streets, walking lets you see who's out and about." There, *walking* is a noun, that is, a "verbal noun" or "gerund." There on the bus line, however, the accountant was surprised that I knew half a dozen others, not so major, besides. You should too.

Big words are fun. It won't hurt you to know that the longest word in the English language is "antidisestablishmentarianism" —or how to pronounce it, or what it means (to be against the separation of church and state). Don't let yourself be stymied by a litotes or an anaphor. Train yourself to distinguish a syllepsis from a zeugma (it takes a little work, but it sensitizes you to the fine points of the language); learn what a syllogism is, a polysyndeton, and an anacoluthon. (You can Google them all directly.) You should be able to spot a dangling participle at fifty paces—and fix it! (It's an error in grammar and logic.) Again, none of this is stuff you have to know for a test by nine AM tomorrow. But certainly you can know it in a month.

Start learning it now.

Why should you learn it? Because it's a game. This is the traditional language for discussing fine points of the game's play. Moreover, the people who can do it have an edge over those who can't, whether or not they use that knowledge directly. (Remember all those people from my introduction who wanted to write? It's such a competitive game, any edge you have is a help.) It promotes sensitivity to your major tool—the language—whatever you finally decide to do with it.

To walk, to see, to hit, to run, to be, these are called the "infinitive form of the verbs," or simply "infinitives"). Latin and most Romance languages that derive from Latin do with one word what English does with two: *marcher* (French: to walk), *videre* (Latin: to see), *golpear* (Spanish: to hit), *correre* (Italian: to run), *dormir* (French: to sleep). In the sixteenth, seventeenth, and eighteenth centuries, with the rise of interest in Latin and Greek, English writers decided that because you *couldn't* break up an infinitive in Latin and the other Romance languages, you *shouldn't* do it in English either (which is a Germanic language, not a Romance language), as part of an attempt to standardize all languages with one another. Thus, throughout the nineteenth century and well into the twentieth, letting a word fall between the "to" part of the infinitive (the infinitive particle) and the verb proper, *walk, see, hit, run,* and so on, was called "splitting an infinitive"—and it was considered an error. Writing "I like to quickly walk where I'm going"—was considered a stylistic gaff: "quickly" falling between "to" and "walk" *still* sounds awkward to many of us. Educated people didn't do it.

Shortly after World War I, however, critics began to notice that Shakespeare (c. 1564–1616), while writing his plays and sonnets at the beginning of the rebirth in England of intense interest in classical learning at the end of the sixteenth century and the beginning of the seventeenth, split his infinitives regularly. As well, however awkward "to quickly walk" feels, "To finally decide what you want will make it easier for everyone," *doesn't* sound awkward to any competent English speaker today, whereas moving that "finally" to one side of the infinitive or the other—"finally to decide" or "to decide finally"—begins to strain the patterns of ordinary English speech.

Today, the general wisdom is, if it was good enough for Shakespeare, it should be good enough for the rest of us.

Thus, after three-hundred-odd years of infinitives never split, today the infinitive can be split with impunity—though, because my childhood education overlapped the last years when it was considered a solecism (a barbarism educated people did not do), I still find split infinitives something I'm more comfortable avoiding.

Read a lot. Listen a lot. Find out who you are. (What forms are you most comfortable with?) Read up on the alternatives. Choose one—and, one way or the other, stick by it. But remember, these are choices, not right and wrong. All choices are culturally conditioned. The writer has a choice over which bit of cultural conditioning she or he accepts or rejects. That's because of the lopsided relationships between production and reception.

Many of these things are matters of taste, temperament, exposure, and—yes—age.

When I was a child, if I wrote "different than," I was marked wrong on any English test or paper. The proper form was "different from," though in journals and letters by many fine writers, you can find "different than" back through the nineteenth century and before. Today both are acceptable and the new form is more and more displacing the older.

When my mother was in school in the 1920s and 1930s in New York City, she wrote "Making your corrections with a green pencil is as good as making them with a red one." The proper negative of that was "Making your corrections with a green pencil is not so good as making them with a red pencil." If, by mistake, she wrote "not as good as" instead of "not so good as," she was marked wrong. Today that's *not* considered acceptable—and what was once right now sounds archaic. Generally speaking, things have moved in the direction of simplicity and consistency. For the first seventy-five years of the twentieth century, deciding when to use "that" and when to use "which" was a nightmare. Today it's all but been reduced to: "that" is restrictive and "which" ("which" is always preceded by a comma, unless it comes just inside a parenthesis, such as this one does) is nonrestrictive—end of story. In the last fifteen years, computers have done much to standardize such prior grammatical confusions, so that the endless subtleties and distinctions that thousands of grammar books tried to instill, about when to use "which" and when to use "that," with or without commas, have pretty much gone by the board. Restrictive "which" ("which" not preceded by a comma) is capable of elegant and nuanced effects. It adds variety and subtlety to English. Still, I suspect, its days are numbered.

Whether they are logical or illogical, however, knowing these things (and their histories) is—once more—purely a game; but it's a game that sensitizes you to fine distinctions in a highly competitive field, where there are many, many thousands—even hundred of thousands—of players.

A writer's reputation and fame develop around the wonderful things she or he does with language, the way he or she makes the language perform, and the things (and their intensity!) the writer makes happen in the reader's mind, as the reader runs his or her eyes along the words in each line. If these things are wondrous, intense, and marvelous *enough* (as Shakespeare's so often are), the occasional thing the writer does that other people frown on—like splitting an infinitive—may also be accepted.

Sentences

Probably the most important grammatical concept—and the most difficult one to discuss with any rigor—is the sentence. The sentence or the proposition (*der Satz*, say the Germans, who have only the one word where English has two) is the basis for modern Anglo-American "ordinary language" philosophy. Whether the sentence and the proposition really are two things or only two names, emphasizing different aspects, for one thing has been debated by philosophers from Ludwig Wittgenstein and Charles Sanders Peirce to Willard Van Orman Quine, Ruth Marcus, and Donald Davidson. (Myself, I accept Quine's argument that says they are really one. But philosophers who claim they are two are still doing very interesting work.)

It's almost impossible to define what a sentence is in any exhaustive way.

Traditionally sentences start with a capital letter and end with a period. But some end with exclamation points, question marks, even dashes, or ellipses. If they are quoted within other sentences, sometimes they end with commas or, if very short, they can have no punctuation at all!

Almost all sentences have a subject and a verb—that is to say, they contain a predicate. This is true, especially if we agree that the subject of the verb can be implied, as in the exhortation "Run!" (where the subject of "run" is clearly "you"). But there are enough one-word exclamations and what are called "absolutes" in grammar to make that a dicey definition in enough cases to be memorable. "A sentence expresses a complete thought." This, too, is almost always true. But what is true of a sentence is also true of a clause—those pseudosentences, distinguished only by their subordinating pronouns, adverbs, and conjunctions (who, whom, whose, as, while, when, where, which, that, because, if, than, . . .), which we string together to make up longer, complex sentences. With those two definitions, inadequate as they are, you should be able to recognize sentence fragments and run-on sentences when you see them, nonetheless. You should be able to understand that they are errors, and learn to correct them.

"I am," is a sentence. "She walks," is a sentence. "They are walking along the street," is a sentence. "Walking along the street," is, however, a sentence fragment. Standing alone as it does, it's a participial (or perhaps gerundive) phrase. In either case it lacks a *main* verb: it has no predicate.

(1) "He saw the clouds in the sky, the cars moving down the street, and the people crossing at the corner," is a sentence.

(2) "He saw the clouds in the sky. The cars moving down the street. And the people crossing at the corner." That's one perfectly good sentence followed by two fragment sentences—an error that more and more of my students at the Temple University Creative Writing Program resort to. It's not poetic. It's illiterate. Turn those periods into commas! Number 1 is correct. Number 2 is simply wrong.

The simplest kind of run-on sentence is "He goes to sleep early she wakes up late." Even with a comma after "early," it's still a run-on—and still an error. If you want to turn that into one sentence, the proper way to punctuate it is either with a semicolon ("He goes to bed early; she wakes up late") or with a comma followed by "and": "He goes to bed early, and she wakes up late."

Finally, what makes a sentence is a matter of some general rules and a few exceptions that simply have to be learned.

When I was in elementary school, from the fourth grade on, if we handed in a paper on any topic whatsoever that had two or more run-on sentences or two or more fragment sentences (or, for that matter, one of each), we got it back, unmarked. We had to write the whole paper over. That seems excessive for such a slight failing. Quickly, though, fragments and run-ons became errors that, by the time we left the fifth grade, we no longer made.

There are, of course, more complicated kinds of run-ons— and more complicated kinds of sentence fragments:

Because the wind was blowing across the sand and the dried seaweed, all along the whole of the three miles below Lowery Hook, on the Massachusetts beach.

That's a fragment. (Not a run-on.) It doesn't need that first comma. What it needs is a subject and a main verb after the second, which will tell us the consequence of that "because"— probably something that happens *on* the beach.

While I walked along in the shadow of the Manhattan Bridge, I found myself remembering that day, last October, when John and Phil sat arguing on the porch of the little Staten Island house near Tottenham, the hickory trees dropped their leaf-shadows across the glasses of cider Margaret had brought out to them after an hour of their intense talk, punctuated by bursts of undergraduate laughter.

That's a run-on; also it's a run-on that, for some reason, my computer's grammar check does not catch. At the very least, you need an "and" before "the hickory trees." The comma after "Tottenham" should be a semicolon; even better, make it a period and begin "the hickory trees" with a capital "T." If you take that second approach correcting it, however, almost certainly you should break the sentence again after "out of them," and make the rest into a *new* sentence: "Their hour of intense talk had been punctuated by bursts of undergraduate laughter."

Sentence fragments and run-on sentences (one kind of run-on has been known for the last twenty years or so as a "comma splice") are still mistakes that suggest as much as, or more than, any other that we are reading an amateur. Learn to spot them in your work. Correct them.

Despite the exceptions, remember that initial capital letter and that terminal period. Remember the predicates (subjects with verbs); and look for that *complete* thought. They'll get you through most problem cases.

One of the best quick courses in grammar is a rewardingly brief book called *The Elements of Style,* by William Strunk, as revised by E. B. White (New York: Macmillan, 1959). Today known familiarly as "Strunk and White," the book is in its fourth edition. For forty-five years it's been a major seller in high schools and college bookstores. Since the second edition, the editors have updated the examples. Frankly, they've done a poor job.

For an example of an error to be a good example, once you correct the error in the exemplary sentence, the corrected version should be well-turned, economical, and efficient. The error discussed should be the *only* thing wrong with the sentence. For most of the new examples in the fourth edition of Strunk and White, however, the exemplary sentences are so clumsy that, even with the blatant error corrected, they remain awkward, limp, and ugly.

Chapters 4 (on "Misused Words and Expressions") and 5 (on "The Elements of Style") are, nevertheless, worth the price of the entire book, each one.* Read them.

Punctuating Dialogue

Dialogue in fiction is, of course, the direct report of what people say to each other. The ways we deal with it go back many years, but the basic rules are simple. This section will talk about those rules. As well, it will cover a few complications.

Consider the sentence

She washed the dog and the car.

"She" is the subject of the sentence, because *she* initiates the action. "Washed" is the verb, because *washed* is the main action the sentence describes. "The dog and the car" are what we call the object of the sentence, because *the dog and the car* receive the action. (In this case, because the object is more than one thing, we call it a compound object. It's two things: a dog *and* a car. But that's a fine point.) They are what receive the action (*washing*) that the subject (*she*) initiates.

Now consider the sentence

She said, "I enjoyed myself; I'd like to come back."

* "Chapters 4 and 5" is, by the way, a zeugma—and a prozeugma, at that.

Yes, this too is a sentence.

Once again, "She" is the subject.

"Said" is the verb.

"I enjoyed myself" and "I'd like to come back" form the object of the verb *said*. (They're *noun clauses* rather than *nouns*; but they're still objects.) Once again, they form a compound object. In this case, however, they are joined not by an "and" but by a semicolon.

The punctuation is, however, somewhat different from the earlier example, "She washed the dog and the car." In "She said, 'I enjoyed myself; I'd like to come back,'" all the words that are directly quoted—the words she actually said—are put inside quotation marks. As well, after "said" and before the quote itself, there's a comma. Why? Because that's how people have been writing it for almost 320 years. The convention of quotations marks and commas is so set that if you do it any other way, editors and copy editors (as well as literate readers) will simply assume you've made a mistake. It stands out and—like fragment sentences and run-ons—registers with readers as an error, and a *very* amateur error at that.

The convention obtains no matter how you rearrange the elements:

"I enjoyed myself; I'd like to come back," she said.

This time, however, the comma goes inside the closing quotation mark, rather than after the "said," which gets a period. The grammatical structure of the sentence, however, is still the same as if somebody had written:

The dog and the car, she washed.

Such inversions are considered archaic in any other situation *except* dialogue—where they have remained useful enough to appear still modern and up-to-date.

We can even put the "she said" in the middle of the object.

"I enjoyed myself," she said; "I'd like to come back."

That is to say, we now have a sentence whose grammatical form is the same as:

The dog, she washed, and the car.

We *wouldn't* punctuate it in the following way, however:

"I enjoyed myself"; she said, "I'd like to come back."

That's because (you remember) the semicolon functions as an "and." If we did, we would have a sentence with a grammatical structure as follows:

The dog and, she washed, the car.

While "The dog, she washed, and the car" is archaic and strained, it's still English. But there's never been a time when "The dog and, she washed, the car," would have been accepted by competent English speakers as correct, even back in Anglo-Saxon times—though, from time to time, Latin did things of that sort.

Sometimes the "she said" (or the words that stand in their place) can fall in the middle of a quoted sentence, when there's a natural pause:

"If George gets here by twelve," I told her, "just give me a call. I'll come back then."

The first thing to note is that this is *two* sentences. Stripped of quotations marks, the first is "If George gets here by twelve, I told her, just give me a call". And the second is "I'll come back then." But the second half of the first, along with the whole of the second, is surrounded by *one* pair of quotation marks, opening and closing. Why? Again, because that's the way it's done. Until the person stops speaking and we leave his or her reported words, we stay inside the same pair of opening and closing quotation marks, no matter how many consecutive sentences he or she utters. (Actually, there's an exception to this: when the speech of one person runs on for more than a paragraph. We will discuss this shortly. But don't worry about it now.) Note also, that there are *two* commas in this case, on either side of "I told her." The one to the left goes inside the closing quotation mark. The one to the right goes *outside* the opening quotation mark and up against "I told her." If this is in any way new to you, take a moment and reread the example, noting where commas fall in relation to the quotation marks. Now read it again. *Now* you're ready to read it a third time—and to learn it!

Here's another fine point to pay attention to:

> "I like coming to visit you," she said, "you're always so nice."

That's a run-on sentence and an error. Unless you're doing something highly colloquial, the words inside the quotation marks should be grammatical in themselves. In this case, if we dropped "she said," we'd have: "I like coming to visit you, you're always so nice." It's easier to see, now, that it's a run-on (of the comma-splice variety). Putting it in quotation marks and sticking "she said" in the middle doesn't make it any less a run-on.

Here's the proper way to do it:

> "I like coming to visit you," she said. "You're always so nice."

That's a period after "she said." What should follow is a new sentence with its own capital letter and its own period, inside its own quotation marks.

Remember: Even though she is still speaking, that's *two* sentences.

Here are a few fine points:

1. "Said she," "said George," "said I," and "said the policeman"—these are all archaic locutions. We don't use them today. They occur regularly in the fiction of the nineteenth century and the early twentieth, up until about World War I. Somewhat more rarely, they occur in the fiction written between the First and Second World Wars. But since the end of World War II (1945), these locutions have come to seem more and more old-fashioned. Except in cases where you're trying to sound outmoded or to imitate a style from the past, avoid them. Today they are errors.

2. For ninety-nine percent of all dialogue, keep everything that one character says consecutively within a single paragraph.

Here is perhaps the *most* important rule for dialogue:

Whenever another person starts to speak, start a new paragraph.

If someone *must* speak for several paragraphs running, the way to punctuate the speech is to leave the final quotation mark off the end of the paragraph. Then, after the indentation, you can start the new paragraph with an opening quotation mark. Only put a closing quotation mark when the entire speech is finished:

> "I would like you all to pay attention," George said, looking down from the podium, "because I only have time to go over this once. I want to keep the discussion short and to the point. I'm happy to let anyone of you speak, but—please—don't hog the floor. There are a lot of us here this evening. Before we get started . . . what?
>
> "Oh, excuse me, Mary." George stepped away from the podium to the front of the stage. "I didn't see you sitting down there." Though everyone could still hear him, away from the microphone his voice was only a third the volume it had been. "You have the key. Could you run up to Mr. Collins's office on the second floor and bring me down the yellow folder of attendance slips on the left side of his desk, there? Thank you.
>
> "All right, everyone. Now." George walked back to the podium, and, as he stepped behind the mike once more, again his voice filled the auditorium. "Let's get started. Who would like to speak first, while we're waiting for Mary to get back with those slips?"

Note (and remember): no closing quotation mark at the end of a paragraph of dialogue means the character has not finished speaking. The opening quote beginning the next paragraph means that he or she has started speaking *again*. If, however, the next paragraph goes on to description, reverie, or action, the previous section of dialogue must end with a closing quotation mark.

(An extended parenthesis that continues on for more than a paragraph should be handled in the same way. Would you like an example? All right. We're in the midst of one now.

(Were there a real reason to start a new paragraph, here,

without ending the parenthesis, this would be the proper way to do it. *Don't* put the closing parenthesis above. Rather put it here.)

3. Here is something to remember about "said" and "speak." "Said" allows quotation marks. "Speak" does not. We can speak words. We can speak speeches. We can speak the dialogue in a play. What we *cannot* speak is directly quoted dialogue.

"That was a really nice lunch, Mrs. Franklin," she spoke.

The above is not English. It's wrong. Don't do it.

The word used most often in dialogue is "said." Others that can be used are "asked," "answered," "told," "called," "yelled," "shouted," and "whispered." For a while, especially at the start of the twentieth century, writers tried very hard to vary their dialogue with a variety of sound-making words. Today, however, most writers get by with the above. Even words such as "cheered," "shrieked," "laughed," "grunted," and "cried" are shunned as dialogue words and sound archaic. They draw attention to themselves when coupled with commas and quoted dialogue. There is nothing necessarily wrong with a story, even a long one, that only uses the dialogue word "said."

This brings us to the most complicated part of this topic: how to mix dialogue and description. The fact is, in many, if not most, situations, people talk *while* they're doing other things. Writers have developed a number of ways to indicate this.

The easiest way is as follows.

In the corner where the dirty ivory walls came together, George squatted, moving the screwdriver blade around the can's top. He pried once more. "You know, this Benjamin Moore stuff costs half again as much as it did eight years ago." Again he moved the blade. "That's the last time I did any painting." Again he pushed the handle down. Faintly, the can top popped. "There we go." He picked it up with thumb and forefinger. Beige drops fell on the newspaper under the can by his worn runner. Wrinkling his nose, George peered down, then glanced up where, across the kitchen, Alice was paying as much attention as she usually did, while she worked on the counter with the onions, lettuce, carrots, and cutting board. "They mixed it pretty well—on that machine they got." Suddenly, grunting, he stood.

Alice looked up from her salad makings. "What did you say, sweetheart?"

Note: The fact that there is no paragraph break between "He pried once more" and "You know, this Benjamin Moore stuff costs half again as much as it did eight years ago, the last time I did any painting?" is the sign that George is speaking. (Because George has been identified as the actor, you don't need any "He said," or "George said.") Even though the sentence "Wrinkling his nose, George peered down, then glanced up where, across the kitchen, Alice was paying as much attention as she usually did, while she worked on the counter with the onions, carrots, and cutting board" switches our attention to Alice, the lack of a paragraph break before the next line of quoted dialogue ("They mixed it pretty well, on that machine they got.") lets us know that the last person who spoke (George) is *still* speaking. Indeed, if we wanted to switch the speaker and change to something Alice said, after that sentence, the way to do it would have been:

. . . Faintly, the can top popped. "There we go." He picked it up with thumb and forefinger. Beige drops fell on the newspaper under the can by his worn runner. "They mixed it pretty well—in that machine they got." Wrinkling his nose, George peered down, then glanced up where, across the kitchen, Alice was paying as much attention as she usually did, while she worked on the counter with the onions, carrots, and cutting board. Suddenly, grunting, he stood.

"What did you say, sweetheart?" Alice looked up from her salad makings.

In the version above, the paragraph break lets us know that the speaker is changing (to Alice)—even though Alice is introduced in the previous paragraph.

If we were not totally set on keeping Alice's salad fixing in the same sentence with George's upward glance, we could of course write:

. . . Faintly, the can top popped. "There we go." He picked it up with thumb and forefinger. Beige drops fell on the newspaper under the can by his worn runner. "They mixed it pretty well—in that machine they got." Wrinkling his nose, George peered down, then glanced up.

Across the kitchen, Alice was paying as much attention as she usually did, while she worked on the counter with the onions, lettuce, carrots, and cutting board—as, grunting, he stood. "What did you say, sweetheart?" She looked up from her salad makings.

Indeed, narrative is at its clearest when a new actor (or a new speaker) gets a new paragraph. Sometimes, though, the shift in the reader's attention is only momentary, or is still so much controlled by the point of view and general perception of the initial character that a new paragraph feels clumsy. (Myself, I prefer the first version.) Still, you need to remember that a *new* paragraph of dialogue will be interpreted as a *new* speaker or actor, wherever it comes. *Same* paragraph means *same* speaker, even if, within it, a new character has been mentioned.

Of course people don't always speak conveniently between prying at the paint can lid and prying it again. Sometimes actions are performed in the middle of speech or simultaneously with it. The narrator can always write, "At the same time, she said. . ." Another technique to render this, however, is as follows:

Stretching as far as possible, George pushed the roller up as close as he could get it to the molding, drew it down and over, then pushed it up again. "Honey, don't you think this is—" with a glance at the counter's colorful plastic bowls and the lettuce piled on the paper towels, he frowned back at the wall above him—"kind of dark for the kitchen?"

Coming from the refrigerator with a stainless steel bucket of ice, Alice said, "Well, you were the one who wanted beige." She put the bucket down, then frowned too at the wall with its lopsided square of new latex. "I thought we could have gone with . . . well, yellow or blue. But—" looking up, she frowned even harder, till, suddenly, drying her hands quickly on a dish towel, she stepped to the counter's end, swung her hips around it, and strode across the gold-flecked vinyl—

"that's *brown*, George! That isn't even tan!" Beside him, she scowled at the wall. Then, tossing up her shoulders, with what she intended to be a forgiving smile (but it only carried all the subdued accusations of every one of his past domestic miscalculations), she declared, "Can't you see that's brown?"

"I told the guy at the store I wanted a rich beige."

"Did you tell him it was for a kitchen?" She tried to hold the smile in place. "Didn't you look at the color sample?"

George took a deep breath and stepped back. "He said I should take that little swatch thing and bring it here and show it to you. But *I* figured beige was beige."

As he backed away, frowning at the dark taupe square, Alice turned to watch him, still trying to smile, till suddenly George whirled and flung the roller to the floor, where it skidded sideways, leaving a smear half the size of the one painted on the wall.

"Oh, come *on*, George!" She flinched with the momentary fear that surged whenever he did something like that. "*Don't* act that way. You don't—" she took a step after him, thought better, and stepped back—"have to make a mess of *everything*! Really, look! It isn't that im—"

"*You* want to cook in a black kitchen?" George grunted, wiping his bony hands on the seat of his jeans. Suddenly, he stalked out the door.

Alice breathed deeply now.

All right, let's go over this carefully:

"You don't—" she took a step after him, thought better, and stepped back—"have to make a mess of everything! Really, look! It isn't that im—"

"*You* want to cook in a black kitchen?" George grunted, wiping his bony hands on the seat of his jeans. Suddenly he stalked out the door.

(That penultimate paragraph is *three* sentences, not two: after he speaks, *then* George grunts. It would work even better if we reversed the clauses: "Wiping his bony hands on the seat of his jeans, George grunted.")

Basically, you need to remember that a dash (or 1/m dash, as it's often called: —) is a mark that signifies interruption. Thus, the clause describing Alice's action ("she took a step after him, thought better, and stepped back") comes along to interrupt what Alice has started to say: "You don't—"

By the same token, after the clause describing what Alice did is completed, the rest of her sentences comes to interrupt that:

—"have to make a mess of everything! Really, look. It isn't that im—"

Clearly Alice is about to say, "It isn't that important," but, in the same way, George interrupts her with his rhetorical question: "*You* want to cook in a black kitchen?" The mark that Alice is interrupted is, however, the dash above.

Remember, too: The first dash (with "You don't—") comes *inside* the closing quotation mark. The quotation mark itself is followed by a space before the description continues. ("You don't—" she took a step after him, thought better, and stepped back—) The dash that ends the interruption comes outside the new, opening quotation (and stepped back—"have to make a mess of everything!"). There is *no space* before it. The dashes fall at the same places commas would, if the interruption was the usual "he said" or "she said."

Why? Because that's the way it's done. Just learn it: Dash/close quote is *always* followed by a space (but never has a space between them). Dash/open quote/word *never* has a space between any of them. (Unless, of course, they come in two different paragraphs.)

"Well, I'm just—" she blinked rapidly—"astonished! Really, I don't know what to say."

The clause "she blinked rapidly" is set off by dashes on both sides. That's why it has no capital letter at the beginning or period at the end. It's inserted where it interrupts the speech. But, again, *note the space* after the close quote after "just—"; and *note the lack of space* before the open quote before "astonished!"

Now make sure you do it correctly.

For many years this was the province of copy editors, typesetters, and compositors. Word processors have dumped much of this, however, back in the writer's lap. You might as well learn it.

Another mark of punctuation that we can use to vary tones of voice is the ellipsis, indicated by three dots (. . .). Basically three dots means that something has been left out, or is fundamentally incomplete.

The official nonfiction use of the ellipsis is when you are quoting a document and you elide (skip over) a passage. The ellipsis represents the missing words. But in dialogue, the two marks, the dash and the ellipsis, suggest notably different tones of voice. The dash suggests words interrupted or broken off sharply. The ellipsis means something has been left out. It suggests that the speaker trails away or is uncertain what should come next.

Thus, when we are reading, we hear, "Oh, I—" and "Oh, I . . ." very differently. Both can be combined with exclamation points or question marks:

"Alice—?"

"George . . . !"

But have a particular reason or an effect in mind when you do anything covered in this section. All of them are effective, but use these techniques sparingly. Quickly they become affectations.

I want to conclude this section with three errors.

The following two sentences are both wrong. Don't write them.

1. "Oh, I really enjoyed that," she laughed.
2. "Really, I just feel so . . ." she sighed.

The punctuation is wrong in both cases. Both *laughing* and *sighing* are fundamentally *wordless* sounds that human beings make. You can't *laugh* words, nor can you *sigh* them. If you are not laughing very hard, you can laugh *while* you speak:

"Oh, I really enjoyed that," she said, laughing.

The same goes for *sighing*:

"Really, I just feel so . . ." As she spoke, she sighed.

But both examples 1 and 2 above are actually run-on sentences.

Either they should be rewritten or they should be corrected:

"Oh, I really enjoyed that." She laughed.
"Really, I just feel so . . ." She sighed.

Neither of these means, however, quite the same thing as 1 and 2. Each example is two sentences. They mean she spoke first. *Then* she laughed—or sighed.

A third and final error is very close to these but has some interesting ramifications. The following is also wrong.

3. "Oh, Billy," she wept, "I've just been so miserable since˜ I've been back from school."

It would be just as incorrect if you replaced *wept* with *cried* or *sobbed*. As do laughing and sighing, "to weep," "to cry," and "to sob" all refer to fundamentally *wordless* sounds people make. The same argument holds for them as holds for laughing and sighing.

Crying presents a complexity, however, because "to cry" is actually *two* verbs in English. One can cry out, or do what the town crier does. You can cry out, "Help!" or, "Wait!" or, "Oh, please! Someone get over here, right away. There's been a terrible accident!" But for the ordinary and garden variety crying that children do when they scrape their knees or that folks do when they are suddenly overcome by misery, while you can cry and weep tears, you can no more cry words than you can laugh them or sigh them. Thus, in written narrative, you have to handle them in similar ways:

"Since I came back home from law school, it's been terrible, Billy. Once I got here to Enoch Hills, my aunt went and told everybody how I'd flunked out! Everyone's whispering behind my back. I mean, this is such a tiny town. On the street, I've caught people looking at me, all strange. And I just—well, I can't *stand* it . . . !" Halfway through her third sentence, Joan had started to cry. With her final exclamation, sobs swept away all words, and she went digging in her coat pocket for her handkerchief.

But if you write

"And I just—well, I can't *stand* it . . . !" she cried.

you're making a mistake. (By the standards of contemporary English, where "cry" means to shed tears, that's a run-on sentence.) It's illiterate. Don't do it. Copy editors should correct that into:

"And I just—well, I can't *stand* it . . . !" She cried.

But remember, that's *two* sentences. They describe a situation in which she spoke first. *Then* she cried. Better rewrite it in such a way that people will know exactly what's happening and what you really intended to convey.

A Final Note on Dialogue

Most dialogue—indeed, most effective dialogue—is not particularly realistic. Generally speaking, dialogue is written in a slightly more colloquial tone of voice than the general narrative. The verbal markers of dialect or class that give individuality to characters are best handled as sparing bits of decoration. Their purpose is to identify the character's origins or position in the social web. They should not get in the way of your understanding what the character is saying.

In the history of English prose fiction or English drama, every once in a while a writer will make a major move toward returning his or her language to the "language really used by men," as Wordsworth and Coleridge characterized it in their preface of their joint book *Lyrical Ballads* in 1798. Mark Twain's colloquial diction in *Huckleberry Finn* is one such example.* The

---

*To experience the contemporary *literary* language, read Mark Twain's 1897 novel *Personal Recollections of Joan of Arc.* Ten years in the planning, two years in the writing, Twain's longest solo novel tells Joan's tale in the words of her single educated childhood friend and later secretary, Louis le Conte. Not only Twain but Twain's friend William Dean Howells and Twain's early biographer Albert Bigelow Paine felt it was Twain's "most important work" [Bigelow, 958], his "supreme literary expression, the loveliest, the most delicate, and most luminous example of his work" [Bigelow, 998], and his best bid for immortality. But while it's written in the highly serviceable prose of the 1890s, still, where Huck's colloquial language [of 1885] is headlong and enthusiastic, Louis's literate discourse is

self-conscious slanginess that J. D. Salinger gives to his spoiled upper-middle-class narrator in *Catcher in the Rye* is another. Following Irish playwright John Millington Synge's country language in his plays *In the Shadow of the Glen* (1903), *Riders to the Sea* (1904), and *Playboy of the Western World* (1907), playwrights such as Joe Orton, Harold Pinter, and David Mamet resorted to far more familiar verbal melodies and naturalist pauses and repetitions in their dialogue, which made their early audiences sit up and realize that the writing here was far more realistic than usual. Samuel Beckett, Ernest Hemingway, and Raymond Carver each made major moves in the direction of making the dialogue in their plays and stories hold closer to aspects of actual speech.

In all of these raids on reality, however, there is a point of diminishing returns. Every once in a while, a writer will try to set down extended conversations exactly as they occur—or might occur. Invariably, the result is confusion, chaos, and—more than all the rest—banality. Whether on the stage or on the page, in dialogue "realism" beyond a certain point can only be achieved in part—by highlighting one aspect or another. For a season or a decade, an audience may applaud it, till it ceases to seem new. But when we try to apprehend and present the whole of the natural thing, the thing itself crumbles, lacking the aesthetic structure, sense of immediacy, and coherence that more artificial writers such as Oscar Wilde and George Bernard Shaw, Thornton Wilder and Maxwell Anderson, Peter Shaffer and Tom Stoppard, Edward Albee and Terrence McNally (or Giraudoux, Ghelderode, and Anouilh in French) have tried for by pitching their diction a point or two higher than naturalism. In the end their work exhibits more verbal liveliness than a Eugene O'Neill or a Clifford Odets. However ambitious intellectually,

----

restrained and thoughtful; where Huck is wry and ironic, Louis is sincere and even mawkish; where Huck is morally non-judgmental, descriptively precise, and sensorially inclusive, Louis is summary, analytical, and, yes, witty. The novel probably influenced George Bernard Shaw, if not Bertold Brecht. But few read it today. Quick overviews of Twain's work—such as the article on Twain in the current *Oxford Companion to English Literature*—don't even mention it.

such works sink beneath the grim gray realism the playwrights have worked so hard to thicken over the imaginative surfaces of their dramatic inventions.

Apostrophes

Because we need to talk about apostrophes somewhere, probably this is the place. I'll assume that you all know when to use apostrophes in words such as "won't," "can't," "don't," and "shouldn't."

"It's" (with an apostrophe) is the contraction of "it is":

It's going to rain tomorrow.

"Its" (without an apostrophe) is a possessive. What follows belongs to "it":

The dog was sopping; bedraggled hair hung from its belly.

(The belly belongs to the dog, which is why we say "its.")

Those two still confuse many people. You just have to learn them. Something that will help: remember, while possessives, singular or plural, formed from ordinary nouns *all* get apostrophes (the dog's collar, the children's games, the professors' robes . . .), *no* possessive adjective (a possessive formed from a pronoun) gets one: *my* car, *your* notebook, *his* hat, *her* idea, *its* weight, *our* apartment, *their* laughter . . . nor do *any* possessive pronouns: *his, hers, mine, thine* (obsolete*), *its, yours, ours, theirs, whose* . . .

See? There's not an apostrophe in the lot.

For the rest, the basic rule is this: Whether at the end, or in the middle, or at the beginning of a word, an apostrophe stands in for one or more missing letters. They *all* curve like little caves opening to the *left*:

Goin', don't, ain't, can't, 'cause.

With a colloquial word such as *'cause* (a contraction, or syncopation, of "because"), where the apostrophe comes at the beginning of the word, getting the apostrophe to curve left can be a problem on some word processors. That's 'cause at the start of the word, what are called "smart quotes" usually want to face right. What you have to do is type a random letter, then type the apostrophe, then type the word: *t'cause.*

Then you must go back and delete the random letter: *'cause.*

But if it comes out *'cause*, it's wrong. Fix it.

Unless you're using single quotation marks instead of double quotation marks, the only time you use a right curving apostrophe is in front of a few vowels in Greek in order to let people know they're pronounced as if they have an "h" in front of them. Otherwise, don't use them at all. Got it? Good!

Dramatic Structure

Dramatic structure is the fractal structure of fiction. Fractals are patterns (structures) that repeat in a picture or a work in both smaller forms and larger forms, the larger forms created *from* the smaller forms. The writer can use dramatic structure to control and organize whole stories, individual scenes, or even paragraphs and sentences.

What is it?

Consider the text of a contemporary drama. The first thing we have is the scenic description, telling us *where* we are and what things *look* like. The play's action follows, telling us what's happening. The vast majority of dramas reserve their highest emotional point for the play's end, the climax to which everything builds. We can synopsize this: location, situation/action, affect.

That *order* is dramatic structure.

To have something to compare it with, however, let's consider what I choose to call "natural narrative structure," the structure many people not noted for their storytelling ability fall into when, in ordinary situations, they recount an incident that recently happened:

> Yesterday I was so scared—I mean, I was just . . . astonished! I wasn't prepared at all. [*The emotions are what remain with the narrator most strongly from the incident—the affect—so he/she starts with them.*] I mean, I really got upset. This guy thought I'd done something to him, I mean to his truck—but I didn't know who he was. I'd never

seen him before. *Or* his goddam truck. But he just started yelling at me. [*The narrator follows the statement of his own current emotions with an assessment of the motivations of his assailant, between protestations of his own innocence. Because his lack of understanding at the time of the incident left him with the greatest anxiety about* those motivations, *this gets interspersed with the discomfort from the accusation, now brought back to him by his own retelling.*] I swear, I was so surprised, I knocked my glass over. He was this big, strong fellow—I mean, talk about tattoos? I'm just sitting there, when I knocked my beer over. You know, you got this stranger, just yelling at you . . . ? That was scary, man! He'd torn the sleeves off his shirt—you know how I mean? Arms as fat as inner tubes! [*Once the affect is more or less out of the way and the anxiety over the motivations and the description has been addressed, the narrator begins to fill in the details of the situation and provide memories of what happened and memories of the assailant, randomly intermixed, followed by some evocation of the character.*] He was down at the very end of the bar but suddenly he leaned forward, pounded the counter, and shouted, "Hey—you! I know who you are!" I was looking at the game on the TV, and this fellow—I hadn't even seen him. He just starts yelling like that. At first, even though my heart was pounding—I mean, he yelled so loud, like that, he scared me! Really, I thought, at first, he was shouting at the bar girl, Meg. But he's looking right at me. I tell you, even before I realized he was talking to me, I half jumped off my stool. That's when I spilled my beer. We were in Red's—I mean, I'd just gone in there for a beer. It was so hot out, and they have the AC on all the time. [*Going back and forth, looking to fill in missed details, which his hearer may need, the narrator finally locates us in a place—as a kind of afterthought, so that the hearer only now gets some picture of the whole situation. Up till here, this hasn't been a major concern of the narrator, who is far more interested in expressing his emotions about the encounter than letting us in on the materiality of the situation.*] The guy's an asshole. I mean, why's he yelling at me? I never saw him before.

He never saw me before. And the guy's stupid, too—you can look at him and see he's stupid. And, of course, he's drunk. [*Only now that this much venting has occurred and the emotional pitch has lowered, can he/she give the most embarrassing detail of the story.*] I got beer all down my slacks.

We can call this "natural narrative structure," though its structure is no more natural, really, than any other. It simply serves a different psychological purpose.

It is the opposite of dramatic structure, however, which is, by comparison, artificial, learned (largely from other texts, the media, and other storytellers), and is more concerned with reproducing the experience and its resultant emotions *in the hearer*. Because of its form, it already begins to partake of some of the "objectivity" of history. This is how someone with a greater distance, who has internalized the order of "dramatic structure," might recount the same incident:

You remember it was so hot yesterday? Well, I went into Red's at about two o'clock to cool off with the AC. I was sitting at the counter there, having a beer, watching the Cardinals on the TV they got up over there, when, from the end of the bar, I heard this *crash*—! I practically jumped off my barstool! Knocked over my beer mug, too. This guy with his sleeves torn off and tattoos all over arms as fat as inner tubes—I swear!—had just hammered both fists on the counter. He's leaning forward. And he's shouting: "Hey, you! I know who you are! *You're* the asshole who messed up my goddam truck!" I'm confused. I'm scared. I'm not even sure if he's talking to me—and beer's running down from the counter, all *over* my khakis! It takes me three seconds to figure out he's drunk as a skunk, he's probably not the swiftest player on the field, and I've never seen him before! I'm still trying to figure out why he's glaring at me—or even if it *is* me he's glaring at. Only besides him and the counter girl, I'm the only one at my end of the bar. And he sure wasn't looking at Meg! I was terrified.

Location, situation/action, affect: in terms of the economy, clarity, and immediacy of information the *hearer* gets, this is a much more effective way to recount the same incident. Some people who have "natural storytelling ability" have learned to recount the events of their own lives using dramatic structure: It allows their friends to see and understand what happened to them more clearly. Because they start with information about the place, they've pulled up to the fore all the associations the hearer has with such places, which, as they move on into the situation, the hearer now has ready. Everything that follows seems clearer, makes more sense. We see the people more sharply. We have a better sense of what happened. Even if one or more of the characters are out of the ordinary for such a place, the narrator can immediately characterize them in terms of their differences from an implied norm. ("You know the kind of beefy Portuguese loaders who're likely to get drunk there before five. But this fellow had on a three-piece suit, a toupee—it was two shades lighter than the rest of his hair—and though he was as big across in the chest as any of the loaders in Maitland Demolition, he wore the thickest glasses you *ever* saw . . . !") As well, the narrator is not afraid to be "objective" about his own clumsiness and its consequences: the overturned beer, his wet slacks . . . Finally, because all this registers so much more forcefully, we are more likely to remember it, to believe it, and to interrogate its causes and take into account its results.

Another advantage of dramatic structure is that you have to spend far less time and words on the emotions. (A few phrases cover them, evoking them far more strongly, as opposed—in the "natural" account—to six or seven sentences, which, while they tell us about those feelings, don't make us experience them particularly.) The location and the situation suggest so much about what the affect is going to be, that the teller can concentrate on what makes the affect specific to the situation and assume a general identification and understanding for the rest.

Immediacy and identification are gained. Little is lost.

Dramatic structure promotes emotional identification with the point-of-view character: it organizes the material in a way that follows the emotions of the point-of-view character *during the occurrence.* Natural structure *discourages emotional identi-*

fication. Instead, it creates a relatively bland field ready for whatever *intellectual analysis* the auditor might bring to the material, because it organizes that material entirely in terms of the situation's emotional aftermath. Instead of an "objective" chronological map of *what* happened *while* it was happening, it's a snapshot of the emotional ruins, taken the next day, of what remains. It's historical evidence. But it's not a history.

Young writers are subject to lots of advice today, much of it contoured by movie and TV writing. Much of it is some version of "Get right to the situation. Don't waste time on description or emotion." But the setting tells us a lot *about* the situation and the possible range of emotions that might occur in it. When a TV show or a movie starts, we get much of that "description of the setting" from a glance at the screen. The reason not to "waste time on it" is only if something else or someone else—the director, the set designer, the cinematographer—is going to do it for you. A novelist or short-story writer doesn't have that luxury.

Consider the following text:

> Our story is about the conflict between a father and his grown son, which almost leads to the son's murdering his father. At the last moment, however, the son pulls back
> . . .

If the conflict takes place in 1938, on a May dawn at the edge of a half-plowed field of kale on a foundering Ohio farm, on which a bank is about to foreclose for the last seed-loan, likely we have one story—one *kind* of story.

If the conflict takes place on the night before Thanksgiving, two hours after the office staff has gone home from the empty executive boardroom of a major law corporation on the twenty-second floor of a Chicago office building, however, most likely it's another story—and another kind of story, even though the conflict can be described with the same words. Start with the setting, and by the time you come to the basic situation or action you will already have implied much about it, so that it will be easier to write.

From the different locations, we can intuit a lot about probable differences in the characters, their education, their dress, speech patterns, their motivations, and a good number of other situational parameters. Set up the location before you establish the conflict situation itself, and that information is already tacitly in place so that you, as a storyteller, can make use of it and develop it.

Characterized as it is by "location/situation-and-action/affect," dramatic structure has two prongs. To slight either makes the other register less forcefully or, at any rate, appear less useful. The added vividness and extra sense of presence to the implied data that comes through generally letting us know where we are before telling us what's actually happening is the first prong. The use of action, incident, and observation in the resultant enhanced data field *to imply* the resultant emotions, *rather than state them*, is the second prong.

We might show a character—call her Lucy—at the end of our tale, doing anything from looking pensively out a window toward the birch trees to huddling on the floor in the corner behind the head-table dining room chair, convulsed with sobs. But if we have told our story right, in neither case should we have to write: "Lucy was feeling wholly miserable about Uncle Martin's having to put down her dog, Archie, despite its arthritis and the tumor in its side, whom she had loved so dearly for seventeen years since it had been a pup." Whether we have seen Uncle Martin take Archie out to the woods with his rifle or off in his pick-up to the North Jersey dog pound, such emotions should be evoked through implication, not stated with words such as "wholly miserable" or "dearly loved." Another way to articulate this advice is, "Show. Don't tell." But it is just as much a part of dramatic structure as the advice to indicate clearly *where* you are, if only by a phrase or two, before you start telling us what's going on.

Bear in mind: stories are not movies.

That opening shot of the old bushwhacker who opens up his canteen and pours out the water happens against a specific background; and the immediately perceived tension between the background and his action produces the initial sense of drama. Is he in a desert, with no other human beings in sight? Then immediately we sense that he is either depriving himself or someone else of precious water, and our curiosity is alerted in one direction. If, however, he is indoors and pouring the water into the sink (which, in a film, takes us no more time to ascertain than the other), our suspicions are alerted in other directions: he's returning from a trip, possibly even getting rid of evidence of something already accomplished, such as poison in the canteen.

But the *written* story that begins:

> He turned up the canteen to let the water pour out.

gives us neither of those sets of possibilities; and when, a sentence or a paragraph later, we find out where we are, the force has gone out of the possibility of evocation; whereas both

> Under widely dispersed clouds in the Wyoming morning, beside the sagging gray-green barrel cactus, Old Jimson snorted behind his walrus moustache and, squinting and showing bad teeth, turned his canteen up to let the water run out over lime-white sand.

and

> Beside the sagging window screen, with three moths still asleep—or dead—on the mesh, Old Jimson snorted behind his walrus moustache and, while the floorboards squeaked under his boots, turned up his canteen and let the water run out over the mess of beans, eggs, and breakfast dishes still in the stainless steel sink.

set up different and contrasting story possibilities.

The fact is, neither example produces the same generic expectations that either would evoke in a film. But both begin a process that we can recognize as dramatic structure, and either might lead to the implied emotions, later in the tale, that would give us the satisfaction of a dramatic structure achieved.

For those interested in literary theory, we can (and probably should) begin to deconstruct any summary opposition between "natural structure" and "dramatic structure" right away. The easiest place to start is the moment in "natural structure" at which the narrator is "going back and forth looking to fill in missed details, now that his hearer may need them" and finally gets around to mentioning that the incident took place in Red's Bar. This is the moment in "natural structure" from which dramatic structure, as a kind of supplement, grows.

We can also put some historical limitations on the process as well. If we actually read the surviving dramas from ancient Greece, especially the tragedies by Aeschylus, Sophocles, and Euripides, it's clear they have more to do with the kind of normalized "natural structure" we've outlined than they do with the dramatic structure as we have described it. They don't take place in "Red's Bar." The fact is, most of them take place on the outdoor platform of a large amphitheater, which, now and then, only when it's relevant, we are reminded represents the courtyard of some palace or the space before a temple (another generic, outdoor, public location); by the same token, most of them start at a fairly high emotional level that they try to maintain through to the end. After the choral introductions, most of the tragedies get under way with one wail of high anguish or another—and stay there.

The tragedies of Shakespeare and the other Elizabethans are only fleetingly congruent to the dramatic structure we've outlined. It is not until the bourgeois dramas of Ibsen and Chekhov toward the last third of the nineteenth century that we can really discern that structure's recognizable outlines—and only its outlines.

Nevertheless, here are the opening two sentences of a recently published short story in a commercial magazine: "The man barreled forward from behind a pile of cartons but just before colliding with him pulled up, there in the corridor cluttered with boxes and half-packed equipment. 'Sir, I'm sorry . . . !'"

From the reader's point of view, the story would take off from a stronger position had it gone: "In the corridor cluttered with piles of cartons and half-packed equipment, a man barreled out and forward, but, just before colliding with him, pulled up. 'Sir, I'm sorry . . . !'"

We can cite all sorts of reason for *not* using dramatic structure. Sometimes the writer starts off in natural structure in order to give a sense of verisimilitude or voice, and only moves on—later—into more dramatic organization. Joyce does this in "The Dead," which starts in the voice of a servant describing Lily, "literally run off her feet," and her back and forth career from doorbell to coatroom. But before the page ends, carefully he is giving us the front hall, the upstairs dressing room, the coatroom under the stairs, and the upstairs landing where, at the party's end, the "climax" will take place, when Gabriel looks up those same steps to see Gretta, his wife, standing there, listening to tenor Bartell Darcy singing from the upstairs sitting room, which, by then, we have also spent time in and have had carefully described.

Still, unless you have a good reason *not* to use it, it's best to let "dramatic structure" be the default structure you use, whether on the small scale of the sentence, on the larger scale of individual paragraphs or scenes or, indeed, for your overall tale.

Excitement, Drama, Suspense, Surprise, Violence

Each of these five nouns names a very different effect. What makes so much popular narrative (especially in films and TV) seem so mindless is that someone, usually a producer, has mistaken one for the other or tried to use one in an attempt to get the effect of another. Most often violence is used in places where one of the other four might have been more interesting or effective.

Consider your response to violence in real life: if you are walking down the street and a stranger thirty feet (or even three feet) away is suddenly injured or hurt, often your emotions lock down. The very shock shuts off any immediate emotional reaction, sympathy, sadness, or empathy. Violence to strangers armors us *against* involvement with them. The fact is, this is a useful reaction, whether we decide to help the person or simply to move quickly away to escape the danger ourselves, or because it's not feasible for us to do anything useful just then and we want to make room for someone who can. Clear thinking is necessary in such situations, not emotional involvement and personal identification. That's probably why we're wired like that.

Numberless times now I've been handed manuscripts by young writers that begin in the darkness with a shout, a scuffle, a thud, followed by the sound of breaking glass, whereupon people rush in to find Colonel Mustard (or his equivalent) dead in the sitting room. Almost immediately the writer follows with the life story of Colonel Mustard, under the impression that, because Mustard has been killed, the reader is now interested in him. But this is to confuse a strategy from the genre of the analytic detective story (where it can indeed be quite effective) with that of general fiction—usually because so many film and TV producers have already made the same mistake, and simply through unexamined exposure it comes to them second nature.

What's interesting about Colonel Mustard's murder is not, of course, Colonel Mustard. Rather it's the twisted iron bar, red paint at one end and blue at the other, which is lying on the floor, beside the mantelpiece, three feet from the body. One end of the bar was on top of a calling card, with no name on it, but which nevertheless showed a golden seven-point star with a black band across it. Now, the bar itself had obviously been used to break three pieces of glassware, which had been sitting on the mantel—the shards were all over the green carpet. Nevertheless, while the side of Colonel Mustard's head had been beaten in with a blunt instrument—surely the cause of death—there was *no blood on the bar*! As is the blue on the other end, the red is clearly enamel paint . . .

In short, the potential for mystery and interest is *entirely* intellectual—for those readers who enjoy a good mystery. The violence at the beginning is precisely what has closed off the possibility for *emotional identification*, however, and moved our interest (if we have any) to the intellectual plane: Who did it? Why? And how? Those Sherlock Holmeses, Philo Vances, Philip Marlowes, Jane Marples, or Matt Scudders are ready to investigate . . .

Violence can be surprising, but it is not interesting or exciting or involving in itself. What caused it may be interesting. Its effects may be of intellectual interest. But it is not *emotionally* interesting in and of itself. On the contrary. The psychological use of violence in art is, paradoxically, not to engage our emotions but rather to put our emotions on hold, heighten our perceptions, and get us ready to think. But since so few public narratives—as offered by television and film—give us much to think about, most of it is wasted.

What does tend to get our emotional interest and identification is watching someone put out energy to get something she or he wants. But, in an attempt to make "something happen," don't confuse that with violence—a murder, a fight, or a robbery.

The great film director Alfred Hitchcock differentiated between surprises, mystery, and suspense as follows:

Surprise (Hitchcock explained) is where neither the audience nor the character knows that something surprising is coming; it just happens, and the character's surprised response becomes a dramatization of the audience's equal surprise.

In *mystery,* the character knows what the situation is (and the audience knows the character knows), but the audience does *not* know: Among the weekend house guests and the servants gathered at the country mansion, there in the sitting room, along with the detective and Mustard's corpse, *we* know one must be the murderer. That person also knows who she or he is and knows as well the answers to our intellectual puzzle. But we (the audience)—and the detective—do not. That's what creates a mystery.

With *suspense,* the audience knows (because we have already seen the psychotic murderer with his gun take refuge from the police in the deserted building on the corner and creep upstairs to hide in the big bedroom closet) what is likely to happen—but the character does not: college student Susan Falcon just happens not to be able to sleep that night and so decides to walk over to the house that belonged to her dead aunt to pick up the old portrait of her mother, left against the wall in the upstairs walk-in bedroom closet. Only when she gets inside and tries the switch, does she remember that the electricity has been off for the last three months. But she recalls where the portrait is, and so—even without a flashlight—starts upstairs to the bedroom to get it . . .

Because all three—mystery, suspense, surprise—involve withholding information (from audience, characters, or both), too much of any one of them easily becomes banal. (Good fiction is about giving as much information as possible; withholding information is an interim or secondary strategy to make the giving of information richer, more poignant, more satisfying.) All of them require careful set-ups. Generally we don't want too much violence in that set-up if we are to become emotionally involved—and stay involved—in what's going on.

Some producers/directors actually like to play a game with their audience, to see if they can get the violence in quickly enough before the audience battens down its emotional hatches. This has its entertainment value, but by and large the long-term effects of such games are simply an increase in the banality of violence, and the numbing of the emotions per se. The unskilled producer/director simply tries to substitute violence for all other possible effects—which accomplishes the same banalization, only faster. The fact is, these games can *only* be played in film. While mystery and suspense have their literary equivalents, surprise and violence *cannot* produce the same effect on the page as they do on the screen. That's a good reason to leave them to the media that do them well.

Point of View

Keep the point of view consistent within a scene. The sudden intrusion of another point of view, even for a phrase or a sentence, registers with most readers today as a narrative error. Unless the story is fairly long, we usually expect a story to be told from one character's point of view, even if the narrator is only looking over the character's shoulder. There is an "omniscient" point of view, a narrator who, God-like, knows—and is ready to tell—everything that everyone in the scene is thinking and feeling. But such stories become rarer and rarer and register as more and more eccentric. Such tales cannot turn on any sort of mystery or character revelation, so that it becomes hard for the writer to keep them interesting.

What point of view should you tell your story from?

Novelist and Joyce scholar James Blish used to answer this question with a counterquestion: "Who in the story hurts the most?"

Do you *have* to tell your story from the point of view of the character who hurts most? I would say only, if you don't, you should have a good reason. If the reader learns toward the end of a story that a character other than the one he or she has been following is also in great emotional pain, that reader is likely to leave the tale at the end, wondering why he or she didn't learn more about that other character.

Characters who want something and exert energy to get it

are usually more sympathetic than characters who don't want anything in particular.

Characters who undergo change are usually more satisfying to read about than characters who don't.

Does this mean that characters who don't want anything or don't change should *never* be the focus of your writerly attention? No. But it means that the writer will have to work harder to keep up the reader's interest in such characters. And it *will* be work.

First Person

"When should I tell my story in the first person?"

Remember, the first person is a far *more* limited way to tell a story than limited third person. Thus, when you take it on, you're taking on an added constraint.

The main reason to give up the freedom of the limited third person (the story about a "he" or a "she," where the narrator still has access to what that person is thinking) and take on the first person is not a matter of information. You can give as much or more of what the character is thinking in limited third than you can in first. As well, you can be more selective about it, offer more commentary on it, and narrate it from a far greater range of rhetorical approaches, from the words the character him- or herself might use (as you would do in first person), to the most ornate presentation of what the character is thinking, feeling, seeing.

So why *would* any writer in her or his right mind want to tell a story in first person?

Here's a rule of thumb: take on the first person only when the character has *an interesting voice.* Limited third is a blessing for writing about the ordinary Joe or Jane, who doesn't have a particularly exciting or even interesting way of expressing him- or herself. From time to time everyone thinks something about his or her own situation that's interesting or insightful for others to hear. When a character does that, in limited third you can always quote that character's own thoughts on the matter. But for the rest, an external narrative voice can be more economical, more evocative, more intelligent than the voice of the character you're writing about might ever be—and just more interesting. You can use that added writerly range to make the character interesting, by showing us what the character sees and feels and telling it in language more lively and insightful than any language the character him- or herself might have access to.

Nothing loses our sympathy faster, however, than an inarticulate person trying to tell the most interesting events that may have happened to him or her, if he or she happens not to have much in the line of narrative or descriptive ability—and that, after all, is most people. Raymond Carver—who made his reputation writing stories in the voices of ordinary people—rarely produced a story even ten pages long. The vast majority of his tales were three, four, or five pages. An ordinary voice going on for even eight or nine pages, much less fifteen, twenty, or twenty-five, will, first, alienate readers and, second, make them really start to dislike the character.

What does it mean, then, to say that a character has an interesting voice? The character him- or herself might be particularly intelligent so that we can believe that he or she writes particularly clearly, concisely, and vividly. One of the most famous first-person passages in the American novel of the past hundred years is Benjy's ninety-two-page monologue that opens William Faulkner's *The Sound and the Fury* (1929). Benjy is a mentally retarded adult who has very little sense of consecutive time and a rather limited perception of space and physical depth. Thus he recounts all of his memories and his current perceptions in pretty much the same flat uninflected way. This is not the way most people speak about either the past or the present. As well, he is totally nonjudgmental—largely because he has no understanding of what he sees. Even though his is a highly limited account, the fact that it is *different* from the normative makes it of interest. But even with that added interest, Faulkner knew enough to stop and take on at least two other voices in order to recount the last two-thirds of his novel.

If the only reason you're telling the story in the first person is to withhold information that a more omniscient narrator would be expected to know, chances are you have a weak story.

Huckleberry Finn has an engaging regional accent that allows him to use all sorts of conventional turns of phrase that are outside the standard bounds of the literary. He is an extremely observant young man—far more than most. He has a feeling for nature that allows his descriptions to compete with, and often win out over, those of many more traditionally literary narrators. His accounts of action are clear and simple, and he is extremely precise on what motivates them. At the same time, because he has not been raised "civilized," a great deal of society's mechanics bewilder him, and—in the course of his telling about them—they come to look pretty unnatural to the reader. Despite his unschooled diction, Huck is smart, observant, and nonjudgmental in a way that is very different from that of Faulkner's Benjy. In short, he's someone it's fun to listen to for long stretches.

In Theodore Sturgeon's short story "The Clinic," a man wakes up in a hospital, with no memory, and starts to tell his story. From the first sentence, we understand that he is not a native English speaker. He puts words together in the strangest ways—sometimes ways that are very interesting. While he recounts other people's attempts around him to decide if he is Italian, Greek, or from some Eastern country, the reader begins to suspect that the man is from *much* farther away than that. While there are aspects of his thinking that recall both Benjy and Huck, not only is his language strange, but his ways of thinking about things are wholly unusual—and often brilliantly original, in ways that Huck and Benjy never come close to. Finally we come to understand that the man is a very intelligent alien from another world . . . For the length of the story (about twenty pages), Sturgeon carries it off pretty convincingly.

Questions of information are going to come into the decision, of course, but, more to the point, your reader must spend the duration of your story or your novel *listening* to this person speak (that is, reading what this person writes). Thus, if there isn't something particularly interesting about his or her voice (and, Benjy aside, that usually means someone of above average intelligence, who sees unusual things in ordinary situations and can articulate what's unusual about them, or who is particularly witty and/or observant and comes up naturally with interesting turns of phrase and clever observations), you'll do better in objective third or limited third.

For a first-person story to work, the narrator should be someone you yourself would find interesting to sit around with for two, three, or four hours while she told you what happened to her during her last summer in Albuquerque, when the ranch boss thought—erroneously, for three days—that they'd discovered oil and everyone on the place was running around all excited, thinking they'd be millionaires. If, however, he or she is just an ordinary Joe or Jane, no matter how likable or pleasant, who tells an ordinary tale, no matter how thoroughly, objective third person or limited third person will give more leeway to vary the kinds of writing you can do within the story. Ordinary Joe or Jane is the character you *don't* allow to tell the story—because the voice (and the lack of narrative skill) will soon tire the reader.

Trust Your Image

Here are some images from published stories or books I've recently read.

> She washed old plastic bags and hung them on the line to dry, a string of thrifty, tame jelly fish.

This is charming. But the very fact that they are on the line suggests, already, that they're tame. If the writer dropped "tame" and made it simply "a string of thrifty jelly fish," it becomes not only more pointed but suggests a wit that, highlighted by one adjective, is obscured by two.

> The train station, its windows as large as those in any cathedral, was a cavernous space inhabited by echoes that seemed to have been cursed with immortality and murmured continually of the past—the foot that had already fallen, the voice that had already spoken, the whistle that had already blown.

The image of the train station as cathedral and the immortal, murmuring echoes are all evocative. The phrase "of the past," is not doing any particularly useful work, however, other than hammering home what the images are already all about. The same goes for the word "already." Also "seemed to have been cursed" compels us to note: if you're going to use a metaphor, don't apologize for it. As well, "cavernous space" and "*cursed with immortality*" are both bits of received dead wood. With the subject joined to verb, the writer could drop them all:

> Its windows as large as those in any cathedral, the cavernous train station was inhabited by immortal echoes, murmuring continually of the foot that had fallen, the voice that had spoken, the whistle that had blown.

That's the cleanest and strongest version of that image cluster you can have, against which the first version seems unnecessarily cluttered.

Having said that, there are questions of sonority that might make the writer want to go back to something nearer the original—which certainly sounds Miltonically grand. (Were it mine, I'd risk pluralizing the final triplet, "of feet that had fallen, voices that had spoken, whistles that had blown," to enhance the iconic sonority, or onomatopoeia.) But the writer has to be aware of the fact that each addition for sonority's sake also blurs, by a bit, the clarity of the cleanest version.

> The children's screams wove a tapestry of sound.

The same sort of critical thinking that we've used before should lead the writer to ask, why do we need "of sound" at the end? Well, it's clear that we need it because "wove a tapestry" is a visual image, not an aural one, and without "of sound," the reader moving through the sentence into the next is likely to be a bit lost:

> The children's screams wove a tapestry.

But this, in its turn, suggests that perhaps it simply isn't that good an image in the first place. As a matter of fact, the sentence here comes from a description of an Indian attack on a bunch of white settlers. The writer could drop the image as not particularly appropriate, at least in this context, and replace it with the more direct "Children screamed" (or "shrieked," or whatever)—or find a completely different one if that seems too thin. In certain kinds of poems, "The children's screams wove a tapestry" might work by itself, if the required effect is one of retardation and consideration. But, as I said, this is lifted from a scene of high action; for that reason, it doesn't work.

When what you're writing about evokes an image that you want to put down, try it. But once it's in place, check to see that, one, it's not just a piece of received language, hackneyed or formulaic. Two, let the image do its work: clean away the unnecessary verbal baggage that most images are likely to come with. Present it with as little ornament as you can—the image itself *is* your ornament. Three, when you've cleared off all the editorializing and repetitious excrescences, decide whether the things the image suggests (and the word *is* "suggests" here; not states) clarify the situation and contribute to the effect you want. If they do, use it. If they don't, consider the possibility that it may not be a good image for what you want. Try the passage without it.

Write What You Know

This very good advice has been given for such a long time that it was already classic when E. M. Forster wrote his *Aspects of the Novel* in 1927. As such, the perspicacious Mr. Forster was able to make some interesting qualifications, even back then. He noted that, while writing what you know is certainly preferable to writing about what you know nothing about at all, you are more likely to be able to write about something well if you've only done it a few times in such a way that someone who has been doing it for years might recognize, because your impressions are clear and sharp.

By the same token, something *you've* been doing for years might not be so fresh or yield the kind of insights that makes for lively fiction.

For forty-seven years I was a freelance writer. After I had become a professor and taught for a year, been department head for a year, then gone and taught in another university as a guest professor (where I became aware of all sorts of similarities and differences between the two institutions), I came back to my home university and wrote a novel in which much of the action was based in a university and where much of the plot leaned on departmental politics and personalities that had been common to both places I'd taught. Today, after having taught for sixteen years, I don't think I could (or would want to) take on the academy as a major setting for fiction, even though I know far more about it today than I did then. I'm now much *too* familiar with the things that make it interesting and am more likely to overlook them in a piece of fiction. Like all rules about writing, "Write what you know" should be taken as a goad toward common sense and a general guide. Cleave to it too closely, however ("Write *only* about what you know. *Never* write about anything you haven't experienced first-hand"), and it becomes a set of severely limiting blinkers. A corollary to the rule can be more useful than the rule neat: Use what you *do* know to write more believably about what you can only imagine.

Probably you've never been in an all-out sword fight on the deck of a pirate ship—a-wash in blood—in the Caribbean at dawn. But if you need to write such a scene, you can start by mining your own experiences for the microexperiences that can contribute to it. Have you ever been on the deck of *any* boat at dawn? Perhaps that experience can provide you with a sentence or so of description that can precede or follow the major action. What are the various ways people might act in such a fight—this one trying to get away, that one, blade out, throwing himself in among the striking blades? As a child, did you ever have a stick fight with a friend? Do you remember how, when your friend really hit your stick hard with his, it jarred you to the shoulder and made you clamp your teeth? Did you ever take a fencing class? What are the moves and positions you can remember from it? Have you ever been in any confused crowd? Have you ever seen anyone cut badly—and noticed how the blood runs out one end first, then spreads to the other? Perhaps you've been in or seen a bar fight. Perhaps you were in a fleeing crowd on the street. A moment or two lifted from such experiences and carefully observed can make your imaginary Caribbean sword fight more believable. Has your foot ever slipped on a board floor where a can of paint had overturned? Your foot slipping on spilled blood is not going to feel very different.

This is the time to do some nonfiction research. Many seventeenth- and eighteenth-century memoirists (Casanova, for example) left first-hand descriptions of such experiences or of experiences very near them, which you can mine for general atmosphere as well as telling details. Perhaps the final thing you need to remember about the advice "Write what you know" is that, if you've been told something by (or read it in) an authoritative enough source, it's now fair to say you *know* it.

Not too long ago, an ordinary surgical incision I'd recently gotten in the hospital developed a staph infection. When it burst open, the overpowering fecal odor suddenly made me understand why two-day, and three-day-old battlefields, strewn with corpses and wounded men, where there are frequently hundreds of such infections, are so often described by their noxious stench, strong enough to make your eyes water, even if you don't gag. Thus, a personal experience allows us to generalize, first-hand, about more sensational experiences we might personally have missed out on.

You can use the same technique of breaking down a spectacular imaginative experience into smaller familiar experiences, supported by research, for a trip to the moon, an expedition to the South Pole, or a diving trip to discover treasure in a sunken military ship lying on its side on the Atlantic floor. Paradoxically, the way to do all these best *is* to write what you know.

—New York City
April 2005

About the Author

Samuel R. Delany is a novelist and critic, who lives in New York City. His work appears in dozens of anthologies, including *The Norton Anthology of African-American Literature* and *The Norton Book of Postmodern Fiction*. Delany's first novel was published in 1962, when he was twenty. His tenth, *Dhalgren* (1975), has sold more than a million copies and is currently in print with Vintage Books. His most recent fiction includes *Atlantis: Three Tales* (Wesleyan University Press, 1996) and *Phallos* (Bamberger Books, 2004). Presently he is a professor of English and creative writing at Temple University in Philadelphia.

 Wesleyan University Press is a member of the Green Press Initiative. The paper used in this book meets their minimum requirement for recycled paper.